In one quick move ~~~~~~~~~~~~~~~~~~~~~~ r the
bed and upon her b~~~~~~~~~~~~~~~~~~~~~~ duc-
tive husband atop her.

"I merely thought to—"

"To steal my treasure," he said, his voice dark and full of sinful promise.

She shivered in response.

Desire coursed through her, making her focus on his every breath. Graeme's arm tightened around her, pulling her into his body so that her bottom nestled snugly against his legs.

Hot breath slid across her neck and down her shoulder as he leaned closer. His well-muscled chest pressed to her back. Even without the benefit of seeing it in the moment, she knew what that chest looked like. Knew every sinewy line that traced the hard muscles of his abdomen.

He kissed her neck. One hot, moist kiss that proved to be her complete undoing. She knew in that moment that she would not leave this bed tonight.

PRAISE FOR

DESIRE ME

"Sexy, daring treasure hunters...wild escapades...This is one great ride of a read." —*RT Book Reviews*

"5 Stars! Robyn DeHart has written a treasure trove of trouble that will have you reading at top speed!"
—HuntressReviews.com

"Adventure, romance, and wonderful writing...a thrilling read...Robyn DeHart writes delicious heroes, sharp-witted heroines, and adventurous plots that rival any Indiana Jones movie...will undoubtedly entertain you and leave you wanting to read the next adventure as soon as possible." —FictionVixen.com

"Great read from start to finish!"
—TheMysticCastle.com

"4 Stars! A delightful story!...kept me turning the pages wondering what would happen next."
—TheRomanceDish.com

"A great addition to any tote bag for a day at the beach or curled up on a hammock for a light and breezy read."
—NightOwlReviews.com

PRAISE FOR

SEDUCE ME

"Robyn DeHart's vibrant characters sweep the reader into a clever and sensual romp that is not to be missed."
—Julia London, *New York Times* bestselling author of *The Book of Scandal*

Also by Robyn DeHart

Seduce Me
Desire Me

Treasure Me

Robyn DeHart

FOREVER

NEW YORK   BOSTON

This book is a work of fiction. Names, characters, places, and incidents are the product of the author's imagination or are used fictitiously. Any resemblance to actual events, locales, or persons, living or dead, is coincidental.

Copyright © 2011 by Robyn DeHart
Excerpt from *Seduce Me* copyright © 2009 by Robyn DeHart
All rights reserved. Except as permitted under the U.S. Copyright Act of 1976, no part of this publication may be reproduced, distributed, or transmitted in any form or by any means, or stored in a database or retrieval system, without the prior written permission of the publisher.

Forever
Hachette Book Group
237 Park Avenue
New York, NY 10017
Visit our website at www.HachetteBookGroup.com

Forever is an imprint of Grand Central Publishing. The Forever name and logo is a trademark of Hachette Book Group, Inc.

The publisher is not responsible for websites (or their content) that are not owned by the publisher.

Printed in the United States of America

First Printing: March 2011

10 9 8 7 6 5 4 3 2 1

To my sister, Rhonda, who named Vanessa so many years ago. Even though you're not a reader, you still pimp my books out to all your friends. Your support means everything to me.

And, as always, to my husband, Paul. No matter what the world throws at us you are there to hold my hand and wipe my tears through the rocky stuff, and buy me chocolate and champagne through the good stuff. You're my favorite!

Acknowledgments

It is often said that books aren't written alone, and I couldn't agree more. To my brainstorming group, Emily, Hattie, and Joey, this book came directly out of our meetings and lunches at Chili's. I couldn't have written it without you. To my brilliant agent, Christina, thanks for your insight and enduring encouragement and for never batting an eye when it comes to my neuroses. To the Grand Central art department, you continue to bless me with spectacular covers; I am grateful for your talent. And to my editors, Amy and Alex, you push me with every book to become a better writer, and I am eternally thankful for your editorial feedback and guidance. I am proud of these Legend Hunter books.

Treasure Me

Prologue

Loch Ness, Scotland, 1881

Thunder crashed and fat, heavy raindrops pelted Graeme Langford as he plunged the oars into the cold, murky depths of Loch Ness. The muscles in his arms burned from rowing, and despite the chill in the air, sweat beaded down his back. The storm made the loch choppy and his trek more difficult. Still he rowed.

Through the sheets of rain, he could see the rocky beach ahead in the distance and the hills that rose behind the shore. Somewhere in those hills, he'd find the abbey. A foolish wealthy American had recently purchased the crumbling estate and intended to restore it to its former glory. They were supposed to start construction next week, so Graeme had to hurry and find what he sought before it was too late.

The small boat rocked against the angry waves, and

Graeme fought against the current. His progress was slow, and he was damp to his bones. The newly formed blisters on his palms ached. Eventually he made his way to the beach. He jumped out and pulled the boat onto the shore, cursing his aching muscles. Clearly life in London was making him soft.

The last ribbons of light were partially hidden behind the storm clouds, compromising his visibility greatly. But he'd climbed enough hills throughout Scotland to know that he would be able to traverse these in limited light. He secured his bag across his body and started up into the hills. The highlands weren't mountains; he'd seen true mountains in Spain. Still, the rocky hillsides were treacherous on their own account, so he minded his steps carefully. The rain slowed, and the thunder softened as the storm faded into the distance.

The crisp autumn air filled Graeme's lungs as he climbed up the hill. As raw and untamed as parts of Scotland remained, he loved this land. Loved the history and the rough terrain, loved the people and their lore. Half of him rightfully belonged here by his mother's blood, but it was his father's English blood that ruled his life. Four years earlier, when his father had fallen ill and died, Graeme had taken his place as the Duke of Rothmore. And he did his duty as an English lord, although he longed for time to spend in his beloved Scotland.

The pull from his Scottish heritage was what drove his quest, his burning desire to find and restore what rightfully belonged to Scotland—the Stone of Destiny, a biblical relic that held mysterious powers. It had belonged to the Scottish monarchy for hundreds of years before it had been stolen by the English. Or so everyone had thought. Graeme had recently come to believe that the stone taken by the English was counterfeit. He intended to be the one to locate the original stone.

According to his latest research, there was a book that he needed to complete his quest. It lay somewhere within the dilapidated walls of this old abandoned abbey.

As if his mind had conjured the image, a massive stone building suddenly lay before him, nestled into the next hill. Arches towered over crumbling stone, like the ribs of some enormous animal picked clean by vultures. Only the building at the main entrance remained. Graeme stepped through an opening in the wall that had once protected the monks, but he was not alone as he'd expected. The workers for the reconstruction were already here, or at least their equipment was, as it littered the hillside. They were early, which meant that he just might be too late.

With night falling, it seemed unlikely that the men would still be working, so Graeme crept closer. He listened intently for the sounds of voices, but heard nothing. Finally he reached the inner sanctum of the abbey. He pulled at the huge arched wooden door, and it opened with an echoing creak. Darkness surrounded him.

From his bag, he withdrew a simple beeswax candle and lit it. He unfolded a map and glanced at the rendition. The candlelight flickered as he studied the drawing, an illustration of this very structure—or more precisely, what lay beneath it.

Graeme stood in what had once been the chapel. Time and thieves had stolen the stained glass from the windows of the once glorious room. Tools and other construction supplies lay up against the wall. He crossed into the next room and found scaffolding between two pillars there.

He moved past the large columns, through the arched doorway, deeper into the ruins. Most of the stone floor remained in decent repair, though there were intermittent holes. When he'd heard someone had purchased the old building, Graeme had wondered if it was for residential purposes or if someone else sought the treasures that were believed hidden beneath. All the construction efforts he saw led him to believe that the new owner planned to live here.

It had been nearly a hundred years since monks had lived in this abbey, perhaps longer. Legend had it those men of the cloth had once been guardians to many of the church's ancient treasures—lost canons, the Spear of Christ, and the item that Graeme now sought: *The Magi's Book of Wisdom*, an ancient text rumored to contain the most accurate description of the Stone of Destiny.

Hot wax dripped onto Graeme's hand, burning and then congealing on his skin. The hall narrowed, then ended at a staircase. Graeme wound down the spiral stone stairs. He ended up in another hallway that revealed several smaller arched doorways. The hidden chamber still lay another level beneath the abbey, dug deep into the bowels of the hill.

Graeme walked through the sleeping quarters, one room leading to another, twisting and turning through hallways until he came to a dead end. He knew he needed to go down below this level of the abbey, but he hadn't come across any stairs. Damnation, he must have made a wrong turn somewhere along the way.

He pulled out the illustration again and studied the image. His destination was a large room filled with books and treasure, where monks had once guarded the entryway. He'd found this bloody picture in the journal of a dead village priest who'd had a penchant for ancient folklore.

A short burst of wind swirled around him. His stubby candle died. Darkness enclosed him. He dug into his bag to retrieve another, then struck a match on the stone wall. The match flickered to life with a spark, and the new candle illuminated the space in front of him. Then the flame died as if someone had blown it out. There was air coming from somewhere.

He leaned against the wall, moving his hands against the cold stone, but found nothing. This entire search might prove futile. He moved his feet, and his boot touched something protruding from the wall. He knelt and ran his hand against the protrusion. It was a lever. He pushed it, shoving it flat against the stone. Something below him shifted. The floor separated and then he was moving downward. It was a lift. Evidently the monks had been rather advanced in their technology. He just hoped this ancient thing worked as well going back up.

The stone chute surrounded him, scraping against his shoulders as he continued to descend, but in the darkness, he still could see nothing. Chains creaked and groaned beneath him. Then the platform jerked to a stop.

Graeme waited until all the noises ceased before he stepped forward. He relit his candle, and to his right, he found a wall sconce with a tallow-dipped torch. Once lit, it illuminated the area around him. He stood on a dirt floor and directly in front of him laid a deep chasm; an underground gorge.

It was far too dark to see what lay beyond the gorge, but if the illustration was correct, then across the expanse he would find a chamber. He stepped to the edge of the cliff and stared out into the dark abyss. How was he to get across? He moved slowly to his left, searching for any sign of a bridge. When his boot scuffed over something, he kicked the dirt out of the way and found a rope stretching out from his feet across the canyon. There was another rope above his head attached firmly to a metal loop anchored to the stone wall. He pulled on it, and it slackened, lowering the rope until it was about chest high. The two-rope bridge provided one rope to hold on to, and one to walk on. These had been ingenious monks.

He inhaled slowly. This was not the sort of bridge that he'd been hoping for. He hated heights. Having nothing but an aged rope between him and the nothingness below did not evoke confidence. But he was running out of time. The American who had bought this place would certainly discover this area eventually. If Graeme didn't find that book now, it would likely be lost forever.

It would be impossible to cross the rope bridge while holding the candle, so he pinched the wick between his fingers and dropped the candle in his bag. The torch lit the area behind him, but once he stepped out onto the rope, he'd be shrouded in darkness. He checked his bag to make certain it was secure, then he put one boot onto the rope. It gave beneath his weight, but held firm to the anchor on the other side.

He took a step with his other foot and grabbed hold of the balance rope. Slowly he began his way across, sliding his left foot and then following with the right. The rope swayed and moved, jostling him around as he crossed over the canyon. What the hell had these monks been thinking? Evidently they'd guarded some valuable pieces to go to such lengths to protect them.

His eyes tried to grow accustomed to the blackness around him, but with no light to be found, he still could see nothing. He kept moving. Finally his foot hit against the rock on the other side. He'd made it.

Graeme stepped onto the ledge. Quickly he relit his candle and found a series of torches along the wall that illuminated a hallway. He crouched as he moved through the space, his height a hindrance in the small area. He lit more torches along the way.

A room opened before him, and Graeme stepped down into it. A large, not-quite-circular space, it was filled with trunks and chests and stone tables covered with a variety of items from goblets to jewels. Alcoves carved into the stone wall held other, smaller trunks. He began his search, opening the lid of every trunk and rummaging through their contents, going over every surface and examining each item. If the rest of these priceless treasures remained, then certainly that book was here somewhere.

One of the smaller trunks contained every gemstone he could imagine, and another overflowed with gold pieces. If the American owner became aware of these treasures, his wealth would more than double overnight. Graeme pulled a trunk out of one of the wall niches. A series of high-pitched screeches filled the area, then bats flew at him. He ducked, but one of them smacked into the top of his head, then kept flying. Dammed vile creatures.

Inside this trunk, he found a map, which he tossed in his bag in case it might prove useful. He searched one trunk after another until he finally came to one that was filled with books. He squatted and picked up each book, carefully checking the titles as well as glancing at the inside texts. He came across two that might be of use to some of his friends at Solomon's and shoved them both in his bag. Then he saw it, a small leatherbound volume encrusted with jewels. Inside he found Ancient Persian text. *The Magi's Book of Wisdom*.

He took one last look at all the glittering treasure,

then extinguished the torches before stepping back onto the rope bridge. It was difficult to leave all of the antiquities behind, but he couldn't excavate all of that alone. He would notify Solomon's and they could send a group in to remove all the historical treasures, but he'd found what he'd come for. The rope beneath his feet wobbled. Somewhere to his right, he heard metal scrape.

Then the rope fell away beneath his feet. He gripped the balance rope firmly as he dropped. It felt as if his shoulders were being ripped from his body at the sudden shift of all his weight, but he would not let go. As quickly as he was able, he started moving to his left. One hand moved painstakingly over the other.

He listened as he moved, waiting to hear the sound of fraying rope, but all he could hear was his own heavy breathing. His heart pounded. Sweat coated his hands, and he prayed that he wouldn't lose his grip. He slowly drew closer to the light from the torches to his left.

Finally he reached the other side. He fell onto the dirt floor and lay there, feeling grateful he hadn't fallen to his death. He was one step closer to finding the Stone of Destiny.

Chapter One

———✦◆✦———

London, 1888

Vanessa Pembrooke crept down the staircase, careful not to make a noise. She would marry in two more days, and thoughts of the ceremony plagued her mind, keeping sleep at bay. It would take hours for her mother and her army of servants to primp and curl and shine every last inch of Vanessa's person. Not to mention the dress that she was expected to wear: She'd be head-to-toe ruffle and lace; a doily with feet. Needless to say, all these wretched thoughts left her wide awake. Currently she tiptoed to the library to find something to occupy her mind.

The house sat void of sound, the servants all off to bed, her family long ago retired. Her fiancé was staying in the house, but he had gone to bed early with a sour stomach. So at this late hour she would have the library to herself. All those books waiting just for her. She'd already read the latest scientific journal from front to back. Perhaps she'd pick up a history text.

A soft noise caught her attention and she paused at the door. She turned behind her, but saw no one there. Perhaps her nerves about the wedding were making her more jittery than usual. With a silent turn of the knob, she opened the library door.

Vanessa paused just short of entering the room when she caught sight of something, or rather someone, on the floor in front of the fading fire. Naked limbs writhed around one another, glistening with sweat. The man groaned, and the woman, who sat atop him as if riding a horse, whispered a series of soft *yesses* again and again.

In all her imaginings, Vanessa would never have guessed that couples could copulate in such a manner, having only been told of the traditional man-on-top-under-the-covers-in-the-dark position. Vanessa wondered what might compel two people to do such a thing in a public room. It was rather scandalous, and were her mother to discover such activity, she would have the servants fired immediately. But then the woman leaned back, giving Vanessa a clear view of the man's face—Jeremy, her fiancé.

Vanessa knew her mouth had fallen open, and protocol demanded that she turn away and leave him to his transgression. It was precisely the advice her mother would have given her. *Turn your head and look the other way. Pretend as if you don't notice.*

She knew men strayed from marriage, but it was that long blond hair about the woman's shoulders that gave Vanessa the longest pause. She knew that hair. It belonged to Violet, her younger sister.

Anger coiled inside her. Vanessa didn't know how long

she'd stood there, but eventually they finished what they were doing. Violet rolled off of Jeremy and lay to his side. They murmured to one another, soft whispers between lovers, their heads leaning close together. It was then that Vanessa stepped into the room. She cleared her throat, and upon seeing her, Jeremy reached for the nearest piece of clothing to cover himself. This happened to be Violet's shift, making him look utterly ridiculous. But Vanessa could find no humor in the situation.

"Vanessa!" he said. "I, uh, we—" He had the decency to blush under her scrutiny, the rosy hue staining his cheeks and neck.

"I can see what you were doing," Vanessa said. She steadied her breathing and selected her words carefully. "You said you were not interested in that sort of relationship. You said you did not believe in passion."

He looked at Violet, then back to Vanessa. "That was before." His eyes cast downward.

"Before this?" She motioned to the floor where they sat. "Before tonight?"

"Well, before I met Violet." He winced, clutched the shift to his chest.

Had they been together the entire six weeks Jeremy had been in London? Vanessa longed to sit down, to take several slow breaths and think on the situation until it all made sense.

"We're in love, Vanessa." Jeremy shook his head, his expression moving dangerously close to pity. "I'm sorry. It happened so unexpectedly."

Vanessa shifted her stance, crossing her arms over her body. "In love. Another thing you said you did not believe in. And when were the two of you going to tell me this bit of news?" She took another step forward. "On our wedding day?" Anger, like a spool of thread wound too tight, unraveled. "After the wedding? Or were you planning to simply ignore it and hope I wouldn't notice?" she asked, knowing her voice was rising.

All the while Violet simply sat there, not saying anything, nor did she even have the decency to blush. She would not, however, meet Vanessa's gaze.

"I don't know," was all he said.

Vanessa didn't wait for further explanation. Instead she simply turned and left the room. She didn't know which one of them had angered her more. She was fond of Jeremy, but she'd thought their relationship had been built on mutual interest and respect. As for Violet, they shared blood, a childhood, memories. Granted those things were the extent of the commonality between the two sisters, but she was family.

Vanessa entered her bedroom and closed the door behind her. Without another thought she opened her trunk, already partially packed with her wedding trousseau, and started tossing clothes into it. Violet was the youngest of the three Pembrooke sisters and undoubtedly the most attractive. Also the most gregarious. She was vibrant and spoiled, and people, mostly men, loved her.

Vanessa loved her, too. Although they were different, they were sisters, and this was the ultimate betrayal.

Three hours later when the carriage finally rumbled down the London street, Vanessa did not dare glance out of the tiny curtained window for fear of seeing her mother's stricken face, or worse, her would-be groom's relieved expression. She was officially a runaway bride.

No one would realize that she'd gone until morning. She removed her spectacles and cleaned the lenses on her skirt. Oh, the scandal this would cause. She sighed heavily. So often it was the man who committed the indiscretion, yet it would be the woman's reputation that lay in tatters.

Well, it could not be helped. Vanessa carefully placed her spectacles back atop her nose. She straightened in her seat. Jeremy P. Morris. She'd carefully selected him as her future partner. An American scientist in need of money for his research—her dowry would have set him up nicely. Together they could have made great scientific discoveries.

She pulled a stray thread off her bodice and wound it around one finger. He'd seemed perfect. Level-headed, analytical, intelligent, and not at all moved by the frivolities in life that consumed most people these days—love and lust and whatnot. He'd agreed completely with her thoughts on those matters. She unwound the thread and balled it between fingertip and thumb. Jeremy had seemed a perfect match for her.

She had even come to terms with copulation with him. They wouldn't be plagued with passion and delusions of love. Instead they'd share relations for reproductive purposes. He'd have made a fine father, being able to teach their children about all the meaningful things in life. But now she'd caught Jeremy in the arms of her sister. A passionate embrace, with nude limbs and moans of urgency. She shook her head to dispel the image.

If anyone could bring about a passionate response from Jeremy, it would have been Violet. What choice had that left Vanessa? She could have gone through with the wedding, married the man whom she'd thought was her perfect match. Then her sister would have been miserable. As her husband would have been. And where would that have left Vanessa?

Clearly the two of them had found something special

together. Whether it would last any longer than a shooting star, Vanessa had her doubts. But who was she to stand in the way of two people who had deluded themselves into believing they'd found love? At least she'd discovered the truth before it had been too late.

Besides, this had conveniently opened up her own schedule to allow for a most important trip. She clenched her fists to stop her hands from shaking, all the while telling herself this was what was important. Her research. This was what she cared about. Thank goodness she'd had a modest stash of money hidden away. It had been intended to purchase hair ribbons and the like, but she'd simply tucked away those funds every time her mother had doled them out.

Once the carriage stopped, she'd board a train that would take her to Scotland. All the way to Inverness, to Loch Ness, where some most unusual finds had recently surfaced. Of course, those with limited imagination saw the fossil as merely a standard bone—they were speculating a bovine of some sort. But Vanessa thought better of it.

Mr. Angus McElroy had unearthed evidence of the legendary creature that supposedly dwelled beneath the murky depths of the loch. She believed the locals called it a water kelpie. Had William Buckland not proved the existence of such massive creatures, though on land? Why would it be such a stretch in reality to believe there were those creatures who lived in water?

But the paleontology community had scoffed at the Scotsman's claims, and her fiancé—rather her *former* fiancé—had led the charge. He'd even published a paper refuting the find and claiming it as nothing extraordinary. She should have known then that Jeremy was not the right man to marry.

He was narrow-minded and lacked creativity. Thank goodness, she would not be passing those qualities on to any future progeny. Worse still, his ideas were scientifically unsound. In short, he was wrong.

And she intended to use her time in Scotland to prove precisely that.

On the other side of London in a darkened carriage, Niall Ludley, Earl of Camden, took a shuddering breath. "I'm getting close. I know I am. I merely need more time." His voice shook with anger or fear. He was not certain which.

He was not accustomed to being questioned so. Under normal circumstances, he would be the one in charge. Not only that, but sitting in the darkness unnerved him. He didn't like being unable to see with whom he was speaking. What kind of man entered into a bargain with someone he didn't know? A desperate man. A man who had no other option.

"More time," the man said, his voice completely void of emotion. A crack of a match, then the small flame held to a cigar. A deep inhale, then a puff of smoke. The scent of sweet, spicy tobacco filled the small space. "How much more time?" the man asked.

Niall shook his head, although he knew the man could not see him. "I don't know. Two weeks. Perhaps longer." The truth was he had no idea. Hell, he'd been searching for the treasure of Loch Ness for nearly six years, and he still hadn't found it. Only recently had he discovered that there was another group of caves beneath Urquhart Castle. He'd searched the known ones, but hadn't been able to get into the ones that reached beyond the fallen rocks that barricaded the rest of the caves.

"I can be a very patient man," the stranger said. "I inquired a very long time about this particular treasure, and I was told you were the expert, the man who knew the most and had gotten the closest. But my patience only goes so far. I could have done what you're doing in half the time."

It was on Niall's tongue to inquire why he hadn't. This wasn't the first time the man had mentioned such a thing. He'd said something very similar on their first meeting. Niall had asked some questions that day and received few answers, and then the man had evaporated as if he'd never been in the room. But he'd said something about how he couldn't be seen in public anymore, that there was a bounty on his head.

So this was what Niall had been reduced to. Bargaining with a man whose identity he did not know but who was undoubtedly a criminal. Not just bargaining with. Pleading with.

"I will find the treasure. I promise."

"Of course you will." Niall could hear a smile in the man's tone. Not a cheerful, encouraging smile, but a sadistic, cruel smile. "You know the consequences if you don't."

"Yes, I know," Niall said.

"Do you know what they call me?" the stranger asked, then inhaled slowly on the cigar.

"You told me your name was David," Niall said.

"It is. No one calls me that anymore. I have a much more interesting moniker." He leaned forward, bracing his elbows on his knees, and Niall got the first glimpse of the man's face. It was barely an outline, a fraction of a view highlighted only by the lamplight on the street outside. It was then that Niall noticed the pistol encased in his left hand. "My associates call me The Raven."

Niall's blood ran to ice, and his hands clenched into fists. He had heard the name on more than one occasion. At Solomon's. Other members had had run-ins with a man known as The Raven, a ruthless treasure hunter that had a proclivity for theft, blackmail, kidnapping, and murder. Niall tried to keep his breathing under control. Panic would not save his wife and son. He had to be strong for them, keep his temper under control, and do whatever this bastard wanted so he could get his family back.

Graeme Langford swirled his glass of scotch as he listened to Fredrick Rigby regale him with the story of how he found the ancient scrolls of some obscure Byzantine king. Graeme took a sip of scotch, then rolled his eyes. As he stretched his legs out in front of him, the wool of his trousers felt heavy and oppressive against his skin. He knew it was time to go to Scotland. He was feeling the need to don his kilt and walk on the Highlands.

It had never been his intention to join the ranks of Solomon's Legend Hunters, but when the invitation had come, he'd readily accepted. Most of the time, he enjoyed his association with the club, as the majority of the men were good blokes. But there were a scattered few who were just plain peculiar.

Nick Callum caught his glance from across the table and gave him a look of pure exasperation. Nick leaned forward and set down his glass, then laid his head on the table. Graeme swallowed a smile. Whenever Rigby was in the club, no one could have a conversation of their own. The damned bastard spoke so loudly and addressed the room like an assembly so everyone was privy to his stories.

"He's never going to shut up," Nick said.

"Move to the main room?" Graeme suggested.

"Definitely," Nick said as he came to his feet.

When they entered the main room, Graeme immediately saw Max Barrett, Fielding Grey, and the newest Solomon's member, Justin Salinger, seated at a table. He and Nick made their way over. Nick turned his chair around to straddle it.

Graeme watched his friend. "It's a compulsion with you to be different."

Nick cursed Graeme in response, then gave him a toothy grin.

"Children," Max said with feigned annoyance.

It was much quieter in the main room despite the number of people. Once Rigby realized the larger crowd was in this room, he'd move in here. If they wanted to have a conversation, they'd have to do it fast. "How goes the Atlantis search?" Graeme asked Max.

Max shrugged. "New research of late, but I'm not certain it will lead to anything."

"He got shot," Justin added from behind his hand.

"Not the first time," Fielding said.

Max laughed. "I forgot I told you that story."

"It was a woman that shot him," Justin said with a smirk.

Max had a way of getting himself into trouble. The fact that it had been with a woman didn't surprise Graeme in the least.

"Who was it this time?" Fielding asked.

"What the devil, Salinger, if you tell all my bloody secrets, I'll tell yours," Max said.

"Hello, darling," Esme Grey said as she swooped down to kiss Fielding's cheek.

Graeme had been of assistance to both of them when

they'd gotten into some trouble with Pandora's box, not to mention a well-known criminal who happened to be Fielding's uncle. There were those that didn't believe either one of the Greys should have been granted admittance into the club, but Graeme hadn't been one of them. Fielding had almost single-handedly saved the crown, and though Esme was the only female member of Solomon's, she was smart and as much an authority on their subject as he was on his.

Nick swiped a chair for her from an adjoining table.

"Thank you," she said as she sat next to her husband.

"Did you spend all of our money?" Fielding asked.

"Perhaps," she said sweetly. Then she began pilfering through her shopping bag. "I know you will all be delighted to know I have purchased a new pair of gloves," she placed them on the table, "a new hat,"—again, it went onto the table—"and some fancy face crème." She set the jar down as well.

"I knew if we allowed a woman in our midst, she'd start bringing in fancy-smelling whatnots," Nick said dramatically.

"I'll have you know that none of this is for here. This is all for me," Esme said emphatically.

Max grabbed the jar of facial crème.

"See there, you've already ruined Lindberg," Nick said.

Max shook his head. "Did you buy this at the little shop in Piccadilly Square?"

"Yes," she said with a slight frown. "A friend suggested it, said it's all the rage right now. It's supposed to remove unwanted lines from one's face." She smiled. "Perhaps we'll use some on you right here." She rubbed the skin between Fielding's brows.

He swatted at her hand. "Those lines make me look distinguished. Otherwise I'd be just as pretty as Nick here."

"Why do you ask?" Esme turned to Max.

"I had the opportunity to meet Miss Tobias recently," he said.

"Isn't she utterly charming and so beautiful?" Esme asked.

"Charming and beautiful?" Justin asked. "You never mentioned that."

"So she's the lass who shot you?" Graeme asked. He laughed at his friend.

Chapter Two

~~~~~~~~~~~~

Vanessa made her way quickly through the noisy pub and took a seat at an empty table. Heavy wood paneling covered nearly every surface in the room. The floor currently acted as a small pool for spilled ale. But she needed to eat.

Gingerly she opened Jeremy's notes and smoothed her hand across them. This was precisely the sort of place that Jeremy would balk at entering. He would despair at even laying his precious notes on the sticky surface of the table. So she did it regardless, knowing that he wouldn't be needing them anymore. Furthermore, he shouldn't have left them lying around while he was off dallying with Violet.

All around her, large and hairy Scottish men sat at the tables slamming their mugs together, cursing and picking fights with one another. Were it not for her considerable practice at ignoring noise to focus on work, she might have been more distracted.

Vanessa was quite used to pretending that nothing

around her was meant for her attention, a skill that had come in handy on more than one occasion when she'd been stuck beside a bore at a dinner party. Or been persuaded to dance with an arrogant, yet ignorant, oaf at a soirée. She'd learned such a skill at home with her family, where her mother and sisters spoke of nothing of more import than the next social engagement and which fabrics best complemented their coloring. Of course, they tried to include her, but Vanessa found none of that the least bit interesting. Instead she wanted to read or study, or more precisely, *she wanted to dig*. Until this very trip, she hadn't yet had the opportunity.

Now Vanessa was finally here in Scotland, where the history was mixed heavily with myth and the soil was rich with undiscovered fossils, all waiting for her to unearth and categorize them. First thing tomorrow morning, she would hike over to those castle ruins and find her way into the caverns beneath. Jeremy was wrong about Mr. McElroy's discovery, and if the poor Scotsman were still alive, she'd find him to tell him so. It had been a point of contention between her and her would-be husband, but he'd taken the time to listen to her argument. She'd thought he'd been weighing her hypothesis. Now, though, she believed that he'd merely been humoring her. Well, she would prove him wrong—him and the rest of the scientific community who believed her to be utterly unqualified.

She had tried to argue Mr. McElroy's point by sending several letters supporting his theory that the bone belonged to what the Scots called the water kelpie. But not one of them had been printed in any of the scientific journals. No; Vanessa didn't believe a mystical creature still lived in those peat-stained waters. But something *had* lived there many years ago, and the evidence was just waiting for her discovery.

She put the tip of her pencil between her teeth as she collected her thoughts, then she jotted down a note.

"What's a purty lass like you doin' all alone?" A large-necked man plopped into the empty chair adjacent to hers. His thick brogue, laced with inebriation, took some concentration to understand. As he looked over her notebook, his nose wrinkled. "What are you doing there in that book?"

She closed the pages over her hand to mark her spot and glanced at him above her spectacles. "I am working, sir, and you are disturbing me." Perhaps she should have stayed in her room. Still, she'd been hungry, and the bar-maid had said this was the only place she could eat. So she'd sat to wait for her lamb stew.

He laughed, a gritty, dark sound. "Disturbing you, am I? Well, we'll see about that." He reached over, and with one swift pull, he'd yanked her onto his lap, knocking the notebook to the floor in the process. She struggled against him, kicking at his legs and trying to pound on his chest, but he clasped both her wrists in his vise-like grip.

"Unhand me, sir!" she said loudly, continuing to fight. She eyed Jeremy's notebook lying facedown on the filthy floor. As gratifying as it might be to destroy something of his, she needed that research. "I must collect my notes!"

"I don't think so. You're a nice little morsel, aren't you?" He buried his face in her hair. "And you smell real nice. Like flowers and honey."

Vanessa's heart thundered in her chest, the sound reverberating to pound in her ears. She had not carefully weighed the situation before she'd acted. She'd been so focused on her research, so intent on her own purpose, that she hadn't bothered to think about this new environment. This was not the sort of place where a well-bred lady should travel alone. Yet here she was. Not very smart of her, she now acknowledged. This was precisely the impetuous behavior that her mother found so taxing.

There was no need to panic; that's the reaction her sisters would have had. Vanessa, however, was level-headed and generally good at sizing up challenging situations. This one would be no different. She merely needed to stay calm, keep her wits about her, and figure out a way to escape. Perhaps she should simply jerk herself away and run up to her room. But with the current hold the man had on her, freeing herself was impossible. She could call for help. Perhaps people simply didn't realize that she wasn't interested in being handled by this man. Certainly a crowd this size would not allow this man to truly harm her.

But as three other large Scots stood and moved to her table, each of their expressions more lascivious than the others', she began to doubt her convictions. These men would not protect her. They would assist her assailant. She saw the great error in her logic. She had grossly underestimated her situation, and now she was in serious trouble. She doubled her efforts. Her legs kicked out, trying in vain to wiggle free from the man's hold.

"What do we have here, Angus?" one man asked as he straddled a chair next to them. He ran a rough hand down Vanessa's cheek.

She frowned at him and tried to pull away from his offensive touch. Had her hands been free, she would have walloped him good. Boxed his ears, or poked him in the eyes.

"A fine piece of muslin," another man said. He moved his eyebrows up and down in a move that Vanessa could only assume meant he found her attractive. The irony of the situation was not lost on her. Finally she had a man sexually interested in her, something her mother had spent hours fretting about. But eligible, appropriate men they were not.

The man who'd imprisoned her on his lap—Angus, the other man had called him—was trying to run his hand up her leg, but she managed to deflect his efforts with an elbow to his abdomen. The man next to him yanked on her hair, pulling her head back so she could see his grimy face above hers. His yellowed teeth smelled foul, a mixture of ale and rot. Her eyes watered.

"Oh, there you are, love," another voice said from behind her. "I'd ask you kindly to remove your hands from my intended."

She could not see the owner of the voice, but this man sounded different from the others. While his voice still had the lilt of a Scottish brogue, his tone was more refined, cleaner around the edges. Though his words were polite, his tone was edged with a threat.

"Your intended?" Angus asked.

"Aye. I said let her go."

"As you wish," the man said, then dumped Vanessa onto the hard wood-planked floor.

Vanessa landed with a thud, her wool dress splayed around her, revealing both ankles. A hand reached out to pull her to her feet. She snatched her notebook on the way up.

She looked up and found herself staring into the most alarmingly handsome face she'd ever seen. His long brown hair hung to his shoulders in a wild and unkempt way, but she could tell he'd washed it recently, not at all like the greasy, matted manes of the other men. A day's worth of beard covered his cheeks and chin, but did nothing to hide his sensual mouth, which quirked in a subtle grin. But it was his crystal clear green eyes that seemed to void her vocabulary. She nodded like a simpleton.

He held her close to his side. So far, no one had resorted to fisticuffs, but two of the Scots still held a stance that suggested they might swing a punch at any moment. Vanessa found herself holding her breath, so she exhaled slowly.

"So, English," Angus said, sizing up her rescuer. "You've come back to the wilds of the hills, have you?"

"Fits you'd find yourself a pretty lady to wed," another said. "What's the matter, the local skirts aren't good enough for the likes of you?" Guffaws of laughter surrounded them.

This close to her rescuer, she could smell him. A delicious combination of soap and leather and the pure smell of the clean Highland air filled her nose. She caught herself before she closed her eyes to inhale.

"Did you bring her home to wed her properly?" Angus asked with a wide grin that highlighted his foul teeth.

"None of your damned business," her savior said. But she noted a slight tic in his jawline.

"A true Scot would wed her here and now," Angus taunted with narrowed eyes.

"Wed her, then bed her," the other agreed with a grin.

"What's the matter, English?" another asked.

Vanessa noticed how the man at her side clenched his fist that rested at her waist. Her savior never once met her gaze as he looked at the other men in the tavern. They were all slightly smaller than he, but two of them were as broad. Still, he was only one man.

"English won't do it," Angus said.

"He ain't a real Scot," the other said. "Too much blue blood."

The taunting reminded Vanessa of her young cousins who teased and quipped back and forth, goading each other into doing something unpleasant. Children's folly, nothing more. But suddenly she realized how quiet the room had fallen. It had been so loud, full of boisterous voices and music coming from an old harpsichord in the corner of the room. Everyone waited, listening for what would happen between her defender and the wretched men who'd attacked her.

"Mavis," Angus yelled. Then he held up his hand. A moment later, a rope soared across the pub, and he caught it in his fist. He took a step toward them. "Well, are you a real Scot or no'?"

"Nah, he's an English," the other man said.

At long last, the man protecting her glanced down and met her gaze. His pure green eyes met hers, and her mouth went completely dry. She'd never been one to become lathered by the appearance of men. Her sisters had certainly fallen into fits of hysteria when handsome men had expressed interest in them, but Vanessa had never looked up much to take notice. But with this man, his rugged handsomeness was hard to ignore. She pushed her spectacles back up the bridge of her nose.

"We'll do the ceremony," he said in his low baritone voice. "I'll marry her right now."

Before Vanessa could ask any questions, she found herself facing the large stranger and both their right hands were tied together with the rope. The man before her repeated vows, and then nodded to her when it was her turn.

Vanessa tugged on her hand and realized it was indeed

tied quite firmly to the man with the beautiful green eyes. The stench of the other men around her assaulted her senses. "Marry this man?" she asked softly, more to herself than anyone in particular.

Loud cheers surged around her. If she wasn't mistaken, she'd just accidentally married a Scotsman.

"Well, kiss her, then. Kiss your bride," the man said.

Graeme took a long look at the woman standing before him. She was not exactly a wee thing, though she was most definitely smaller than him. But for a lass, she was tall. And pretty, with her bright blue eyes and dimpled cheeks. Though her beauty was understated because she hid it behind drab colors and spectacles.

With his right hand tied to hers, he used his left to pull her close. Then he bent and pressed his lips to hers. It was intended to be a brief kiss to seal this foolish ceremony. Instead, the instant their lips touched, he forgot about the fact that he didn't even know her and kissed her soundly. Her soft lips opened, and her warm breath mingled with his own. And in that moment, it felt as if they'd kissed a hundred times before.

He abruptly ended the kiss. Still she stood before him, eyes closed, lips parted. Damn if she wasn't beautiful. He needed to get her out of here and soon, before he ended up doing to her precisely what he was trying to rescue her from.

"Get these bloody rags off our hands," Graeme said.

"Eager to get to the bedding!" one man shouted. Raucous laughter followed.

The man unwrapped their hands. Graeme slid his hand protectively around his counterfeit bride to guide her out of the pub. She halted, slid her hand out of his, and turned to face him.

"Thank you very much for coming to my rescue. I can assure you it is most appreciated. I was not certain what those wretched men had planned to do with me, but I knew I was not in the least bit interested," she said, her tone filled with indignation.

Did the lass actually believe that he'd leave her here? Alone?

She nodded once, then turned in the direction of the stairs that led to the sleeping quarters.

He moved them in the direction of the stairs, trying to ignore the bawdy shouts around them. "You cannot stay here," he said.

"And why not?" she asked. She placed her hands on her hips and eyed him defiantly.

"Because had I not interfered, those men would no doubt have taken turns with you." He paused to see if she understood his meaning. When her blue eyes rounded and her head tilted, he wagered she'd comprehended perfectly. "Staying here would only give them an invitation to do so in your room instead of on the dirty pub floor."

Her mouth formed a silent "o."

He turned her back toward the door.

"My belongings," she whispered as she came to a stop.

"What?"

"The items I brought with me are in a room upstairs. I had intended to stay here," she said.

"Let us collect your things," Graeme said. "And then we need to remove ourselves from this place. Those men believe us to be husband and wife, and they might expect us to prove that."

Again her eyes widened. Then she hurriedly made her way up the stairs.

He followed behind her, enjoying the way her skirt

cupped her backside as she climbed upward. Her height intrigued him; her legs must go on forever. He'd best stop the direction of these thoughts. But before he did, he took a moment to imagine what it would be like to press her up against the door and kiss her again.

He reached over and assisted, sliding the key into the lock and turning hard to the left. He'd seen the way that she'd handled herself with the other men. She was smart, but foolish in not knowing her own limitations and what a dangerous situation she'd been in.

The room was a tiny space with only a narrow bed, the mattress no doubt stuffed with moldy hay, and what Graeme could only guess was a washbasin.

"How long were you intending to stay here?" he asked.

"As long as it took," she said as she gathered her belongings.

"As long as what took?" he asked.

She closed the trunk, then stood there glancing first at the trunk and then the door. "Do you suppose I could call a footman?"

He plucked her trunk up off the floor. "You didn't answer my question."

"Right." She surveyed the room, presumably searching for anything that she might have left. She chewed at her bottom lip, then shoved her spectacles up further on her nose. "My research." She turned to face him, a small shoulder bag pressed against her chest. "Precisely where are you taking me?"

"Somewhere safer than this," he said.

"How do I know I can trust you? That you're not simply leading me out of here so you can ravish me?" she asked. Then she rounded her shoulders and eyed him across the top of her glasses.

He suppressed a laugh. "You don't." He stepped closer to her, his large frame looming over her. "But I would wager I smell better than those blokes downstairs." He made to put her trunk back on the floor. "If you'd prefer—"

She held a hand up. "No."

He braced the trunk on his shoulder, then turned for the door. "Follow. And stay close." Quietly they crept down the stairs, then out the door. The cold night wind had calmed, but the chill still hung heavy in the air.

"What am I supposed to call you?" she asked.

"Husband," he said.

She caught up to walk beside him. She opened her mouth to say something, but words failed her.

"My name is Graeme," he said, interrupting her protests. She was more than annoyed by their little ceremony and by being removed from her room; he could see the frown settle on her brow. He had to admit, though, that seeing her with her feathers all ruffled was vastly entertaining.

"Graeme. Very well, and I am Vanessa." She fell into step beside him, still clutching her bag to her chest.

"It's not far, where we're going. Just over that small rise," he said, gesturing up ahead.

They walked in silence for a few moments before he spoke. "Research?" he asked, curiosity getting the better of him. "What sort of research does a lady of good breeding busy herself with?"

She cut her eyes at him, and he knew instantly that he'd somehow offended her. "Fossils. And old bones."

"Bones," he repeated, unsure whether he'd heard her correctly.

"Precisely." She juggled her bag to try to better grasp it, and he realized that two rather large volumes had been stuffed into the bag. Briefly, she paused to straighten her glasses. "They are most fascinating."

"Indeed." She was a most peculiar female. Beautiful and obviously intelligent, in a bookish sort of way, but fascinated by strange things. Granted people could say the same of him; some had. "They call that study Paleontology, I believe," he said, then wondered why he'd tried to impress her.

Her eyes brightened, and she gave him a brilliant smile. "That is correct. It is a relatively new science compared to other fields of interest."

He reached over and grabbed the bag out of her arms and slung it over his other shoulder. Now weighed down with both her trunk and her bag, he silently wished that he'd brought his horse. But there really wasn't much farther to walk.

"Thank you," she said, sounding surprised. "Might we talk about that ceremony?"

"It wasn't real," he said, finally ending her misery.

"I beg your pardon?" She turned around to look back in the direction of the pub. "But those men said—"

"I know what you heard. Fools," he said. "Handfasting is an old Scottish custom, but it's not widely practiced anymore. It's not a legally binding ceremony."

She stopped walking, and her hand came up to her chest. "So we are not married? Oh, that's a huge relief. Not that you're not husband material, though certainly not husband material for me." She began moving forward again. "Not that I'm looking for a husband, because I most assuredly am not. In fact, I only recently escaped from my own unwanted betrothal only to stumble into our little union."

She took a great gulp of a breath, then flashed him a

blinding smile. "In any case, I do appreciate you coming to my rescue. Although I'm certain I would have escaped unscathed somehow, it was much easier, not to mention faster, that you came along to save me."

Graeme was relatively certain that she hadn't taken nearly enough breaths to get through all of that. Not only did she speak incredibly fast, but her thought process jumped from one subject to the next with nary a pause.

So she didn't believe him to be husband material. Was it because she thought him a dirty Scot? Oh, perhaps he was more passable than the others from the pub, but not as refined as a stodgy Englishman that was more to her taste? He'd be a liar if he said that didn't offend him, but he was used to the English judging him by his Scottish heritage as well as the Scots ridiculing him for his English title.

She was full of surprises, though, and that certainly kept his curiosity piqued. From studying fossils to breaking an engagement, she had him wondering what she'd reveal next. Damned if instead of finding her behavior annoying, she made him smile. Annoyed by that revelation, he forced a frown.

"Escaped your own wedding?" he asked. They crested the hill, and down the path sat his mother's white stone cottage. The stones reflected the moonlight, taking on a nice sheen. Though he knew the inside was spotless and tidy—his mother took to heart the old proverb that cleanliness was next to godliness—the cottage would be a far cry from anything Vanessa was used to in London. Though she *had* been willing to stay in that pitiful excuse of a room at the tavern, he reminded himself.

"I did. Just yesterday," she said. "Got on a train and immediately came up here."

"Old or fat?" Graeme asked.

"I beg your pardon?"

"Your groom. Was he old or fat?"

She chuckled. "Neither, actually. He was rather pleasant in appearance, and I *thought* we would make a brilliant pair. He is a researcher as well. He's an American, though." Then she shrugged. "But I did not hold that against him."

It was his turn to laugh. "Kind of you." He waited a few more steps before asking, "If you were so perfect for each other, what happened?"

"I found him in bed with my younger sister," she said without even pausing. "Well, on the floor in front of the hearth in the study, to be exact."

Graeme released a low whistle. Evidently that fiancé of hers was a complete and utter idiot. Though Vanessa was certainly not your typical English lady, she was beautiful and definitely more interesting than the rest of them. Perhaps American men were even more foolish than Englishmen.

"I suppose it's not entirely surprising," she continued, not pausing to pity herself. "Most men can't walk away once they've seen Violet. She's lovely." She sighed. "But Jeremy had seemed so level-headed. Above all that passion nonsense."

Graeme bit back a laugh. He stopped in front of his mother's cottage. Despite the late hour, two lanterns still burned bright, welcoming any visitors. Come springtime, the front of the house would be covered with brightly colored flowers, and in autumn, the hills behind the house would be bright purple with heather. But now in the dead of winter, the earth slept, and the grounds around them were nearly colorless. Though it wasn't a sprawling estate,

it was a sizable house with several bedrooms and a study
that he used when he visited.

"We're here," he said.

"We're where, precisely?" she asked.

"My home. My mother's home." It occurred to him in
that moment precisely what he'd done tonight. Yes, he'd
rescued the girl from a dangerous situation. But he could
have done so without allowing Angus and the rest of those
men to goad him into a meaningless ceremony. He could
have simply swept the girl out of the room and brought
her to another, safer inn closer to Inverness.

But instead he'd brought her home.

Chapter Three

Once Graeme had safely deposited Vanessa in his old bedroom, he made his way to the small kitchen at the back of the house. There was no reason to wake his family to notify them that they had guests; tomorrow morning would be here soon enough, but he was hungry.

The kitchen looked the same as it always did. A table with six chairs was off to the side, calico curtains hung in the small window at the back wall, not a crumb, nor any dish left out of the cupboards. A loaf of bread rolled up in a towel sat on top of the stove. He took a seat at the wooden table with a hunk of the herbed bread slathered in butter.

Tomorrow Graeme would convince Vanessa that Scotland was no place for an unaccompanied single lady. She should make her way back to London. Certainly her family would understand her need to flee her wedding under such circumstances.

Graeme needed her off his hands so he could focus intently on catching up on his own research. It had been several long months since he'd been able to get back here, and his work locating the Stone of Destiny had suffered.

While he was here in Scotland, he hoped to finally be able to locate an artifact that would enable him to decipher the secret code of a handwritten section in *The Magi's Book of Wisdom*. He'd tried without the decoder. Ever since he'd first glanced through the book, he'd worked on that code, employing every tactic he could to uncover the meaning. But so far nothing had worked.

He'd searched for it every time he'd returned to Scotland, but he'd had no luck thus far. But he'd recently found some old letters between two monks that said "the key had been hidden away to protect the royal ones." Because the Stone of Destiny had been fought over by kings for generations, Graeme felt certain the key was the decoder he sought.

Graeme had been so deep in thought that he hadn't heard his mother's approach until she appeared in the kitchen, a huge log held over her head.

She took one look at him and closed her eyes in relief. "You scared the devil out of me, boy." Moira stepped over to him, set the log on the floor, then popped him on the head with her open hand. "Coming in to the house and not even letting us know you're here. Where is your head, Graeme? I could have killed you, you know?"

He chuckled. "Of that I have no doubt." He'd been in many dangerous situations, yet being clubbed to death by his mother, who barely reached his chest, seemed a humorous way to perish.

"What were you doing sneaking in like that?" she asked.

"I brought a woman here," he said. Not the best way that he could have alerted her to Vanessa's presence. He chalked it up to being tired after a long journey.

"Did ya now?" Moira asked. She dropped herself into a

chair across from him and smiled. She clutched her dressing gown tighter around her body.

"It's not what you're thinking, Mother. She's English and was at the pub. Alone. Got herself into a bit of trouble, and I figured she'd be safer staying here."

"Right you are. That place is none too gentle on the fairer sex." Moira took a bite of Graeme's bread and chewed thoughtfully.

A knock sounded at the front door of the house.

"Expecting someone?" Graeme asked as he came to his feet.

"Not at this hour," she said, following close behind him. "Hurry, before they wake the rest of the house."

Graeme opened the door to find Jensen, the leader of Solomon's, standing in the cold. A hired hackney waited behind him. "Jensen. Come in."

"I do apologize for bothering you here. I tried to catch you before you left London, but I missed you. This is of dire importance. Is there somewhere we can speak?" He eyed Moira, but said nothing.

"I'll leave you two to your privacy," she said, obviously taking the not-so-subtle hint. She left them standing in the front parlor, a room not quite big enough to do significant entertaining, but it would serve the purpose of a late-night meeting.

"Someone has broken into Westminster," Jensen said as soon as Moira was out of earshot. "The police are not even certain how the perpetrator got inside, as the guards remained in place through the night."

"Bribery," Graeme said. "I don't suppose even the queen's guards are above that."

Jensen nodded. "Indeed." The man stepped over to a chair near the hearth and sat.

"What did they take?" Graeme asked, but somehow he knew precisely what Jensen was about to say. Why else would the man be here to talk to him?

"The Stone of Destiny," Jensen said.

"The counterfeit one," Graeme corrected.

Jensen nodded. It was common knowledge in Solomon's that Graeme fervently believed that the Stone of Destiny housed within Westminster Abbey was a forgery.

"Can't say I'm surprised. It seems a worthy token to have, if one believed it to be the true piece," Graeme said. "But there are certainly other treasures, more valuable ones, housed elsewhere in London."

"Precisely. Why would someone want," Jensen paused, "pardon the disrespect, a piece of sandstone?"

Graeme had to smile. There were plenty who didn't understand his quest to find the real Stone of Destiny. Hell, there were times when even he wasn't certain why he felt such a burning desire to locate it. But he knew it was an artifact that the Scottish people revered. King Edward I had stolen it from Scotland, and Graeme wanted nothing more than to return it to them.

"The answer to *that* question is what's bothering us," Jensen said.

"Well, there are those who believe the stone to be a biblical relic," Graeme said.

"Yes," Jensen said. "The pillow stone upon which Jacob had his prophetic dreams." Then he paused a moment before adding, "Graeme, please sit."

Graeme did as he was bade, not out of obedience, but more from curiosity. Jensen had been a member of Solomon's for more than twenty years and, for the most part, kept to himself. He tended to engage other members only when it was time to invite someone new into the club, or if there was a problem that needed an immediate solution. As in this current situation, Graeme assumed.

"Recently some potentially troubling things have come to our attention," Jensen said.

The man always spoke in the plural. Graeme knew there were others that worked in the background of Solomon's, but for the most part "we" usually meant only Jensen. "And?" Graeme said.

Jensen clasped his long fingers together across his lap. "I'm afraid it's in reference to your cousin."

"My cousin?" Graeme asked.

"Yes, Niall Ludley," Jensen said.

Ah. He nodded. Graeme, of course, knew Niall. They'd grown up together. But he rarely considered him family. His father's side. The English side. Niall was Graeme's father's sister's son and now bore the title of the Earl of Camden. Graeme had assumed that Niall would be more like Graeme's father and the rest of their English peers—cold. So he'd not invested much time in having more than a friendly relationship.

"I'm afraid if this is in reference to Niall," Graeme said, "I won't be of much service. We aren't exactly close."

"Meaning what precisely?" Jensen asked.

"Meaning I know him." Graeme shrugged. "We're courteous, but we aren't close like brothers." Like family ought to be.

"But you knew he was a member of Solomon's as well," Jensen said.

Graeme nodded slowly. "I do recall reading about his membership a few years ago in the newsletter."

Jensen's eyebrows rose. "I'm surprised." A small smile played at the corners of his mouth.

"Because you keep close watch as to what all of your

relations are doing?" Graeme asked. He uncrossed one leg, then crossed the other.

Jensen chuckled. "No, of course not. But I would have thought his particular interest would pique your own curiosity."

"Remind me," Graeme said. He leaned back in the chair, resting his hands across his abdomen.

"The Loch Ness treasure."

Graeme did remember reading about that. "Right." It hadn't surprised him. Even as a child, Niall had always wanted to go with Graeme to Scotland. Thankfully Niall's mother had had prejudices against the "wilds of the north" as she'd called them and never let her son go. But it stood to reason that as a boy, he'd been interested in the land, and as a man, he'd come to study a bit of it. Graeme remembered now when Niall had built another home here, and how he'd invited them all over for dinner.

"Are you familiar?" Jensen asked.

"With the legend of the treasure? Aye, I have heard tale of it."

Jensen leaned forward. "And the connection to the Kingmaker, have you heard of that?"

Something tickled at the back of Graeme's mind, but he couldn't recollect any mention of a Kingmaker. "There are many theories involving the Stone of Destiny, but I've never heard it referred to as a Kingmaker."

"The Stone of Destiny and the Kingmaker are not synonymous, Graeme, but rather two separate items," Jensen said.

"I do not mean to be rude, Jensen, but I'm unsure of why you've traveled all this way. Merely to educate me on my cousin's research? Or to discuss Scottish lore of ancient treasures?" Graeme said.

"Bear with me a moment longer, and I believe it will all begin to make sense to you," Jensen said. Once Graeme had nodded, the older man continued. "The legend of the Kingmaker states that any person to have the four royal stones in their possession would, in turn, become King." Jensen shook his head. "The idea that a mere legend would jeopardize Her Majesty's claim to the crown is, of course, ridiculous."

"Of course," Graeme agreed, but that thought continued to nag his mind. The missing decoder was supposedly hidden to protect the royals; perhaps that too had something to do with this Kingmaker.

"However," Jensen continued, "We cannot ignore that the situation is troubling. If someone is indeed moving to collect these royal stones in an attempt to complete the Kingmaker, then the intent behind the threat is real, if not the danger itself. There are many who believe this is precisely how William of Normandy claimed the crown of England. Of course we have no actual proof of that." Jensen paused, then cleared his throat. "As for any mystical powers the Kingmaker might actually possess..."

Jensen let his words trail off. Another man might have infused the words *mystical powers* with scorn, but not Jensen. By and large, the men of Solomon's were scientists and explorers. Rational men. Yet they were also adventurers. And Graeme had witnessed firsthand the cursed bracelets when his friend Fielding had unearthed Pandora's box. He knew all too well the mysteries that lay between reality and legend.

"And the Loch Ness treasure is one of those four royal stones?" Graeme asked.

"We believe so. Supposedly, the others are guarded by similar creatures," Jensen said.

"You mean the water kelpie," Graeme said with a smile.

"Indeed." Jensen did not sneer, but his tone held a hint of cynicism.

Evidently Jensen was not a believer. Graeme had many a memory of listening to his family weave tales of kelpie sightings. As much time as he'd spent in these highlands, he'd never even seen a glimpse. However, he knew his family believed. Most Scots did. But he never questioned it one way or another. What did it matter to him if there was a beastie swimming in the dark waters of Loch Ness?

"The fabled dragon guarding the treasure," Graeme said. "So what does this have to do with Niall?" Graeme drummed his fingers on the side table. "You believe *him* to be after this Kingmaker? Because someone took the stone from Westminster."

Jensen released a heavy breath. "Either he is or he's working with someone else who is after it. Either way, his behavior before he left London had been curious for several weeks. We need you to check in on him. See if you can't discover precisely what he's working on, and who he's working with, if he has a partner."

"Where is he?" Graeme asked.

"Here. Loch Ness. He's been here for a few days. We've also intercepted some of his communication, which is oddly vague. The evidence is not conclusive, and we merely need to be certain before we confront him."

"I see." Graeme leaned forward, bracing his elbows on his knees. "So you want me to spy on him?" Graeme asked.

"Precisely. Extend your visit with your family. It's lovely up here this time of year, isn't it?" Jensen asked with a mischievous grin.

"Ah yes, winter in the Highlands. Nothing like having only a few hours of daylight."

"Reconnect with your long-lost cousin," Jensen said.

"One more question," Graeme said. "What does all of this have to do with the Stone of Destiny?"

Vanessa pressed her ear against the heavy wooden door to try to hear more of their conversation. She assumed the speakers sat in the room directly outside of hers. The walls in the cottage were not thin enough to hear everything, but she was able to decipher some key phrases. She knew she'd distinctly heard something about a hidden treasure. Certainly she would not have misheard something that intriguing. She stood up straight.

There had also been mention of Westminster. A treasure hidden in the abbey; is that what they meant? She'd never heard a tale of such a thing.

When Graeme was talking, his deep brogue seemed to penetrate the walls and breeze over her skin. He spoke of the Stone of Destiny. Counterfeit? Certainly not; that stone had been in the abbey for hundreds of years. Was that the treasure of which they spoke?

She pressed her ear tightly to the door and held her breath. The other gentleman certainly sounded English, and she could tell from his manner of speech that he was educated.

"Loch Ness treasure." She heard those three words perfectly. It would seem in her quest to find fossils, she had stumbled upon a most captivating mystery.

Perhaps when the voices stilled, and the house grew quiet, she'd sneak out to do some investigation. Graeme was hiding something. Clearly he was no simple Scotsman. And she could rarely resist a good puzzle. Granted, her inquisitive nature had gotten her in trouble on more than one occasion in the past, but she had learned from some mistakes and now was more careful, more guarded.

Vanessa sat on the floor, leaning against the door, and continued to listen. Their conversation had quieted to whispers now, but she did not know if they had retreated to another part of the house or if they had simply lowered their voices. Twenty minutes later, Vanessa heard only silence. For good measure, she waited another hour before venturing out of her room.

The house wasn't large, the rooms close together, so she was thankful that she'd had the good sense to remove her shoes. Any noise she made could easily wake Graeme and his family. If she was caught, she would simply say that she'd gotten thirsty and had gone in search of something to drink.

The three doors down the hall from hers were most likely other bedchambers, so she decided to go back the way Graeme had brought her in. She passed through the parlor, a small dining room, and then stumbled upon what appeared to be a study. She crept through the partially opened doorway and examined her surroundings. A fire still burned in the hearth, though it had not been stoked for a while, and the flames were beginning to die out. She found a lantern on the desk and lit it so that soft light flooded the area.

On the desk, she found some texts lying open, but they were nothing particularly out of the ordinary. However, beneath them, she found handwritten notes as well as a journal and two maps spread open. The notes detailed the existence of something called the Kingmaker. She'd heard the man who visited Graeme mention a word she hadn't quite understood—but "Kingmaker"—that was what he'd said. She fell into the chair behind the desk and pulled the notes to her.

According to legend, the Kingmaker was precisely what it sounded like, a relic that would make someone a ruler once they had it in their possession.

Only it wasn't simply one relic. It was composed of four royal stones—the Stone of Destiny, and then three gems, all named for important kings. King David's stone, a sapphire, represented wisdom. King William I's stone, a ruby, represented courage. And King Robert Bruce's, an emerald, represented authority. Certainly it was the latter whose treasure was tied to Loch Ness.

Surely no one actually believed that if they had a certain collection of rocks in their possession, they would magically become king? Still, Vanessa knew that people could believe in nearly anything. And it seemed people these days were eager to believe in the unexplained. Hadn't she seen an advertisement in the newspaper of an exhibit at a London museum featuring relics rumored to be cursed? So it was feasible that someone might accept the legend of the Kingmaker as truth.

She set aside the notes and moved on to the maps. They were both hand drawn, and while one depicted the inner workings of a series of caverns, the other appeared to be where those caverns were located.

While it was clearly not a professional map, the level of detail was admirable. The loch covered a small portion at the bottom of the drawing, but just above the water's edge she could see what appeared to be an entrance into a cave. Then high upon the hill, above the loch, sat Urquhart Castle, with a staircase that led into yet another set of caverns. Judging by the distance between the two entrances, Vanessa would wager these were the same set of caverns but with two separate entries.

There were marks on some of the caves as if they had already been searched and marked off the list. Excitement bubbled inside her. It would seem that she had found the very caves she needed to visit for her own research.

Oh how she wished Mr. McElroy were still alive so that she could find out precisely which caves he'd explored to find that bone. Of course, she had the man's crude drawing amidst Jeremy's notes, but it was just of the actual cave. But even without a guide to the correct spot, she now knew where to start.

The journal was the most interesting item, though. It detailed several years of research for the legendary Stone of Destiny. If she wasn't mistaken, the penmanship looked similar to that on the maps, but it was hard to tell due to the limited words on the maps. There was mention of a group of men called Solomon's, *The Magi's Book of Wisdom*, and many other resources.

Vanessa's heart beat quickly with her excitement. Was this Graeme's journal? Vanessa read on, fascinated by the detailed research. Although the subject wasn't one grounded in science, the reasoning was purely logical.

Her breath caught as, page after page, she was entranced by the quest. To this researcher's mind, the Stone of Destiny stolen by King Edward I and placed in Westminster Abbey was a fraud. So this was the counterfeit bit she'd heard the men discussing. Evidently the Scots had known the English were coming, and they'd taken measures to hide the true stone. But now no one knew where it had been hidden.

Vanessa was not one to spend much time reading fiction, but she admitted that on more than one occasion she'd been swept up in an adventure novel. These notes certainly had the making of a brilliant adventure. And the person who had written this journal, perhaps Graeme, had been searching for nearly eleven years. Whoever this person was, they could lead her into the caves and guide her so that she might find the spot where Mr. McElroy had been working.

She had been nearly ravished tonight, then almost married to a Scot who appeared to live quite a secretive life. Lost treasures, legendary quests, and maps of caves—it would seem that she'd stumbled upon a man who could provide her invaluable assistance with her own journey. And she intended to utilize that circumstance to the fullest.

Chapter Four

————— ❧ ❧ —————

The following morning, Vanessa awakened and dressed herself. She'd stayed up far too late reading the night before. As she glanced around the room, she realized her dress had been laid out on a chair in the corner, but her trunk appeared to be missing. Perhaps someone had moved it to another room.

She stepped out of the bedchamber and retraced the steps they'd taken the night before. It did not take her long to locate the kitchen. Inside the room, she found two women. One was bent over in front of the oven, the other was searching for something in a cupboard.

"Pardon me," Vanessa said. She took a step further into the room.

"Good gracious," the woman at the oven said with a start. She stood upright and turned to face Vanessa, her hand resting over her heart. "You startled me."

"Who is that?" the older one asked, her voice aged. She still stood in front of the cupboard, but she'd angled her body in Vanessa's direction. She had sun-weathered skin and white hair that hung down her back in one fat braid. Wrinkles masquerading as dimples warmed her smile. Her blue eyes were cloudy as if she'd spilled cream in them.

"I'm sorry," Vanessa said. "Evidently Graeme did not notify you of his hospitality. I'm afraid he rescued me last night. At the pub. I inadvertently got myself in a tangle with some of the local men, and they did not want to allow me to go on my way."

The younger woman stepped away from the oven carrying a steaming loaf of bread. Her hair was a riot of bright red curls tied back in a scarf. Her bright blue eyes and rosy cheeks all came together in a picture of pure loveliness. The yeasty aroma of the fresh bread hit Vanessa and instantly her stomach growled in response. She put a hand to her abdomen to hide the noise.

"The men around here can be like that," the younger one said with a smile. "And my son did tell me last night you were here. How fortunate that he was able to rescue you, my dear." This petite woman with her cloud of copper hair and cheerful disposition was Graeme's mother? They seemed so different in both appearance and temperament. Not to mention her brogue was thicker than Graeme's. Vanessa had to concentrate to catch every word.

Graeme's mother pulled a chair out from the small table. "Please sit. The bread is ready, and I've no doubt you're hungry. You're thin as a rail."

Vanessa released an unladylike snort. "I don't know that anyone has ever considered me thin. But thank you." She sat and waited patiently while the women busied themselves about the small kitchen, then returned to the table with a jar of fruit preserves, butter, and the hot bread. "Where is Graeme?" Vanessa asked.

"Can't say that I've seen him this morning," his mother said. "I'm Moira, and this is my mother. Everyone calls her Old Mazie."

"I'm Vanessa. Very nice to meet both of you," she said. "And kind of you to allow me to spend the night. I'm certain I'll find more suitable lodgings today and be on my way."

"You had a room at the pub?" Old Mazie asked.

"I did," Vanessa said.

"You'd have better luck in Inverness," Moira interjected.

"I have no doubt that Inverness, being a larger village, has better options," Vanessa said. "But I'm here for research, so I need to be close to the loch."

"Research?" Moira asked. She placed a plate piled with warm bread smothered in butter and fruit in front of Vanessa. "Eat, then you can tell me about your work."

Vanessa smiled and took a bite of the food. She was alarmingly hungry. Obviously not eating dinner last night had done that to her.

"What is there to study around here?" Old Mazie asked.

"There is so much. Much of your land is undeveloped, unlike England. But I study fossils."

"Fossils?"

"Yes, imprints in the rocks from plants and animals that once lived in these areas. And, of course, bones. It's all utterly fascinating," Vanessa said.

"Well, I suppose it could be," Moira said. "And we do have a bunch of bones around here. Why, a few months ago, someone found something buried down in those caves. Said it proves there's a kelpie in our waters. 'Course we've all known that for years."

"Seen him with my own eyes," Old Mazie said with an affirmative nod.

Before Vanessa could comment, Graeme stepped into the room. He'd clearly taken the time to bathe, because he came in the room with his long hair wet and dripping onto his white shirt. Not only that, but this morning he'd donned a kilt. Vanessa's mouth went completely dry at the sight of his long, bare legs. Of course his entire legs weren't bare, only from his knees down, but it was enough to hint at the pure masculine strength in them. He padded into the room on bare feet, and carried a pair of boots and long woolen socks.

He was a fine specimen. But that was all this was, admiration and appreciation for a body well sculpted. The way she might admire Michelangelo's *David*. Graeme sat on the bench beside her and bent to put on his boots. She watched him methodically roll up one sock, then the other, and then he laced his worn leather boots. His long fingers, dusted with dark hair, made quick work of his task.

As a scientist, she was, of course, familiar with the work of Charles Darwin. She may not agree with all of his ideas, but seeing Graeme, she could certainly imagine that the sheer perfection of this...um, physical specimen would provide a decided advantage when it came to wooing women.

"Are you ready?" Graeme asked.

"Ready for what?" Vanessa asked in return, her voice sounding slightly breathy to her own ears.

"I was going to take you into town."

"Oh." She came to her feet, embarrassed to be caught woolgathering. Especially since the wool she was gathering was of such a decidedly personal nature.

"Thank you for breakfast. It was delicious. And it was

lovely to meet you both." Vanessa was unsure if she should say that she would see them again. It seemed unlikely. She'd find a new room, and then she'd get to work.

But she wanted to discuss the conversation she'd overheard last night, not to mention all the notes that she'd read. She needed to find a way to do so in a way that didn't reveal she'd been eavesdropping and sneaking through his house.

Vanessa followed Graeme out the door and down the rocky hillside to the path below. Her height had always enabled her to keep up with the pace of an Englishman, but matching Graeme's pace was another matter entirely. He stood at least a head taller than she and was rather broad. Standing before him in that ceremony last night was the first moment she ever remembered feeling feminine and dainty.

Vanessa's height had been one of the things her mother had fretted about, wringing her hands and chewing her lips, so concerned about the wedding. Vanessa had stood the slightest amount above Jeremy, and Vanessa's mother had worried herself into the vapors one afternoon deciding which shoes Vanessa would wear.

What a shame that Graeme was not a real candidate for her groom. His sheer masculinity and undeniable good looks would have made her mother swoon—until he opened his mouth and revealed his uncivilized Scottish brogue. The second her mother realized he was a simple Scotsman, the vapors would return.

"I trust you slept well," Graeme said, though he did not turn to look at her.

"I did. Thank you." She thought about inquiring where he'd slept, but thought better of it. Why did it matter where he'd lain his oversized body for the night? "Why are we going into town?"

"To put you on a train back to London."

She stopped walking; he did not. "I have no intention of returning to London," she said loudly so he could hear her down the path. "At least not now. I have much work to do."

He halted and turned to face her. So she caught up with him. "This is no place for an unmarried woman," he said through gritted teeth.

"Yes, you made that quite clear last night when you tricked me into marrying you." She crossed her arms over her chest and met his gaze straight on.

"I told you, our marriage," he said loudly, then took a steadying breath and continued speaking in a much lower tone, "is no more legal than had we found a drunk sailor on the street and asked him to marry us. It's a foolish old ceremony that no one recognizes anymore."

She realized then that Graeme's hands gestured more when he was angry. As much as she didn't want to admit it, he was an interesting specimen to study. And the fact that she was so bloody curious about him was vastly annoying, especially since he was behaving like an over-bearing brute.

He dropped his arms to his sides. "And I can't offer you protection. I have work to do."

"Work? And what sort of work do you have to do?" Perhaps if he told her about the hidden treasure and the quest for the Stone of Destiny, she could offer her assistance. She was excellent with research, not to mention that she could read and write in seven different languages.

"Certainly I don't have anything worthwhile to do," he said, his brogue growing stronger with every word. "You believe me to be nothing but a lazy Scotsman who spends his days swigging ale and reaching beneath the nearest skirt."

She opened her mouth to argue, then promptly shut it. She had not thought anything of the sort. He'd completely misread her question. Of course, she certainly had thought such things about the other men last night, but not Graeme. He was more educated; anyone could see that. Still, he was a Scot.

"My work is none of your concern," Graeme continued. "Now stop being so damned stubborn and let us get you to the train station." He tugged on her arm, but she held firmly to her place.

"I'm sorry, but since you are not my husband, you cannot tell me what to do." And because she simply couldn't help it, she smiled smugly.

"I suspect that even if I were your husband, you would not obey my wishes."

"That is probably true."

"Then you have left me with no other option." And with that he picked her up and tossed her over his shoulder as if she weighed no more than a child.

Once the shock wore off, Vanessa realized how very intimate their current position was. She lay across Graeme's shoulder, her bottom directly in the air for anyone to see. Granted it was covered, but still that did not erase the fact that his arm nestled directly under her curves.

"This is unacceptable," she said. "I demand that you put me down straightaway."

Graeme not only ignored her, he moved his arm so that he was able to put his hand atop her bottom. He gave her a pat, and she heard him chuckle.

Vanessa ran through her mind, searching for the appropriate thing to say. A sharp insult, a pithy retort, something—anything—that would make him put her down and stop manhandling her. It occurred to her that while she had found the touches from the men the previous night utterly revolting, Graeme's hand on her created no such feelings. Quite the contrary, his hand felt intimate and inappropriate and, though she would never admit it, not entirely unappealing.

Graeme carried her in that fashion the entire way to the train station. They passed a few people who did stare, but not one of them stopped to inquire if she needed assistance. When he finally placed her upright, Vanessa landed with a thud on the wood-planked floor. Beside her, she found her own trunk.

"But how did this get here?" she asked. She scrambled to her feet.

"I brought it by this morning when I purchased your return ticket to London. I have no doubt that your fiancé and family will be thankful to have you safely back," he said.

"Whether or not my fiancé or anyone else is concerned is... well, none of your concern. You are not my father or husband, nor do you have the authority to tell me when I have to leave this country." She stood close to him, standing as tall as she could, and jabbed her finger into his solid chest. "I will leave when I am ready to leave and not a moment sooner."

His lips quirked in what could have been the start of a smile, but it never quite made it to fruition. "Have safe travels. It was interesting to make your acquaintance, Vanessa." Then Graeme turned and walked away.

Vanessa's first thought was to chase after him and continue to give him a thorough tongue-lashing. But she stopped herself. It would solve nothing, and none of it mattered. She could remain here, find somewhere else to stay, and keep away from Graeme. She had research to do, and she could find another means to get into those caves. This was why she'd come to this frigid country. She exhaled and her breath fogged in front of her. She would not leave until she'd accomplished her work.

Vanessa watched Graeme continue to walk away. His kilt kept close to the back of his legs, and she found herself hoping for a gust of wind to blow it upward. Then she stopped herself and turned away from him. Gracious, she'd never ever had the desire to see a man's backside. Infuriating man!

Vanessa flopped onto a bench and stared at the train tracks before her. Perhaps she *should* leave. Come back when she had more protection. She could hire someone to be a travel companion. Women were always safer in numbers. But whom would she hire? And what would her parents say when she returned? They'd force her to marry Jeremy, which she had no intention of doing. Not now or ever.

No. She came to her feet. She would find a way to stay here and get her research done. Certainly not everyone was as rough as those men in the pub. Clearly she needed to steer clear of that establishment, but there must be somewhere else for her to find suitable lodging while she continued her research.

When the attendant tried to stop her, she quickly learned that Graeme had plied the man with money. Well, as the saying went, if the sauce was good for the goose. Only in this case it was the gander. Vanessa dug money out of her bag.

Vanessa hoisted her trunk by the side handle and dragged it down the grassy hill that led back to the village. The frost that covered the blades made them crunch lightly beneath her boots. She was resourceful. Simply because some brute of a man told her she couldn't survive here didn't mean anything. She would prove him wrong. The trunk wobbled and rocked as she dragged it behind her. Her belongings shifted within, knocking the trunk off balance and twisting her wrist.

Living in London where one could hire a carriage on every street made life so much easier. Here in the village, people walked or rode horses. She certainly had no aversion to walking, but doing so while dragging a large trunk created a struggle.

And so her journey began. She'd pull the trunk for a while until it became unstable, then she'd stop and sit upon it and catch her breath. She supposed that she had one thing to be happy about: the exertion from lugging the trunk was preventing her from becoming too cold. The brisk winter wind swept around her, whipping her hair about and making her eyes water.

On one such break, she opted to crack open her volume of *Grayson's Exploration of Scientific Discoveries* and read through some of the text. She had tried once to correspond with Mr. Grayson about some of the information in said text, but he made it perfectly clear that he would not entertain letters from a lady. Still, she found his book helpful, so she used it often as a resource, but it didn't make her think kindly about the man.

She folded the book onto her finger to mark her spot and looked down on the village below. There was still a ways for her to travel with her trunk in order to make it to the main street. There was the Cow and the Dog Tavern & Inn, where she'd been the previous night, but she obviously couldn't return there.

Perhaps she could approach Graeme's mother and offer

a boarding situation. He wouldn't be able to say no if she offered his family money. No man would ignore financial gain if it took care of his relations. She eyed the path that led from the inn, then went directly over the hill to their cottage.

He'd said her family would understand why she'd left. That once everyone knew about Jeremy and Violet, no one would blame Vanessa. That only proved he didn't know her family. Oh, she doubted they'd expect her to still marry the man, but somehow they would twist the situation and blame her. And frankly she wasn't ready to face her sister. She hadn't yet decided what she wanted to say to her, and when the moment came, she wanted to be prepared.

She blew out a breath. "That's a damned long way to drag this bloody trunk," she said aloud.

"Pardon me, madam, but is that a copy of *Grayson's Exploration of Scientific Discoveries*?" a man's voice asked.

Vanessa looked up to find an attractive and well-groomed man standing over her. "It most certainly is."

"Do you mind?" he asked, pointing at the book. "I have been trying to locate a copy of this for some time."

"No, of course not," she said. "You're English."

He smiled. "Yes, I am." He was a tall gentleman, though not as tall as Graeme had been, not that he was the standard by which she would measure all men. She shook her head to rid her mind of him. The gentleman opened up her book ever so gently, clearly a lover of the written word as well, and thumbed through some pages. "Excellent illustrations," he remarked. He was fair in complexion and features, with light blond hair that waved against his scalp and warm brown eyes.

"Yes, the drawings are quite good. Overall the text is

wonderful, though I've been told Mr. Grayson is a bit of a prig," Vanessa said.

He chuckled and met her gaze. "Oh, where are my manners? I am Niall Ludley, Earl of Camden. I'm a scientist, here working on a project."

Vanessa's heart beat faster. "Indeed? I am a scientist as well. And my name is Vanessa Pembrooke." She held her hand out, and they shook. Perhaps she wouldn't have to pay Graeme's family after all. This gentleman could certainly point her in the right direction for appropriate lodgings. "Might I inquire as to where you have found lodging? I am having a terrible time of it."

The man smiled warmly. "I work here in Loch Ness so often, I actually own an estate in this area," he said.

Her heart sank. "I see." But if she were willing to pay Graeme's family, why not offer this gentleman the very same deal? He was an aristocrat, more than likely from London. And she felt safe in his presence. It wasn't quite the same feeling she'd experienced with Graeme; she doubted this gentleman could have saved her from those men last night. But she also doubted he would ever treat her disrespectfully. She took a deep breath. "Lord Camden, I don't suppose you have a room you would be willing to rent to me?"

She could tell her request surprised him, and for a moment, she thought he might decline. But then his features softened and he nodded. "Allow me to rescue you, then, fair lady. I would be most pleased if you agreed to join me, and no boarding is required. You would simply be my guest."

She had asked, and he'd agreed, and yet she felt a slight moment of hesitation. Her reputation could be sullied, that was true. But was it not already irreparably damaged simply from her taking this trip? She was damaged goods now. Nothing she did would change that.

"I would consider it a great honor to assist you, a fellow scientist," he continued. "People around here are not too keen on men of science." Then he smiled warmly. "Or women of science, as the case would be."

The fact that he so readily accepted her as a scientist despite her sex made her trust him all the more. Not since she'd met Jeremy had she found that kind of reception in a fellow researcher. Perhaps this man was the answer to her worries. She eyed the inn down the hill and then rose to her feet. "I really do appreciate your hospitality."

"I even have a carriage waiting. Come along." He held his arm out to her. "I'll send a footman down here to retrieve your trunk."

They walked back up the hill to the waiting carriage. It was a shiny black landau with his family crest emblazoned on the side, just as she'd find in London.

"I do hope you'll allow me to peruse that book of yours for a longer period of time. I really have been searching for a copy for such a long while."

Chapter Five

———— ✿ ✿ ————

Graeme stepped through the back doorway of his mother's house. The kitchen area was empty, but he was fortunate enough to find leftover breakfast still sitting on the table. He dropped into a chair and grabbed a hunk of bread and some fruit preserves. He chewed thoughtfully, wondering—as he'd done the entire walk home—if he'd done the right thing for Vanessa. Of course, there was no place for her here in Scotland. She was far too refined, far too delicate, to survive without a chaperone or guardian, and he certainly didn't have time for such a task. He'd even slipped the train attendant some additional monetary compensation to keep an eye on the chit while she waited.

His mother walked into the room and right up to him. Without so much as a good morning, she slapped him on the back of his head.

"If you're going to keep doing that, I'm going to start wearing hats made of iron," Graeme said, rubbing the abused spot.

"Do you know what I heard this morning in town?" she asked.

"How am I supposed to know?" Graeme frowned at her and set his bread back down on the plate.

Moira shoved his plate to the middle of the table. "A handfasting ceremony? In a bloody pub?" she asked, her voice rising in volume with every word. "And then you don't have the decency to tell me that that charming woman is my new daughter-in-law?"

But she didn't pause long enough to allow him to answer. "How do you think," she asked, jabbing him in the shoulder with every word, "it makes me feel to hear that my eldest son has gotten himself a new wife and doesna even tell me?

"And I had to hear it from Mary McDonald." Moira made a sound that resembled a growl. "Mary McDonald. How embarrassing. You're lucky your grandmother wasn't with me. She'd have done more than smack your head."

"Mother, calm down. It was nothing. We're not really married," Graeme said. "It was a foolish ceremony in the pub, not even overseen by a priest." Frankly he didn't want to be reminded of how he'd succumbed to Angus and the rest of those men ribbing him. He should have taken a stand and rescued the girl without allowing them to bully him into an unwanted marriage.

He'd rescued the chit, and first Vanessa herself had ridiculed him about it, and now his mother. Would they have felt better about the situation had he stayed out of it, minded his own affairs, and looked the other way as those brutes molested her? He doubted that. No, he'd done the right thing.

"Where is the girl now?"

Graeme shrugged and pulled his plate back to him. "I

dropped her off at the train station. She should be heading back to London very soon." He sopped up some preserves, then popped the bite in his mouth, but he tasted nothing.

"Aye. So that is how it is. You marry the girl, then you ship her back to your house while you continue to play in the hills." She shook her head while clucking her tongue.

Graeme continued to eat. Perhaps he should have told his mother about the handfasting, but he hadn't realized that the gossip mill was as active here as it was in London. He'd never imagined she'd actually find out.

"Disappointed, that's what I am," Moira continued. "What's the matter, Graeme? You don't think we're good enough for your fancy London wife? Are you embarrassed by your simple Scottish family?"

"First of all, I am not now nor have I ever been embarrassed by any of you," he said. "Secondly, we aren't truly married, not really. There was no priest. It was only the handfasting ceremony, nothing more. And there's not a court in all of England that would deem that a legal marriage."

"Ah," Moira said, holding her hand up in the air. "But you're not in England now, are you?" she asked, her tone dangerously close to yelling.

"Are you trying to tell me that people still believe in that old ceremony?" he asked.

"Not only do they *believe* in it, it's a legally binding marriage. In the eyes of the civil authorities, the church, and everyone in that pub, you and that girl are husband and wife."

Graeme opened his mouth to argue, then shut it. He felt his frown increase. "That is ridiculous."

"Ridiculous or not, it's a fact." Moira paused and pressed her lips together, clearly hiding a smile.

"I'm glad you find this so amusing," he said.

"Didn't think it all through, did ya, boy? What happened anyway?"

Graeme relayed the story of the men who were bothering Vanessa and then the goading he'd endured. "At the time, it seemed the only option." He didn't explain how the men's taunting had gotten to him, how their childish teasing had pushed him into action. Admitting to that wouldn't solve anything.

"So you married her." Moira was quiet for a few moments before she nodded knowingly. "You made the right choice, I suppose. But now you have to live with the consequences. You'd best be off."

"Off where?"

"To claim your bride. Go find her at the train station and bring her back. Whether you wanted to or not, you are married to the girl. For now. The two of you can decide on what to do next. Get an annulment if you like." Then Moira slanted him a look full of mischief, and perhaps a tad more satisfaction than he'd like. "Or perhaps you'll decide to keep her."

Graeme swallowed hard, unable to fully comprehend what his mother was suggesting. He didn't want a wife, let alone one that would no doubt cause him more trouble than she was worth. "Keep her?" He came to his feet. "Why in blazes would I want to do that?"

"Well, you'll need a wife eventually. An heir for your family name. And I'd like grandchildren. Don't you want to be married, boy?" Her eyebrows rose, and then her lips quirked in a half smile.

Clearly his overreaction had not gone unnoticed. He took a steadying breath. "Not particularly." He grabbed a chunk of bread for his walk. "Marriage certainly didn't work out so well for you."

"That was my own stubbornness." She turned away from him and busied herself with stacking some dishes.

More like his own damned father had chased her away. Had never accepted her Scottish heritage and hadn't made it easy for her to fit into Society. Vanessa, though, would fit perfectly in Graeme's world, the English side at least. She was a well-bred lady, attractive, tall—not that her height had much to do with anything, but she was an appropriate height for him to reach down and kiss if he so chose.

But Graeme had never wanted to marry. His parents' terrible marriage was enough proof to him that people shouldn't join in a union they didn't intend to keep, especially if they brought children into it. Graeme had no desire to be a husband, for all of those reasons and plenty more. They would get an annulment.

But he supposed his mother was right. If Vanessa was legally his wife, then he best go and find her until the annulment was legal.

Graeme had started searching for his errant bride at the train station, but had found no sign of Vanessa. The attendant had reluctantly admitted that she'd doubled Graeme's original fee, and the man had looked the other way when she'd left the train station. He hadn't seen her since.

Damned stubborn girl not to heed his warnings. He'd told her this place wasn't safe for her alone, yet she'd stumbled off, dragging that trunk of hers behind her. Admittedly, though, he was glad that he didn't have to board a train himself to chase the girl down to London.

Graeme made his way to the inn where he'd found her two nights before, but he found no sign of her there, either. Of all the damned ways he could be spending his time. He had work to do, not only on his own research, but now this business for Solomon's.

He searched the only store in the village, and she was nowhere to be found. But as he was stepping out the door, a man remembered her. He'd seen her sitting on her trunk in the middle of the hill for a long while until a gentleman had come over to her, and they'd disappeared in his carriage.

In Graeme's experience, only one man used an enclosed carriage in this village, but to be certain he asked, "What did the man look like?"

The grizzled man shrugged. "That English lad. The one who has that house up on the hill."

That certainly sounded like Niall. "What color hair?"

"Fair. He was fair. They left, went that way." He pointed to the right.

Niall. Well, at least this was one way to make contact with his cousin. But what would Niall want with Vanessa? If his cousin was involved in some dangerous undertakings, the last thing Graeme needed or wanted was for his temporary wife to be involved. Wasn't Niall married himself? Until now he'd always assumed his English cousin was as harmless as a mild English winter. He hated being wrong. It seemed that he could no longer ignore the English side of his family.

Graeme thanked the man, then left. It took him nearly twenty minutes to make his way to Niall's house. It would have been faster on horse, but he hadn't thought that he'd needed one. Niall's estate was just outside of the village. It still overlooked the loch, but did so from above the rest of the town.

Graeme walked down the drive. The red brick manor with large white columns boasted three stories and a perfectly manicured lawn. He made his way up the stair-case and slammed the knocker against the shiny door.

The butler answered the door and nodded at the sight of Graeme. He stood aside and allowed him entrance. "Your Grace," he said with a nod. "My lord is in his study. He has company."

Graeme didn't bother to comment. Instead he simply walked past the servant and into Niall's home. Niall's study was the second door on the right, and though the door wasn't precisely closed, it was nearly shut. He nudged it open and immediately Niall came to his feet. The situation, however, was completely innocuous, with Niall behind his desk and Vanessa in a chair opposite it.

"Graeme," Niall said, clearly surprised. "How did you know I was here?"

"I am not here for you," he said, never taking his eyes off Vanessa. Though he certainly had business with his cousin, he wanted to follow him first, see what he could discover without simply asking the man. To further muddle things for Graeme, now he had this business of a marriage to handle.

Vanessa's eyes rounded in surprise, then a frown settled on her face. She stood. "I have nothing to say to you." Defiantly, she crossed her arms over her chest.

"You have to come with me," Graeme said.

"Why? So you can drop me off at the train station again?" She turned abruptly to face him fully and faltered, her pale hands gripping the chair in front of her. "No, thank you. Niall has offered to be of assistance to me. Take me into the caves."

"Is that so?" Graeme eyed his cousin, who in turn was glancing from Graeme back to Vanessa, looking not in the least manner guilty. "Still, you must return with me."

Graeme made his way to stand next to her, but did not touch her.

Niall straightened some papers on his desk, and Graeme couldn't help noticing how the study looked precisely like every other English study he'd ever seen. All the accoutrements of home brought here to make Niall's stay in the wilderness more comfortable. The man might be fascinated by Scottish lore, but he didn't have a drop of true Scottish blood running through his veins.

"I don't *have* to do anything with you," she said. "You made it abundantly clear earlier you were finished with me. And now I am to follow you? I think not."

"Graeme, it appears the lady is not interested in going with you," Niall said, coming around his desk. "Perhaps you could come back at a later time and visit with her." He smiled. "Perhaps we can arrange some dinner or a tea."

"No. We don't need a bloody tea," Graeme said. He turned his attention to Vanessa. "We can argue about this later, but now, come with me."

She shifted her body away from him. "Are you going to toss me over your shoulder again?"

"If I must. You are behaving like a child." He grabbed her arm and pulled her to him. He knew Niall was watching him carefully, ready to step in should the moment call for action. Graeme only hoped his cousin wouldn't, out of some misplaced gallantry, challenge him to a duel to defend Vanessa's honor. He lowered his voice before speaking again. "That subject we discussed this morning. It appears as if I've made a mistake," he whispered.

"To what do you refer?"

"Our little ceremony," he gritted.

"And?"

"It appears as if it was in fact legitimate," he said.

Delicate brows arched over her cerulean eyes. "Truly?" she asked.

"We need to rectify this issue. Or at least discuss it more. Please come with me." Graeme loosened his hold on her arm.

She was quiet for a moment, then nodded. "Very well."

"Vanessa, you aren't required to go with him if you feel at all, um, uncomfortable," Niall said.

"Nice, cousin." Graeme rolled his eyes. "I won't hurt the girl if that's what you're worried about. And believe me, she's more trouble than you have the skill or energy to manage."

"I take great offense at that," she said. Vanessa held her hand out to Niall. "I appreciate your kindness, and I do look forward to seeing you again." She handed him her book. "You are welcome to examine my copy of Grayson's. Return it to me when you are finished."

The Raven stood in the darkened closet waiting for Niall's guests to leave. He'd caught a glimpse of the man as he'd entered the room. Once the loud talking had begun, The Raven had cracked the door to take a peek. After the man and woman had left, he stepped out of the pantry. "I know that man," The Raven said as he entered Niall's study.

Niall started and released a string of curses. "Why the hell are you here?"

"To keep track of you and ensure you remember what you're looking for and why," The Raven said. He had arrived that morning on the train and had been given instructions on how to get to Niall's estate. At the time, Niall hadn't been here, so he'd helped himself and taken a look around. It was perfect, with all the comforts of home. Niall knew how to live.

"I would never forget," Niall said.

"Of course not. How could you?" The Raven so enjoyed toying with Niall. It wasn't that he relished hurting people, but he wasn't above doing so if it got him what he wanted. He lit his cigar.

The Raven was almost certain the large Scotsman who had just left was a member of Solomon's. In fact, he believed he was one of the men that had been with Fielding that day at the Tower of London. He'd helped to ruin The Raven's plan for Pandora's box.

Now The Raven was after the Kingmaker, a much more powerful antiquity, and he only needed two more stones to complete it. The Loch Ness treasure, however, had proven particularly difficult to locate. He'd looked on his own for months, but had had no luck. That's when he'd stumbled upon Niall. The Raven knew he could find the bloody thing eventually, but it would be a far faster search with Niall's assistance.

"That man," he said, "he is a member of Solomon's as well?"

Niall inclined his head. "He is." He fell into his seat.

"And a relation of yours?"

"My cousin." Niall picked up a torn piece of paper and rolled it between his thumb and forefinger.

"How charming." The Raven inhaled his cigar, then allowed the ashes to fall onto the carpet beneath him. Niall's cousin might prove a problem. But The Raven was used to cleaning up such problems. Given the right opportunity, he could rid himself of that man.

The study door opened again, but this time a young man entered. He was truly no more than a boy, perhaps sixteen. Obviously one of the local boys, he wore the traditional kilt and tartan, and his hair looked shaggy and tangled. He had several dirt smudges on his cheeks.

"Niall," the boy said with obvious excitement. "I heard you were in town." His brogue was thick. He smiled broadly.

The Raven tried not to roll his eyes or show his exasperation. They had work to do, details to discuss, and all of these interruptions were seriously trying his patience.

"Dougal," Niall said as he came to his feet. He came around his desk and went to the boy. "It's lovely of you to visit, but as you can see," he motioned to The Raven, "I already have a guest. Perhaps another time."

The boy's smile wilted; he was clearly hurt. He was too young and self-involved to notice the tension eating at Niall, the nervousness that shortened his sentences and made his hands shake subtly. "Graeme was here, I know. I heard him yell at you."

Niall smiled reassuringly, all the while trying to usher young Dougal out of the room. "Nothing to worry about. He was frustrated," Niall said. "Your brother is merely loud. We were discussing politics from London. Nothing to fret about."

But the boy seemed unsure.

So this was Graeme's younger brother. Very interesting. And evidently very interested in his English cousin. The Raven stepped forward and held his hand out.

"Leave the boy be, Niall. I should like to meet a relation of yours since I missed the previous one," The Raven said with a smile.

Niall's eyes narrowed, but he held back any argument that he might have had. The Raven had him precisely where he wanted him.

"My name is David," he told the boy.

Dougal smiled and came forward, clasping his hand in a hearty clasp. "Dougal, sir. Are you from London as well?"

"Indeed I am." The Raven pulled his hand back and fought the urge to wipe it on his trousers. The boy's nails were caked with dirt, and The Raven had to redirect his attention to avoid staring. "I came up to see Niall. We're good friends."

"He's my cousin," Dougal said cheerfully. "My father was from London."

"Perhaps you can come visit me in London," Niall said. "But we really must get back to discussing our business." He put his hand on Dougal's back and led him to the door.

"So that must make you half English," The Raven said, knowing full well the more he allowed this brat to stay, the longer Niall was away from the caves and his quest. But The Raven couldn't resist playing for just a little while.

"Yes, I am," Dougal said enthusiastically. "But I was raised here in Scotland. My brother lives in London most of the time, though."

"And your brother inherited your father's title?" The Raven asked.

"Right. He's a duke of London," the boy said.

"How charming." And utterly asinine. This pup left nothing hidden. "I suppose you mean the duke is his title and he resides in London."

The boy's cheeks stained with embarrassment. "Yes, that is what I meant to say."

The Raven could clearly see the boy longed for the life of an aristocrat. Well, The Raven could certainly show him one.

Niall tried to plead with his eyes, tried desperately to shield Dougal, and finally The Raven said nothing more. He'd gotten bored with the boy in any case. And he wanted to know about Niall's plans for the search.

This boy could be perfect for ridding himself of Graeme should the man prove to cause problems. And The Raven fully expected Graeme to cause a multitude of problems, so he'd have to make certain that he made young Dougal's acquaintance again.

Chapter Six

～～～❧～～～

Niall had graciously offered Graeme and Vanessa his carriage, which they had gladly accepted. Vanessa was not about to try to lug her trunk around again, and she wasn't interested in asking Graeme for assistance. They rode in silence for several moments, and she was perfectly fine with that. She was trying to figure out precisely what had happened. She'd come to Scotland to do research. To prove, once and for all, that a woman could be as legitimate a scientist as any man could.

She had planned to prove Jeremy wrong about the Loch Ness kelpie. When she did so, she could hope to take her rightful place among the rest of the names in Paleontology. Unfortunately, her father was no longer alive, so he wouldn't get to see it. But now she would no longer have to worry whether or not her discoveries would embarrass her husband. Jeremy might disagree with her, but he could make no claim on her now.

Vanessa pulled back the tiny curtain on the carriage window and watched the scenery go by. The landscape here was so raw, so untouched by man, a sharp contrast to the hustle and bustle of London's busy streets.

So while she'd escaped a marriage she'd never really wanted to begin with, she'd stumbled headfirst into another. She'd already seen Graeme's temper flare, so it seemed his character ran quite differently from Jeremy's. For all of Jeremy's flaws—flaws that were now only too apparent—at least he had been a man of science. He'd been logical and dispassionate—when it came to her, at least.

Although marrying Jeremy was certainly out of the question now, she had still hoped that, if she did one day decide to marry, she might find a husband like him. One who shared his better qualities, albeit one who did not fornicate with her sister.

Instead, she'd married Graeme. She'd attached herself to an overbearing, stubborn man who cared not one whit what her opinions were. Nor had he expressed any interest in her research, aside from his initial question. Though he hadn't ridiculed her, he hadn't shown interest, either. In fact, the only thing he had to recommend him was that he had never met Violet.

She let the small curtain fall back into place and met her husband's gaze. "Why did you come back to get me?" she asked.

"Because we're married," he said simply, as if that explained everything.

"Why the sudden feeling of responsibility?" Impatience gnawed at her. "You seemed quite content to deny the entire episode this morning."

"I did not deny anything," he said harshly. Then he cleared his throat and said in a more gentle tone, "I didn't believe it was legal. I've been told otherwise since we departed this morning. Don't fret. You won't be saddled with me for long."

"You intend to get an annulment?" she asked, unable to hide her surprise.

He eyed her. "Isn't that what you want?"

"Of course," she said quickly. Though was it? She had no desire to be married to him or any other man. Independence called to her on the chilly wind, a siren song meant only for her. She exhaled loudly, then said nothing more for several moments. Memories of that morning, when he'd hoisted her onto his shoulder, flooded her mind. As if his hand still rested on her bottom. She could almost feel his touch. Well, *that* was unusual, and most unwelcome.

"You never told me why the men in the pub called you English," she said, attempting to divert her thoughts.

"Because I live in London. I'm half English," he said.

That explained why he spoke the way he did. While he had the brogue of a Scot, his vocabulary and speech were more refined, better educated. She remembered then the way the men had used the moniker as a taunt.

"And you don't like that they call you that?" she asked.

"No, I do not." His jaw clenched.

"Why do you come here if you live in London? You said you had work to do?" Now that she would be spending more time with him, she wanted to discuss the late-night visitor he'd had the previous night. And the notes she'd read.

Vanessa smiled at him.

It took Graeme a minute to notice, then he tilted his head ever so slightly. "What?"

"I will cooperate with you. Give you the annulment you desire, if you answer some questions for me."

"You have been asking questions already, and I have been answering them." He seemed amused, but he did not smile. "What more questions could you have?"

"Tell me specifically about this work of yours. Is it family work?" she asked.

"No, it's not exactly family related. I'm doing some investigative work. For some associates of mine."

She knew that she was treading on dangerous territory. Curiosity could betray her. "Associates from London?"

His hands clenched at his sides. He crossed one leg over the other, bringing them much closer to her. The dark hair curling over his muscular calves intrigued her. Would that hair be soft or crisp to the touch, and precisely how hard was the sinew beneath his skin?

"Why the sudden curiosity about my life?" he asked.

She shrugged, trying to look indifferent. "I'm merely a curious sort."

"I don't believe my work is any concern of yours, despite your innocent curiosity," he said. But his shrewd eyes kept focused on hers, making her feel as if he could see inside of her. To those hidden parts she never revealed to anyone.

She shifted in her seat and decided to change her tactic. "How about this? I will remain married to you, be a thorn in your side, so to speak, if you do not answer my questions. Take your pick." She crossed her arms over her chest to show him her determination.

But instead of appearing threatened by her blackmail, he tossed his head back and laughed. A riotous belly laugh that made her want to smile and laugh with him. But she forced herself to remain stoic. These were serious negotiations.

"I am quite serious," Vanessa said.

"Of that, I have no doubt. Very well, I'll tell you." He still smiled, though, as if taunting her with his humor. "I was asked to look into something that another man is doing. Make certain that he's not doing anything illegal or dangerous."

"By whom?"

"Some men that I work with in London."

"Your flair for detail is astounding. Truly, the entire situation makes perfect sense to me now," she said.

"That's all I can tell you about them."

Who was he protecting? The other men or himself? Was he hired to do the work these men could not manage on their own? Graeme was large, larger than most Englishmen in height and breadth. Perhaps they used his strength to intimidate others. But what did that have to do with stolen treasure and the Stone of Destiny? The carriage came to a stop in front of Graeme's cottage.

Graeme stepped down from the carriage, then helped her do the same. He lifted her out of the rig, then set her down directly in front of him, no more than a breath away. "That man you went home with is not a true gentleman. He is potentially involved with some very dangerous people, and I'm here to see if I can discover the details surrounding his situation."

"You are speaking of your cousin, Niall?" She waved her hand dismissively. "He is harmless enough. He is a scientist."

He cocked an eyebrow. "Scientists can be deceiving, can they not?"

"Not generally. They don't bother themselves with those matters and instead focus on their studies."

"Like your fiancé?" he asked.

It was not the kindest remark, but she deserved it. And

it was a good reminder for her to keep her wits about her and not be deceived by someone simply because he claimed to be a scientist. "*Touché.*"

They walked toward the cottage as the carriage rolled away down the drive. "Why was Niall so interested in that book you loaned him?" Graeme asked.

"I'm not certain. It's a common enough book in my field of study. Perhaps Niall is interested in fossils as well," she said.

"I'd wager he has a much more specific need for the text."

"You think he was merely using that as an excuse, and he intends to ravish me?" Vanessa asked. "When he returns my book?"

Graeme smiled. "I suspect had he wanted to ravish you, he would have done so earlier today."

Vanessa nodded. She hadn't even considered that as an option. Men scarcely ever noticed her, so she never thought about that. Perhaps that was why she'd gotten herself into so much trouble the night before.

They entered the house, and Graeme brought her trunk to the room that she'd slept in last night. "Why don't you get settled while I go and talk to my family. Let them know you're here."

"What about our bargain?" she asked. "You answer my questions, and I give you that annulment?"

He smiled. "We'll negotiate that later."

Graeme stepped out of Vanessa's bedchamber and went in search of his family. He didn't have to journey far, as his mother had magically appeared in the parlor.

"Were you spying on me?" he asked.

"Aye," his mother said with a grin. "So I see you found the girl."

"Indeed. She had not yet left for London." He decided that there was no reason to tell his mother about Vanessa's interaction with Niall.

"So have you made a decision?" she asked.

"About what?" Graeme had no interest in discussing this matter with this mother.

"About staying married to the lass," his mother said impatiently.

"We will get an annulment," he said. "And then I will promptly send her back to London. But she needs somewhere to stay until the legal matters are resolved."

"It shouldn't take too long," his mother said.

"I hope not."

Later that night, Vanessa remembered the words she'd overheard through the door. She sat upright in bed, and the coverlet fell around her. Graeme had told his mother that they would get the annulment. He'd already made the decision, without her, not that she disagreed. She didn't want to be married any more than he did.

But it was what he'd said after that, about how he'd send her back to London. She refused to return to London just yet. Therefore, she could not allow him to dissolve this marriage, at least not now.

Allowing the annulment would mean returning to London without accomplishing her goals. And who knew what awaited her back at home? Had Jeremy and Violet gotten married instead? Were they all relieved that finally the one family member who had never truly belonged had simply disappeared? Of course, she had left them a note, not very detailed, but something that let them know she was leaving.

She needed to stay married to Graeme long enough

to get herself into those caves and to find the fossils she needed to prove her theories.

But how could she ensure that Graeme did not seek out the annulment? She supposed she could simply ask him. She was normally forthright with people. But hadn't her mother always told her that there were better ways to deal with a man? You had to be crafty. Clever. And hadn't being straightforward with Graeme only made him evasive? The man had yet to give her a detailed answer.

"A man will give you anything if you wait for the right time to ask for it." That's what her mother had always said.

Select the perfect time.

But what made a man not want to leave?

She closed her eyes to mentally search her thoughts for ideas. An image of Jeremy and Violet flashed through her mind. They'd been writhing on the floor of the study, both completely nude, glistening with sweat from the nearby fire. It had taken both of them several minutes to even notice that she'd entered the room.

She'd stood there like a damned fool watching them copulate, her face flaming with humiliation. Even now, she could feel the heat settle in her cheeks. Jeremy had claimed to not believe in love. He'd said he agreed with her that it was based on nothing more than a bodily reaction and more akin to lust than anything.

She herself had never felt even a twinge of lust, even when she and Jeremy had kissed. It had been a scientific experiment. They'd both been utterly unmoved—proof that their life together would never be so distracting that they'd forget their heads and their work. It had been perfect. But Violet—passionate, beautiful Violet—had ruined it.

That was it. *Passion.*

Men were defenseless against passion. And were she to ruin herself by consummating their marriage, Graeme could not send her away. She'd worry about the long-term repercussions later. Right now, she had a problem, and this was the perfect solution. She had to seduce her husband to keep herself married. That way she could stay here and complete her research. She couldn't bear to go home and face Jeremy and Violet if she hadn't at least accomplished something worthwhile with her studies.

It seemed such a simple solution, but she didn't have the faintest idea of how to seduce anyone. She jumped from the bed and moved about her room searching for something, anything, that would guide her in this quest. She frowned, wishing that she'd paid more attention to her mother when she'd tried to teach Vanessa how to flirt—how to use her womanly wiles, as her mother had called them. At the end of the day, her mother had declared that Vanessa possessed no wiles, womanly or otherwise. Vanessa exhaled, and her hair fluttered above her eyes. What had Violet done to get Jeremy in that position?

Vanessa stopped pacing. They had both been nude. And Violet had rubbed her naked body against Jeremy's, ran her hands over his torso. Perhaps that was it. Perhaps all that was required to produce passion was a lack of clothing. She glanced at her reflection in the mirror. She must have briefly fallen asleep, as she still wore her brown wool dress, which did absolutely nothing to enhance her figure. That had never been anything she'd taken care with, choosing her clothes for their durability rather than those that made her bosom look the most voluptuous.

She was attractive enough, she supposed, not too round, but not too thin, either. Of course, it mattered not because there was absolutely nothing she could do to enhance her figure right now. She would merely remove her clothing and press herself against him, and perhaps he would take over and do the rest. Then the damage would be done.

She stood in front of the mirror and methodically removed all of her hair pins, laying them in a neat row on the dressing table. Next she pushed down her stockings. She unhooked her dress and slid out of it, then removed her undergarments until she stood in the middle of the small bedchamber completely nude. The chill in the air scattered gooseflesh over her unprotected skin. She hoped that didn't make her look unappealing.

What would she do if he sent her away? Refused to touch her and walked her back to her room?

No, she wouldn't think like that. She could do this. She was an intelligent woman, and according to her mother, men were simple creatures who paid attention to their own pleasures in life.

Without another thought, she pulled on her nightrail, tugged it tight against her, and then went in search of her husband. She knocked on his bedchamber door, and he grunted what sounded somewhat like "enter," so she pushed the door open, then closed it behind her.

He sat in the corner of the room in a wing-backed chair poring over a small leatherbound book. He looked up and his eyebrows rose with surprise. His eyes roamed the length of her, obviously noticing she wore only a nightrail. "Vanessa, what's the matter?"

She cleared her throat. "Nothing. I merely wanted to discuss something with you."

He set the notes aside and rose to his feet. He'd changed into trousers, and his white linen shirt was open at the neck, revealing a swath of dark chest hair. His long hair was pulled back and tied at the nape of his neck, and his shirtsleeves were rolled up to reveal well-muscled forearms.

He was muscular and strong, a fine male specimen. He had lovely eyes; she'd noticed that about him from the first, and so she deduced that the rest of him would be equally attractive. She might not be interested in matters of the heart or loin, but she knew a handsome man when she saw one.

If she stood here much longer, she'd start talking, and then she might just ruin her plan. So she took a deep breath, and in one swift movement, she untied the night-rail and let it fall to her feet.

His eyes widened, then he swallowed visibly.

"What the bloody hell do you think you're doing?" he asked. A frown settled on his forehead, suggesting that he was displeased with her seduction efforts. But then his gaze took in her body, his eyes moving over her as intense as a touch.

She tried to think of the appropriate response, but remembered that Violet and Jeremy had not been talking. They'd only been touching and kissing and moaning. And she tended to get into trouble, especially when she spoke to men. She closed the distance between them and pressed her body to his.

"Vanessa," he told her, "you are dancing too close to the devil."

Again she said nothing. She continued to stay precisely where she was, her breasts pressed against his chest, her legs against his. He sucked in a breath as she rubbed her nipples against his chest. Nothing about this was as she'd imagined. She knew that he'd be firm, but she'd never thought he'd be this warm. She took one hand and ran it up his arm. He was strong, stronger than she'd realized, and his arm was as hard as the marble statue in her mother's garden. Her heart beat wildly, her nerves prickling her skin. If this seduction didn't work, she was in trouble. She remembered what she'd seen her sister do, and so she closed her eyes and tossed her head back, releasing a low moan.

"God's teeth, woman," Graeme said. He grabbed both of her arms and held her to him, then he slammed his mouth down on hers. The sudden kiss alarmed her. This was not the kind of kiss that she'd shared with Jeremy. He had simply put his lips to hers; Graeme devoured her. His lips were hot and hard against her own, and when his tongue invaded her mouth, she gasped. It wasn't unpleasant; quite the contrary.

He took with this kiss, demanded, and her body seemed to react by itself. Something was definitely happening inside of her, as if her skin had taken breath.

Perhaps she *was* capable of lust.

And that was the last coherent thought Vanessa had as Graeme took over the seduction. She vaguely noticed when he removed her spectacles and placed them on a side table. But then he continued to kiss her, his hard body melding against hers, and she forgot everything else. She was no longer cold; the gooseflesh had long since disappeared and, in its place, heat and fire skimmed across her skin.

When Graeme's hands left her arms to stroke down her back and across her abdomen, flames followed in the wake of his touch. And when one hand moved up to cup her breast, she involuntarily cried out.

Lust. She was experiencing lust. Her whole body felt alive and full of energy and sensations. She wished she could simultaneously experience this and watch it so she could examine her own facial expressions, record her every sensation. This was science in the making.

Graeme pulled her to him and kissed her again, this time more slowly and with more tenderness. He picked her up, cradling her to him as he carried her to the bed and gently laid her down. In no more than a minute, he'd removed his clothes and climbed atop her, the weight of his heavy frame unfamiliar, but not altogether unpleasant. The hairs along his legs and torso tickled her own flesh every time he moved over her.

His kisses continued. And desire continued to soar through her body. So new were the experiences that Vanessa reveled in each one, every touch, every breath, every kiss.

He moved his hand between them, ran his fingers up her thigh and then into the curls nestled between her legs. As if he'd shot electricity through her body, jolts of pleasure tingled over her. She jerked beneath this touch, but he continued his exploration until he'd plunged a finger inside her. She cried out again. Her body was ready for him, she knew that. Knew what would happen next. Her mother had explained coupling to her, had said it could be uncomfortable, perhaps even painful if the man did not properly prepare the woman. But Graeme had done everything right, had known precisely where to touch her and how.

She opened her legs knowing that he would want to enter her, and she relaxed, closed her eyes, and waited for the next sensation. Thrills shimmied through her stomach when she felt him, hard and warm, settle between her thighs. Instinctively she moved her legs, pulling them up and then wrapping them around his body.

He groaned, then thrust into her body. There was a pinch of pain as her body took him in, but as he began to move, the delicious sensations started to build. He nibbled at her neck and her collarbone as he moved within her, and she kept her legs where they were, tightened around his waist. Over and over, he pushed in and out, and the pleasure crescendoed until she thought she would go mad from it. Again he slipped his finger in between them, but this time he found the nub hidden between her folds.

She sucked in a breath as he ran his finger against her, all the while thrusting. *Oh. Oh. Yes.* Her breathing was labored, and perspiration slid down her neck and between her breasts.

This was it, something was happening—and then it did. His finger flicked one more time, and pleasure exploded within her, creating wave after wave of sensations she'd never felt before.

Oh yes!

Then she felt Graeme's release as he fell onto her. Their labored breathing was the only sound.

She smiled. There would be no annulment now.

Her mother hadn't told her about this. No one had warned her. No one could have. She wouldn't have believed them.

Chapter Seven

~~~

Graeme lay there for several minutes, not quite believing what had just happened. He'd never intended to lay a finger on Vanessa. Although certainly the thought had occurred to him, they'd agreed on an annulment. Now that was impossible. Now she was his wife in every way. Had that been her intention?

He looked at her sleeping form, her arms flung above her head, hair splayed across the pillow, pleasure staining her cheeks. She slept hard, her rhythmic breathing slow and steady. What the hell was he supposed to do?

How could any man have resisted her? Her attempt at a seduction, he realized now, had been rather awkward. She knew nothing about the subtleties of luring a man into bed. Yet that was precisely where they'd ended up, because he'd taken one look at her body and desire had surged through him. Even now, with the sheet draped around her waist, she looked beautiful. Unlike most women, she seemed not overly concerned with her appearance. What other woman would wear her spectacles to a seduction?

And she wasn't shy about her body, which in and of itself was arousing.

Her pert breasts rose and fell with each breath; the rosy hue of her nipples enticed him even now. Her body was not as overly curvy as he usually preferred in his lovers. Vanessa was thin, but her waist narrowed and then her hips were rounded nicely. She was beautiful.

And his wife.

He hadn't even wanted a damned wife. He leaned against the headboard, his arms cradling his head. Didn't that just damn it all.

Before this night, he'd never lain with a virgin. This woman was his in a way no other woman had ever been. A surge of protection welled inside him. He'd be the only man to ever touch her. The only man to cup her breasts and bite her neck. The only man to enter her, spill his seed within her. Again lust filled his body, and he grew heavy with need for her. Well, if he was to remain married to the woman, at least he desired her.

He leaned over and covered her breast with his mouth. She stirred, then moaned as he continued to lave kisses on her tender skin. Her hand reached up, threading her fingers through his hair.

He'd take her again this night.

She moaned again as he slid into her. God, she felt good—hot, slick, and tight. And as her pleasure mounted and her soft cries came faster and faster, he thought again and again: his woman, his wife and no one else's.

The following morning, Graeme sneaked out the back door of the cottage and nearly ran into his brother.

"Dougal, what the devil are you doing up and about so early?" Graeme hissed.

"I had to tend to the animals. You've been out of Scotland so long you've forgotten where your dinner comes from?" Dougal teased.

His brother's words jabbed at him. They were meant in fun, but the boy was right. England made him soft, made him pampered and forgetful that his family didn't live in the same luxurious lifestyle he did. Not for lack of trying on his part. As soon as his father had died, he'd begged his mother to move the family to London, but she'd refused. She would not leave her beloved Scotland, not that Graeme blamed her in the least.

"I've got to go," Graeme said. He wanted to be far enough behind Niall to not be noticed, but not so far that he lost him.

"Where are you off to this morning?" Dougal asked. "I could help." He set the bucket down. His brother's face was sharpening, becoming less boylike and more like that of a man. But a determined jaw could do nothing to hide the youthful enthusiasm shining in his eyes.

"Not this time; I need to do this on my own." He patted the boy's shoulder. "But we'll talk later today." Graeme turned and walked down the path away from the house.

He climbed the hillside to the castle ruins. If Niall was searching for the legendary Loch Ness treasure, then more than likely he was doing so within the caverns that wove beneath Castle Urquhart. The very caves he'd been in many times searching for his own bloody treasure. Today was not the day to look for the decoder, though. He only wanted to follow Niall a while, and see if he met anyone there.

Graeme thought of Vanessa while he climbed. He had consummated a marriage he hadn't intended to stay in, and he'd done it three times. The rocks from the hillside bit into Graeme's boots, but he didn't care. He'd come here with a task to complete, and if he wasn't careful, he'd get so distracted by his new bride that he'd fail to accomplish it—not to mention the work Solomon's had requested of him. Hell, he was curious himself about what his cousin was up to.

Niall had been helpful to Vanessa, offering her a place to stay. In his experience, the English were not overly friendly; instead they were polite and proper to a fault. Yet Niall had brought her back to his home, and they had been chatting in his study when Graeme had found them, as if they were old friends.

There had to be something more. Niall had borrowed that book of Vanessa's. She'd said it was a book about fossils, though. It seemed unlikely Niall would take time out to study fossils. Solomon's, though, would not be suspicious without reason. Niall had been behaving in such a way that Jensen had traveled all the way up to Scotland to enlist Graeme's help. No, there had to be something more useful to him in that book, and Vanessa simply was unaware of it.

Once Graeme discovered Niall's secret, then he could focus on his own interests. In the meantime, he needed to get Vanessa back to London, where she would be safe.

Graeme continued climbing the hill, and the castle grew closer. Much of the castle's outer wall remained intact, but the structure itself was composed of mostly crumbled-down walls with one partially standing tower. The entrance to the caves lay deep within the belly of the ruins.

Quickly, yet quietly, he moved, trying to make good time before his wife woke up and realized he'd deserted her—and to prevent Niall from discovering him. Niall had crept past Graeme's family's cottage in the early morning hours, and Graeme had waited fifteen minutes before following his cousin. Niall was a talented explorer, or else Solomon's would not have welcomed him into their fold, so chances were he'd be watching for anyone coming behind him.

Graeme climbed over a collapsed wall, then skirted beneath what remained of an archway as he entered the ruins of Castle Urquhart. He'd always loved this old place. Despite its condition, it still looked very much a fortress guarding over the loch. There was another entrance into the caverns, below the castle and above the rocky shore, but it was difficult to get to. And Niall had been heading in this direction.

Stepping inside one of the few remaining rooms of the castle that still claimed four walls, Graeme made his way down a stone staircase.

He hit the bottom of the staircase and then started down the tunnel to his left. At first the area resembled a stone hallway, but the farther he walked, the narrower the passage became, until he found himself standing in a cavern. Gone were the manmade bricks. In their place were the slick, moss-covered sides of a cave. Graeme's lungs chilled as he took a deep breath. The air was heavy with the scent of his stale, cold, and chalklike surroundings.

He moved farther into the darkness and was pleased to see that Niall had already lit some of the torches attached to the wall. They were far apart, so the light was spread thin, providing only enough visibility to keep moving forward. Graeme was glad of the torches, although he had brought his own lantern, along with some tools and a gun, in the pack he carried over his shoulder.

There was a slight thump from somewhere behind him, then several rocks broke off the wall and crumbled to the ground. Someone was following *him*. Graeme stopped walking, molded himself to the damp cavern wall, and listened. Definite steps moved through the tunnel behind him.

Perhaps his cousin's partner? Graeme started moving forward again, trying to gain some ground on the intruder. The deeper into the cave he walked, the colder the air became. A draft shuddered around him, and the torches nearest him were extinguished, leaving him in darkness. Again he molded himself against the cavern wall and waited. The footsteps grew closer.

Graeme inhaled slowly. Soft footfalls beat against the ground of the tunnel as the intruder approached. A breeze fluttered against him when the person passed in front of Graeme's hiding place. Graeme reached out, grabbed the body, and slammed it against the cavern wall.

Upon impact, the person released a groan that was decidedly more feminine than Graeme had been anticipating. The arms beneath his hands felt far too soft and small to be a man's.

"That hurt," she said softly.

"Vanessa!" he whispered. "What the devil are you doing following me?"

"You left early, and you were so careful, so quiet. I deduced you were attempting to conceal something from me." Then she was quiet for a moment before continuing, and he wished he could see her. "It is my wifely duty to investigate such matters. That is, until I am no longer your wife."

He exhaled loudly, and the sound echoed around them.

"Precisely where are you going in the dark?" she asked. "I brought along some candles, in my bag, for precisely this purpose. Shall I light one?"

"No, you shall not."

"Are you going to release me?"

He hadn't let her go yet. He was enjoying the feel of her womanly curves pressed against his own body. He had her pinned to the wall, and that was precisely what he wanted for the moment. He dipped his head so that his breath brushed against her shoulder. "Perhaps I had other things in mind."

She shivered beneath his hands. Her breath caught, making her words husky. "I'm not certain that would be a prudent activity in such a place."

"Probably not." But it didn't mean that he couldn't kiss her. Just one sweet taste. He caught her lips and kissed her hard. She whimpered against his mouth as her body relaxed against his. More than anything, he wanted to take her back to the house and properly bed her. But he couldn't afford to ignore his duty to Solomon's. He'd made a commitment to them, and he couldn't ignore it. He'd be damned if he'd be the man his father was.

Vanessa was prim, yet not so proper, and it was a heady combination. Damnation if he couldn't forget his own name while touching this woman. There was work to be done. He pulled back from her.

"Be careful; follow behind me. And don't talk," Graeme said. He grabbed her hand and pulled her in the direction that he'd been headed. He could attempt to send her back to the house, but he knew that would be wasted words and effort. She had already shown him once that she was not the sort of woman who would behave or do as she was told.

In fact, she seemed far more likely to do the exact opposite of what she'd been told. It seemed increasingly unlikely that he'd be able to send her to London unless he'd be willing to escort her there himself or tie her to the train. Neither option guaranteed she wouldn't follow him right back here.

They crept along in the darkness, and Vanessa neither stumbled nor said a word. He tried not to be impressed that she could match his stealth and keep his pace. But that probably explained the smile that he knew played at his lips.

Somewhere to the right, Graeme heard a rock scrape down the stone wall. He stopped moving, and she halted along with him. Up ahead, he could see a slight flicker of light. Perhaps the torches there remained lit.

"It's coming from over there," Vanessa whispered, and he knew she probably pointed as well, but the tunnel was too dark to make out her precise position.

"Quiet," he whispered into her ear. She smelled good, like springtime and clean linens, and he wanted nothing more than to bury himself in her until her scent enveloped him. He stepped away to clear his head, then moved them in the direction of the noise.

The light grew brighter as they stepped forward, and Graeme knew they'd reach Niall soon. He just hoped there would be enough darkness to conceal themselves so they could watch his cousin.

Another bang of something, then Niall swore. Graeme found a wall to the right that they could hide behind. He moved Vanessa in that direction.

"You stay behind here," he told her.

She nodded, her eyes wide.

Graeme looked around the corner and saw Niall

moving rocks as if building a barricade. Over and over he bent, then rose to stack them until he'd walled off a section. What the hell was he up to? If he was searching for the treasure, why would he build a wall?

Graeme wasn't certain how long he watched, peering around his hiding place but keeping most of his body huddled next to his wife's. Her hand rested easily in his own, and she made no effort to move from her position. Most women would not be this comfortable shrouded in near darkness and hiding in a cave. But Vanessa stood there as if this were nothing more than a friendly game of hide-and-go-seeking.

Graeme leaned against the wall next to her, his breath labored, but quiet. She was keenly aware of him standing beside her, his body heat chasing away the chill of the cave. For the last few years, she'd longed to explore these very caves. Yet now that she was here, it was not the prospect of scientific discovery that excited her, but rather the man beside her.

He was handsome, intensely so, she had to admit that. Here in the cave, she couldn't make out all of his features clearly, but she closed her eyes to remember them from the night before. His crystal green eyes had darkened when he'd lowered himself on top of her, turning the color of a spring field. It was a marvel really, the way her body had responded to his touch. Interesting. And the sensations had been mesmerizing. As if her body was no longer her own, and she was merely riding in the vessel and reveling in the experience. She'd had no idea her body was even capable of such things.

A most interesting experiment. Perhaps those feelings were what Jeremy had mistaken for love. He and

Violet had writhed around on the floor for so long, panting and moaning, and now Vanessa knew what they'd experienced.

But could she and Jeremy not have shared the same in their marriage bed? Was the reaction to touch dependent on the other person so greatly that with one man you could share explosive passion and with the other feel nothing?

Perhaps she should try again. Kiss Graeme and compare it to the kiss that she'd shared with Jeremy. Last night, she'd been too nervous about her seduction to pay close enough attention.

Without another thought, she pressed her hands to Graeme's chest, reached up on the tips of her toes, and kissed him.

Immediately he responded. His arm snaked around her waist, pulling her close to his warmth. Possessively close. His kiss was not rough, but tenderness was decidedly absent. Instead his kiss was urgent, his tongue deep, his lips intense, but just as pleasant and thought-scattering as she'd remembered from the night before. Coils of pleasure wound their way through her extremities, up her legs, down her arms, around in her stomach, all swirling and moving toward the center of her body. The hidden area where Graeme had put his fingers.

Heat flamed in her cheeks and chest, and she knew pink stained her skin. The mere thought of their union brought color to her face. Not out of embarrassment, but pure unadulterated desire. She longed to get closer to him, longed to wrap her legs around him and have him ease the lust that pounded through her. Most interesting indeed.

They continued to kiss, and he kneaded her bottom, but she wanted more. No, craved more.

Without further thought, she hiked one of her legs

up and wrapped it around his waist. He lifted her off the ground and pulled her tighter to him, pressing her to his erection. Yes, that was the spot; the pressure of him against her was precisely what she desired. In one swift movement, he flipped their positions so that her back pressed into the wall, and he pinned her in place. He lifted her other leg, and she wrapped both of them around him, her dress bunched up at her waist. In this position, nothing save her undergarments and his trousers stood between their skin.

He kissed her, and she bucked against him, rubbing herself along the hard ridge of his erection. Again and again, she moved until the pleasure unwound and the spiral of sensations burst through her. She did her best not to make a sound as her climax exploded through her.

Good gracious, but it was most fascinating how she reacted to him. He leaned against her, his warm breath scattering gooseflesh across her neck. Perhaps she'd misjudged lust, placing it in the same useless category as love. Lust was most pleasant, and between husband and wife, certainly it was appropriate, although perhaps too distracting to accomplish much.

Graeme lowered Vanessa's legs to the ground and stepped away from her. Damned if she wasn't a tempting little minx. And now he was so hard that he wanted to rip off her clothes and pound himself into her, but he couldn't do that. Not here and certainly not now. He took a deep breath and pulled his mind out of his pants. He knew how to control himself. Hell, he'd been doing it his entire life.

He strained his ears to listen, trying to hear what Niall could be doing. He moved over to the wall and peeked around it, but Niall was gone. The stone barricade he'd made stood, but there was no other sign of the man. Graeme swore. He couldn't even keep his hands to himself long enough to complete the task that he'd started this morning.

"This way," Graeme said to Vanessa. He made no move to touch her this time since he struggled to keep his hands off her body.

But she followed obediently. They stepped around the boulder and entered the area where Niall had been working. Directly above them, the ceiling towered high, covered with long reaching stalactites. Then the chamber narrowed, rounding downward to form a tunnel. Damn it all, but Niall had already escaped. Gone into that tunnel? Or passed beside Graeme and Vanessa without being seen or heard?

"Son of a bitch," Graeme bit out.

"What's the matter?" Vanessa asked.

Plenty was the matter. While he'd been pleasuring his wife up against a wall, he'd allowed his target to escape. He exhaled slowly.

"The man you were watching, he left," she said.

"My cousin," Graeme corrected.

"Niall was here?" She stepped out into the open area of the cavern and started examining her surroundings. "Then for whatever reason were we hiding? If you wanted to know what he was doing, why would you not simply ask him?"

There was a simple logic to her question, and for a moment, Graeme wondered if that tactic would work. But he didn't know if Niall trusted him enough to answer truthfully. Chances were he would not. Were their positions traded, it was unlikely that he would trust Niall. But if the men of Solomon's were suspicious, then they had good reason to be. They were cautious men, and by no means alarmist.

"It seems such a simple tactic is not possible."

She shrugged. "Asking questions has always been preferable to me, than to wonder endlessly what someone is thinking or doing." She looked around them, her nose wrinkled. "What is he building?"

"I don't know. I need to look around," he said, expecting at any moment that she would begin complaining about the temperature or the darkness or simply the fact that they were in a cave. But Vanessa seemed as at home here as he did. She nodded, then turned to investigate the stone wall Niall had constructed.

Graeme moved to the opposite side of the wall. Stone by stone, Niall had stacked rocks to the cavern ceiling. There appeared to be no significant reason, but that was unlikely. Graeme turned and looked back up at the high ceiling. Those long, narrow, and nearly flesh-colored stalactites pointed down at him. Accusatory fingers ready to blame him for failure. Echoes of his father's voice whispered inside him. But Graeme wouldn't give up so quickly.

He deliberately looked away, glancing down to examine the cavern floor. They continued looking for several minutes and still Graeme had found nothing that indicated what Niall might be up to. If the man was searching for the bloody Loch Ness treasure, why the hell would he build a wall? It made no sense.

Unless he'd already discovered the stone and was trying to block it off until he could remove it. Graeme turned in the direction of the wall just in time to watch Vanessa take a step around it, and then there was a huge blast. Dust exploded around them, and rocks tumbled to the ground.

A stalactite dropped, knocking Graeme to the ground. He tried to move and realized that the stalactite had speared through his arm, pinning him to the floor. Blinding pain surged through him, and he growled in response.

As the dirt cleared, Graeme saw that the explosion had split open the floor of the cave, creating a huge gash separating him from Vanessa. She, too, lay on the ground, but seemed unscathed.

"What the devil happened?" he asked.

"Some sort of explosion." She came to her feet and brushed the dirt off her skirts. She looked around her. She came to the edge, where dirt continued to fall into the hole below.

"Don't move," Graeme warned, holding up his free arm. "That ground is still unstable."

She took several steps backward. "It's too wide," she said calmly. "I don't think I could cross it."

"No, it's far too wide. I couldn't even cross it," he said.

It was then that she seemed to look up and realize where he was. Her eyes widened—and she pointed. "Graeme, your arm. Are you bleeding?"

"A little. It isn't that bad. It's barely engaged my skin." Not completely untrue, though he would lose more blood when he pulled the damn thing out. While the stalactite was not that large in circumference, it was brutally sharp, and had it fallen a few inches over, it would have gone straight through his heart.

He gritted his teeth, closed his eyes, and pulled up on the stalactite with all his strength. It tore through his flesh on the way out, and he knew that echoing sound filling the cavern came from his throat. But finally he was free.

Blood oozed from the wound, running down his arm. He struggled to sit up, the pain swirling nausea through his stomach.

"You're bleeding faster," Vanessa said. "You need to stanch the bleeding. Create a tourniquet."

He nodded, knowing what she said was true. He was thankful she said it aloud to remind his clouded mind what to do. He ripped his other sleeve off and wrapped it around his arm, then used his teeth to help tie it off. The fabric strained as he pulled it tight, and the blood slowed to a trickle before eventually stopping.

Graeme didn't move for several moments, merely concentrated on inhaling and exhaling. Breathe in, breathe out.

Then he looked across the gap to where his new wife stood, her face concerned, but without fear. Injured or not, he couldn't leave her over there. He came to his feet, using only his good arm as leverage. The empty chasm was far too wide for him to jump. If he had two good arms, he might risk it, but even then it would be a stretch.

Graeme looked around. "I'm going to have to find another way to get you out."

"I don't think you're in any state to rescue me," she said.

"You just sit still and don't touch anything." He glanced around them, surveying their surroundings once more. Several other stalactites had also fallen, and the blast could have caused additional structural instability. "I don't want to cause any more shifts, or else we'll never get out of here."

She nodded, but continued to look around her.

"I'm serious, Vanessa; don't move. The caves here go down so deep, if you fall down there"—he pointed at the gap between them, then shook his head—"I'd never be able to save you. But I think I can circle around and find another tunnel that leads to you."

She took a steadying breath. "I'll be safe. You just work on a way of getting me out of here. And concentrate on not bleeding to death."

"I'm working on it right now."

Chapter Eight

Niall made haste returning to his home. He knew The Raven had been following him, had heard his steps near. Had the bastard followed earlier, Niall might not have accomplished his task. But he'd heard the explosion. The man had stepped around his barricade to appease his endless curiosity, had fallen into Niall's trap, and now was trapped himself.

Niall would wait a while to allow The Raven to take in the gravity of his situation. Then Niall would return to the cave and do a little blackmailing of his own. He had leverage now, and soon he'd be able to walk away from all of this. There had been a day when he'd longed to find the Loch Ness Treasure, but the quest had brought him nothing but pain and grief. No more.

The only thing that he wanted now was for his family to be safe. And he had The Raven right where he wanted him.

Vanessa surveyed her surroundings, knowing that Graeme was out there looking for a way to save her.

Thank goodness that Niall had had the foresight to leave a lit lantern in this area. She assumed it meant he would be returning soon to his work, whatever that might be.

Graeme's wound had been a nasty one, but the stalactite had missed any organs or arteries, so in time he should be fine. It seemed likely, though, that he'd need stitches. She considered this, and in the meantime decided that while she waited for him she might as well use this time to explore. Perhaps she'd find something useful. She did not think she was in the precise cave where Mr. McElroy had discovered his fossil, but that did not mean there weren't discoveries to be made here. Or perhaps she'd even rescue herself.

She made her way over to the wall that had crumbled, hoping she'd find something buried within the stone. Fossils had a way of showing up inside of rocks. The crumbled wall dissolved into a pile of rocks about three quarters of the way down on one side. The only opening was considerably narrow. She reached into her bag and retrieved a candle and lit it. The flame sputtered to life, and she held it in between the narrow opening to see what was beyond.

It was yet another cavern, but because of the fallen rocks, the opening was far too narrow for her to pass through. It might be a way out, but in its current state she'd never be able to fit through the passage, not even by turning sideways. She needed to remove more of the rocks to widen the opening. She extinguished the candle.

She took one glance behind her, but Graeme was nowhere in sight. He'd told her to stay where she was, but what if his wound had started bleeding again? What if he'd passed out somewhere and needed her help? There was no waiting in a situation like this. There was only action.

Vanessa set the lantern aside to give herself free use of both hands. She bent to retrieve the first stone, lifting it to cradle near her body. The chalky exterior flaked against her skin, making the rock difficult to hold on to. Then she picked up another. This one scraped against her fingernail until it tore off so close to her finger's tip that she fully expected it to bleed. But her tiny injury shrank in comparison to Graeme being impaled by a stalactite.

One by one, she removed rocks, setting them off to the side behind her. Though the air surrounding her was chilled, her exertion caused sweat to bead and roll down her back so that her dress began to stick to her skin. Almost there; the passageway was almost wide enough. She worked to pull some additional rocks out of the way. Finally she'd removed enough that she'd be able to squeeze through.

Retrieving her lantern, Vanessa sucked in her breath and climbed through to the other area. Gingerly, she stepped into the other tunnel and waited for another explosion. Only the sound of her own breathing filled the space. So she took another step, the ground firm beneath her feet. She only hoped where it led her wouldn't bring additional danger.

Chalky dust filled her lungs as she inhaled, and the chill emanating off the stone walls seemed to close in on her. But she'd never been one to allow fear to stop her. She would simply walk down this way for a few meters and see if she could detect a way out, a way back to Graeme. If nothing came of her search, she'd return and wait until Graeme found her.

To keep herself company, she talked as she walked. Recited formulas, poems, and even bits from Jeremy's notes. She walked down the tunnel until she came to a large boulder. There was no way to get past it, so it appeared she'd come to another impasse.

The large rock took up nearly all of the space leading through the remainder of the cavern. Upon closer inspection, Vanessa could easily see this large rock was not of the same stone as the rest of the cave. This boulder had been placed here on purpose.

Vanessa had learned long ago that no scientist achieved greatness by giving up at the first obstacle, so she would not turn back until she had exhausted all efforts to move past this rock. She knelt and dug into her bag, searching her tools for something that might assist her. But the instruments she carried were for more delicate work.

Still on her knees, she bent and felt around the base of the rock. Someone had placed the thing here; certainly that meant it could be removed. She'd read about such things in her scientific journals. Men on the hunt for antiquities often ran into clever traps and mechanisms meant to divert the average adventurer.

Her lantern didn't afford her much visibility, but that didn't prevent her from exploring with her hands. She moved her fingers over the walls that surrounded the boulder, searching for a lever or something that would shift the rock out of the way. Cobwebs matted to her fingers, and she ignored the urge to swiftly pull back her hand. No, she was a serious scientist, and that meant getting your hands dirty. A shiver crawled down her spine.

Momentarily she lost her balance, and her left arm reached behind her to grab onto the wall. She steadied herself just as her hand ran over something ridged and rough. It certainly didn't feel as if it belonged in the cavern wall; perhaps this was her lever. She turned, holding the lantern closer, and saw an imprinted image of a fern. It was a perfect rendition, and her very first find.

She had gotten close to a discovery several years ago

in some cliff caves near her family estate. But her mother had found out and had locked her in her room until the family had returned to London the following morning. But no one was here to stop her today.

Today she'd be a true scientist out on an actual expedition. Not merely one who theorized things and wrote articles, but a real paleontologist who had found an authentic fossil. It might simply be a fern, but it was hers.

She squatted and dug around inside her bag, searching for the appropriate tools. This set of tools was the one thing she owned that had belonged to her father, the one possession she truly treasured. She unrolled the leather pack and hand selected a small chisel and pick.

She knelt and positioned herself to carve out the fossil. But there was no way she could do it with only one hand. Odds were good she'd destroy the fossil should she attempt to remove it without adequate lighting. So she did the only thing she could think of: she put the lantern handle between her teeth and went to work.

Vanessa marked a space far enough outside of the fossil so as not to destroy her treasure. She hit the rock and the sound reverberated through the small space. She winced, drawing up her shoulders. But upon examination, she saw that she'd done as intended and started extracting the fossil. She continued striking the rock in precisely the same manner, only pausing to remove the lantern handle, swallow, and take a few deep breaths, then returning to her work. Finally the fossil broke free from its stone prison.

She held the lantern steady, then held the fossil out in front of the light. Her heart beat like thunder in her ears. It was perfect. A delicate template of a fern leaf, with every line and detail immortalized in the rock. She smoothed her thumb over the surface. Her first discovery.

Accomplishment surged through her, bubbling to the surface. She smiled until her face hurt. No more was she simply a student of Paleontology. No; she was out here using actual tools and unearthing real fossils.

Vanessa took one last look at the fossil, wrapped it in a cloth, then dropped it into her bag. Perhaps there was more of interest within this stone. And she still needed to get around that boulder. If it was put here for a reason, then it would move somehow. She felt certain about that.

Her hands made quick, but thorough, work of the rest of the boulder. She had inspected almost every inch when she felt a piece of metal jutting out of the floor, lodged far beneath the great stone. She knelt and tugged on the metal, but it did not move. She tried pushing it but still gained no ground.

Trying a new angle, she turned it and the boulder creaked, then shifted. The floor beneath the boulder opened, like a trapdoor hidden beneath a rug, and the large rock disappeared into the ground. The floor did not seal back over; instead the missing stone left a sizable gap in the flooring.

Vanessa came to her feet and gauged the distance before she leapt across it. This side of the tunnel was short, and soon she found herself in a chamber shaped much like a wagon wheel, with narrow caverns leading off it in every direction.

She was quite unsure which direction she should go in first. She didn't want to go far away, in case Graeme found a way across. If she journeyed too great a distance, she might not be able to hear his voice if he called to her.

While the boulder that had hidden this area had clearly been brought here by man, this ring of tunnels appeared to be naturally formed caves. Vanessa started down the first tunnel to her left, and it was darker and narrower than where she'd been before. The ceiling sat heavy above her, not even an inch from her head. Cobwebs lined the walls and brushed against her arms as she moved deeper into the cave.

Of course, exploring crevices and caves for fossils entailed a certain amount of nasty creatures, she reminded herself. But she loathed spiders. Still she persevered and sent a quick prayer heavenward that none of the creatures would crawl on her. Or bury themselves in her hair. A chill prickled up her spine. She wished now she'd braided her hair or worn a cap.

Her foot stumbled against something, and she stopped and lowered herself to shine the light better on the ground. She looked down into the hollow eyes of a human skull.

Graeme continued searching the area where the explosion had occurred, but he still could not find an opening to lead him to Vanessa. What the devil had Niall been doing to create such an explosion? Had he gone mad?

The chasm provided no way for him to cross here. Clearly he'd have to find another way around. Graeme coughed, trying to clear his lungs of all the dust from the explosion. Pain screamed up his arm, but he had no time to pity himself. The bleeding had stopped, for the most part, and now he only needed to concern himself with infection. However, there was nothing he could do to prevent that now, so he'd simply have to take the necessary precautions once they returned home and hope for the best.

He moved off in the direction from which they'd come. While he hadn't been in this particular area of the caves before, he knew from previous experience that these hillsides were riddled with interlocking caverns and passageways that doubled back on themselves.

Hopefully Graeme would discover another route that circled around to where Vanessa sat trapped. He moved quickly, not wasting his time on being careful and quiet. Right now, what he needed to do was save Vanessa before she got herself killed.

She'd been his new bride for only a day, and he'd already led her into a harrowing situation. Well, he hadn't precisely led her. He'd thought he was leaving their bed without her knowledge, but clearly he had misjudged her. That did not speak well of his abilities as a husband.

Granted he hadn't anticipated excelling in that area. His own father had been a piss-poor husband, as had his grandfather. Neither one remained faithful, and his own father had gone so far as to bring his wife back to her home country and simply leave her here. He'd deserted her and expected her to live without one of her sons, once he'd reached a certain age.

At least his mother had fought back. She'd managed to keep Graeme's younger brother Dougal home with her, but Lord Rothmore had not allowed his heir to leave England, except for a few weeks each summer when he'd allowed Graeme to visit. Once his father had died, Graeme had come to Scotland far more often than he'd been permitted to as a boy.

Finally his trek brought him back to the fork where he'd hidden earlier when he'd captured Vanessa. This time, though, instead of going to his left, he went to the right. This might angle over to where she was now. He hurried through the tunnels, not minding the stones that bit into the bottom of his boots or the cobwebs that tangled in his hair. She was in danger, and he'd be damned if he'd let her get hurt. Not his wife.

Vanessa was not the sort to simply stay out of trouble.

He could see that clearly enough, so he needed to remove trouble from her grasp. Now that he knew she was prone to following him, he'd be more careful about keeping an eye on her.

Graeme knew that for these reasons it would be best if he could persuade her to return to England, where she would be safe. Perhaps he wouldn't even take her to London, but rather one of his country estates, where she would be away from danger. He wondered if there was something he could offer her, making a bargain to persuade her to leave. But even as the thought hit him, he knew it would not work. Vanessa was smart. She would not be bribed into obedience by pretty baubles.

He hadn't wanted a wife, but that mattered not now, regardless of how much trouble she'd get into. And that inquisitive nature of hers was likely what had fueled the intense passion he discovered last night.

He kept moving and entered a spot where the tunnel narrowed. He hunkered down to fit his too-large frame in the smaller area and kept going. Pain radiated up his arm as he clutched it tightly to his body to fit through the tunnel. His light flickered, and he knew there was more air up ahead. Encouraged by the new source of airflow, he increased his pace.

"Vanessa," he called.

There was no response. Hell. He might have gone completely in the wrong direction. But he kept going. Finally the tunnel opened up, and he found himself in the spot where Vanessa had been standing earlier—the open gorge to his left and a partially crumbled wall directly in front of him.

"Vanessa?" he called again.

Where the hell had she gone?

• • •

Vanessa stared at the skeleton at her feet, wondering what precisely had caused his or her demise. She saw no obvious sign of death, such as a sword or any such weapon protruding from the body. Had the person been shot, she wouldn't be able to tell now, as the flesh had been eaten away. Now all that was left were bones wearing clothes that appeared too large for them, like a young girl playing in her mother's dress—something Vanessa had never done, but both her sisters had. Perhaps this unsuspecting soul had been lost and simply lay down, gave up hope, and starved to death.

She knelt and searched around the skeleton but found nothing of interest, so she simply stepped around him and moved forward. The tunnel continued to narrow.

Her body practically hummed with excitement, though she knew fear contributed partly to that. She'd never before seen a dead body, and she couldn't help but shiver a bit every time she envisioned its hollow eyes. She was thankful that only bones were left.

Up ahead, Vanessa could see stone formations, and she held out her candle for a better view. Rough grooves ran down the wall and floor, as if water had sliced into the rock and left scars in its wake. Stalagmites stood from the cavern floor like old men in drab robes, and stalactites hung from the ceiling in a haphazard, jagged pattern.

This certainly appeared to be an older part of the cavern. Water trickled through a small crevice at her feet, and the sound of it had a musical quality. Vanessa stepped deeper into the cavern, careful of each placement of her feet. The sharp stalactites clumped together, making some areas look nearly impossible to traverse. When coupled with some of the massive formations sculpted from the ground, the cavern became a veritable maze.

Unable to resist the temptation, she reached out and ran her fingers across one of the lumpy stalagmites to her right. It was cold and damp and quite solid, feeling almost like a roughly carved statue.

"Vanessa!"

She turned at the sound of the voice echoing far behind her.

"Vanessa!" That certainly sounded like Graeme.

Had Graeme discovered a way to save her? That was indeed good news. But what should she do about her discovery here?

"Where are you?" he asked.

"Just a moment," she said. She eyed her surroundings once more, knowing she must return to investigate. A cavern this old promised wonderful finds. This was a prime fossil-hunting ground.

"Vanessa, now!" he bellowed.

"Graeme?" Her voice came from far off in the distance.

"Where are you?" he asked.

"Just a moment," she said casually, as if she were doing nothing more than entertaining friends in her parlor.

Just a moment for what? Damned if her curiosity hadn't lured her in another direction. But with the instability caused by the explosion, Graeme couldn't allow her to simply explore these caves on her own.

"Vanessa, now!" he demanded. He stood over the partially crumbled wall, noting the tidy pile of rocks where she'd removed them to make the space large enough. She had evidently crawled over this and made her way down that tunnel. But she hadn't removed enough rocks to make way for him to crawl through, and he didn't dare remove any additional stones lest he permanently trap Vanessa on that side.

She came out of the tunnel with her skirt and boots damp and cobwebs hanging off her hair. Her eyes widened with exasperation.

"What is the emergency?" she asked.

Chapter Nine

Niall climbed the hill up to his home, his heart beating fast. He merely needed to bide his time and allow The Raven to sit there, trapped, for a while until he was ready to negotiate. Niall threw open his front door, then made his way to his study. It was far earlier than he would normally seek out a stiff drink, but today he needed one. He believed that he had some scotch lying around from his previous visit.

He couldn't wait to confront the bastard. Demand to know where his family was, and then and only then would he consider releasing The Raven from his trap. The dynamite would have created a blast large enough to strand the man in a desolate part of the cave with no discernible way out. It was a perfect plan.

He poured the amber-colored liquid into a glass and brought it to his lips.

"Do you think me a fool?" The cold voice came from behind him.

Niall stopped. As if he'd downed a chilled drink, icy

cold spread through his body. He set the glass down before turning to face The Raven. "Of course not."

"If you think to outsmart me, you had best consider your family dead now." He fell into a chair across from Niall's desk, then propped his feet up on the mahogany furniture. "You'll never find them, and I'll never let them go. And if you try to kill me," he released a low chuckle as he lit a cigar, "not only will you fail, but your family will suffer for your stupidity."

The Raven took a slow drag, then shook his head. "I've killed men for lesser offenses." He eyed Niall's glass. "I once stabbed a man because he spilled scotch on my favorite boots. I've always hated the stench of scotch. Terrible stuff, don't you agree? I much prefer brandy."

Niall thought to argue, claim ignorance of what the man accused him of, but he knew better. This man was no fool. Defeated, Niall picked up his drink and settled in. His nerves needed steeling.

"I'd kill you right now if I hadn't already invested so much time and energy in you. Between kidnapping your family and arranging for their care all these weeks, it simply wouldn't be efficient to find someone else to do the job I've arranged for you." The Raven lowered his cigar and leveled his soulless gaze on Niall. "But do not test me again. I have two members of your family in my care. I would hate for something unfortunate to happen to one of them. Though I suspect you would hold up your end of our arrangement to ensure the safety of only your son."

Niall took a step forward. "Don't you hurt my wife."

"Find my treasure, and I'll disappear from your life," The Raven said matter-of-factly. He inhaled deeply on his cigar, then released a puff of smoke.

"Please, if you would let me know they are safe." Niall

leaned forward on his desk, meeting the other man's gaze. Cold blue eyes stared back at him. "Please." The Raven's stare never changed. Niall sat back in his leather chair. "I would be able to concentrate more if I knew they were safe and healthy," he added softly.

The Raven paused as if truly considering his offer, but Niall knew it was merely a cruel illusion; this was not a man to be reasoned with. Still, he couldn't help begging for his family's safety. His wife and son meant everything to him. And this—this obsession for the Loch Ness treasure that used to fill his life—had become little more than a casual hobby that he tinkered with every now and again. Spending time with Penny and Jonathan had become so much more important than a frivolous treasure. But now their lives depended on the bloody gems. He ran his hand through his hair.

The Raven laughed. "I never give anything for free. You bring me what I want, and you can have your precious family back."

"My son is just a boy."

If it was possible, The Raven's features hardened even more. "I have a son, too," he said. "They're not worth the trouble."

Niall turned away from the man now, unable to look upon him any longer. He had no choice. He had to find that damn treasure. And quickly. The terrifying thing was, he wasn't any closer today than he'd been three years ago.

The Raven stood from the chair. Niall heard the leather creak as his weight lifted.

"If I don't have that stone in my hand by next week," The Raven said, his tone steady, "I'll kill them. And I won't be gentle. I'll start with your wife, take my pleasure with her, and rough her up a little, but not enough so that she isn't alert when I kill your son. For him, I'll start at his throat, and I'll drag my knife all the way down to his groin, completely gutting him. I have no pity for those who fail me, nor their loved ones. Don't forget that." With that, he strode out of the office.

Niall downed his drink and then forced himself to take steadying breaths. His stomach rolled with the thought of that bastard laying a hand on his sweet wife. But he couldn't afford to panic now. Penny needed him. As did young Jonathan. His fingers curled around the glass in his hand, then he fired his arm back and hurled the glass across the room. It shattered against the heavy wood paneling, falling to tiny shards on the floor. Like a million sparkling gemstones, mocking him.

He'd searched every bloody cave that he could get to, and he'd never found anything that resembled a treasure. But he also knew there were more caverns hidden in the depths of that mountain. He only needed to blast his way into them. He was running out of time.

Vanessa still felt the hum of discovery coursing through her as she and Graeme walked back to the cottage. Not only had she discovered her first fossil—she gripped the stone, which sat at the bottom of her bag—but she had come upon another cavern, ripe with potential discoveries. She wanted to tell Graeme about it, but decided it might be best to be more discreet about the exchange of information. She was still quite curious about the notes she'd read in the study.

If she wanted him to give her additional information regarding the treasure hunt and the search for the Stone of Destiny, perhaps her discovery would provide her with some negotiating room.

"What were you doing in there?" Graeme asked.

"Exploring," she said simply. "I am a scientist. It is in my nature to be curious."

"And?" he asked, prodding for more information. His eyebrows arched up from his warm green eyes.

"And what?" she said, feigning ignorance.

He actually huffed like a little boy, then released some sort of frustrated growl.

She was annoying him; that much she could tell. There was some small part of her that relished the thought. Childish, she recognized, but still it was there. She knew what he wanted, and she even had something specific to tell him. Something about his own personal interests. But dragging it out was informative and revealing about his character.

"Did you see anything?" he asked slowly through gritted teeth. "Or find anything of interest?"

"Such as?"

"Vanessa, stop playing games with me." He pulled her close to him. His green eyes bore into her own. "Tell me what you discovered."

She exhaled slowly. Perhaps she had tested his patience more than was necessary. She kept her gaze on his eyes for a breath, before looking pointedly down at his hands, then back up. He released her. She caught sight of the bloodied shirt piece tied across his injury, and guilt gnawed at her.

"For starters, I came upon a body," she said. "Though I could not determine precisely how, I decided he must have died a most painful death."

A heavy frown creased Graeme's brow. "You're quite serious."

"Oh, indeed." Vanessa began walking again.

"He was dead, though?"

She smiled. "Oh, most decidedly. He had decomposed almost entirely." When his frown had not resolved, she touched his hand. "It was skeletal remains, Graeme. There is no need for concern. So I suppose I cannot be certain it was a man." It suddenly occurred to her. "Though he did seem to be wearing trousers. Not to say women don't on occasion don a pair of pants, but it isn't common. Unless it is more so here in the Highlands."

When he said nothing, she said, "Graeme?"

"What?" His brow was still heavily creased.

"Do you suppose it could have been a woman?" she asked.

"It's doubtful other women have been traipsing about in those caverns," he said sardonically.

It was a thinly veiled chide, one which she would completely ignore. "I don't think we can assume that. Scottish women are strong and courageous." She smiled sweetly.

"You're not going back into those caves. As soon as the weather allows, you'll be back on a train to return to London."

There he went again assuming he could control her behavior. Yesterday at the train station he'd been overbearing and demanding. Trying to send her home. As if he could assert some manner of control over her. And that was before he'd known they were truly married. Honestly.

She stopped short of rolling her eyes. Clearly he had a very specific idea about the rights and duties of a husband. It may take a fair bit of work on her part, but she would have to disabuse him of that notion.

"That is utterly ridiculous," she said. "I have work to do in those caverns. But for the sake of your argument, why? Because I found a dead body? I can assure you he was long since dead. No harm could have come to me."

"It's far too dangerous for you. And no, not simply because of the body."

"I think I managed just fine today even without your assistance."

He nodded. "Yes, discovering a skeleton is precisely what every man desires for his wife."

"So far I have not heard a sound argument. Not only did I discover a fossil today—a perfect one, I might add—but I came upon a new cavern," she said.

"You went down a new tunnel?"

"No, I found an entirely new cave. There was a hidden passage that led to it." There, now he knew that if he wanted to find it, he'd need her assistance.

They descended the hill from the castle ruins and skimmed the shoreline of the loch. The cottage was not far, and though she was eager to get back to the cavern for more exploring, Graeme's wound needed tending.

"What do you mean you found another cavern?" he asked.

"I'm not speaking in riddles. I said precisely what I meant." Why was it that men assumed women needed help expressing themselves? She'd always said what she meant, how she meant to say it, yet people were always asking her for additional clarification. Vanessa stepped through the gate that Graeme held open for her. The cottage sat in front of them. Smoke billowed from the tops of the chimneys, promising warmth.

"I thought you might find the cavern interesting considering your own research," she said. Of course she didn't know for certain that any of those notes had belonged personally to Graeme, but it did seem that, at the very least, he'd been hired to do some investigation in those caves.

He stopped walking and eyed her, his green eyes narrowing. "What research?"

"There's no need to be so secretive." Perhaps she had crossed a line reading through that material, but it had been left out in the open in an unlocked study for anyone to read. She waved her hand in front of her dismissively. "Now that we're married." There, she could toss that about just as he did.

"Yes, but how do you know I even have research, as you call it?" he asked.

"I read through your notes. In the study." She shifted her weight, uncomfortable in the cold now that they were no longer moving. "The ones on the Loch Ness treasure."

He said nothing, but he was listening very carefully to her words.

"*And* the Stone of Destiny." Gooseflesh covered her entire body, and her teeth began to chatter.

"Indeed," was all he said. But she noted a slight twinge along his jawline.

"Could we perhaps go inside and continue this conversation? It is rather frigid out here," she said. No amount of wool could have stifled the chill that permeated her body, as if her very bones were cold. "Not only that, but I am concerned about your injury. We should get that cleaned and make certain you don't need stitches."

He nodded and led them inside and into the very room in question, his study. "Wait here," he said. He was gone but a moment and then returned with a bowl and some torn pieces of fabric.

Once they were seated and the fire stoked so that the flames spread warmth into the small space, Vanessa continued. "While I might ordinarily think that chasing treasure is a waste of time, it is my understanding that you've been commissioned to do this work. At least that is what I gathered the other night."

"I beg your pardon," he said. Vanessa untied the tourniquet. Graeme removed his shirt, wincing when he pulled the sleeve off his arm.

"When that gentleman came to call upon you, I could hear the conversation." She picked at her fingernail, the one she'd snagged on the stone. "Small excerpts are truly all I heard, but I put the pieces together later that night when I read through the books and notes. I wasn't precisely trying to invade your privacy. I'm afraid my curiosity simply got the better of me." She smiled with a slight wince. "My mother always said it would be my downfall."

"Reading?" he asked.

"No, my curiosity. But now that you mention it, she probably thought reading as well. She's from the generation that believes that women are better uneducated. The fewer ideas a woman has, the fewer disagreements she can have with her husband," she said.

"I see."

That was all he said. Vanessa was uncertain if that meant he agreed with her mother, that if they were to stay married, he'd prefer that she sit at home and not read or think or speak her mind. But nothing in his demeanor nor words gave her a hint to what he was thinking. She ran the dampened cloth over his injury to wash off the blood. He sucked in a breath through his teeth.

"In any case," she continued, "back to the subject at hand. I suspect my expertise could prove useful to you." And perhaps it could, but in all honesty, all he needed was to know where the cave was, and she wanted to show him, if doing so would provide her the additional time in the caverns that she needed. Again she gripped the wrapped fossil that was tucked into her bag. She was eager to get back to her room, wash it up, and spend some time examining it beneath the light.

"Your expertise. Please enlighten me," he said.

"I believe I've mentioned before that I speak and read a number of languages which can be helpful in deciphering ancient texts. I'm rather clever, so figuring out riddles comes easily to me." She continued to clean his wound as she spoke. It was a rather deep cut that could probably warrant a stitch or two.

"You haven't yet convinced me," he said.

At least he was gracious enough to give her an opportunity to make her appeal. In the end, it would matter not what he said; she'd do as she chose. Exploring the caves with him would be infinitely preferable, though, considering he could offer her additional muscle. Not to mention a measure of protection if a spider should appear. Or something more nefarious.

"Do you want me to stitch this up for you?" she asked.

"Have you done that before?"

"No; in fact I'm terrible with a needle and thread, but it didn't seem the time to discuss one of my weaknesses," she said.

He smiled. "I'll get my mother to do it."

Whether he *thought* he needed her help or not didn't matter. "I didn't want to handle things in this manner, but you leave me no choice. I will not show you the whereabouts of the new cavern I located unless you share details of your research with me." She held up a hand to ward off his protest. "And if you think to leave me behind, you can rest assured that I will follow you or wander through those caves myself." She shook her head and did her best to appear innocent, silly even. "And you never know what can happen when a woman is left to her own devices."

"You think to blackmail me, woman?" Graeme asked.

He released a string of curses that should have had her blushing, but for whatever reason, she found it fascinating. The angrier he got, the thicker his accent became. He rose to his feet. A large, angry Scotsman towered over her.

She came to her feet and did her best to glare up at him. He wouldn't bully her. She wouldn't stand for it. "I will do whatever is necessary to continue my research. You," she poked him in the chest for emphasis, "might be my husband now, but you will not prevent me from doing my work."

He opened his mouth to say something, then shut it. He glared at her for a few seconds before saying, "You could draw me a map."

"No, I don't think so." She moved to stand in front of the hearth. Slowly she rubbed her hands together in front of the flames. "I truly think it would be best if I showed you." Heat radiated up her arms and warmed her legs through the heavy fabric of her skirt. "That is my price."

"You think you are clever." He stood behind her now. He'd moved there so silently, so quickly that she had not heard his approach.

A different kind of heat shimmered over her skin, one that had nothing to do with the flames from the fireplace. Vanessa closed her eyes and fought the urge to lean into the man standing behind her.

"I don't take kindly to these types of games." His deep brogue was soft, close to her ear. His hot breath slid over her exposed neck.

Her nipples hardened, and she inhaled a shaky breath. She waited for his touch, but it never came. Instead she felt a draft behind her as Graeme moved to the door.

"Two hours," he said. "Eat something, rest or whatever it is that ladies need to do, then meet me outside."

Graeme stepped outside the cottage, the cold winter wind biting into his cheeks. He needed to clear his thoughts. How the devil was he supposed to focus on his bloody work when he had to deal with that woman? She infuriated him. And damned if all he could think about was making love to her, slow and sweet.

He was quickly learning that his duchess would not be controlled no matter what his reasons. She would do as she pleased. So far, she'd managed to keep herself out of too much trouble. Still, he knew he'd have to keep an eye on her.

Hadn't she just admitted that she'd sneaked into his study and read through not only his notes, but all of the notes that Jensen had given him regarding Niall's research? Which meant she knew about everything.

Hell, maybe she would prove useful. But he'd been so bloody distracted by her...hell, her hair distracted him, the way the fiery curls hovered around her face begging to be brushed behind her ears. And the way her nose wrinkled when she thought.

Yet she'd faced the sight of a dead body today. Most women would have fainted at the sight of such a thing and needed smelling salts to be awakened. Then they would have had to take to their bed to recover. But Vanessa not only managed to survive the incident on her own, she intended to return. She was not an ordinary lady.

Chapter Ten

Two hours later Graeme walked beside Vanessa, trying to keep his focus on the task at hand. His immediate purpose was to investigate his cousin, but he couldn't ignore his own interests. Graeme had searched through these caves looking for possible hiding places for the Stone of Destiny. If Vanessa had truly located a new cavern, then he wanted to look around. He was not without his own curiosities.

Vanessa walked next to him. He liked that she was tall. His mind flashed to this morning in the cave when he'd pressed her against the wall and how close her sex had been to his. He'd almost lost control and taken her up against that cavern wall. Certainly not the way to treat a lady. Lust stirred in his loins.

That direction of thinking would not prove useful for this task. He concentrated on the frigid temperatures as they descended the hillside to get to the next. The frost-covered grass and leafless trees formed a barren landscape.

"You read all of my notes?" he asked.

"I did," Vanessa answered without hesitation. "I heard you speaking with that gentleman outside my door."

"We weren't precisely outside your door. We were in the next room."

She shrugged and smiled broadly. "I might have pressed my ear to the door a few times to amplify the sound."

"That conversation was really none of your business," Graeme said.

"Perhaps not, but you did leave the notes out on the desk for anyone who was walking by to see." She smiled. "Not only that, but I could make the argument that whether or not I dig around in those caves is none of your business," she said.

"I am your husband, and it is my duty to protect your welfare."

"Indeed. And I am your wife, and it is my duty to over-see what happens in my household. Granted that was your mother's home, but you had a visitor, and his comfort could have fallen to me." She carefully skirted some slippery stones; the ice atop them shone. "I was listening so intently to ensure he didn't need anything."

He hid a smile. He could find no fault with her line of reasoning, even though he knew her argument was weak. "You read the notes on the Loch Ness Treasure," he said.

"And the research on the Stone of Destiny, which I can only assume is your vocation."

Her tone revealed nothing about what she thought on the matter. Some people thought treasure hunting was a waste of time, nothing more than chasing a fantasy, but he'd seen evidence to the contrary. A friend found Pandora's box, and Solomon's was full of other men who'd discovered hidden treasures. "I have a friend who located the last library of Alexandria," he said abruptly. Then felt foolish for trying to impress her.

"Truly?" Vanessa asked with interest, her eyes widened. "Now, *that* is a treasure I would find worthwhile and most interesting. Could you introduce me to him?"

"He's married," Graeme said dryly.

"I wasn't asking you to find me a paramour, Graeme. My only interest would be his scholarly work."

At that Graeme snorted. "Fielding would never consider himself a scholar. I suspect you might get along famously with his wife, though." Fielding had always said that Esme had a special knack for finding trouble. He suspected that the two women would get along quite well. Of course, he wasn't certain that either he or Fielding would benefit from the women's combined propensity for mischief.

Suddenly Graeme realized that in his mind he was building a life for them. Fitting Vanessa into his world in England.

"So why the interest in the Stone of Destiny?" she asked, bringing his focus back to the present. Her cheeks were flushed a pretty pink with exertion, and her breath was coming more rapidly than normal.

He noted that Vanessa never complained about the rough terrain as they ascended the hill above the loch and approached the castle ruins. Most English women, in their dainty shoes, would not make it across the narrow shoreline, given the large stones edging the water, let alone the rocky cliffs above the loch. But Vanessa said nothing and continued to climb beside him.

"Might I remind you that I will only reveal this cavern to you if you share your research with me," she said.

He supposed there was no harm in having a discussion about the treasures. She'd already read through the notes and heard much of his conversation with Jensen. "It is part of Scotland's heritage," he said simply, answering the question that she'd asked a moment ago.

"I was under the impression it did not need to be located since King Edward I stole it from the Scots in 1296. Is it not sitting in Westminster Abbey, where it has been since then?" she asked. She held her hand out to him so he could assist her over several of the larger rocks. At least she was intelligent enough to wear boots and not try to maneuver out here in those flimsy soft-soled slippers that many women wore. Although her dress seemed like it might hinder her, she managed to maneuver quite well within her skirts. "Or rather *had* been in Westminster. Did your friend not inform you that it had been recently stolen?"

"Yes, someone absconded with it. And yes, most people believe it to be the true Stone of Destiny," he said.

"But not you," she said. "You think the real stone is still out there waiting to be found."

"I do." He paused before continuing. "Well, I believe that a counterfeit was made, and that is the one that was stolen—the one that was in Westminster," Graeme said. "I'm merely trying to find the authentic stone."

"You believe that the Scots knew the English were coming, and they hid the real stone, replacing it with a fake one before the theft?"

He tried to gauge her expression to see if she believed him to be utterly mad. But she was not hiding a smile or snickering at him; instead her questions and tone all seemed to express genuine curiosity. "Something like that," he said.

"And once you find it, what do you plan to do with it?"

Before Graeme could answer, they'd reached the mouth of the cave. "Be mindful of your steps. We do not want a repeat of this morning. Let's not set off any other disturbances or explosions," he said.

"Of course." She nodded. "I should think the Stone of Destiny's proper place would be in a museum, rather than Westminster," Vanessa continued. "It is a biblical treasure, Jacob's pillow, as it has been called. Do you believe it reveals prophetic dreams when you sleep upon it? I read about that once and thought it sounded interesting, although certainly it must be untrue."

"I've never given that much thought." Though he'd read about that theory as well, he'd only ever wanted it because it was a Scottish relic—their coronation stone—and he thought his kinsmen deserved to have it back.

"It would be nice if it were true," Vanessa said, and a hint of wistfulness tinged her tone. "Did you know that some believe it was the cornerstone upon which the Tower of Babel was built?"

Graeme had to admit that she surprised him with her knowledge of the antiquity. Not many people ever gave the Stone of Destiny a single thought, let alone were aware of the number of random facts she'd been rattling off. And none of what she'd just said could be found in his notes. This was information she'd gathered from reading elsewhere. "You seem to know an awful lot about this particular relic."

Vanessa shrugged, a pleasant smile on her lovely face. "I know about many different things. I very much enjoy reading, and history is one of my favorite subjects."

"What else do you read?" he asked, finding himself genuinely interested.

"Science, of course, philosophy, and religion."

"I came back around this way to find you yesterday," Graeme said, leading the way down the tunnel. His lantern funneled light ahead of them.

"I suspect there are many ways to connect all these caverns," she said.

"Indeed." More than likely he could find the new cavern on his own. Yet he'd allowed her to convince him that he needed her assistance. Allowed her to blackmail him into accepting help. He still was unsure of his reasons, although he suspected it had more to do with the pleasure of her company than any research necessity, something he didn't want to think about for any length of time.

Once again they found themselves in the area with the crumbled wall where she'd originally been trapped. "We'll have to tear more of this down to make room for all of you," she said, letting her eyes roam the length of him.

She didn't wait for him to take action. Instead she immediately went about moving rocks out of the way, building a larger opening for his broad frame. Not to be outdone by a woman, Graeme helped, grabbing the larger stones, carefully pulling them down, and then setting them aside. Finally their efforts paid off; they had created a big enough entrance.

"That should do it," Vanessa said, exertion lining her voice, making it husky and as rich as it had been when they'd made love. Perspiration dampened her hair, and tight wispy curls now framed her face. Delicate brows arched over her eyes, and here in the darkness of the cave, her long black lashes highlighted the blue of her eyes. Her rosy-stained cheeks and labored breathing spiked his desire. Damned if he couldn't take her right there on the cold stone floor.

She stepped through the entryway, then turned expectantly toward him. Her head tilted, and again her eyes traveled the length of his body. "I do believe you'll fit, although you might have to turn your body and perhaps bend some." She demonstrated the motion, bending her body to illustrate how it was done.

He suppressed a laugh. He'd been climbing through these caves since he was a small boy, but he'd let her play the expert. He did as she'd shown him and followed her down the tunnel and into the chamber.

They walked in silence for a while, the sounds of their footfalls echoing in the cavern. Soon they came to an area in the passageway with a gap in the floor. "Vanessa?" he asked. "Are you certain this is the right path?"

She maneuvered herself around him. "Of course I am. See down there? That's the boulder I was telling you about, the one attached to some manmade structure."

"Precisely how did you manage to get across?" he asked.

Before she answered, she shoved him out of the way, then ran and jumped across the gap. "Like that. It's not that difficult."

Graeme swore, then rubbed the back of his neck. This was going to be a trying marriage, full of surprises both pleasant and nerve-racking. He followed behind her. "You really must try to be more careful."

"I was quite careful," Vanessa said. "I have jumped it twice now without even a scratch.

"Look at all of these new caverns I've discovered," she said. Her eyes lit with enthusiasm. "But this isn't the one I was so excited about. There are more, and one deeper in. This is the tunnel I took." She pointed to her left. "I had to crouch, so it's likely you'll have to crawl through." She eyed him, then the tunnel. "It's a tight space."

"I'm certain I've been in worse."

She was right. He did have to crawl. The space was far too small for him to even bend over and walk, so he had to get on his knees and move through it that way. Tiny rocks lining the floor punched into his knees.

"Because this particular cavern is so difficult to get to, I believe that it is quite special. Especially because of the manmade contraption farther back. It does seem as if perhaps someone might be protecting something," she said brightly. "I, for one, hope it's fossils."

They came upon the skeleton, and Graeme, already on his knees, used his position to investigate the remains. He ran his hands along the outer edges of the remaining clothing, looking for anything that would indicate the person's identity. But he found nothing.

"If I had to guess, based on the type of clothing," Vanessa said, "this was a man, and he's been dead for many years. Look at the style here of his shirt." She pointed, her long fingers pausing over the collar. "Clearly a style long since passed."

Graeme sat back on his heels. "You surprise me," he admitted.

"How so?" She looked at him inquisitively.

"I would not have expected you to care a whit about fashion, let alone pay that close attention to it." Judging from the clothing he'd seen her wear, she only had an arsenal of practical dresses cut from wool.

"Oh, I don't care at all." She waved her hand. "But my mother does, and she has schooled my sisters and me on the intricacies of fashion, both for males and females. A good wife should know how to select a tailor for her husband."

She was quoting her mother there; on that he'd wager

money. Despite her odd interest in the bones of creatures long dead and her decided lack of delicate sensibilities around dead bodies, Vanessa had obviously been raised a gentlewoman. She had all the knowledge and skills to make her the perfect duchess. His perfect bride. On the other hand, whether or not he had what it took to become an ideal husband was still very much up for debate.

Graeme glanced back at the body and found her assessment to be true. He'd seen his own father wear a shirt with a similar cut, but his father had been dead for nearly ten years.

"I don't believe this man is going to offer any further assistance to us," he said.

"Shall we continue, then?"

Graeme nodded and motioned for her to move farther into the tunnel.

"It's right up this way," she said.

The area opened slightly, enough that Graeme was able to stand and move his arms freely.

She was right. This cavern was spectacular, formed and shaped by water flowing in and out. Their damp, cold surroundings seemed untouched by man. Vanessa immediately went about exploring. She walked slowly, holding her lantern just so as she scrutinized the cavern walls.

"Be careful," Graeme said. The small puddles around his feet sat stagnant, but as he moved forward they rippled around his boots. There was something almost familiar about the cavern with its many stalactites and stalagmites. Not that he hadn't seen such shapes before. Hell, he'd been intimately acquainted with one earlier that day. The two stitches in his arm still pinched where his skin had been pulled tight to close the wound.

It was something else that called to him. A certain

recognition felt deep in his gut. There was a passage in *The Magi's Book of Wisdom* that immediately came to mind: *The three guard the secret, and swords from above point the way.* He'd never known precisely what those words had meant, and it seemed odd that he'd think of them now, but looking straight in front of him he knew why.

Hunkered in the darkness, three large stalagmites stood looking very much like monks wearing their tunics and hoods. Directly above the formations, sharp stalactites pointed down at the cavern floor, almost illuminating the area nestled at the would-be men's feet.

Perhaps he was imagining things. Perhaps he'd searched for the damned thing for so long that his mind conjured clues where there was nothing to be found. But he'd followed lesser hunches. He fell to his knees and felt around the base of the largest stalagmite, the center of the three. Chilled mud oozed around his fingers as he explored.

"Graeme?" Vanessa asked from behind him. "Whatever are you doing on the ground?"

"Looking for something," he said.

"Indeed." And then she was at his side, on her own knees.

The additional light from the lantern better illuminated the entire area. More than ever, the formations before him resembled three men, and above, the sharp tips reaching down toward him appeared swordlike. With renewed effort he dug through the mud.

"Whatever are you searching for?" she asked, her voice breathless with excitement.

"A medallion." He laughed. "It's probably a futile quest, but something about this area seemed right."

His fingers moved through the mud and water searching for anything that felt out of place. He searched all over in front of the three figures, but found nothing unusual. "It's a decoder," he found himself saying. "For *The Magi's Book of Wisdom.*"

"That handwritten bit in the back of the book," she said.

He chuckled. "You really did read through everything. I don't suppose that's some ancient language you're fluent in?"

"Unfortunately, no," she said.

He sat back for a moment and looked up. "They're supposed to point the way," he said absently.

She reached into her bag for her tools. She unrolled the pouch and withdrew what looked like a miniature shovel. "Perhaps you only need to dig a little deeper."

Graeme took the shovel and drove it into the muddy water. Almost immediately, it struck something that would not give way with mere pressure. He moved the instrument around in an effort to outline the object. It could be nothing more than another naturally formed cavern structure. But what was it?

With one hand, he held the miniature shovel in place and with the other, he dove in. The hole was much deeper than where he'd previously been looking. Now his arm was buried in the cold, murky water all the way up to his elbow. His finger moved over something decidedly hard and round.

"Did you find something?" she asked.

"I think I may have." He worked the object free of its muddy imprisonment, then pulled it out. Mud caked to his arm and fingers and all over what he felt certain was the decoder. "Son of a bitch," he swore.

Graeme rinsed the artifact in the muddy water, then held the light over the metal disc.

"That's it, isn't it?" Vanessa asked. "The decoder you've been searching for?"

His pulse thundered. "Aye, it seems to be," he said. The medallion dated back to the third century and yet still displayed every original carving. Now he could decode the last portion of *The Magi's Book of Wisdom*.

"Had you been searching these caves for that piece?" she asked.

He shook his head, but never took his eyes off the metal disc in his hand. "No, I looked for this for several years after locating that book, but to no avail. Eventually I stopped. I figured if there was more than one way to bed a woman, certainly there had to be more than one way to find that bloody block of stone." Then he looked up and met her gaze, only just realizing to whom he'd been speaking.

"Sounds logical," Vanessa said. She swallowed, then came to her feet. She eyed their surroundings. "I'm going to go back to my search and see if there is anything else important in this cavern."

He'd obviously flustered her, and ordinarily he wouldn't have said such a thing to a lady. But she'd been down there on the ground helping him, providing encouragement and suggestions, and he'd simply said the first thing he'd thought. He'd momentarily forgotten she was his wife and instead had spoken to her as if she were a friend or a partner.

Decidedly male voices echoed somewhere behind them. Graeme pulled Vanessa close and motioned with his finger to his lips. He strained his ears to listen to the men's words. Two distinct voices, but he couldn't make out what they said.

He pulled her close and bent to her ear. "We'll move closer, but stay behind me."

She nodded.

Together they crept down the tunnel, in the direction from which they'd come. Graeme suspected the men were in the central chamber that led to the various tunnels. Their voices still echoed around them, their words becoming clearer.

"The Loch Ness treasure is what he really wants. It's here somewhere," one man said.

"We'll find the stone before he does," the other said.

Graeme held an arm out to stop Vanessa's progress. She pressed her body up against the wall, effectively hiding herself. "Stay hidden," he told her, then sneaked closer to the main chamber. He caught sight of one of the men standing at the mouth of a tunnel. He had dark blond hair cropped short, and his leather coat sported dust and debris from the cavern, but there was something oddly familiar about the material.

Only one man that he knew wore a coat like that. Anthony Braden was not a member of Solomon's, but Graeme knew all about him—the man was a bounty hunter. Wealthy collectors paid him huge sums of money to find their treasures. Graeme's friend Fielding had once earned this same living before he'd joined the ranks of the men of Solomon's.

"What the devil are you doing here, Braden?" Graeme asked as he stepped out of the shadows. It was risky to confront them, especially since he was unfamiliar with the other two men, but sometimes surprise could work in one's favor.

Though Braden didn't start, Graeme knew his abrupt appearance startled the man. He turned and met Graeme face to face. The man was younger than Graeme, but by no more than a few years. "I should ask you the same question, but then your kin are local to these parts, aren't they?"

Graeme nodded, but said nothing. The man standing next to Braden stepped forward, his hand moving to the pistol strapped to his leg.

"Sam, that won't be necessary. Graeme here is merely being cordial," Braden said.

Sam eyed Graeme for a moment longer before crossing his arms over his chest.

Graeme had no weapon with him. Unless he could count the small sharp instruments that his wife used to scrape things out of stone. Hardly a man's weapon.

A third man stepped back out of the tunnel: Rodrick Fitch, longtime associate of Braden's. Fitch was slightly shorter than Graeme, but as broad. He was known as an accomplished athlete, a man who favored bare-knuckle fighting inside the ring.

"I heard the Stone of Destiny was stolen from Westminster," Braden said.

"A fool has wasted his time and efforts," Graeme said.

Braden bowed slightly. "Naturally you would believe that instead of recognizing that bloody thing had been sitting under your nose the entire time." He glanced around at their surroundings, then took a few steps forward. "What are you skulking about these caverns for?"

"A simple exploration," Graeme said.

"Coincidence. That is precisely what we are about." Braden smiled. "Isn't that right?" he asked, eying his companions.

"Absolutely," Fitch said, his deep voice vibrating off the cavern walls.

Sam grinned, though it looked more like a sneer. "We'd best be getting on with that *exploration*."

Graeme still blocked any view of Vanessa with his body. There was no need for the men to know she was even there. He'd never known Braden to be violent, but these other men might have more dangerous appetites.

But Graeme was tired of skirting around the subject at hand. "What do you want with the Loch Ness treasure?" he asked.

Braden's brows rose, and then he and Fitch exchanged glances.

"I heard you," Graeme explained.

"Wealthy client's obsession," Braden said with a shrug. He eyed Graeme a moment and then slowly smiled. "Solomon's sent their dogs here to protect it?" But the man didn't wait for an answer. "We have bigger foes to worry about." He motioned to Fitch to return to the tunnel they'd started down. Sam reluctantly followed.

"Watch your step, Braden," Graeme said.

"You just stay the hell out of my way." Braden turned and disappeared into the darkened tunnel.

Chapter Eleven

Who were those men?" Vanessa asked.

Graeme faced her as they stayed hidden inside the tunnel. "Filthy scavengers," he said, unable to keep the disgust from his tone.

"You mean like pirates?" Vanessa asked.

"I suppose you could call them that. They're treasure hunters for hire," Graeme said.

"And you know them?"

Graeme shrugged. "More or less." Solomon's, on principle, did not approve of men who earned their living hunting treasure for profit. A life like that tended to lead to greed, and greed fed the need for power, which only caused greater problems.

"Do you believe they're working with your cousin?"

"No, I don't. Niall isn't the sort to hire help for his own search. He knows more about this damned treasure than anyone." Graeme looked out in the direction that Braden and Fitch had retreated. "Something doesn't fit."

"Should we follow them?" Vanessa asked.

"No. We aren't prepared in case things become less friendly. Besides, I suspect we'll see them again," Graeme said with a shake of his head. "I want to venture down where we were yesterday. Investigate a little more of what Niall has been working on."

"This is becoming quite the puzzle," Vanessa said. They walked through the central chamber and back around the way they'd come.

Graeme agreed, but said nothing. Niall wanted the Loch Ness treasure, but his efforts in the last month had created concern among the men of Solomon's. Braden and his two cronies were also after the Loch Ness treasure. Too much interest in a single treasure in a short amount of time might have triggered Jensen's concern, especially when that treasure was a part of the Kingmaker.

The individual stones posed no threat, but when combined, they could potentially create trouble for Her Majesty. But why would Niall have changed his course, changed his focus from simply craving the Loch Ness treasure, to wanting to possess a dangerous artifact like the Kingmaker? Niall had more money than most men, and he'd never been particularly ambitious. So why the sudden interest in a relic associated with great power?

Quietly they'd circled back, heading down the tunnels where they'd followed Niall yesterday. Vanessa reached into her bag and retrieved some folded parchment. She scanned it, then glanced up at the cavern walls.

"What are you doing?" he asked.

"Research," she said. "While we're in these caves I would like to find additional evidence to prove Mr. McElroy's theory."

"Who?" Graeme asked.

She handed him the notes that she held. "Mr. McElroy

was a farmer who did a bit of exploring on the side and came across a bone he claimed proved the existence of the water kelpie."

"Our beastie?" Graeme chuckled. "Interesting."

"Indeed." She took back her notes. "Somewhere in these caves is the cavern where he found that bone. He also has an illustration of a cave he could see, but not get into, that had several bones. I intend to find them," she said. But then she abruptly stopped walking, and Graeme nearly slammed into her. "Oh my."

"What?" he asked.

"Dynamite. A lot of dynamite."

Graeme pushed Vanessa behind him and stepped over to where she'd been. Inside a small alcove were several sticks of dynamite.

Graeme glanced at his wife. She seemed as unruffled as she had been when facing down the corpse.

"The explosion," Vanessa said.

"I was hoping that had been a one-time event," Graeme said. "But it does appear there are plans for additional blasts." Using such material could make these caverns far more dangerous than they already were. Cave-ins occurred naturally, but to accelerate such events with explosives—Niall must be desperate.

"We need to leave," Graeme said. He needed to have a conversation with his cousin. Warn him to cease his blasting or else he'd chain the bastard in that damned house of his. And he'd leave the man there until he decided to stop behaving like a lunatic.

"Leave?" Vanessa asked.

"No more exploring until I know for certain this area is safe." Graeme put his hand on the small of her back and pushed her gently toward the cave's opening. "Besides,

Duchess, we have the party tomorrow night. I'm assuming like most women you'll need at least a day to ready yourself."

"I need no such amount of time. Without the army of my mother's servants, I should need only to put on a dress." Then she paused and looked up at him. "What party?"

"Our party. To celebrate our marriage." He paused a moment, noting that only days ago his life had seemed so simple. But now he had a bossy bride, and the new marriage had given his mother an excuse to muck around in his life. "My mother is organizing the entire thing." Then he shook his head and continued to guide her back down the tunnel.

"I don't have party clothes," Vanessa said, although judging from her weak tone he'd guess that wasn't precisely true, but rather an excuse she thought he might accept. "At least not the sort for a wedding party."

"You'll look beautiful no matter what you wear. By the by, I sent a telegram to your family announcing our nuptials and your safety. There will also be a formal posting in the newspapers."

She stopped so quickly that he ran into her. She turned to face him and he grabbed her arms as her large eyes peered up at him in wonder. "You did?"

He shrugged. "Seemed the appropriate thing to do."

Graeme left Vanessa in the care of his mother and grandmother to help her decide what she should wear to the party. He then made quick work of the stairs leading to Niall's front door. There was no need to bother with propriety; instead he stormed into Niall's house, not waiting for an invitation or announcement. He made his way into his cousin's study and threw the door open.

Niall immediately came to his feet from behind his desk. "Graeme, what are you doing here?"

"What kind of bloody fool are you?" Graeme asked as he breached the threshold.

Niall shook his head. "What are you talking about?" he stammered. Odd, because Graeme had never noticed Niall stammering before.

"The dynamite in the caves. Are you mad? You could destroy the entire system of caves. Bring that side of the hill sliding into the loch."

Niall's face went tight, his lips nothing more than a line. "I don't know what you're talking about."

"The hell you don't. I saw you the other day. Saw you sneaking around, building that wall." Graeme glanced around the room. Unlike the other day, where everything had appeared neat and orderly, today everything sat in shambles. All of the furniture remained the same, but now stacks of books littered the floor, and Niall's desk was covered with papers and maps as well. There was a large ink stain on the expensive rug. Evidently Niall had become haphazard in all areas of his life.

Graeme exhaled slowly, then moved to Niall's large desk. He sat in one of the chairs opposite the desk and leaned forward. "My wife was nearly trapped there thanks to the addle-brained trap you set."

"Your wife?" Niall's tone rose in surprise.

"Yes. My wife."

"But you're not—"

"We are newlyweds," Graeme bit out slowly. "The point is, that explosion you set off trapped her in a secluded area of the cave, and the results could well have been disastrous had I not been able to circle around and get to her through another tunnel."

Niall slowly lowered himself to his chair. It was then that Graeme noticed Niall's appearance. Normally he was the picture of an English gentleman: hair sculpted into the perfect style, clean and starched clothes with a crisp white cravat, bright, alert eyes. But the man standing before him had limp hair that hung around his face, and his clothes seemed as if they'd been picked up from the floor, wrinkled and stained.

But it was his face that showed the most difference. Dark circles lay heavy beneath eyes that now appeared hollow and gaunt. His shoulders slumped forward. He wiped at his mouth, then looked at Graeme. "That was you?"

"Yes, that was me. And Vanessa. She could have fallen, Niall. Been killed." Graeme leaned back and eyed his cousin. They had never been close, but he was family. For that reason alone, Graeme would give him the opportunity to explain himself, give some damned excuse as to why he was acting reckless and crazy.

"I'm sorry. It wasn't meant to be a trap." He tried to laugh, to appear light, but Graeme knew better. Niall's face, his entire body, jittered with a sense of anxiety. The man sat in his chair as if any moment he would spring to his feet. His eyes darted around the room, searching, but his gaze never settled on anything for any length of time. His skin tone was now almost gray in color, and he looked as if he hadn't eaten or slept in days.

"What is going on, Niall?" Graeme asked. "You look like hell, man."

Niall released another weak laugh. "I'm merely trying to find that treasure. Getting impatient, I suppose." He wiped his hand down his face, and for a moment his façade cracked, and Graeme saw panic lurking in his eyes. Niall was terrified.

Graeme put his elbows on the desk and met his cousin's gaze. "No, there's more. What kind of trouble are you in? Do you owe someone money?"

As far as Graeme knew, Niall had always had plenty of money, but wiser men had lost fortunes at the gaming tables or in risky investments. Graeme could think of no other explanation for Niall's odd behavior.

"I'm not in any sort of trouble." Niall shook his head fervently and again attempted a light-hearted chuckle. "I'm merely searching for that treasure. It's elusive, and I suppose it's been driving me a bit mad as of late." He scraped his fingers through his blond hair, then set his jaw. "You have no reason to be concerned," he said, his casual tone forced.

Graeme could see the lines of resolve in Niall's face. It was an expression Graeme was familiar with because it was one he himself wore all too often. He had not thought his English cousin had such spine in him, but obviously Graeme had been wrong. Niall would tell him nothing more.

"I see," Graeme told him. But Niall was hiding something. Graeme could tell. It was in Niall's voice, his movements, the shifty twitch in his gaze. Something had him scared as hell. Even if he would not ask for the help he so obviously needed, Graeme could not allow him to continue.

"If you keep using that dynamite, you'll end up destroying those caves and making them all but impassable. If you think finding your damned treasure is hard now, try doing so when you can't even pass through the caverns."

Niall was quiet for several moments. "I have to do what I have to do." His jaw set as he raised his gaze to meet Graeme's.

Graeme looked around the room, seeing no one else, but he would have sworn that Niall was looking at someone behind him.

"You're going to get yourself killed or end up killing someone else," Graeme said.

"I am careful," Niall said. "The dynamite is merely an easier mode to break into some of the tunnels that have long since closed up with fallen rock."

"And you're certain you'll find that treasure in those caves?" Graeme asked.

Niall nodded. "Positive. There is no other place it could be."

"Unless someone else already found it," Graeme said.

Niall's eyes widened, and fear shone brightly in their brown depths. "Has someone found it?"

"Not that I know of." Graeme thought of mentioning the presence of Braden and his men, but thought better of it. If Niall was working with them, he didn't want his cousin to know that he'd discovered his alliances. "And I suspect had it been found, Solomon's would have heard tale of it."

Niall seemed to relax a measure. "True." He paused for a moment, then stood. "You mentioned a wife. I wasn't aware you had married."

"Vanessa; you've met." Graeme came to his feet. "It's a recent union." He paused before adding, "Mother is having a party to celebrate. You could come."

Niall nodded. "Congratulations."

Graeme put one hand on the desk. "If you need help with anything, you need only ask."

Niall again looked behind Graeme, then back into Graeme's face. He gave him a brittle smile. "I appreciate that. But I'm perfectly capable of handling matters myself."

• • •

Two hours later, The Raven sat across from Dougal and waited for him to speak. He slowly drank his whiskey-infused tea and eyed the boy, who seemed beyond excited to receive such an invitation. The young Scotsman shifted in his seat, seeming uncomfortable in the delicate chairs that adorned the parlor.

After Graeme had left Niall's, Niall had wasted no time in excusing himself as well. He had said that he wanted to get back to the caves to try another path, but The Raven suspected it had more to do with not wanting to discuss Graeme's visit. Or the man's speculations. All the more reason to otherwise engage Graeme so he would cease paying attention to Niall and his quest.

The Raven could be a patient man. He had to be in his line of work. But he wasn't used to extending his patience to sniveling boys like the one before him. Still, The Raven wanted to see what Dougal might be able to offer him. Clearly the boy hungered for attention, and his brother simply wasn't providing that. Might be Graeme's new wife that was demanding his time. The Raven felt certain the boy would prove useful, but he'd require guidance, guidance with a delicate hand.

Dougal sipped his tea, the dirt beneath his fingernails a stark contrast to the elegant teacup.

Filthy mongrel. He really was a hulking lad, meant for plowing fields and throwing back drinks in the pub. However, he clearly yearned for the finer things in life. And that yearning would be his downfall. The Raven pushed the tray of cakes toward the boy, then crossed his legs. "You do not care for your brother's new wife," The Raven finally said, taking a careful guess.

Dougal had already grabbed a sugared cake and poked

a portion into his mouth. He shrugged. "She's all right, I suppose," he said, once he'd swallowed most of his bite. "Though I haven't seen much of my brother."

The Raven nodded knowingly. "That's what happens. Life will never again be the same for you and your brother. She will now be his top priority." He sighed wistfully. "I'm surprised they're still here. I suspect since she's English she'll want to get back to England soon rather than stay here."

Dougal hadn't responded, but his lips had compressed, and he didn't take another bite of cake. He was listening to every one of The Raven's words. And believing them. He nodded some, then set the remainder of his cake back on the plate. His shoulders sank.

"More than likely you won't see Graeme as often," The Raven continued. "Perhaps they'll invite you to their house in London." He tossed out that last bit to see what sort of relationship the brothers had. He'd never particularly gotten along with his own brother. The bastard had never respected all that he'd been given, but had never been willing to step aside and allow The Raven to take his place.

"Oh no," Dougal said, shaking his head. "Graeme has never invited me to London."

The Raven tsked in sympathy. "Never?" He feigned shock. "But is it not your family estate as well?"

"Never," Dougal spat out.

The Raven nodded. "As I expected. He simply doesn't appreciate you. Or what he has." He leaned forward, allowing his cigar to rest in the ashtray. This would be too easy. He knew all too well from his own life what it felt like to be the brother that should have been born first. The one who deserved to be heir but instead was resigned to a life of nothing better than a peasant.

"You and your mother live in a house of modest means here, but compared to the wealth and opulence of Graeme's estates in England . . ." He let his words drift off. Again his shook his head. "Pity."

"What?" Dougal scooted his chair closer. "What's a pity?"

"That you could not change places with him. You would make a much better duke. Much more honorable and worthy of the title, a man who would fully recognize what he had. You would care about the duties and responsibilities and the respect that goes along with such bloodlines."

Dougal's eyes narrowed. "I've never even seen our English estates," he said.

"Never?" The Raven asked with feigned surprise.

Dougal shook his head. "No, Graeme thought it best if I stayed here in Scotland. Said England was full of judgmental blue bloods who would look down upon me because of my Scottish roots."

"Lies, all of them. You would be readily accepted. You could dress in the finest of fashions." He held his arm out. "Feel the fabric on my sleeve." Dougal did as he was instructed. "Do you feel the difference, feel the luxuriousness of the silk? These are the sorts of clothes you would purchase for yourself. And warm, heavy coats so that you would never again be cold."

The Raven watched the boy's expression soften. The anger disappeared, and in the place of the hard lines, wistfulness filled his eyes. "Then you'd have your own fleet of carriages and drivers willing to take you anywhere you so chose." The Raven continued. "Not to mention a bevy of servants waiting for any command you could give them."

Dougal's eyes glazed with dreaminess. "What of London itself? Is there much to do there?"

"More than any one person can do. There are lavish parties every night with gourmet foods and the finest of liquors. You would never have your fill," The Raven said. "And you could have your choice of any number of beautiful women."

Dougal's shoulders slumped, and he looked down at his hands. He picked at the dirt clumped beneath his fingernails, then he folded them in his lap, out of sight.

"It could be yours, but instead, all of it belongs to your brother," The Raven said.

"And he doesn't appreciate it. Doesn't even want it," Dougal said, the anger seeping back into his voice.

"Quite true." The Raven lit another cigar. "But your brother would have to die in order for you to inherit it, and then only if he doesn't get his new wife pregnant with his heir." He held out a cigar for Dougal, which the boy greedily accepted.

Dougal inhaled on his cigar, coughing a few times but managing to get things under control. He was quiet for several moments, then he nodded slowly. "You know, he used to let me help him with his research, but not anymore." He shook his head. "Not since she came along."

Dougal was quiet for several moments before he asked, "Do you truly believe, now that he's married, Graeme won't return to Scotland?"

"Chances are he won't. They'll be awfully busy in London. English dukes are very important, and he has his duties to Parliament. And now his wife is a duchess, and she'll have many parties and other functions to be involved with. Not to mention the children they'll have. Scotland is . . ." he let his words trail off.

"Dirty," Dougal supplied, his jaw set at a tense angle, resentment simmering just below the surface.

The Raven shrugged. "I would never be so unkind. But it is rougher than London. Not the place for genteel ladies. It is unlikely he'll leave her in London and travel up here. So it is quite probable that this is his last trip."

The Raven barely suppressed his smile of satisfaction. Resentment, he could use. Resentment was as familiar and comfortable as an old friend.

"You know, I am a second son as well," The Raven told him. "My older brother was the heir and didn't appreciate any aspect of it. He was given every opportunity, and instead of seizing them, he simply whiled away his life, content to dangle from his wife's apron strings." The Raven took a sip of his tea. "Of course, I'm certain your brother is quite different from that."

Dougal made a noncommittal sound, so The Raven continued. "Second sons never have an easy path. *We* aren't given anything; nothing is handed to us. *We* have to create our own destiny. Have to work and scrape for the things we want. And sometimes, we have to make tough choices. Make sacrifices for the greater good."

Dougal nodded, and then was quiet for several moments before admitting, "I wish he wouldn't have married her."

"Indeed. Not much you can do about her. Unless," The Raven said, then shook his head. "No."

"What?"

"If they weren't married any longer, but you can't very well do away with her, now can you?" He laughed a casual laugh to plant the seed, but not allow Dougal to know he was quite serious.

For several moments, Dougal was quiet, his mind obviously running with ideas. The Raven watched the boy intently. He couldn't risk saying too much and having the boy run off to Graeme. The last thing The Raven needed was for the men of Solomon's to descend upon Scotland in search of him.

The following afternoon Graeme found Vanessa in the study poring over the notes that Jensen had given him. She was clearly unrepentant about sneaking in here the other night. She glanced up, then went back to her reading, but at least she was doing so without hiding it from him.

"What did you say to him?" Vanessa asked.

Graeme crossed the room to where she sat at a reading table. He leaned against it. "To whom?"

She smiled up at him. "Your cousin." She marked her place in the notes with her hand. "I assumed you went to confront Niall on his reckless behavior."

"Indeed?" Graeme felt his brow rise with his surprise.

"It seemed a logical conclusion." She shrugged. "Did you convince him he's behaving the fool?"

"I don't believe so."

"I do hope he'll be more careful. He could destroy countless fossils with his haphazard explosions."

"Or get someone killed." Graeme paused while she considered his words. He nodded to the notes. "Find anything of interest?"

"Not particularly. I was reading through the information on the Kingmaker again. To refresh my memory. More important, though, I was waiting for you to arrive back home so we could put that decoder to use."

That simple word seemed to stand out among all the rest. A stab to his gut. *Home.* He'd always considered this house as his home, this country, these people. The pull to his Scottish heritage had always been greater, yet he spent so much more of his time in London. Vanessa, though, seemed quite comfortable no matter where she was.

He mentally shook himself. The decoder, the Stone of Destiny: *that* was his focus. But the business with Niall and the dynamite and then Braden and his men had pulled his attention away. He withdrew the metal decoder from his coat pocket.

The Magi's Book of Wisdom lay on the table with the rest of the materials Vanessa had been perusing. She reached over and pulled it to her. Gently she opened the book to the inscription that required the decoder. He'd looked at the message hundreds of times. At first glance the writing appeared to be nonsensical, random letters, both Roman and Greek.

"Ready?" she asked with a smile. The enthusiasm in her expression tugged at him, drew him in. What other woman of his acquaintance would express such joy at deciphering an encoded message from a dusty old tome?

Graeme leaned over her, medallion in hand. "Hell, I've tried to decipher that damned message for years now." The decoder was a metal disc comprising of three smaller discs soldered to it. Letters were engraved on each disc. All they had to do was figure out where to start it, then spin the dials until they lined up. That would reveal the code.

"It's a basic coded inscription," he said, "and I tried every combination of letters I could think of. But without knowing which letter corresponded with what, it was impossible to figure out."

"It certainly didn't help that there was a page that had been forcibly removed from the book," she added. She stood to pace the room, her tall, willowy figure walking back and forth past him. Her wool skirt billowed as she moved, flaring slightly at her rounded hips. She was lovely.

Graeme examined the decoder once more. A symbol of a lion hovered between two of the Greek letters. They could try every possible formation with this and see if together they could decipher the message. He tried to turn the wheel, but it would not budge. "This should be able to move," he said.

She smiled. "I thought the same thing earlier when I'd examined the thing. The wheels should spin, and once you know your starting point, you should line up the letters to reveal the code."

He tried again to spin each dial, but none of them would shift even slightly. "It's as if a piece is missing." He tapped on the center of the medallion. "Something right in here that would allow the joints to turn."

She walked over to him, and, mimicking his earlier actions, she leaned against the desk. With determination, she picked up the book to re-examine it. Her teeth caught her bottom lip as she contemplated.

Desire surged through him. There was something about the way she stood there, holding his book, concentration furrowing her brow.

He cradled the decoder in his palm, frustrated that the damned thing wouldn't cooperate. Hell, he'd searched for this for years, and now it didn't even matter. It wasn't useful.

Vanessa still stared at the book, her index finger following along as she read. There was nothing particularly seductive about her stance, yet she beckoned to him.

He moved to stand in front of her, so close their thighs touched. His mouth hovered a breath away from hers.

She looked up. He became trapped in her blue eyes. "What are you doing?" she asked. There was an innocence to her direct gaze that called to him more strongly than a thousand seductive glances.

He removed the book from her hands and placed it on the wooden chair she'd been sitting in earlier, along with the decoder. He leaned forward, and her arms fell backward until she was bracing herself on the desk. Still he was caught in her stare.

"I'm trying to read that to assist you," she told him.

His mouth found her throat, her collarbone. He nibbled and kissed, the feel of her soft skin sultry against his tongue. Her head fell back, relishing the feel of his lips. She caught herself and tried to stand straight, pushing slightly against his chest.

"Graeme, we have work that needs to be done," she said. "What of the decoder? Certainly we can take a closer look, see if there isn't something we can do to fix it."

He agreed. There was work to be done. But first he needed to have her. Needed to touch her, to love her, every last silken inch of her. With his hand, he tilted her chin up, then met her lips. Slowly he kissed her, a gentle but passionate seduction. She stopped pushing against his chest. Now her hands clutched at his shirt, pulling him closer, kissing him more deeply.

It was enough encouragement for Graeme. God, he wanted her with a bone-deep need that startled him.

He left her lips, trailed kisses down the column of her throat, and bit her where her neck met her shoulder. Vanessa released a little moan, then craned her neck, giving him better exposure. He continued kissing her while his hands worked the back of her dress, one button at a time, until the fabric gaped open. Slowly, intentionally, he slid the wool down her arms.

He wanted it to rub against her skin, to increase the sensations as he undressed her. The other night when she'd come into his room, removed her dressing gown, and stood

before him as God had made her, he'd responded with lust
as any man would have. Tonight, though, he wanted to
see her, look at her, as his wife. Memorize every line and
curve of her flesh.

With the bodice at her waist, he was able to pull the
dress completely off her body. Impatience ate at him,
spurring his desire and fueling his urgency. Without
another thought, he took her shift in his hand and pulled.
The fabric gave way with a tear as he ripped it from her
body. He nuzzled her close.

"I'll buy you another," he managed to say.

Next he pulled off her drawers until she stood before
him, still pressed against the desk, in nothing but her
shoes and stockings. He bent and pulled one nipple into
his mouth. She didn't have large breasts, but they fit perfectly into his hands. He cupped one, suckled the other.

Suddenly her nimble fingers were at the fastenings of
his trousers, deftly unhooking them as if she removed
men's trousers all the time. The unexpected expertise was
a sharp contradiction to her clumsy seduction from the
other night, and he realized that, seductress or virgin, he
wanted her any way he could have her.

He pushed her down onto the desk. Her loose hair
spread behind her like a russet waterfall. She arched up to
him, her pert breasts beckoning him.

"God, you're beautiful," he gritted.

He stepped out of his trousers and plunged into her.
The desk was a perfect height, and with her lying back
like some Grecian nymph, he pounded into her. With one
hand, he cupped her right breast, flicking her nipple. With
the other, he found her center and ran his thumb across it.

Her eyes widened and then fluttered closed. With every
thrust, he brought her closer to release—he could see it in

her abandoned expression, hear it in her labored breaths. His own climax approached, boiling inside him and threatening to explode. And then hers hit. She slammed her hands against the desk, arched upward, and whispers of "yes, yes, yes" fell from her lips.

He was lost to her then as his own release thundered through him.

Chapter Twelve

Vanessa lowered herself to her bed. She sat on the edge, the soft coverlet cushioning her, but she felt no comfort. The envelope was clasped in her hand, as yet unopened. Before she'd left Graeme's study, he'd handed it to her. Vanessa had instantly recognized the graceful, swirling penmanship. It was a letter from Violet.

It shouldn't come as a huge surprise considering Graeme had written to her family and told them they were married. But Vanessa had never guessed anyone would write. Least of all Violet. She must have somehow sent the post by special courier to get it here so quickly.

Vanessa released a puff of air. She could sit here all afternoon and try to imagine what the letter said, but she may as well simply read the bloody thing. With renewed fortitude, she tore open the envelope.

My dearest sister, it began. Vanessa rolled her eyes. Dearest sister, indeed! Where was that affection when Violet had been stealing Vanessa's fiancé?

I began this letter the day after you ran away. I've

re-written it so many times, I believe I've used all of Mother's fine stationery. But now thanks to your new husband, we have your address. We were all so relieved to hear that you are safe. Mother worried so.

Vanessa set the letter down. Mother would only worry about how Vanessa's actions would reflect upon their family. Still, Vanessa could not deny there was a hope that perhaps her mother had shown true concern for her welfare. She went back to the letter.

A mere apology seems incapable of expressing my sincere regret. But please know, dear sister, that it was never my intention to hurt you. My relationship with Jeremy started innocently enough. I had gone to him because I'd always longed for a greater understanding of what Papa had worked on. You and Victoria knew him well, but I was so young when he passed. And I'd always been curious about his research and studies, but knew Mother would never approve of my curiosity.

I went to Jeremy simply so that he could explain a few things to me. The more he explained, the more intrigued I became. Truly, I understand more than ever your desire to be a scientist, dear sister. But the more time we spent together, the more drawn to him I was. Not simply because of his charm—

Vanessa snorted. What charm? Vanessa had appreciated Jeremy for his intellectual pursuits, and he had been pleasant to look upon, but the man had no discernible charm.

—but also because of his mind and his passion for his work. The love between us developed quite rapidly and without either of us fully realizing what was occurring until it was too late. And it pains me so how you discovered us. What you must think of me, Vanessa. I do hope

someday you will begin to understand and forgive me.
Perhaps since you are married now, you have found the
love and joy that I have found. Perhaps you now know
what it is like to have your every waking thought con-
sumed by the presence of another person. I hope you too
have experienced the bliss of the true joining of souls that
comes with finding the love of your life.

With all my love, Violet.

Vanessa dropped the letter onto the bed, then she stood
and made her way to the opposite side of the small room.
She rubbed at her arms, a vain attempt to warm herself.
Even standing so near the hearth, she felt a coldness deep
inside. So Jeremy and Violet had not simply been together
that one night in a fit of physical passion. No, it sounded
as if they were still together and that they believed they
were utterly in love.

It was bothersome, though, how Violet had gone to
Jeremy looking for an explanation of her father's work.
Vanessa had studied her father's notes for years, and she
was the one that was most like him, whether or not he'd
accepted that while he was alive.

Why, then, had Violet not come to her for guidance?
Was she such a foreigner to her own family that they
would choose a stranger over a conversation with her? If
Jeremy was going to mistake himself in love with any of
them, why, then, would it be Violet, whom he had to teach
in the ways of research when Vanessa had already been his
intellectual match? How was it possible that Vanessa had
so completely misjudged both her sister and her fiancé?

Part of Vanessa wanted to pity them, that they could
continue to fool themselves. Of course she certainly
knew now what it was like to get lost in the passion, to
have someone touch you and make the rest of the world

disappear from your vision. But that was lust, purely a physical reaction. Love, though, was fleeting, and soon enough Violet would realize that.

Even now Vanessa's skin tingled from Graeme's love-making. She wondered if in these moments she looked different to people. Could they take one glance and know she had shared passion with her husband? She knew it wasn't wrong; intercourse was a part of any marriage.

It wasn't so much the act itself, but her reaction to it. For so many years she'd believed herself above those baser needs, believed that if given the opportunity, she could pass on something so primal as lust. That hadn't been the truth at all. Her first taste of it, and she'd devoured the entire plate. Several times.

It wasn't the lust per se that frightened her, but what would come next. If she could allow herself to stumble, be so susceptible to a simple touch from her husband, what more could he evoke from her? She wasn't a believer in romantic love, but she hadn't thought herself capable of lust, either. Was she so different from her sister?

She quickly went about dressing herself for the evening's festivities. As she yanked her simple gown into place, she glared at her reflection in the mirror. Yes, yes, she was quite different from Violet. Her younger sister might have fooled herself with fancies of love and romance, but Vanessa would not be so naïve. Now was not the time to reevaluate her theories. She still firmly believed that love was fleeting, and she wanted no part of it, but right now she had to finish getting ready for the wedding reception.

Vanessa sat at the dressing table putting the last hairpin into place. She wasn't completely unaccustomed to doing her own hair, because she'd stopped using her chambermaid for everyday life years ago. She simply hadn't seen the need. Her mother had still required Vanessa to have a proper toilette before attending any soirees or balls, but Vanessa had grown used to dressing herself.

She glanced at her reflection, noting how very different this wedding reception would be compared to the one she would have had with Jeremy. There she would have been wearing that ridiculous ruffled dress her mother had loved so dearly. Tonight she'd donned a simple but pretty green velvet gown. It was far too formal for anything she would have thought to pack for her research expedition, but her trunk had been partially packed with her trousseau when she'd escaped. So the emerald confection, with its cap sleeves and seductive neckline, had come along.

She was thankful the gown had come with matching elbow-length gloves, considering the chilled winter air. As she rolled the satin gloves up her arms, she wondered what her family was doing tonight. Graeme had notified them of their marriage, but she hadn't yet had the fortitude to send them a letter herself.

What would she say? She knew she had been impetuous and somewhat reckless fleeing the way she had, but she'd been ill-prepared to face Jeremy and Violet. Not to mention the flood of tears her mother, no doubt, cried. Once she and Graeme returned to London, they would face her family together.

They might not be a love match, but he was her husband and she knew that he would stand by her. Perhaps with him at her side, she'd be able to face her family and gracefully accept their apology. But tonight she didn't have to think about unfaithful fiancés or betraying sisters. Tonight she was a bride.

• • •

Graeme led Vanessa out through the back garden, where the path to the barn was lit by several hanging lanterns. His mother and Old Mazie had decorated the barn itself with more candles than he'd ever seen in one place.

The barn had been cleared of any livestock. All that lingered was the earthy scent of dry hay and well-oiled leather tackle. The large doors were left open to allow guests to come and go freely and enjoy the outside air if the temperatures stayed this pleasant. While it was certainly not warm, the wind had died down considerably.

"Looks like a garden in springtime full of fireflies," Vanessa said. "It's lovely."

Out here in the candlelight, her smile seemed impossibly bright. "*You're* lovely," he said before he'd thought better of it.

She looked at him, surprise lining her features. She didn't wear her spectacles tonight, and he could see her beautiful eyes. Her copper-colored curls were swept up from her face and hung in a cascade down her back. Her simple green gown looked perfect on her, molding to every curve and accentuating her best features.

"Thank you," she said. And if he didn't know better, he would have sworn he'd seen her blush. What kind of woman blushed like a girl at so simple a compliment? One would think that she'd never had a serious suitor before. Graeme was starting to think that Jeremy was a complete idiot.

"You're welcome."

He took a moment to wrap her cloak around her shoulders. Perhaps it wasn't fashionable, but Scottish nights this time of year were very cold. Still, tradition brought everyone outside, and the dancing and the ale kept them warm.

They walked silently for a moment. Not many guests had arrived yet, and they were able to find some privacy beneath a large oak tree. She turned to him, looked up and met his gaze, and said, "I've been considering the matter, and I've decided that we shouldn't have relations anymore."

"What?" he asked, unsure he'd heard her correctly.

"Yes, it seems to me that it is far too distracting for me." She crossed her arms over her body. "It takes my focus off my research, the entire reason I came here to begin with, not to mention assisting you with the work you're doing." Her arms uncrossed, and she clasped her hands in front of her.

Graeme thought if given the choice, he'd certainly choose to make love to his wife over having her assistance with his search.

"Up until now," she continued, "I thought that the reason I'd been unable to complete any work, outside of my study, was because of my family. First my father refused to allow me to entertain thoughts of being a scientist. Once he died, I was finally able convince my mother, but she'd have a fit of the vapors if I went anywhere near caves or spoke of traveling to far-off lands for more exploration. She wanted me to be content with merely reading books."

Graeme certainly knew what it was like to have your parents not understand aspects of your life. His own father had never understood, nor accepted, his desire to embrace his Scottish heritage.

"I merely need to know that I can do this, actually search and locate fossils."

"Did you not already collect one?" he asked. She'd already shown him the small fern fossil that she'd removed from a rock.

"I did, and that was wonderful, but it is only the beginning. And I still need to locate that cave where Mr. McElroy found that bone." She sighed heavily. "I do realize that as your wife, it is a required activity some of the time, and I will do what is necessary"—she held a finger up—"for procreation, but recreationally, I find it far too distracting." She released a heavy breath. "So if it is all the same to you, I would prefer if you kept from touching me in any fashion."

Graeme fought a smile. There was no need to embarrass her. "I see. And you've been thinking about this for a while?"

She nodded. "Ever since that first time." Her forehead looked pinched as she frowned. "This afternoon confirmed my feelings on the matter. I admit that relations are far more pleasurable and entertaining than I would have guessed." Her head tilted. "I suppose I fully understand poor Jeremy's infatuation with my sister."

Graeme's stomach muscles tightened. "Are you saying that you're infatuated with me?"

"Heavens no." She brought a hand to her chest in relief. "But I believe I was on my way to being precisely that. Had I not had the mind to put a stop to the foolishness."

"You believe sex is foolishness." Now he couldn't help himself; he smiled. She found their lovemaking distracting because she enjoyed it. Regardless, Graeme determined there was more research to be done in the area.

"I suppose it has the potential to become a vice. Just as gambling does if one isn't careful, especially for people who have great passion." She frowned and looked up at him. "That is how it is between us, intense passion. Correct?"

Graeme swallowed, thankful that the guests hadn't yet

started to approach them, but he could hear voices coming from the pathway. He nodded. "Yes."

"But it is not always so explosive," she said.

"No, it isn't."

She nodded. "As I suspected. I merely need to focus on my research, and we have this puzzle to figure out about your cousin. And we mustn't forget your own search." She exhaled slowly. "We have much to accomplish."

Her logic was faulty, but her belief solid. It would take considerable persuading to sway her position. "And to do all of that means we cannot have relations?" he asked.

"Precisely. We'll be so busy we probably won't even notice."

But Graeme was not so certain of that fact. Even now, he remembered how it had felt to plunge into her on that desk, to feel her shudder with release. Desire stirred through his groin.

"Come and enjoy," his mother called out as she walked toward them. "Guests have been arriving for a while now." She clasped Vanessa's hands. "This isn't as grand a party as you would find in London. We're simple people. But hopefully it will suffice."

"It's perfect. Better than any party I've been to," Vanessa said, and though he didn't know for certain, he would guess she was being completely sincere.

Moira glowed. "Thank you, dear." She pulled Vanessa forward. "I have some people I'd like you to meet." And then his mother took his bride away from his side.

He watched the two women walk through the crowd, stopping to greet people. Vanessa never faltered in shaking someone's hand or offering them a warm smile. She seemed to shine beneath all the candlelight. Her skin was ivory and flawless. And the stars above seemed to agree, shining down upon her as if she were one of them, misplaced and walking the earth tonight.

Graeme spied his brother standing off to the side, leaning against a tree. He made his way over to him.

"Why the deep scowl, Dougal?" he asked. He playfully punched him in the arm.

Dougal's frown only seemed to deepen. He shrugged.

"Why are you not out there asking the pretty girls to dance?" Graeme would have thought this was the perfect place for a seventeen-year-old boy. It seemed the entire village had turned out, and the barn was practically crawling with girls Dougal's age.

"Not interested," he said with a shrug. "We could go inside, though, and talk the way we used to. About all of your research and the men in your club."

"Well, you know I can't leave the party, boy. Mother hosted this for me and Vanessa. But we can talk later if you'd like." He knew he'd been the only father Dougal had ever known, and he'd tried to do right by the boy, but his duties in London kept him away from Scotland longer than they used to. "Besides, you know how Mother can be when you do something that annoys her."

Dougal eyed him, then nodded. He was quiet for a few moments before he spoke again. "Do you love her?"

"Of course I do; she's our mother," Graeme said.

"No, your wife." Dougal never took his eyes off of Vanessa, who currently was shaking hands with the neighbors.

"No, I don't. But I only recently met her. It's far too soon to love her." He wasn't even certain that he ever would. It didn't seem that marital love was found in his family. If he were like his father, he probably wasn't even capable of love.

"Why'd you marry her, then?" Dougal asked, meeting Graeme's gaze.

That was far too complicated to answer honestly. The question wasn't so much why he'd married her, but why had he *stayed* married to her. And his lustful reaction to Vanessa's seduction was not something that he wanted to discuss with his younger brother. "A man needs a wife," he said simply. Not completely untrue.

"Father and Mother never stayed together."

"But they remained married." As if that meant anything. He shook his head. "Our father was a bastard."

Dougal's expression pinched, and something akin to hatred lined his features. "I don't believe you; he was a good man."

"Well, you never met him, did you?" The lad knew nothing. Although their mother had always spoken kindly about their father where her boys were concerned, Graeme knew the truth. He saw no reason to paint a sweeter picture for Dougal. He was old enough now. "I lived with the man, and I know what I'm talking about."

Dougal shook his head and stared straight ahead.

Graeme followed his brother's gaze and found him once again staring at Vanessa. "She's beautiful," Graeme said.

"I guess."

Perhaps Dougal hadn't gotten to the age where he noticed much about women. Although that didn't seem right: Graeme had been chasing skirts before his fourteenth birthday.

"Someday you'll understand."

"I'm not a child," Dougal said, then stormed off.

Graeme sighed. Perhaps he'd forgotten how it was to be a boy. With a shake of his head, he made his way back over to Vanessa. The band was getting ready to start, and the makeshift dance floor sat empty. It was a far cry from a London ball, but there was laughter and good music and ale.

"Care to dance?" he asked.

Vanessa smiled, but looked up at him shyly from beneath her lashes, a move he wouldn't have thought that she would know how to do. Evidently she knew how to flirt, or perhaps that sort of behavior came natural to all women. "The band hasn't started yet," she replied.

"They'll know what to do." He pulled her to him, then headed out to the dance floor. Four topiaries marked the corners on the square ground, creating the boundary. They were alone there, dancing beneath the stars and surrounded by the candlelight. He pulled her tight to his body, and the band followed their lead.

The Raven stood in the trees hidden by the darkness. Silently he watched the boy in front of him aim the pistol. The boy's arm shook as he focused on his target. The Raven looked past Dougal to where Graeme and Vanessa stood talking to some guests. The party had been going on for hours now, and Dougal had left nearly two hours before. The boy had paced in the woods for a while, holding the gun at his side before he'd finally made his way to a grove of trees close enough to actually hit his target.

All the while, The Raven had hid in the darkness watching and waiting. It was not often that he misjudged people, so he fully expected Dougal to take action. Especially after their conversation earlier that day.

Dougal had sought him out at Niall's house and had seemed relieved when he'd found The Raven alone. "I am grateful for your counsel, but there is nothing to be done about my brother's wife," the boy had said.

The Raven had contemplated a moment before speaking. "That's not entirely true." He selected each word before he spoke. "If she were injured, she would have to leave here. You don't have the requisite medical attention to handle certain types of injuries."

It wasn't the plan The Raven had hoped for, but it was a start. And chances were it would get Graeme out of his way. No doubt the doting husband would follow his injured wife—go along with her to ensure her safety and healing.

Dougal said nothing, merely stood there silently considering The Raven's suggestion.

"You should shoot her," The Raven said. "Aim for her leg or somewhere else that wouldn't threaten her life."

The Raven merely hoped the boy was a wretched shot and mortally wounded the girl. That would get Graeme out of the picture long enough for The Raven and Niall to complete their work here.

"I will meet you in the woods and show you precisely how easy it is to hurt someone." The Raven sipped his tea. "Don't disappoint me, Dougal, or perhaps it will be that brother of yours who is injured."

Now, here in the woods, the boy stood holding the gun, aiming it in the direction of the party. "Shoot her," The Raven whispered, although he knew he was too far away for the boy to hear.

The Raven needed Graeme out of Scotland, and killing or wounding his wife seemed the easiest solution. Graeme would be far too distracted to continue nosing into his cousin's practices. The Raven had seen such behavior with Fielding when the fool had been so worried and protective over Esme. The man had been unfocused, and he'd made mistakes. Men became weak when it came to women. The Raven had once been so foolish, but never again. He was certain the same thing would happen with Graeme as soon as his wife was in danger. He'd be consumed with concern and leave The Raven and Niall to finish their work in peace.

No more Graeme meant no more Solomon's to prevent him from achieving his goal.

It was a perfect plan.

But only if the boy actually fired the shot. Every moment that ticked by decreased the odds of it happening. It was time to intervene, encourage the boy.

The Raven silently made his way to where the boy stood. "Problem?" he asked upon approach.

The boy started at The Raven's voice. "I haven't had a clean shot," Dougal said.

"You have one now," The Raven said. At the moment Graeme and Vanessa were standing alone beside a large tree.

Dougal's arm shook. "She's ruining everything," he said. Then he cocked the gun. There was a sharp pop, and a moment later, The Raven watched as the girl fell to the ground.

Party guests screamed, and Graeme, instead of falling to his knees to tend to his dying wife, looked out into the trees. He would not see anything. The area where he stood amidst the candlelight was far too well lit, and the surrounding woods conversely dark as pitch. Still he looked out, and The Raven felt as if the large Scot stared directly at him.

The Raven took several steps backward. If Graeme were to see anyone there, pistol in hand, he'd only find his younger brother. A realization such as that should keep the man doubly occupied. With a dead wife and a murderer for a brother, Graeme would be far too busy to worry about what his cousin was up to.

Perfect for The Raven to complete his plan. The King-maker was almost his.

Graeme stared out into the woods, toward where the shot must have come, but he saw nothing. He wanted to run out there, but whoever had shot her would see him coming and have plenty of time to flee and hide. What Graeme needed to do now was tend to her wound. With one last look into the darkness, he cursed, then turned to face his wife.

"Move!" he shouted, trying to clear the crowd of people out of the way. He knelt and scooped her into his arms and carried her into the house. Without a word to anyone, he brought her all the way into his bedchamber and laid her on the bed. His hands moved all over her, checking for any sign of injury. Her body was limp, her skin cold to the touch, but he didn't find much blood.

He didn't wait to patiently unfasten her pretty gown. Instead he ripped the bodice until he'd revealed the wound. Her shift stuck to her side where the blood slowly seeped. He gently tugged the fabric away until her torso was mostly uncovered. The bullet had entered her side, and then exited in a similar place on her back. It was not a dangerous injury, as only the fleshy part at her waist had been pierced.

"Get me some water," Graeme shouted, but his mother was prepared and already by his side with the items he would need. He knew he could leave the tending to his mother and grandmother, but Vanessa was his responsibility.

Vanessa's eyes fluttered open, but were still heavy-lidded

and glazed. "What happened?" she asked, trying to sit up.

"Lie still," he demanded. He'd already soaked the rag in the water. He ran the damp cloth over her injury, and she jerked away from him.

Her brow furrowed with her wince. "That burns."

"Keep still; I'm almost done." He exhaled. "I've got to get the wound cleaned."

"I don't think it's bad," Moira said from behind him. "I believe it merely grazed her."

"What grazed me?" Vanessa asked.

"You were shot, dear," Moira said. "Probably some drunken fools shooting guns off to celebrate."

"I don't think so," Graeme muttered as he continued to clean the wound. He met his mother's gaze, and she clearly didn't believe what she'd said, either. She was obviously trying not to concern Vanessa.

As the blood cleared and the wound became visible, his heart slowed. What his mother said was correct; it was little more than a light grazing. Enough to draw blood, but not deep enough to require stitches. She'd probably be sore, though.

Vanessa blinked up at him. She shook her head in disbelief. "You believe someone tried to kill me?"

"Aye," he said. He smeared some of Old Mazie's salve on the wound, knowing Vanessa would stink like death for the night, but tomorrow she'd feel much better.

"Probably because I'm trying to confirm Mr. McElroy's initial theory about his fossil," she said.

"I don't think that's why," Graeme said, sharper than he'd intended. If he wasn't so bloody angry, he might have found it charming that she thought people were as passionate about fossils as she was. Enough so to try to kill her. But as it was, he was in no mood for humor.

"Then who? Why?" she asked.

"I don't know." Graeme exhaled through his nose, trying to keep his anger at bay. He wasn't mad at her, and getting frustrated when she asked a legitimate question wasn't fair. "But I fully intend to find out."

Graeme left the room to give Vanessa some quiet so she could rest. The wound was cleaned and dressed, and she'd been given a shot or two of whiskey to dull the pain. She was barely injured, yet the thought of someone hurting her...

Who the hell had tried to kill her? Or had they been aiming for someone else? Namely him. He'd been standing right next to her. For a poor marksman, it would have been a simple mistake.

Graeme made his way into the study. There he found Dougal flipping through his notes scattered across the desk.

"What are you looking for?" Graeme asked.

Dougal looked up and shook his head vigorously. "Nothing. I was—" He shook his head again. "Nothing."

Graeme poured himself a drink and downed it in one gulp, then poured himself another. He swore and fell into one of the chairs.

"Mother told me she didn't die," Dougal said.

It was a sad attempt at comfort, but Graeme offered his brother a nod. "No, she'll heal quite nicely. It wasn't a very good shot. Makes me think that perhaps they were aiming at me."

"You?" Dougal asked, taking a step closer to his brother. "Why would anyone want to kill you?"

"A variety of reasons, I suppose, though none immediately spring to mind." Graeme eyed his brother, and something in his demeanor seemed out of place. He couldn't make eye contact with Graeme, and his hands alternately fisted at his sides, then clasped in front of him. He was nervous. Very nervous. Graeme leaned forward, bracing his elbows on his knees. "What do you know, Dougal?"

Dougal frowned, but then took two steps backward. "About what? I don't know anything."

"You know who shot Vanessa." Graeme came to his feet, walking toward his brother. "Don't you?"

"Why would I know that?" Dougal asked, his voice hitching in mid-sentence. Again he shook his head.

"I don't know why." The urge was there to grab the boy by his shirt and shake him until he admitted it. But Graeme swallowed the impulse. This was no common thug; this was his brother. The boy had seen or heard something, and now he was scared. "What do you know?"

Dougal said nothing, merely looked out the window.

"Is it someone I know?"

Again Dougal said nothing, but his eyes jerked to Graeme's face and then down to the floor.

"Is it Niall?" Graeme didn't think the man had it in him to murder. Hell, he had his own wife and child. He was a doting family man, madly in love with his wife. But greed or obsession could corrupt the most genuine hearts. And Graeme had threatened him, not to mention told Niall about Vanessa. Perhaps he should have kept his wife a secret to protect her.

Dougal kept his gaze averted.

"Have you seen Niall since he arrived?" Graeme asked.

Dougal shrugged.

"You went to see him?"

"Perhaps I did." The boy looked up at Graeme for the first time since he'd entered the study. "It's none of your damned business." Again Dougal's eyes flashed with intense anger, much as they had earlier that night.

Graeme ignored the anger. Hell, he remembered being furious at that age; having a reason had never been necessary. "Who was with him?" It seemed quite likely that his brother might have seen Niall's partner.

Dougal did not look away, but he didn't answer.

Graeme put his hand on his brother's shoulder. "Dougal, it's important. Niall might be in trouble. The men of Solomon's even asked me to look after him, ensure he was safe." Graeme knew he was being unfair adding that last part. Dougal had always been a little obsessed with all things English, in particular Graeme's affiliation with the exclusive club.

His brother exhaled slowly. "An Englishman. Older, said he was a treasure hunter."

Hairs along Graeme's neck stood on end. "What did he look like?"

Dougal winced. "Fair-haired. He dresses well. His name is David."

An older treasure hunter with blond hair and his name was David. But certainly he wouldn't be so bold as to come here to Scotland and attempt to manipulate Graeme's brother? Graeme shook his head. Of course he would be that bold, and bolder still. Graeme swore. "Stay away from your cousin and that perfect gentleman. He's more dangerous than you realize."

Dougal exhaled loudly and walked to the door. Then he paused. "I'm sorry, Graeme."

Graeme shook his head. There was no reason to blame his brother. "You didn't know."

Dougal opened his mouth to say something, then stopped and instead simply slipped out of the room.

Graeme sat and put pen to parchment. He had to get notice to Fielding immediately. It appeared as if Graeme had just located The Raven.

Chapter Thirteen

───────※────────

Vanessa was sitting up in bed, leaning against the massive wooden headboard, when Graeme entered the room.

"How are you feeling?" he asked.

"Fairly well, all things considered," she said.

He came toward her and sat on the edge of the bed.

With one leg folded beneath him, his kilt revealed a fair amount of his thigh. Well-muscled legs with dark hair covering the tanned skin. Legs she knew were strong enough to hold her up against a cavern wall. Her face flushed, and heat crept up her chest to settle in her cheeks. She had not wanted a husband. Especially one with such... legs.

Even without his touch, she found his very presence distracting. This confirmed her belief that for the time being, there should be no more touching. Touching of the sexual nature, that was, because certainly he had been most kind to treat her wound.

"It wasn't precisely a serious injury," she continued. "Not certain why I fainted."

"I suspect you fainted because you've never been shot before," he said.

"I suppose you might be right," she said. And if she were completely honest, she'd admit that she was terrified. It helped to have Graeme by her side; his presence had a calming effect. Still, someone had tried to murder her. "Do you know who was trying to kill me?"

"I have my suspicions," he said.

"And?" she asked.

Graeme stood up from the bed and loomed over her. "*I* will look into these matters."

"You can try to intimidate me, but I am not afraid of you. Besides, I should think I have a right to know considering it was *my* life in jeopardy."

He scowled at her. "I'm not trying to make you afraid of me, but damnation, woman, you should be afraid of something. Anything." He exhaled. "I have reason to believe that you weren't the intended target."

Vanessa paused and considered his words. But if she weren't the target, then who was? She'd been standing directly next to—she pushed the covers back and swung her legs off the bed. "You?"

He nodded once.

"Who would want to kill you?" She came to her feet and moved to stand beside him. Without thought, she placed her hand on his arm.

"A bastard." His jaw tensed, revealing a flicker of anger that seemed to simmer right below his surface.

"Oh, so generous with your details. Have you considered being a poet?" she asked, infusing her tone with a dose of sarcasm. She crossed her arms over her chest and did her best to glare at him.

"Very funny," he said.

"Was it Niall? Are you trying to protect him?" she asked. There had to be a reason why Graeme was behaving so evasively.

"No. Suffice it to say I don't think my cousin held that pistol," Graeme said. "But I do believe he is part of this somehow. He's involved with the wrong man. A deadly and ruthless man."

"Those men from the cave?" Vanessa asked.

"I don't believe they're connected." His eyes narrowed, and he looked as if any moment he would slam his fist into something. "But you remember what I told you about those men? That they're treasure hunters for hire? This other man is like that, only he's the worst of them. He's deadly and cruel."

"But this other man, is he after the treasure of Loch Ness? Perhaps using Niall to get to it?" she asked.

Graeme forked his fingers through his hair. The unruly mane curled to just below his shoulders. She knew that it was soft and thick, and she longed to plunge her own hands into it. But touching Graeme was far too dangerous, letting him touch her more dangerous still. She could forget anything in his arms. Forget her fossils, forget her research, forget why she wanted it all to begin with. And then wouldn't she be just like any other woman in London? A wife who lived for her husband but had no joys of her own? That was terrifying.

"I think this goes beyond the Loch Ness Treasure. Those other men, now this." Graeme shook his head. "I think they're all after the bloody Kingmaker. The lot of them."

"Ah, yes, I read those notes. Interesting theories, but I still don't believe that a supposedly mystical object is somehow going to allow them to dethrone Queen Victoria," Vanessa said.

"I'm not certain how the Kingmaker is supposed to dethrone the queen," he said. "But if this man is truly involved, then he will have no qualms about killing Her Majesty."

Vanessa knew such a statement should spread fear through any gentle-bred lady. Of course she was concerned for the safety of Her Majesty and the kingdom; however, she also felt a most unladylike excitement to be involved in this adventure. Here was proof that her mother had always been right about her. She didn't understand genteel ladies, didn't precisely belong in their world.

Thrill or not, Vanessa certainly didn't want the queen to be harmed. "She is in danger, then," she said. "Someone must warn her."

"I have already sent a warning to Solomon's, and they will handle matters. And I've notified a friend of mine, Fielding, as he has a personal relationship with the gentleman in question," Graeme said.

Of course he had already sent warnings. He'd been the one to send notice to her family of her safety and their nuptials, when the thought of that had completely escaped her. She wasn't certain if she wanted to examine what that said about her.

"The legend states that once someone has the three stones, the Kingmaker will be complete." Graeme rubbed at the back of his neck.

"Right, the three royal stones—King David, King William, and King Robert Bruce," she said. "Clearly the Loch Ness Treasure is Robert's stone, because he is the only Scottish king."

"I suspect you're right," he said.

"Perhaps what we should do, then, is locate the Loch Ness Treasure ourselves," Vanessa said. "Before your cousin or that nasty man can get their hands on it. Without that stone, the Kingmaker will be incomplete, correct?"

He nodded, and a smile played at his lips. "That is precisely what I had been thinking," he said.

"Do we know where it is?" she asked. "Other than somewhere in those caves?"

He smiled, and the devilish nature of the grin seemed to tickle her insides. "No. I believe we might need to borrow my cousin's notes for that task."

"Borrow them?"

"I have a plan," he said.

Vanessa had a plan as well. They still couldn't get the decoder to work, but she refused to believe that was the only way to decipher the secret text. She hated to do it, but it was time to ask for help. She looked down at the writing in *The Magi's Book of Wisdom* and was once again struck by a slight twinge of familiarity. She could swear she'd seen some of the symbols before, but nothing specific came to mind.

Still, it was enough to spark her curiosity. Perhaps the answer lay somewhere in her father's library. He had a large number of volumes on many different subjects, and perhaps she could find something of use. Of course she didn't have access to those books while she was here in Scotland, so she needed a proxy.

The logical choice for assistance would be Jeremy, but she could not bring herself to ask him for help. Besides, Violet had admitted she'd had a curiosity about their father's work—Vanessa would let her demonstrate her recently acquired research skills by letting her assist with the code. She scrawled a short note at the top of the parchment without an endearing salutation, a mere plea for assistance and instructions to respond through telegram so that Vanessa would receive it quickly.

She would have sent this request in the same manner, but she wanted to send along examples of the symbols to aid in the research. Carefully Vanessa mimicked the style of a variety of the drawings. Then she signed the letter and folded it into an envelope. She would send it out now so it made the evening train.

"Are you certain you feel well enough for this?" Graeme asked for the third time since they had left his mother's house.

Vanessa rolled her eyes, though she doubted that he could see her in the black of night. It had been a full day since she'd been injured, and she hadn't even required stitches. "Yes. I am a touch sore, but otherwise feeling as right as the day is long, as the saying goes."

Then she paused before continuing. "I am in no way saying that I do not feel healthy simply because the days here in Scotland this time of year happen to be quite short."

He chuckled, and the low rumble of his baritone warmed her insides. He finished tethering their horse to a tree.

"Careful where you step," he said. His large hand clasped hers as they made their way through the trees to the back door of Niall's home.

From her previous trip here, Vanessa knew the lawn to be well-manicured, in sharp contrast to the wilds of the rest of the landscape in this area. But Niall's manor house, built of brown brick and accented with ivy climbing up the sides, looked as if someone had picked it up from the English countryside and transplanted it here in the Highlands.

"This way," Graeme said. "There's a back door that leads from the gardens directly into a parlor."

The gardens, as it were, consisted more of statues than of actual plants. Granted it was quite cold up here, and Vanessa doubted one could have much success with flowers. She followed him to the French doors that led into the house.

Instead of opening the door, Graeme turned to face her and bent as if requesting a kiss. His breath whispered across her cheek. Her own breathing seemed to stop—as did her heart—as if her very body waited for what he'd do next. Would he ignore her request that he not tempt her with the pleasures of the flesh? But then he stood to full height again, now holding a pin he'd swiped from her hair. He turned back to the door, and a few wiggles of the pin later, the lock released.

Silently he opened the door, and he and Vanessa slid inside. The parlor was dark, but the lamplight left on in the hall provided enough visibility for them to move through the sitting room.

Graeme glanced into the hallway before leading her out into it. She recognized it as the main hallway that led directly to Niall's study. If Niall worked similarly to the manner in which she did, then there was a chance he'd still be awake working through his notes. When they reached the door, Graeme stood still and silent for several moments, simply listening.

A faint light peeked from below the door. It could be a lamp left burning like the one in the hall, or it could mean that Niall sat in that room reading or working. Nerves beat inside her chest, an internal drum that fired her heart and sped her breathing.

One second more, and then Graeme opened the door.

She knew that he'd tucked a pistol into the waistband of his trousers, but he did not draw the weapon as they entered. A single lamp flickered from the top of Niall's desk, but no one was inside the room.

"We must be quick about this," Graeme whispered.

"Yes, you mentioned that several times earlier when you were trying to convince me I shouldn't come. But so far I don't think I've held you back," Vanessa told him. She waited for him to argue the point further, but he simply sighed.

She nodded and immediately made her way to Niall's desk. The large mahogany surface was empty save for a partially written letter to a woman named Penny. Vanessa could only guess she was Niall's wife. She opened the drawer in the center of the desk, but found only a letter opener and some ink.

She continued to search the drawers while Graeme went through books and items on the bookshelves. In the drawers, she found two additional letters addressed to Penny. Why had he not mailed them? Perhaps Niall had secrets from his wife as well. Vanessa also found some banknotes, blank parchment, and a handful of candles. Nothing useful.

She looked over toward Graeme and found him engrossed in a book.

"Did you find something?" she asked as she walked over to him.

"Perhaps," he said.

The book, a handwritten journal, had been shelved among the other books. Quite clever to hide something in plain view. Graeme flipped pages, finding more notes and a drawing. He stopped and held the book closer to see it better in the poor lighting.

While he examined the journal, she caught sight of

her Grayson's manual that she'd loaned Niall. It was open and lay facedown on a chair. She retrieved it, careful not to lose the place. He'd been reading the chapter entitled "Extreme Measures and Other Necessary Tactics." It was a part of the book she hadn't thoroughly examined yet because of her limited dig experience.

At the bottom right corner of the left-hand page was an illustration showing how to set up dynamite for use in an excavation. "Graeme, I think I know why Niall wanted this book." She walked over to him. "Look." She held it open for him to view the illustration.

Footsteps sounded in the hall.

She grabbed Graeme's elbow.

He ripped the page from the journal he'd been reading, then replaced the book. His large hand grabbed hers and pulled her through a door at the back corner of the room. It was a closet lined with shelves from floor to ceiling and now, with the door closed, as dark as the night outside.

Pressed against Graeme's chest, she could hear the thundering of his own heart.

They were going to get caught.

Niall wandered into his study. He'd thought he'd heard a noise, but lately he hadn't been sleeping much, and his mind conjured images and noises. Even if he did sleep, all he saw was Penny and Jonathan trapped somewhere—scared, hurt, hungry, and waiting for him to save them.

The study was empty, but he had left a lamp burning. Or The Raven had been down here. The man had nearly taken over the entire household. Under the guise of a guest, The Raven had Niall's servants bend to his every whim. If only they knew what a monster he truly was.

If it weren't for fear that he'd never find his family,

Niall would sneak into the man's room right now and kill him. Wrap his hands around his neck and squeeze until no sign of life lingered. He closed his eyes and took several steadying breaths. He had to find that bloody stone soon. His family needed him.

He doused the lamp, then left for his bedchamber.

The sound of footsteps in the study disappeared. Vanessa relaxed into Graeme, her warm breath pouring over his arm. Graeme held them there for several more moments before he opened the door. He didn't want to risk being caught.

The study, now shrouded in darkness, was empty. Vanessa replaced the book she'd been holding, then he led her through the room, back down the hall to the parlor, and out the garden doors.

Neither of them spoke while they hurried to where they'd tied the stallion. Graeme climbed atop the beast then helped Vanessa up, and they rode back to his mother's house.

"That was close," Vanessa said as he helped her down from the ride. "He could have caught us."

"Indeed."

"What did you find in that book?" she asked.

They entered the study and Graeme stoked the fire until the flames roared back to life. Vanessa stood with her back to the hearth, warming her backside and hands.

"I'm not certain, but I believe I've found the answer to that clue," he said. He withdrew the piece of paper that he'd torn from the journal and examined the illustration, a large piece of stone with three carved divots, where the three royal gems were to be placed. "*This* is obviously the Kingmaker," he said.

She left the fire and came to his side, glancing at the

illustration. "It is how I imagined it would look." Then she met his gaze. "But something in this image troubles you."

"Not as much troubles me as annoys me. It is of the stone in Westminster," he said.

"The counterfeit Stone of Destiny," she said.

"Right. It had these three divots." He pointed to the illustration. "It was one of the reasons why I thought it was a fake. Nowhere in my readings had I come across mention of carvings made into the stone, so I thought the divots proved it was not the real Stone of Destiny."

"And why is that annoying?" she asked.

"Because I could be wrong," he said. "Suppose Westminster's Stone of Destiny was the authentic one, and now The Raven has it. Suppose for years I've been searching for something that was right before me?"

"Graeme, I don't think so. Your theory is sound. It makes sense that the Scots would have tried to hide the real Stone of Destiny. If it is the base of the Kingmaker, then hiding it could protect the throne."

She was right.

"It would seem we have our task set before us," she said.

"And what would that be?"

"We must find the true Stone of Destiny," she said with a toothy grin.

He'd wanted to find the stone and return it to the Scots. After all, it was their antiquity. Now, however, it seemed that this quest was no longer simply to appease some great void inside him. Rather, Graeme had to find the Stone of Destiny to keep the Kingmaker from falling into the hands of The Raven.

At some point, he'd have to decide if it was worth the risk of returning it to the Scots or if the damned thing shouldn't just be destroyed.

Chapter Fourteen

The Raven eyed Dougal. He was out of patience. He'd tried to mold the boy, tried to fill his head with ideas to encourage him to get rid of Vanessa, but the boy had failed and now he could potentially be a liability. But he couldn't very well kill the boy here in this tavern. Although it was at the edge of the village, there were still people around.

"You failed," The Raven said.

"She's injured, but not badly," Dougal said.

"If you knew what lay ahead of you, you would have killed her. She will bring you nothing but trouble. If you think you aren't seeing enough of your brother now, wait; it will only get worse. Tell me, dear boy, has your brother ever offered to send you to school in England the way he was educated?" The Raven asked.

A frown creased between Dougal's eyes. "No, he never has. And I've asked," he added softly.

"I suspected as much," The Raven said.

Dougal rounded his shoulders. "None of that matters. He's my brother, and I can't believe I allowed you to talk me into any of this." The boy shook his head, his expression tight with regret. He came to his feet. "That's all I came here to tell you. I can't, I won't, help you anymore."

The Raven wrapped his fingers around the boy's wrist. "Keep in mind, dear boy, that it was you who pulled that trigger. Once your brother discovers your part in this, he'll walk away from you. He'll have you arrested and imprisoned, and then who will take care of your poor mother?"

Dougal swallowed.

"Do as I say, or I'll kill them all and save you for last so you can watch them all plead, watch them all die. And I'll make certain they all know how you led them to the slaughter."

Two days later, Vanessa took the telegram from the attendant. It was not from Violet as she'd expected, but rather from Jeremy.

Vanessa, first I much congratulate you on your nuptials. STOP. It is most pleasing to hear you have found happiness of your own. STOP. Your letter was most interesting, the symbols most intriguing. STOP. We have found information. STOP. Too much to include here, must write lengthier letter. STOP. Look for correspondence soon. STOP. Yours truly, Jeremy.

"Is this all that came?" she asked impatiently.

"There is this telegram for your husband," the man said.

She glanced over the short message sent from Graeme's friend Esme. Vanessa sent a quick response back inviting Esme and her husband to Loch Ness.

As Vanessa stepped out of the telegraph office, excitement bubbled through her stomach. It certainly sounded as if Jeremy had discovered something useful. But why was he the one responding? Obviously her sister had run to her lover for help. Not that Vanessa could blame her; the task was probably better suited to someone more familiar with ancient texts.

Still, it was curious that he'd used "we" when referring to the discovery of information. Were he and Violet working together? Perhaps it was much in the way she and Graeme worked together, although she and Graeme were not foolish enough to entangle their hearts.

Later that day, Graeme came into the small dining room where Vanessa already sat with a plate piled high with food. He could still feel the lack of sleep gnawing at his mind, yet she appeared well rested and perfectly alert.

"They should arrive soon," Vanessa said gleefully. She continued to enjoy her meal, taking a mouthful of quail eggs.

"Who?" Graeme asked.

She swallowed her bite of food. "Your friends Esme and Fielding. I intercepted a telegram and invited them to come here."

"Why would you do that?" he asked.

"I was already picking up a telegram of my own and I happened to be at that office. It seemed logical that I would respond on your behalf. Besides, we might need their help. You said yourself that Fielding has personal ties to this Raven fellow." She shrugged daintily. "It seemed logical he might provide insight into dealing with him. Do you not agree? I was under the impression that the men of Solomon's stick together."

"I hadn't given it much thought." Graeme took a

seat at the table. "I sent a message to alert him of The Raven's presence out of courtesy, as I knew he'd been looking for the man. The Raven is a relation of Fielding's."

"Well, then, I suspect they would have come up here had I invited them or not. But as your wife, I've decided it is time for me to play the hostess to some degree." She drummed her fingers on the table. "Although I did not invite them to stay at your mother's house."

"How kind of you."

She flashed him a brilliant smile. "I thought so. It seems I'm better at the minutiae of domesticity than I anticipated."

Graeme chuckled, but said nothing further.

"I suppose we should have them here for a meal," she said, her brow furrowing with thought.

He held up a hand. "No more parties. It's dangerous. Too dangerous."

"Don't be ridiculous."

"I'm not being ridiculous." He spoke slowly, struggling to control his frustration. "I'm being logical. Have you forgotten that the last time we had a party, you got shot?"

"Of course I haven't forgotten, but honestly, Graeme, it was barely a grazing," she said. "They will be guests—"

"Vanessa—" he growled in warning.

"Very well." She inclined her head, playing the part of the acquiescent wife, despite the conniving gleam in her eyes. "But remember, you can't protect me from everything."

There had to be thousands of eligible, *biddable* Scottish lasses in the region, and he'd ended up accidentally handfasted to the most stubborn English chit he'd ever met.

• • •

The Raven walked in silence. The fresh covering of snow blanketed the landscape in front of him. The winter precipitation still fell from the sky soundlessly, cold and wet as it landed on his hands and cheeks.

His boots crunched into the snow as he climbed the hill to the castle ruins. Below him, the loch shimmered against the snow. The sun already fought to be free of the cloud cover; he suspected the snow would be melted by noon.

He entered the remains of the castle, stepping over what had once been the stone wall that encircled the fortress. The caverns were below, in the hillside, where Niall swore they would find the treasure of Loch Ness.

Voices came from inside the castle. He stopped and moved to hide behind a staircase that now led to nothing. The ceiling above had long since crumbled, and the open sky sat heavy above him. The voices came closer. Two men, if he had to guess. Niall and Graeme?

Damnation if Graeme hadn't continued to be a thorn in his side. If provided the opportunity, The Raven would simply kill the man. Yes, he risked bringing the full wrath of Solomon's down on himself, but it wasn't as if they weren't all hunting him anyway.

But today was not the day for Graeme to die. The two men who emerged from the castle were neither Niall nor Graeme, but instead two men he knew from London. One man, Braden, he knew particularly well. Until The Raven had been forced underground a year ago, they had been competitors, both treasure hunters for hire. Since The Raven's forced retirement, Braden had acquired most of The Raven's previous clients.

The Raven had taken revenge on the man, though. Not

two months earlier, he'd broken into Braden's house and stolen King David's stone, a relic the man had found himself and opted not to sell. It was one of the three stones necessary to complete the Kingmaker.

No doubt Braden had traveled here thinking that he would find the final stone and barter with The Raven. He was a fool to think The Raven would ever make such a deal.

"Find it, then get yourself back here," Braden was saying to his companion. When the man didn't move, Braden released a heavy sigh. "We will discuss the other matter later. Go." And with that Braden disappeared back into the castle.

The other man, whom The Raven did not know by name, but knew to be a close associate of Braden's, stood for a moment before turning to leave. The Raven allowed him to exit the castle before he followed him.

Braden's associate was larger than The Raven in both height and breadth. But when it came to being cunning, no one matched him. They were nearly to the bottom of the hill, almost to the edge of the rocky beach, before the man noticed he was being followed.

The Raven stopped walking as the man turned around.

"You there," he said, his voice low and full of gravel. "What are you about?"

"I want to talk," The Raven said.

"So talk," the man said, clearly annoyed by the intrusion.

The Raven made his way closer. He eyed his surroundings. There was nothing the man could use as a weapon unless he had one on his person. At this moment, The Raven had three: a knife lodged in his boot, a pistol tucked into his waistband, and a dagger attached to his belt. One could never be too careful.

"Hey," the man said. "Don't I know you?"

The Raven shrugged. "Perhaps." He reached into his coat and unfastened the dagger. This was turning out to be a perfect day.

The man stepped closer. "I know you. You're the man who stole Braden's treasure."

The Raven said nothing, merely laughed.

The man came even closer. He braced his legs into a fighter's stance. "You want a fight, old man?"

True, he was old enough to have fathered this man. His own son couldn't have been much different in age. But age mattered naught.

"Tell me," The Raven said. "What is it that Braden is after here in Loch Ness?"

The man's eyes flickered past him to the castle ruins at the top of the hill, perhaps surprised that The Raven had seen Braden.

"It can be our little secret," The Raven said. Then he laughed, enjoying his own jest. He withdrew the dagger and turned it over in his hand, the silver blade shining brightly against the snow.

"Do you honestly think I'd betray Braden to you? I'd just as soon kill you first," the man said as he lunged forward.

He landed a blow to The Raven's stomach, hard and forceful. It nearly knocked him backward. Nearly, but not before The Raven was able to slice the dagger into the man's side.

"Is he after the Kingmaker?" The Raven asked, shifting out of the way as the other man's fist came down again, this time hitting nothing but the air between them.

"Kingmaker? I don't know what the hell you're talking about," the man said. He ran at The Raven, this time ramming him with his head at the center of The Raven's gut.

"You can't protect him," The Raven said once he'd recovered from the blow. He leapt forward and managed to jab the man again with the dagger. Blood seeped from the man's leg and dripped onto the snow. Crimson covered alabaster as the blood stained the frost.

The man's eyes widened with surprise. He grabbed his thigh, trying to stanch the bleeding.

The Raven took the opportunity to strike again, this time slicing the man across the torso, not deep enough to cause too much damage, but enough to cause pain.

The man cursed, coming at The Raven again, but his coordination was off this time, and he missed.

"All you need to do is tell me what Braden is after. Then I'll leave you alone," The Raven said.

"I'm no fool," the man said.

The Raven smiled at him. "Perhaps that was a tiny prevarication. Still, the sooner you tell me, the sooner I'll stop toying with you."

"Go to the devil," the man said.

"Admirable. What has Braden done to deserve such extreme loyalty from you?" The Raven danced around him, ducking to miss another blow from the man's fist.

The man said nothing, merely growled and came at him again. This time, The Raven was able to grab hold of him. He held the man by the arm, dagger pressed intimately at the man's side. "Tell me what I want to know," The Raven said close to the man's ear.

"Go to hell," the man said.

"You first," The Raven said, then slid his dagger across the man's throat, the blade sinking into the man's flesh. Blood sprayed upward and outward. It fell onto The

Raven's face, splattering onto his cheek, a drop flickering into his eye.

He dropped the man, who sank to the ground. Scarlet droplets scattered across the snow, pooling where the man had fallen. The Raven stepped away to avoid getting too much blood on his shoes.

He withdrew a calling card from his coat and tossed it onto the body. Let Braden see firsthand what fate awaited him.

Vanessa walked beside Graeme, bundled into her warmest cloak, hat, and mittens. The snow was beginning to melt, but the chill lingered, brisk and sharp in the air. "I am most eager to meet your friends," she said. "I never thought I would say this, but I am missing London, and it will be nice to see some people from there."

It was not surprising that the wilds of the Highlands were beginning to wear on her. London got cold, but snow was not as common and the wind wasn't as bone-chilling. They were on their way from the caves, where they'd spent a frustrating morning discovering nothing new. Something ahead caught Graeme's attention. He stopped walking and held his arm out to block Vanessa.

"What?" she asked.

"Wait here," he said. He cautiously moved forward. A body lay in the snow, but it wasn't until he was right upon it that he could see the damage. Fitch lay slumped on the melting snow, his throat slashed and blood sprayed everywhere.

"Oh God," Vanessa whispered from his side.

"Damnation, woman, do you ever obey?" He tried to turn her away.

"When it suits me," she said. She knelt and picked

up the card lying on the man's chest. She looked up at Graeme. "The Raven."

He took the card from her and dropped it back onto the body. "Ah, Duchess, we need to get away from here," he said.

"Do you suppose he's still here somewhere?" she asked, looking around.

"No," Graeme said, "but this is a threat meant just as much for us as for Braden."

Chapter Fifteen

The Raven sat on a darkened pew in the center of the small chapel. His feet rested on the kneel bar. It was a strange meeting place, but the small size of the village required that he be more careful.

A thin shaft of light appeared on the floor as the outer door opened. Soft footsteps came from behind him. Instinctively he gripped his blade, his hand resting securely on the hilt. Then the kneel bar shifted beneath the other man's weight as he lowered himself next to The Raven.

"Sam," The Raven said. "I suppose condolences are in order for your lost comrade."

"Fitch was an arrogant bastard," Sam said. "It rattled Braden. More than ever, he's looking over his shoulder."

"Where is he now?" The Raven asked.

"In the caves, searching. If anything, Fitch's death fueled his drive to find the treasure."

"Perfect. Between him and Niall, someone will find my stone." The Raven wanted to light a cigar, but the vicar would not take kindly to smoking in the sanctuary.

"Your clever plan is working," Sam agreed.

Sam was unlike the men who'd previously been in his employ. He wasn't simply strong and willing to live at the edge of the law. No, Sam was clever. He'd been the perfect person to infiltrate Braden's group.

Two months of watching Niall had shown The Raven how weak the man was, fawning all over his wife and son. The Raven had simply reminded him what his life's work was all about. He'd removed the distraction so that Niall could focus on locating the treasure. But The Raven had known that his odds for success were greater if there was more than one person searching for it.

So he'd come up with the perfect solution, and Sam had already been in place. Braden had one of the royal stones in his possession, a gem that The Raven needed to complete the Kingmaker. So he'd broken into Braden's home and taken it, deliberately leaving the man his calling card so he knew precisely who had been the thief.

Then it had been up to Sam to plant the seed. To whisper a solution to Braden: find the Loch Ness Treasure and The Raven would consider a barter. So now Braden unknowingly worked for The Raven.

"What is next?" Sam asked.

"I intercepted a letter intended for Graeme," The Raven said.

"We saw him in the caves. He was asking questions," Sam said.

"Of course he was. Damned Solomon's is forever in my way." The Raven drummed his fingers on the pew in front of him. "But they can often also be most helpful. The letter instructed Graeme to visit Cawdor Castle, where he would find the final royal stone."

Sam shifted himself off of the kneel bar and onto the

pew. He leaned forward, his arms resting on the pew in front of him, almost as if he were praying.

"I'll rewrite the letter with additional instructions for Graeme to enlist Braden's assistance for the quest, in case they come against any villains," The Raven said.

"Graeme will heed such advice?" Sam asked.

"Coming from Jensen, yes," The Raven said. "No one questions that man."

Graeme tossed the letter onto the desk, then paced the small study like a caged beast.

"How did he even know that Braden was here?" Vanessa asked. She picked up the letter and glanced down at the florid penmanship.

"Jensen has his ways. He always seems to know what is going on," Graeme said.

"So this isn't completely unusual?" Vanessa looked up, but Graeme's pacing made her nervous.

"No, not in the least. Just as when he appeared here that one night. He has all manners through which he acquires information." Graeme stopped and braced his hands on the back of a chair.

Vanessa set down the letter. "Do you trust him?"

Graeme met her gaze. "Jensen? Absolutely."

"Then we should heed his advice." She nodded with resolution.

He pushed away from the chair. "His logic is sound. We don't yet have other members of Solomon's here with us, and I don't think we have time to wait for Fielding and Esme. We might need some assistance if the residents of the castle don't take kindly to unwanted visitors."

"Indeed," Vanessa said. "Additionally, if Braden and

his men were working with The Raven, then he wouldn't have killed Fitch."

Graeme was silent for several moments as if considering her words, then slowly he nodded. "Then I suppose we have some new partners."

Convincing Braden to join their merry quest had been as simple as offering him a sum of money. Graeme opted to go with what the man knew instead of attempting to appeal to any sense of honor. It had worked, and now Graeme and Vanessa, along with Braden and Sam, walked quietly toward Cawdor Castle. The moon hung low and heavy, illuminating the landscape before them.

Unlike the ruins of Urquhart, Cawdor was a fully functioning estate for the Earl of Cawdor. The manicured lawn led to the gray stone fortress. A drawbridge led into the main gate and overlooked a dry moat. Thickly wooded trees lined the back of the castle.

"Where do we look first?" Braden asked.

"Evidently the Cawdor family has protected King William's stone for centuries," Graeme said.

"So it will be heavily guarded," Braden said.

Graeme nodded. "More than likely. We'll try the non-sleeping quarters first to avoid rousing the residents."

Walking straight up through the main entry gate didn't seem the best way to remain undetected, so they searched for an alternate entrance. They found one on the east side of the castle. Before Graeme could withdraw his tools to unlatch the lock, Sam had shouldered the door and broken the bolt. Effective, but not with as much finesse as Graeme preferred.

Graeme exhaled slowly. He still didn't trust Braden or his associate Sam. He could adhere to Jensen's advice without completely agreeing with it. Besides, Jensen would have wanted Graeme to be cautious.

They stood quietly in the dark for several moments waiting to see if they'd drawn any attention, but no one came.

"We'll take this side; you and your woman go search the other wing," Braden said.

Graeme was not accustomed to working with other people, especially ones who wanted to dictate his moves. But now was not the time to argue about it, and searching separately they would cover more ground faster. He took Vanessa's hand and pulled her toward the hall.

Soon they'd come to the main entrance of the castle, a grand foyer with a staircase at the end and a balcony overlooking the first floor. No doubt the earl had hosted more than one ball in this very area. They moved out of the wide open space and into the opposite wing.

Every room Graeme and Vanessa came to, they'd search, opening cabinets and drawers, peeking in vases, and moving books and pictures.

"Do you know they refer to this as MacBeth's castle?" Vanessa whispered. They walked through a small dining room and into a parlor.

"Indeed?" Graeme said.

"True. In the play, the three witches tell MacBeth that he will become Thane of Cawdor, and it is the first of their prophecies to come true. It is what sends him on his quest to overtake King Duncan and steal the throne." She gasped, then stopped walking.

"What?" Graeme glanced around to try and see what had grabbed her attention.

"Do you think that's what Shakespeare was talking about? The Kingmaker? MacBeth was after the King-maker," Vanessa said.

Graeme shook his head. "Vanessa, it's a play." He pulled her forward, and they entered a library. So far they'd found nothing indicating where the stone might be hidden. Graeme feared they'd have to search the bedchambers, as that was where most people hid their valuables.

"I am quite serious," she said. "If King William used it to become king, why could the Bard not have used it in a play? A play about Scottish kings, no less."

Graeme chuckled. "It's an interesting theory, but it doesn't have any bearing on our current search."

But Vanessa wasn't listening; she'd marched off to a room at the front of the castle. "Don't be so certain of that, my husband." She pointed to a sign, then smiled broadly.

"MacBeth's Museum," Graeme read. "So the Cawdor family is capitalizing on the literary fame of their estate."

Vanessa tugged on his sleeve to pull him into the room. "We must search everywhere."

They stepped into the large room. Posters of various performances hung on the walls, and glass cases held props used in the play: robes, swords, and a handful of scripts.

"Fascinating," Vanessa said.

Graeme walked the length of the room until he stood before a large glass case. Inside was a purple and red robe, clearly designed for royalty, and above it sat a jewel-adorned crown. Emeralds, rubies, and sapphires covered nearly every inch of the gold crown, and in the very center sat a huge ruby.

"Vanessa," Graeme said.

She came to his side and looked up at the crown.

"Hiding something in plain sight can oftentimes be most effective," he said.

She pointed to the plaque next to the case. "MacBeth's crown."

• • •

The Raven stood in the doorway watching Sam and Braden search the study. His own presence went unnoticed by the men, who were focused on their task. That was the problem with most people; they simply weren't observant enough.

Braden paid no attention to the mess he left, overturning drawers and tossing books on the floor. The Raven shook his head. Before Solomon's had interfered with his career, The Raven had been the best antiquities man in the business. For a hefty price, he had tracked down and retrieved more artifacts than most so-called scientists could ever dream of finding. But since Solomon's had forced him into hiding, his former clients had had to rely on this bumbling idiot to find their treasures.

He'd never seen the man work, had only heard from others about his discoveries. And Braden had, of course, found King Solomon's stone, the royal sapphire, which The Raven now possessed. But perhaps all of that had been sheer good luck. Watching the man now, The Raven was unsure he could find his own arse.

Enough of this. He withdrew his dagger and gripped the hilt firmly. Then he quietly stepped into the room. He was halfway across the study when Braden looked up.

"Well, well, well, if it isn't the devil himself," Braden said. He dropped a book on the floor, then stepped on it coming toward The Raven. "Can't ever find anything for yourself, can you? Always have to swoop in and steal from other people." Braden cocked his head to one side. "Is that why they call you The Raven? Because you're nothing more than a filthy scavenger?"

Sam raised one eyebrow.

The Raven nodded in response.

Braden smiled until Sam grabbed him from behind, imprisoning his arms. "What the hell?" He looked from side to side. "Sam? What are you doing?" And then the obvious must have dawned on him. He swore.

"You're a sorry excuse for a treasure hunter, Braden." With that, The Raven plunged his dagger into the man's left side and rammed it upward into his heart.

Braden's eyes widened. He coughed. Blood sprayed all over The Raven and the carpet. Braden choked on his last breath. Sam dropped him, and he slumped to the floor.

The Raven withdrew a handkerchief from a pocket and wiped his face and hands, then dropped it on the body. He sheathed his dagger. "Now I suppose it is up to Niall alone to find the Loch Ness Treasure." He eyed Sam, whose stoic expression gave nothing away. "Shall we see if Graeme has found anything?"

"It's brilliant," Vanessa said. "No one would suspect that to be one of the royal stones. The entire crown looks like a prop."

"Exactly," Graeme said.

"How do we get it out, though? Breaking the glass will cause too much noise and alert the family," Vanessa said.

Before Graeme could think of a solution, Sam ran into the room.

"You found it?" Sam asked.

"Yes," Vanessa began. "But—"

Sam interrupted Vanessa's sentence by slamming his elbow into the glass. It cracked, then shattered, pouring glass all over the stone floor.

"Where's Braden?" Graeme asked.

"He got caught," Sam said. "We need to get out of

here." He glanced behind him. "Now!" He turned and ran out of the room, holding the crown.

Graeme and Vanessa followed after him. "Something isn't right," Graeme said.

They ran after Sam into the main foyer, and then out the front door. They followed him into the courtyard that led to the drawbridge.

"Sam! Wait!" Graeme called. But his words fell on deaf ears.

Then Sam stopped, turned, and pulled the lever that would close the large iron gate. The metal creaked downward. Graeme cursed. They weren't going to make it in time.

"What is he doing?" Vanessa asked through labored breaths.

"I believe we've fallen into a trap," Graeme said. "Hurry." And she did; he couldn't fault her for not trying. She wasn't slowing him down that much, but they'd never reach the gate in time.

Sam stood there watching them, holding the crown in one hand and the pulling the lever with the other.

"You're a bastard," Graeme said as they reached the gate. It slammed closed, locking into the stone floor, trapping them inside the courtyard.

Sam simply smiled.

And then it all made sense. The Raven stepped out onto the path at the edge of the drawbridge and walked slowly toward them.

"Graeme, is this your lovely wife?" The Raven asked, a deadly smile on his lips.

"Go to hell," Graeme said.

"No introduction? Pity." The Raven directed his attention to Sam. "It's time."

Sam turned to follow, but he couldn't move. He yanked on his leg, but it wouldn't budge. He was caught. "I can't move," Sam said.

The Raven stopped. "What do you mean, you can't move?"

Sam jerked his leg again, but he was firmly trapped. "My leg is trapped. My boot is caught on something in the drawbridge mechanism." He continued pulling on his leg, his movements becoming increasingly frantic. "It's stuck."

"Give me the crown," The Raven said.

"Don't do it, Sam," Graeme warned. "He's only using you. When it serves him, you'll be dead." Graeme paused before adding, "Is that what happened to Braden? Did The Raven tire of his service and kill him?"

"That idiot never worked for me," The Raven spat.

"Open the gate and we can help you," Graeme said to Sam.

The Raven didn't wait for further negotiation. He simply walked over to Sam and elbowed him in the nose. Blood exploded from the man's face, and he howled in pain. The Raven ripped the crown out of the man's hand, then ran off the drawbridge.

As soon as he stepped off, the bridge started to move. The chains creaked and gears shifted. Sam yelled and grabbed at his leg.

"Graeme, what's happening?" Vanessa asked. "Can you stop it, stop the bridge?"

Graeme searched all around the gate and the stone wall surrounding it, but found nothing that would enable him to stop the bridge. "It must be inside the castle. Someone inside there has closed the bridge."

The closer the bridge came to Sam, the more he yelled.

This was not going to end well, and Graeme couldn't stand here and allow Vanessa to watch it happen. He pulled her to him, then ran back toward the castle. They skirted the outer edge of the building until they reached the forested area at the back.

As they rounded the corner, the drawbridge slammed into place, and Sam let out his final cry.

Chapter Sixteen

———— ❧≈❧ ————

Vanessa and Graeme returned to the village sometime after mid-morning. They hadn't made it back in time to meet Esme and Fielding at the train station, but had received a note saying the couple had arrived safely. Additionally, the train ride had afforded Esme the time to make the acquaintance of the American man who had refurbished the abbey hidden up in the hills. He'd insisted that they stay with him, and they had readily agreed.

Esme had already accepted an invitation for all of them to attend a dinner party at the abbey that very evening. So it was that Graeme and Vanessa, along with the rest of his family, stood at the man's door and waited for entrance.

"Oh, come in, come in," the American said at the opened door.

Vanessa stepped into the abbey right in front of Graeme, his hand at the small of her back. The warmth of his hand seared her skin beneath her gown, reminding her what it felt like to have those hands touch her most intimately. Heat spread through her body and flamed in her cheeks.

This was no doubt why most women were content to stay at home and drink tea and gossip. Passion and desire had a way of melting your thoughts right out of your head.

"A duke and a duchess," the American man said. "I'm such a goose I don't even know how to address you."

"'Your Grace' is the proper salutation," Esme said. She stood slightly behind their host, a lovely smile upon her face. Fielding kept her close to his side with an arm snug about her waist.

"But there is no need for such formalities," Graeme said. "You may simply call us by our given names, Graeme and Vanessa."

"And I am George Randolph," the man said. "Welcome to my castle."

It was on Vanessa's tongue to correct the man. This was an abbey and not a castle, but she was still contemplating what Randolph had said. A duke and a duchess?

"You're a duke?" she whispered to Graeme. "And you never thought to bring that to my attention?"

He guided her forward with his hand, grinning. "I thought I had told you."

She turned to face him. "I'm fairly certain we never had a conversation involving my being a duchess." Then it hit her; that was why he called her so. It was not a term of affection as she'd thought, but simply the truth. She swiveled herself back toward the rest of the party, putting her back to her husband. Wouldn't her mother absolutely love this? But she probably already knew. Hadn't Graeme sent an announcement to her family and the newspapers? It was possible everyone in London knew before she did. She felt an utter fool.

"This must be your sister." Randolph stepped up and took Moira's hand in his. "*Enchanté,* Mademoiselle." He bent low over her hand, brushing it with his lips.

Vanessa couldn't help but be amused by the American's weak attempt at flirting. Although she was hesitant to group their host with Jeremy, she briefly wondered if all American men were fools when it came to women.

Moira smiled prettily. "His mother, actually." She looked around the foyer. "You've done truly amazing work with this place," she said.

"You've been here before?" Randolph's eyes lit with excitement.

"Aye. We used to play here as children," Moira said. "I live just across the loch from here."

He linked his arm with hers and led her forward. "You must tell me all about it. Everything. I did my best to match what had been here before, based on journals and drawings."

"Fielding, Esme," Graeme said as he came forward. "How charming of you to organize such a gathering."

Fielding smiled broadly. "Esme does have a knack for making friends wherever she goes." He playfully jabbed his elbow into Esme's arm. "She and Mr. Randolph chatted nearly the entire duration of the train ride."

Graeme chuckled. "This is Vanessa," he said.

"Your wife," Esme said with a huge smile. "It's truly a pleasure," she said as she gave Vanessa a tight squeeze.

Together they walked farther into the foyer.

Vanessa's breath caught as she took in the ceiling overhead. It was a perfect rendition of a fresco painting. Bold colors accented the Biblical scenes. One in particular drew Vanessa's eye. Adam and Eve stood in front of a massive tree, the green limbs spreading far across the ceiling. In Eve's hand, she held a piece of fruit so ripe, so irresistibly red, Vanessa was certain that if she reached out, she'd be able to claim it.

It was a not-so-gentle reminder of her own life at the moment. She was finally in a position to do her research freely, and instead, she faced the distracting temptation of her new husband. She took her eyes away from the painting to glance at him. She realized with sudden clarity that he looked very much a duke tonight with his black coat and black trousers, a high sheen on his black boots and the white of his shirt at his throat.

She'd thought that she'd married a simple Scotsman with a penchant for adventure, but looking at him now, she realized she didn't know him very well at all.

His long hair had been tied at the nape of his neck, pulling it away from his handsome face. Long lashes framed his startling green eyes, and although she knew he'd shaved earlier today, stubble lined his cheeks and jaw, giving him a somewhat dangerous look.

This was not deceptive: He *was* dangerous. One touch and he made her forget everything, everything she thought she'd wanted. He made her doubt this woman she'd fought very hard to become.

"The fresco is magnificent," Vanessa said, trying to distract herself, trying to rein in her thoughts.

"Ah yes, that was not original to the abbey," Randolph said. "But I couldn't resist. Let us convene in the dining room."

They all followed his lead. Graeme stepped closer to Fielding, and the two men spoke quietly. Vanessa was certain Graeme had decided to tell Fielding about the men who had died by The Raven's hands, not to mention the stones he now possessed. The man was getting dangerously close to the Kingmaker.

"You look very pretty tonight," Esme told Vanessa.

"Thank you," Vanessa said. "This dress was to be part

of my trousseau, the dress my mother had intended I wear when I hosted my first dinner party."

"Well, it's lovely," Esme said. Vanessa wondered what Graeme had told his friends of his sudden nuptials.

They gathered around a large table, hand carved out of mahogany. It sat in the middle of an ornate dining room, accented with another painted ceiling, this one highlighted with gold paint and cherubs. If Vanessa had to guess, she'd wager that painting was also not a replica of an original, but rather for Mr. Randolph's own enjoyment. Clearly the man loved opulence.

The wall opposite Vanessa's dinner seat was nearly completely covered by what appeared to be an ancient tapestry. Beautiful and elegant, the woven picture depicted this very building as it had once been, as a family's keep jutting high out on the hills. Before they left, she definitely wanted to take a closer look.

Graeme watched their host fall all over himself trying to impress Graeme's mother. And if Graeme wasn't mistaken, she was flirting in return. He'd never seen his mother happy with any man, as his parents had separated shortly after his birth. The only interaction he'd seen them have was to argue mercilessly.

On his other side, Dougal sat quiet and surly, his young features marked by a constant scowl.

Graeme had been to this abbey nine years earlier, before this man had refurbished it to its former glory. But Graeme knew what lay beneath—a deep chasm and a secret chamber filled with treasures. He couldn't help but wonder if Randolph had ever discovered the secret lift that led down to it. But he most definitely was not going to ask.

. . .

They all arrived home nearly four hours later. Vanessa and Moira had already excused themselves. Graeme grabbed Dougal to stop him from leaving the room. "What the hell is wrong with you lately?"

Dougal jerked his arm free. "I don't know what you're talking about," he said, but never glanced at Graeme's face.

"You can't even look at me. You're nervous around my wife. You barely look at her, and when you do, you glare. You stay out all the time. You talk back to Mother." Graeme shook his head. "None of this is like you. I know something's wrong."

"It doesn't matter." Dougal finally met Graeme's gaze, and for the first time Graeme realized how much his brother physically resembled their father. The same height, although Dougal still had the thin and narrow body of a boy not yet a man, and the same light brown hair, the same brown eyes. "I'm a man of my own now," Dougal said. "What I do, it's no concern of yours."

Graeme nearly argued, but Dougal was right to an extent. At least, he believed he was right, and Graeme remembered feeling the same way once upon a time. He'd had this argument, or one very similar, with their father. And it hadn't gone well.

Graeme had two options. He could force the boy to talk and risk losing him forever, or he could allow him to continue down whatever road he'd chosen and more than likely get himself into trouble. Especially if he'd involved himself with The Raven.

"You don't know that man," Graeme said slowly. "The kind of danger you could get yourself into with him."

Dougal's eyes widened with brief surprise, then narrowed. "You don't know what you're talking about."

"Perhaps not, but I know what I see. And I know more about the aristocratic world you're so bloody interested in. Those English men, regardless of what they've told you, sure as hell won't keep any promises they might have made."

"What do you know of promises?" Dougal tossed back, his eyes burning with anger.

Just then Vanessa came in. "Graeme, I'm sorry to interrupt, but I have something most important to discuss with you."

Graeme turned to his wife. "Can it wait?"

She shook her head. "I think you'll want to know this straightaway."

He nodded, then turned back to Dougal. "We're not finished with this." In that moment, he caught sight of Dougal's expression toward Vanessa. His jaw fixed in a tight line, and his eyes widened with something that looked like fear.

"We're finished," Dougal bit out, then slid from the room.

"I'm sorry," Vanessa said.

"I'm not." Graeme yanked the tie from the back of his hair and shook it free. He took a deep breath, then swore. "I think my brother is the one who shot you."

"What?" Vanessa asked. "Certainly you're mistaken, Graeme?"

"No, I've looked at this from every angle, and it has to be him."

"What about The Raven?" she asked.

"No," Graeme said. "If The Raven had held that gun, he wouldn't have missed."

She released a shaky breath. "But why? Why would Dougal want to kill *me*?"

Graeme shook his head. "That I don't know. I think he's gotten himself somehow involved with The Raven." He came and sat next to her, and though he put his arm behind her on the settee, he did not touch her. "What was so important that you wanted to discuss with me?"

"The Stone of Destiny. I think I found another clue," she said.

He frowned and shook his head. "Where?"

"There was a tapestry in the abbey I noticed during dinner. Randolph said he'd purchased it from a family in London but it was one of the original pieces that belonged in the abbey. I noticed it because it was beautiful, so large and lush and full of detail. It had an image of the stone structure itself, off in the distance, but a closer image of a knight hiding what appeared to be a large stone."

"That could be anything," Graeme said with a shake of his head. His brow still furrowed, no doubt concerned about the fact that his brother obviously wanted her dead.

"True, but it could be something, another clue. We should investigate it further."

"Yes, but I need to confront Dougal first." He turned to leave the room.

She put her hand on his arm and met his gaze. "He's not going to talk to you right now. Especially now that you're both angry," she said.

He exhaled slowly, then cursed again. "You're probably right. But damn. My own brother."

"Dougal is merely upset because I'm taking time away from him. Time he normally spends with you," she offered.

He clasped her hands in his, his large hands dwarfing hers. His green eyes bore into her. "Vanessa, he might have shot you, tried to kill you. There are no reasons. You are my wife."

Of course, he was right. There were no legitimate reasons for anyone to attempt to kill her. Regardless of the motivation, one thing didn't change. "But he is your brother. You share blood, a family, and a history together," she argued. Wasn't that supposed to matter? Wasn't she expected to forgive Violet for her indiscretion with Jeremy? Vanessa knew her mother would expect so.

"But you are my wife. If given the choice..." His voice trailed off, and he left it unsaid. But Vanessa knew what he was saying. If given the choice, he'd choose her. His wife over his brother. The fierceness of his loyalty shot straight through her. He would choose her. Something she doubted her own family would do. In fact, she didn't think anyone had ever chosen her.

She longed to say something. To thank him, but words failed her. But then it occurred to her: Graeme hadn't chosen her either. Oh, he just said he would if it came down to it. Their marriage had been a spontaneous accident, at best. Neither of them had chosen this union. And perhaps if given *that* choice, Graeme might not be so loyal to her.

"Let us go and look at this clue you've found," he said, then squeezed her hands. He rose to his feet.

"Didn't you tell me you found *The Magi's Book of Wisdom* in that abbey?" she asked.

"Beneath the building. There's an ancient chamber where monks hid the church's treasures. But the men of Solomon's emptied it out years ago, right after I discovered *The Magi's Book of Wisdom*."

"Perhaps you were looking in the wrong place," she suggested. "The abbey is a large building."

"I don't know." He growled in frustration. "But if the bloody thing has been there the entire time—" He shook his head without finishing his statement.

"I told Esme we would be coming so they could let us in a door without alerting the household to our presence," she said. "Let's go and take a peek at that tapestry, and if you think I'm wrong, we'll leave. It's that simple."

"Nothing is ever that simple with you, Vanessa," he said.

Chapter Seventeen

⋙—⋘

They made their way through the hills and up to the abbey. Darkness had long since fallen, but the bright light of the moon illuminated their path, and Graeme's lantern helped when trees shrouded the silver moonbeams. Soon they found themselves hiding against the gate that protected the outer property of the abbey. A large lock secured the gate in place.

"I hadn't anticipated this being locked," Vanessa said.

Graeme said nothing. Instead he reached into Vanessa's bag and retrieved her tools. He carefully selected a flat metal instrument and started to work on the lock.

"Where did you get these tools?" he whispered.

"They were my father's," she said.

"He was a scientist as well?" he asked as he maneuvered the instrument up to the bolt.

"He was," she said.

"Rather progressive for him to leave his tools to a daughter," Graeme noted.

"Oh, no. He never would have left these to me. In fact,

he'd be quite furious to know that I have them. I stole them from his belongings before my mother shipped his clothing to a charity."

Graeme looked up to eye his wife, and just as he did, the lock shifted and the gate swung open. He tried to quickly gauge her expression, but could read nothing in her glance.

"Shall we?" She pushed past him and entered the yard leading to the abbey.

They approached the building and headed directly to the side door that she and Esme had previously agreed on.

"Vanessa, I'm here," Esme whispered.

Vanessa grabbed Graeme's hand and pulled him to the door. As they stepped inside, Vanessa came face-to-face with Fielding. His droll expression took her in and then moved to Graeme.

"Did you know about this?" Graeme asked him.

Fielding shook his head. "No, but I'm not surprised. My lovely wife would not be herself if she wasn't trying to get into trouble somewhere."

"Don't be such a bore. They needed our help," Esme said.

It was late enough that Randolph and the servants should be sleeping, but if they came across anyone, Graeme and Vanessa could convince them that they too had decided to stay the night. Not too difficult to believe, since several servants had seen them there as dinner guests only hours before.

"This way," Vanessa said. She quietly led the way through the first floor to the dining room where she'd seen the tapestry. "There it is," she whispered.

The four of them walked over to the huge tapestry

hanging along the stone wall directly above a sideboard. The tapestry, like most from its time period, depicted everyday life: an homage to the family's estate and life. Women kneaded bread, men hunted, other men fought battles, and the castle loomed over all in the background.

"What are we looking for?" Esme asked.

"That." Vanessa pointed to the image in the right corner.

A knight carried a stone. "It looks like every description or illustration I've ever come across for the Stone of Destiny," Graeme said. In the second image, the knight was hiding the stone somewhere in the abbey. A partially constructed abbey, as if the tapestry hinted that the stone was literally part of the abbey itself.

"Looks as if the stone is built into the abbey," Fielding said, verbalizing Graeme's very thought.

"But that can't be," Graeme said.

"And why not?" Vanessa asked.

"This place was nearly destroyed, and then Randolph reconstructed it." Graeme ran his hand along the threads. "If the stone had been here all along, it could have been destroyed or moved elsewhere." Graeme was silent a moment before adding, "unless there is a part of this building that Randolph left untouched."

"If the Stone of Destiny was added during construction, I suspect we'll find it on one of the exterior walls."

"Everything on the floors above has been reconstructed," Esme said. When her husband eyed her suspiciously, she shrugged. "Mr. Randolph gave me an extensive tour while you were in the village asking questions."

"Any part of the tour include an original part of the abbey?" Graeme asked.

She looked upward as if scanning her mind for the answer, then she smiled. "Yes, the chapel." She moved away from the dining room. "This way."

They followed her down a long, darkened hallway that led them directly to two double doors opening into the small chapel. Graeme lit the wall sconces, and the warm firelight scattered over the sanctuary.

Seven wooden pews were lined up in the middle of the room, and the altar still hosted the carved wood pulpit where the priest would have given his homilies.

"We didn't look around in here on our tour. He merely opened the door and showed me the inside," Esme said.

"Well, it certainly looks original," Vanessa said, running her hand over one of the pews. "It's not as polished as the rest of the abbey."

"I don't think this part of the abbey was destroyed, so that's probably the reason Randolph never touched it," Graeme said.

"So we're looking for a stone," Fielding said. "Like the one in Westminster?"

"Precisely," Graeme said.

Four arched windows lined the right exterior wall, while the wall behind the altar was solid stone. Together they made their way to the wall.

Graeme watched Vanessa run her hands over the stones with purpose. She had no claim to this journey of his, yet every day she worked beside him. Tirelessly. And rarely, if ever, complained. She expressed interest in his work and research. Granted, she was a curious sort; still her understanding moved him. She was a good mate for him. A good partner.

She was beautiful and intelligent, and she made him laugh. Precisely the sort of woman he would have searched for had he known they existed. In his previous experience, women were either smart or attractive, but rarely both. They would have a good marriage together; a good partnership. No matter what, he vowed to never desert her the way his father had done. Nor would he ever ask her to leave, or make her feel as if she wasn't a welcome addition to his life.

"It has to be here somewhere," she said.

"Unless it was removed or destroyed," Graeme offered. But he didn't stop examining their surroundings. He'd come too far in this damned quest to stop. Though he longed to return the Stone of Destiny to the Scots, he knew it belonged in Solomon's, with the rest of the Kingmaker, for safekeeping.

Graeme ran his hands over the wall once more, but still felt nothing save the cold, uneven surface of the stones and mortar. He stepped up into the pulpit, getting a better glimpse of the carvings. His foot hit something as he entered the priest's lectern, and a loud thump sounded around him.

"Vanessa! Quick, grab my hand." She did as he bade, and he had barely pulled her against his body when the floor beneath them began to shift. There was another loud noise and they began to sink, the floor shifting downward.

"We'll stay here, and if you don't come out, we'll find a way to get to you," Fielding said.

"Good luck," Esme added.

"A lift," Vanessa said, her voice tinged with wonder. "These monks were highly advanced in their technology." She allowed him to hold on to her, but she held her lantern out and watched as they sank farther and farther below, the cold darkness covering them up to their waists and then chests. "Where do you think it leads?"

"I'm not certain, but we've got to be on the right track."

"I believe you are correct," she said.

The darkness surrounded them until they were completely swallowed below. The area around them was icy, and the echoes traveled far.

"Clever monks," she said.

"Indeed," Graeme said with a smile.

Finally the lift jerked to a stop, and they found themselves in a much smaller area. Their lanterns didn't disperse much light, but gingerly Graeme stepped off the lift and motioned for her to follow. Vanessa exhaled slowly, trying to relax the excitement in her stomach.

They walked closely together to investigate the space. Gooseflesh covered Vanessa's skin. "It's very cold," she said, then rolled her eyes at her need to state the obvious.

"And dark," Graeme added, which only served to make her smile. Her husband had a keen sense of humor. He was quick and witty, and she couldn't help but appreciate it. Graeme lit their lanterns, then used the match to also light the torches attached to the wall.

They were in a hallway directly beneath the chapel, made of four solid stone walls. The wall at the end of the narrow room looked to be made entirely of sandstone bricks, all of them slightly reddish in color, different from the rest of the stone walls they'd seen. "It could be any one of these," she murmured.

"Precisely." Graeme didn't seem unnerved or frustrated, merely intrigued and focused. His shrewd gaze never left the wall, and when he stepped forward toward the wall he nearly lost his footing. It was only then that they realized there was no floor between where they stood and the stone wall.

Vanessa grabbed Graeme's jacket and pulled backward. "You almost fell," she said, her heart thundering in her ears.

"So I did. Evidently the monks were not only clever, but diabolical as well." He crouched down to better examine the area in front of them. "Shine your lantern outward."

She did as he bade and shone the light over the empty space in front of them. It no longer appeared empty. Instead, spanning the length of the gap between them and the stone wall were a series of bridges. Several boards of differing breadths traversed the area.

"With so many options, this seems like a test. Which one do we take?" she asked.

"That does appear to be the question," he said.

Graeme came to his feet, and one by one he examined the bridges, pressing his hand against them. He would find the way across, and he would know the stone when he found it. This was his quest, his passion.

Vanessa understood that, understood the overwhelming desire to prove something, whether to prove it merely to yourself or to prove it to others. It was the primary foundation between the two of them, something they would be able to stand upon together for years to come. Perhaps she could have the science-minded marriage she had sought.

Of course, all of that depended on him keeping his hands off of her so she could keep her wits about her. If other women felt this way with their husbands, no wonder they fancied themselves in love. No wonder they became simpletons with nothing more in their brains than dresses and flirtations.

Well, Vanessa had no intention of allowing that to happen to her. If that meant she had to spend less time in Graeme's bed, then so be it. She would have to comply every now and again. She couldn't forsake her wifely duties—she wasn't without certain conventions.

But to allow him to touch her whenever he wanted was out of the question. And she did not have the strength necessary to deny him. One simple kiss, and she'd be lost. She'd never again accomplish anything.

Even now, just thinking about him, she could feel her body betraying her, distracting her beyond reason. As if her memory could recall the sensations of their last lovemaking, her breasts tightened. She closed her eyes and took a deep and even breath.

"In the image of the tapestry," Graeme said, "the knight was placing the stone into a partially constructed wall."

Vanessa shook herself, annoyed that even the mere thought of his touch could so easily distract her from the task at hand. She was supposed to be assisting him, not standing here like a schoolgirl mooning over him. Perhaps she was deficient in some capacity, more susceptible to a lover's touch, as even the mere thought of it made her reasoning disappear.

"So you think it's one of the ones in the center of that wall?" she asked.

He exhaled slowly. "I don't know. From this angle, they all look the same."

"I suppose you'll only know if you try," she said.

"Very true." He took off his jacket and handed it to her. "You stay on this side." He put her pouch of tools into the waistband of his trousers, then went to stand in front of the bridges. The one directly in front of him was wide, large enough for him to simply walk across. It certainly appeared to be the most sturdy of the group. The other boards varied in breadth, the one on the far left being the most narrow.

He put his foot on the wide plank in front of him and pressed downward; it held steady. "Here goes." Graeme lifted his other foot off the ledge and set it on the bridge. It remained firm. He turned to face her. "It appears I've found the right one."

But the words were no sooner out of this mouth than the board cracked. Vanessa grabbed his arm with both her hands just as the wood gave way, and he fell. He grabbed onto the ledge and hoisted himself up.

"Evidently that was not the correct choice," she said. She swallowed hard against the fear that lodged in her throat. She smacked his arm. "That scared the devil out of me."

"I didn't much enjoy it myself." Together they sat and eyed the wood planks in front of them. "No more guesses," he said.

"Yes, please."

They were quiet for several moments. All the while Vanessa contemplated the changes in her life since she'd met Graeme. She was not yet ready to be a widow, and it was on her lips to tell him so when he spoke.

"I think I've found it," Graeme murmured.

She stepped forward. "Which one?"

He pointed to the one in the far left corner.

"Why that one? Simply because it is the most narrow and therefore the most dangerous?" she asked.

"No, because narrow is the way of the righteous," Graeme said as he came to his feet.

"Of course, how foolish of us," she said. Then before she could think better of it, she grabbed his face and pulled him in for a quick kiss. "Just in case."

He nodded. "I believe this wall faces east, though without the sun I can't be certain. Despite the image in the tapestry, I should think if the knights intentionally put the Stone of Destiny in this wall, they'd lay it first. The cornerstone, if you will," Graeme said.

"Well, there are those who believe the Stone of Destiny was the cornerstone of David's palace," she said. " 'Tis excellent logic."

"True." He exhaled slowly. Then, without another word, he stepped out onto the board. It creaked beneath his weight, but did not move. One foot and then the other, and the bridge held firm until he was on the other side.

"You know if I remove it, there could be negative repercussions." He met her gaze. "The wall could tumble down, and we could get trapped here." He paused for a breath. "Forever."

Vanessa released a shaky laugh. "No, Fielding and Esme know where we are, and they'll rescue us should something go horribly wrong."

Vanessa couldn't see his face clearly enough from this distance, but she could imagine his devilish grin and beautiful green eyes. Then she sucked in a breath and waited.

He put the chisel into the mortar line, then slammed his hammer against it. The noise reverberated across the chamber, echoing again and again. Little by little, he worked the mortar away until he was able to shift the stone. He inched it to the left, then the right, rocking it against the floor in an attempt to free it. A crack started in the mortar to his right and climbed up the wall, creaking as it went. Graeme stopped moving.

Vanessa stood still and watched, afraid to even exhale lest she risk blowing the wall down. She felt her eyes widen as she waited to see if the wall would crumble. But the cracking stopped, and everything fell silent again.

Graeme went back to his work until finally he was able

to wiggle the stone free. He stood, holding the sandstone brick in his hands. Quickly he traversed the wood plank.

The stone was nearly identical to the one she'd seen many times in Westminster, including the divots on the backside.

"This is it," he whispered.

"You're certain," she said.

"This, see." He pointed to a small engraving that was nearly worn off. "That is the sign of King David, something that is decidedly missing from the stone in Westminster. And these"—he turned it again to show her the bottom side; there three divots were carved in a line—"are for the other stones. This is the true Stone of Destiny."

Graeme and Vanessa made their way to the small boat they'd taken across the loch. He set the Stone of Destiny down and assisted her into the vessel before joining her. The first fingers of sunlight were caressing the edge of the horizon.

Graeme pushed off the edge, then dipped the oars in the black water and rowed. He observed Vanessa—her eyes wide as she watched the dark water move beneath the boat. Her hand reached over the edge, and her fingertips lightly grazed the water.

"Be careful or the beastie will nip your fingers," he teased.

She jerked her hand back into her lap, never taking her eyes off the water.

His chuckle filled the quiet dawn, drawing her eyes to his face. She smiled widely at him. "You have an infectious laugh," she said. "No matter what, it always makes me smile."

"I'll have to remember that," Graeme said. He allowed

his gaze to roam over her. Her bent knees created a tent with her dress that pooled around her feet.

"We found it," she said. "You finally found the Stone of Destiny. How many years have you been searching for it?"

He exhaled slowly. "Ten, maybe eleven years. Perhaps longer. I became fascinated with the legend when I was a boy, and when I would visit my mother and Old Mazie, they would speak of the story. Then I'd go back to London and go to Westminster to see the one housed there." He shook his head. "I don't know; it became a bit of an obsession, I suppose."

They reached the shoreline, and Graeme pulled the boat onto the rocks. "Be careful where you step," he reminded her. "The rocks are slippery."

She gripped his hand while she exited the boat, and they walked the rest of the way to the cottage. Quietly, they entered, and he stopped outside her room. The Stone of Destiny fit snugly under his arm.

"Where are you taking that?" Vanessa asked with a grin.

"Well, you know what they say. If you sleep on it, you'll dream of your future." Graeme bent and kissed her gently before walking to his own bedchamber.

Graeme sat up abruptly. He'd shifted the covers off his legs and now could feel the chill, since the fire had probably long since faded away. He hadn't bothered to stoke it when they'd returned. He'd been full of excited energy, then had abruptly fallen asleep, but not before maneuvering the stone beneath his pillow.

He'd been teasing Vanessa about it and hadn't even intended to do it. But once he'd been enclosed in his room, he'd been unable to resist. It was a foolish thing, a childish fantasy to have, but who would be able to resist sleeping upon the Stone of Destiny in an attempt to glimpse your own future?

Of course, all he'd dreamt of were bones, a big pile of bones. Interesting notion. He supposed becoming a pile of bones was in everyone's future. But he would have hoped for something a little more telling.

He lay back down, bracing his hands under his head. He stared at the dark ceiling above. Bones. But there had been something else there, too, hadn't there? Something lying amidst the bones. He closed his eyes to try and recapture the image, but the vision seemed cloudy now, blurred by heavy sleep.

Perhaps if he fell back asleep he'd be able to remember what it was. But then he heard a noise at his door, and all his senses came to attention. Someone was in his room.

Chapter Eighteen

———————❧❧———————

Vanessa quietly moved through the darkness of Graeme's bedchamber. She crept across the rug and made her way to the large bed in the center of the room. She knew that her husband was a fairly heavy sleeper, so she should be able to uncover the stone. She only intended to borrow it for the night. While she found the superstition foolish, she could not help her curiosity.

She'd sat up in her own room for nearly an hour arguing with herself about her silly desire. She wanted a reminder, reassurance that she could survive being a wife while continuing in her own pursuits. She realized it was foolish to believe that sleeping upon a piece of stone could do that for her.

But what if she dreamed of something important about her future? Reason won in the end; after all, it was a purely scientific experiment. She would sleep one night upon the rumored prophetic stone and see if it could help her locate the rest of those bones she knew she was meant to find.

Vanessa walked alongside the bed, moving her hand

gently up the mattress to avoid falling. It seemed unlikely Graeme would be so foolish as to sleep upon it himself, but she would search beneath his pillow first.

She made her way to the head of the bed and found the pillow. Her fingertips brushed across some of Graeme's hair, and she stopped, listening for any sound that indicated she might have awakened him, but his breathing remained steady.

Slowly she slipped her hand beneath the pillow, and her fingers met cold stone. So he had decided to try it himself. She couldn't help but smile. He did not seem to be a superstitious man, yet he too had been curious about the legend. What would he dream of? What destiny would Graeme have learned tomorrow morning when he awoke?

To remove it without waking him would take patience and skill. She tugged on the stone, and it shifted slightly beneath his pillow.

His hand clasped onto her wrist. "Looking for something?" In one quick movement, she found herself flipped onto the bed and upon her back, a large and heavy and very seductive husband atop her.

"I merely thought to—"

"To steal my treasure," he said, his voice dark and full of sinful promise.

She shivered in response. "No, of course not. I only wanted to sleep upon it." She laughed. "I know 'tis foolish, but I couldn't resist."

"Not too foolish, considering you found it beneath my pillow." His rich voice caressed her in the darkness, shrouding them in intimacy. It occurred to her that this was the way husbands and wives spoke to one another. Quiet murmurs in bed with the inky night around them. Whispers between lovers.

She tried in vain to remove herself.

"You want to sleep on it, you sleep on it in here," he said. He shifted their positions so that she now lay where he'd been, the hard stone beneath her pillow. His body cradled up against hers. His arm snaked around her waist, lying heavy on her far-too-sensitive, much-too-aware flesh. As if she wore nothing at all, she could feel the heat of his arm against her abdomen. Desire coursed through her, making her focus on his every breath—every inhalation, and then the slow, warm exhalation of air that fluttered over her skin.

Graeme's arm tightened around her, pulling her into his body so that her bottom nestled snugly against his legs. They lay there in silence for several moments, and he made no other move to touch or seduce her. She tried to fall asleep, tried to will herself to forget where she was, tried to simply relax into oblivion, but it seemed impossible.

Perhaps it was merely because of the stone. She knew it was there, knew she craved sleep and dreams, and because of that desire, sleep evaded her. *That* was a logical explanation. But it wasn't the accurate one.

The truth was she couldn't sleep because of Graeme's body pressed to hers. His fingertips gently rubbed across her abdomen. Through the veil of her shift, she could feel his subtle touch.

Desire pooled through her, shutting off all coherent thought. She wanted him. Wanted him to touch her, kiss her, make love to her. But she would not seduce him as she'd done the first time. Instead she'd keep to her word. If he pursued her, she would comply as was her duty as his wife.

Instinctively she shifted her body, and became abruptly

aware of his erection straining against the thin fabric of her shift.

His hand grew bolder, his palm flattening against her stomach. The other hand dipped lower to rest on her thigh. Her bare thigh. How had that happened? Had he moved her shift up and she hadn't noticed? Certainly she would have felt that. More than likely, the fabric had gotten twisted when he'd pulled her into bed and now lay askew. She tried to concentrate on keeping her breathing even, slow, and steady. She could accomplish this wifely task without losing complete hold of her senses. Women did this all the time.

His hand on her thigh moved up and down her leg, coiling desire through her veins. She longed to open herself to him, to fall onto her back and part her legs and urge him to come to her. But she held her ground. If he wanted her, he would ask for what he desired and give her no choice in the matter. She would not deny him.

His warm palm against her thigh made her skin feel alive, as if her very flesh shimmered with sensation. Fingers pushed at her shift, sneaking beneath and sliding up her leg. Vanessa sucked in her breath. What was this spell he held her under? As if his very touch bewitched her mind, emptying it of any coherent thought so she could only focus on the desire he created.

Hot breath slid across her neck and down her shoulder as he leaned closer. His well-muscled chest pressed to her back. Even without the benefit of seeing it now, she knew what his chest looked like, knew every sinewy line that traced the hard muscles of his abdomen.

He kissed her neck. One hot, moist kiss that proved to be her complete undoing. She knew in that moment that she would not leave this bed tonight.

His lips and tongue laved kisses over the tender flesh at her shoulder and across her upper back. He nipped lightly, and gooseflesh shivered over her skin.

His hand found its way to the rounded part of her hip and at the moment simply rested there, warming her skin. His other hand, though, the one wrapped under her body, slid up her stomach to cup her breast. Already her nipples were hard, tight with need.

Vanessa panted, her lips parting and her eyes fluttering closed. Moisture pooled between her legs, but she lay still. She wanted this seduction, wanted to know what her husband would do and say to make her his.

His hand at her breast cupped and kneaded the tender flesh. He tweaked her nipple, rolling it between his fingers. She arched into him. He bit her shoulder, and pressed his erection against her bottom.

Oh mercy, how she wanted him.

His hand slid from her hip to the front of her body. His fingers threaded through the curls at the juncture of her thighs, one fingertip brushing across the tender nub hidden within her folds. Vanessa's legs parted. *Now*, she wanted to say, but she pressed her lips together as she opened her legs.

He rolled her to him, laying her flat on the bed. He loomed over her—large, handsome, and passionate. She could not see the features of his face, but knew his green eyes would have darkened a shade and that his mouth would be set in a hard line.

His lips brushed across hers. His tongue plunged between her teeth in a greedy and hot kiss. She held nothing back as she kissed him in return, cupping his face in her hands. They continued kissing, giving and taking from one another. His hands roamed all over her body, caressing and tantalizing wherever they touched.

She tried more than once to pull him between her legs, but he stayed in his position, lying next to her on the bed. His mouth left hers, then covered the tip of her breast. Through the filmy material of the shift, his hot, wet mouth suckled until she thought she would go mad with desire. But he gave her no relief. Instead he moved to the other breast to continue his sweet torture.

Vanessa grabbed handfuls of the sheets and clenched them at her sides. He kissed his way down her torso, barely stopping over her center so that she could feel the hint of his warm breath. She shivered. Then his hot mouth was on her thigh, nibbling and kissing the tender flesh at the top of her leg. One, then the other, he kissed and teased. She bucked against the bed, knowing she needed relief and knowing only he could give it to her.

He continued kissing her leg as one hand reached up and pulled the shift all the way up her body. He ran his hand over her breasts, then slid it down her torso. Then he shifted himself until he rested between her legs, but instead of thrusting inside of her as she expected, he lowered his mouth and kissed her inner core.

His lips and tongue played her; a master musician perfectly strumming his instrument. She'd wrapped both of her legs around his back and was holding herself as close to his mouth as she could. He dipped his tongue inside her, then moved to suck at the hidden nub. One finger slipped inside of her, and both hand and mouth worked brilliantly together.

And then she was lost. Pleasure fractured inside of her, exploding from her center and rocketing down all of her limbs. She threaded her fingers through his hair and held on as he took her from one height to another. Finally the climax subsided, and he kissed his way up her torso.

His erection pressed into her opening, and before she could completely recover from her ascension, he plunged into her. Again she wrapped her legs around him, pulling him farther inside, deeper still. She ran her hands down his back, feeling the strong cords of muscles playing beneath her fingertips as he thrusted. Her climax began again. She called out his name. He groaned and collapsed atop her.

Now she knew precisely how her husband would seduce her. And she also knew that she'd never be able to resist him. She might be in more danger than she'd first thought.

Vanessa awoke the following morning alone in the bed. She stretched lazily, parts of her body tinged with soreness as the previous night's events came flooding back. Graeme had seduced her. Several times. They'd spent the night making love, yet instead of feeling disappointed with herself, she found herself smiling.

The sun peeked through the window to her left, an unusual occurrence in a Scottish winter. She stretched again, and her arm brushed cold limestone. *The Stone of Destiny.* She'd slept on it. But had she dreamed?

She sat up. Yes, she had. A very real and lengthy dream about Graeme and herself, and there had been children, several of them. Two boys that resembled their father, with wavy brown hair and lovely green eyes, and then three little girls who all looked very much like she had as a child. But surely *that* was not her destiny.

Vanessa remembered many details of the dream. They had been on a picnic near a pond, much smaller than the loch, and it had been warm and sunny, the children running through the grass giggling as their father chased after them. She remembered that she had sat upon a blanket beneath a great tree, and she had watched her family, laughing while she'd readied a light meal of bread and cheese and candied figs. Mostly, though, she remembered the way she'd felt: utter bliss and happiness. Sheer, unadulterated contentment.

Decidedly absent had been any thoughts of her research. She hadn't envisioned any plaques or awards or publications for the strides she'd made in the field of science. No display shelf featuring the fossils she'd found. There had only been Graeme. Their family. And that soul-consuming feeling of joy.

Sitting in the bed, she propped her elbows on her knees and starred at the blank wall, frowning.

No, that couldn't be her destiny.

Her destiny involved great scientific discovery.

All her life, she'd never fit in with other girls, never felt part of her family, never felt her mother's love. It was a struggle, but she'd made peace with it, because she'd realized that was the cost of her studies. It was the price she'd paid. In exchange, she'd been sure that she was destined for legitimate scientific discoveries.

But her dream spoke of nothing scientific. It meant nothing. She propelled herself from the bed and shook off the last of her sleep.

Quickly she scurried to her room and dressed for the day. She wound her hair into a braid, but left it hanging, long and heavy down her back. Then she found her way to the kitchen, the favored room of Graeme's family. She found her husband sitting and leaning his chair back against the wall. His head was thrown back, and he was laughing joyfully at something his mother or grandmother had said.

Warmth spread through her entire body at the sound of his mirth—a sensation she remembered from her dream, happiness and sheer contentment. She shook her head. His was a carefree laugh, one that would inspire anyone to smile.

Smiling was all well and good, but she was a woman of science, she reminded herself. A researcher.

"Good morning," Graeme said with a grin. He moved his leg off the bench, turning to face the table. He patted the seat next to him. She sat down, but with enough room for another person to sit between them.

His mother stood to get another plate out of the cupboard, and Graeme slid closer to Vanessa, leaning down to her ear. "I trust you slept well."

She twisted her body to put some space between them, then nodded enthusiastically. "I did, thank you."

"Have any special dreams?" he asked.

She met his gaze and found only humor there. "Nothing in particular," she said. "And yourself?"

"I dreamt of something, but I haven't quite figured it out yet myself." He took a thoughtful sip of his coffee.

Did he have a similar dream? One of their family picnicking by the water and of their children running and laughing through a field? Had he also seen them strolling together, fingers linked, sharing stories and gazing adoringly at one another?

She scanned his face for a sign, but she saw nothing that gave her any indication. And she most certainly wasn't going to ask.

While it had only been one experiment, in her scientific estimation, the Stone of Destiny was most definitely not prophetic.

Chapter Nineteen

An hour later, Graeme sat in the study recording the details of his dream in his journal. Since this morning, he'd remembered more, not simply the pile of bones, but the treasure. It had to be the Loch Ness Treasure. Somewhere in those caves, he'd find the treasure lying amidst bones. Perhaps the legend had been right and the beastie had guarded the treasure, but now the beastie was gone and the gems lay unguarded.

He had to find them before Niall did. No matter what the cost, he had to prevent The Raven from laying claim to the Kingmaker.

Of course, now that Graeme had the true Stone of Destiny, it would be impossible for anyone to complete the Kingmaker. Still, he wanted to be certain. Solomon's had entrusted him with this task, and he would not let them down. They had been the only true friends he'd found in London.

In England, people had always given him respect because of his family name, because of his title, but begrudgingly. He was not a pure blue blood. In their eyes, he was tainted with poor Scots blood from his mother. Here in Scotland, people thought he was arrogant, that he believed himself too good for them with his fancy title and money. Well, to hell with them. To hell with all of them.

The Stone of Destiny lay on the corner of his desk while he made his notes. He'd considered sending it by post to Solomon's so they could lock it up with the other potentially dangerous relic they protected, but then he'd run the risk of someone intercepting the package. He could not afford to be reckless with such an artifact.

No, he'd wait until he could deliver it in person. He'd keep it here with him. As soon as they found the Loch Ness Treasure, they'd be on their way with both artifacts.

The study door flew open, and Dougal stepped inside. "Graeme, there's something we need to discuss," he said. He stood tall, with his chin held firm.

Graeme set his pen down and waved his brother into the room. He'd decided not to confront his brother, and instead had decided to wait and see if the boy would confess. Perhaps the guilt was proving too much for him. "This is your house, Dougal. You don't need an invitation from me."

His brother sat, then rubbed his palms against his kilt. He sighed.

"What are you working on?" Dougal asked.

"My research."

Dougal's eyes fell onto the sandstone sitting on the edge of the desk. "You found it, then?"

Graeme's hand came down on the Stone of Destiny. He nodded.

Dougal met his glance then, and his eyes brightened for a moment. "Truly?" Then his lips tightened into a thin line. "Did she help you?"

"What is it that you have against my wife?" Graeme asked.

Dougal leaned back in his chair and slowly exhaled.

Perhaps he was going to tell Graeme, admit that he'd tried to kill Vanessa. Graeme had considered what she'd told him, that Dougal was probably feeling neglected and jealous about all the time Graeme was spending with his new wife. It certainly might explain his actions to an extent, but it most definitely did not excuse them. Still, Graeme wanted to hear what Dougal had to say, wanted to hear the admission directly from the boy's lips.

"I don't care for her," Dougal said.

Graeme might desire a confession, but he wouldn't allow the boy to disparage Vanessa. He'd already caused enough harm. Graeme leaned forward and tapped his fingers on the desk. "Tread lightly, brother; she is my wife."

Dougal threw his arms up in frustration. "Don't you see what she's done to us? Before she was here, I was the one who assisted you with your research. She's probably only after your title and your money." He sat forward, his expression tight.

Dougal was utterly serious and truly concerned for his brother's welfare, that much was evident. But sentiments mattered not when it came to attempted murder. Anger welled inside Graeme like a great wave rolling in to crash upon the shore.

"Not that I owe you an explanation, brother, but Vanessa did not even know I was a duke when we got married. As for her coming between the two of us, that's simply untrue," Graeme said.

"But she trapped you into this marriage. I heard you say so yourself," Dougal argued.

"No." Graeme forced himself to take three steady

breaths. "I said *we* were trapped into marriage. But how it happened no longer matters. She's my wife. End of discussion."

Graeme picked up his pen and looked down at his journal, though his anger blurred the words. He was too furious to confront the boy. The last thing he wanted was to behave like his father had, yelling and causing fear.

"What if she puts you in danger, Graeme?" Dougal came to his feet, but he made no move to leave the study. "What will you do then?"

Graeme tossed his pen down and came to his feet. "If you're asking me where my loyalties lie, rest assured that she is my wife and I will not walk away from her."

At full height, Graeme towered over his brother, and at seventeen, Dougal had yet to fully broaden. But the boy stood his ground.

"I suspected as much," Dougal said.

Graeme closed the distance between them and stood over his brother, no longer caring if he caused fear. Hell, right now he was ready to pound his brother. "I know you did it. I know you shot Vanessa."

Dougal's eyes widened. He opened his mouth to say something, then swallowed. "I was trying to protect you. You'll see that someday."

"Get the hell away from me. And I don't want to see you again until you've gotten over this nonsense. Then we'll talk. Is that understood?" He jammed a finger into the boy's chest. "And don't even so much as glance at Vanessa. We'll be out of your house this afternoon."

"Vanessa, come and visit with me for a moment," Moira said.

Vanessa stepped into her mother-in-law's bedchamber

at the invitation. She didn't know Moira all that well, but she knew the woman had stayed by her side and tended her wound when she'd been shot, and that Moira loved her family.

There was a small sitting area next to the window. Vanessa took the empty seat next to Moira.

"I wanted to see how you were doing," Moira said.

Vanessa touched her side. The wound was nearly healed now, mostly an uncomfortable memory. "I feel fine. Thank you for taking such good care of me."

"Oh no, dear, I didn't mean your injury. I meant here, in Scotland, with Graeme." Moira smiled warmly.

Vanessa folded her hands in her lap, unsure of how to answer. Was Moira asking if Vanessa loved her son, if he made her happy? She wasn't certain how to answer the question. "Scotland is beautiful. The land is so untamed."

"Savage beauty. That's what Old Mazie has always said," Moira offered.

Vanessa inclined her head. "Yes. I haven't gotten as far into my research as I'd intended. Graeme and I have been"—she searched for the right word, unsure of how much Graeme shared with his mother about his job for Solomon's—"preoccupied with work on his studies."

"I wanted to give you something." Moira stood and went to her dressing table, then returned with a small bag. "Hold out your hand," she instructed.

Vanessa did as she bade, and Moira emptied the bag into Vanessa's palm. A single ring fell out.

"It was my wedding ring," Moira said.

The gold band was accented with a large round amethyst encircled with small diamonds. "It's lovely," Vanessa said.

"I want you to have it."

Vanessa shook her head and held her hand out to her mother-in-law. "I couldn't."

"Yes." Moira closed Vanessa's fingers over the ring. "Graeme's father gave that to me nearly forty years ago. It's been a very long time since I've worn it. But it belongs in the Rothmore estate, and now you are the duchess."

Vanessa's hand still enclosed the ring.

"Shall we see if it fits?" Moira asked. She withdrew the ring, then slid it onto Vanessa's left hand. "Perfect."

The metal was cold against Vanessa's skin, the ring delicate and beautiful. She looked up at Moira. "Thank you. I really don't know what to say."

"You don't have to say anything. But if I might offer some advice, from experience." Moira didn't wait for approval before she continued. "Don't be a fool like I was for so long." She sighed. "Graeme's father and I had a tumultuous marriage. We were both passionate and stubborn, not to mention prideful, and"—she shook her head woefully—"we gave up on one another. And when that happened, I gave up on love." She held up a finger and smiled. "That isn't to say I ever stopped loving his stubborn hide. No one in the world could infuriate me the way he could."

Vanessa listened intently to Moira's words. She wasn't certain how she felt about any of it yet, but she knew sharing it wasn't easy for her mother-in-law.

"That man has been dead for several years now," Moira continued, "but I've been so fearful of getting hurt that I haven't let another man get close to me."

Vanessa sensed there was more, something Moira hadn't yet said. "Until?" Vanessa prodded.

Moira gave her a wide grin. "Perceptive. I like that. Until I met George Randolph. He came calling this morning after our lovely dinner last night." Moira chewed at her lip, and the movement made her look younger, much like a lovesick girl. "He's charming. Perhaps not as refined as my last husband, but not as overbearing and loud either."

She covered Vanessa's hand with her own. "I don't know if this will go anywhere, but I'm not running. I'm going to allow that man to court me, though heaven knows why he would want a lass such as myself. I'm going to enjoy every moment of it."

Vanessa knew that this entire conversation had been planned. Not simply to give her the wedding ring, although that had been so considerate, but to tell the story she'd shared. Moira was obviously trying to tell Vanessa something—to not be afraid of love. Vanessa wasn't afraid of it; she simply didn't believe it existed. At least not for a long term.

Hadn't Moira said so herself when speaking of Graeme's father? Their passion had burned bright and hot for a short time, and then they'd lived separately. Though Moira had said she'd loved him still, she'd simply been too stubborn to reconcile with him.

Moira squeezed Vanessa's hand.

"Thank you for the ring." Vanessa came to her feet. It was then that she noticed the painting hanging over Moira's bed. It was a simple watercolor landscape of a pond with a large tree off to the side. The image looked vaguely familiar.

Vanessa walked over to it for a closer look.

"I haven't painted in years," Moira said. "But that was always my favorite."

Vanessa closed her eyes, and pictures came vividly to her mind. She and Graeme sitting beneath that very tree, having a picnic, their children running in the grass beside them. Her heart stopped. She opened her eyes and examined the painting. It was precisely the image from her dream.

Vanessa reached out, but stopped herself before she touched the painting. "Where is this?" she asked.

"The Rothmore country estate in Nottingham. I'm certain Graeme will take you there sometime. It's quite beautiful in the summertime," Moira said.

But Vanessa didn't hear all of Moira's words, because all she could think about was the dream she'd had upon the Stone of Destiny.

The Raven sat in the darkened room at the pub waiting for his young protégé to arrive. It didn't take him long. It never did. They had met here, at a pub on the edge of the small village, on occasion since the day he'd invited Dougal to tea.

Dougal entered the room and made his way immediately to the table. The Raven inhaled slowly on his cigar, then exhaled right into the boy's face as he sat. He crossed his legs and eyed the boy. Dirty, with shaggy hair; he would never amount to anything.

"How do you fare today, Dougal?" he asked, feigning interest.

Dougal exhaled loudly. "My brother told me who you are. Told me that you are dangerous and not to be trusted."

"Did he indeed? He warned you to stay away from me, didn't he?" The Raven asked. He was intrigued that Graeme hadn't sought him out. Hadn't called the authorities to pick him up. "I warned you about sharing too much with your brother."

Dougal paled a little. "I didn't tell him anything about you. Only that we'd met."

"Indeed." Of course, Graeme was fully aware of what The Raven was capable of. He'd seen, firsthand, what The Raven did to those who betrayed him, or those who simply had worn out their usefulness. Poor stupid Sam.

The Raven took another lengthy drag on his cigar, pulling the smoke through his teeth. "I can honestly say, Dougal my boy, that I have barely met your brother. So whatever he thinks he knows about me, he's mistaken. I am a gentleman. More than I can say for those renegades your brother associates with in that club of his."

Dougal's eyes widened. "Solomon's? But they are affiliated with Her Majesty."

The Raven laughed, a true and hearty laugh that he didn't even have to conjure. "Is that what he told you?"

This time, the boy did not speak. He merely nodded his head, and his tangled mop of hair bobbed.

The Raven leaned forward, lowering his voice. "That is a lie. Let me tell you a little something about Solomon's. My brother was also a member, and they got him killed. He left behind a young son and daughter. Very tragic." He shook his head and clucked his tongue.

The Raven waited a moment before continuing. "It is true that they have, on occasion, assisted the crown, but they are not affiliated with Her Majesty. Quite the contrary, they work for their own means, their own purposes." He stopped, annoyed with the discussion of Solomon's.

"Some of his friends from Solomon's are here. We met them for dinner last evening," Dougal said. "I overheard them talking last night, and Fielding has come for you." The boy had the impertinence to look smug. He thought the mention of Fielding would threaten The Raven.

So Graeme had called for Fielding. Did he think simply because Fielding and The Raven were related that he would have a better time getting rid of him? Well, The Raven would not allow that to happen. But he knew that he needed to leave sooner rather than later. Fielding would find him and would stop at nothing to bring him in. Damnation, but he needed Niall to find that bloody stone!

The Raven met the boy's gaze. He raised his eyebrows.

A pity Fielding had come all this way right before The Raven planned to leave this desolate country. He would have enjoyed another confrontation with the man.

Nothing could ever be regained once in the possession of Solomon's. Their security was like no other. Of course, The Raven had his ways, such as kidnapping a member's family. But that took so much time and organization. And even then, the results were hardly guaranteed, as was evidenced by Niall's lack of success. It would be far easier were he to find the treasure himself.

"Would you like to know a secret?"

Dougal shrugged.

"Your brother's search is for naught. I stole the Stone of Destiny from Westminster shortly before I left London." There was no reason not to tell him. He would be dead before too long, as soon as his usefulness wore out. They always ended up that way.

A crease slid between Dougal's eyes. "That cannot be."

"Oh, but it is," The Raven said. "I know precisely where it is."

"Yes, I know there was one at Westminster, one believed to be true, but it was a counterfeit. A trick the Scots played on the English long ago. The real one has been here in Scotland the whole time," Dougal said.

Fanciful thoughts no doubt brought on by his foolish brother. "And how do you know this?" The Raven crossed his arms over his chest, ready to enjoy an entertaining tale.

"Because I've seen it with my own eyes," Dougal said defiantly. "Graeme found it last night. I saw it just this morning sitting on his desk."

"Vanessa," Graeme yelled as he stormed from his study into the main hall of the house. He started toward the bedchambers. "Gather your belongings," he said. "We're leaving immediately."

"What the devil are you hollering about?" his mother asked. She wore an apron tied around her waist and wiped her hands on its worn calico fabric. "I could hear you all the way to the kitchen, boy."

He stopped and eyed his mother. "Dougal." Graeme shook his head. "Vanessa and I are leaving. We'll be staying in Inverness for the duration of our stay."

"Don't be foolish." Moira frowned and shook her head. "Your brother is a child. Whatever he's said, I'm certain he doesn't mean it," Moira said.

Graeme didn't see a reason to tell his mother what Dougal had done. "You didn't hear him, and he did mean it." Graeme took a deep breath and put his hand on his mother's shoulder. "I think he's gotten himself tangled with some people, dangerous individuals he has no business dealing with. Still I cannot and will not stay in this house considering his attitude toward my wife."

"He spoke ill of Vanessa, then?" Moira placed both hands on her hips. "I'll box his ears, I will."

"No, Mother." Graeme took several deep breaths, trying to rein in his anger. "This is his house. He's the man here. I can make no claims on this house, nor would I take that from him," Graeme said.

"This is *my* house," Moira argued, placing a hand on her chest. "And you'll stay if I say you'll say."

"I'm not discussing this, Mother."

"Neither am I. Don't test me on this, Graeme. You know you will not win." She narrowed her eyes at him. "Do you think you boys come about your stubbornness by accident?" She didn't wait for him to answer. "You should protect your wife, but don't you forget that you have a brother who loves and admires you. He might have rocks for brains, but he's a good boy."

That was it. He'd had about as much as he could stand, and protecting Dougal no longer seemed important. "Mother, he's the one who shot Vanessa. Do you still think he's a good boy?"

"What are you saying?" she asked, wrapping her arms across her body.

Graeme shoved his hand through his hair. "I told you I think he's gotten involved with some dangerous people."

His mother wrung her hands on the apron. Worry etched lines into her face. "You think the boy is in serious trouble, then?"

"I do."

Moira set her mouth and nodded, her mind already made up. "Still, you will stay here until you leave for London." She held up a hand to prevent him from arguing. "This is my home, Graeme, and I will say who stays and who goes."

Graeme nodded. "Keep in mind it is best if I don't see the little bugger anytime soon, so don't be planning any kind of family discussions." With that, Graeme continued toward Vanessa's bedchamber. He entered the room and found her sitting on the bed looking rather forlorn. "You heard?"

"I did." She looked up at him, her blue eyes large. "But I knew you were talking with your mother, and I didn't want to intrude." Then she paused for a moment. "Your brother truly does not care for me?"

"My brother is an idiot." He came toward her. She was upset. Her feelings were hurt, and he could sense that, but he didn't know what to do or say to make it go away.

He lifted her chin. "He'll come around. Don't fret, Duchess."

The Raven stood in the darkness waiting for the boy. He hated having to rely on inferior assistants, but here in this Scottish wasteland, he had very little choice. Niall was busy in the caves setting up the dynamite for the explosion tomorrow. The fool had said he'd finally discovered the location of the Loch Ness Treasure, but the tunnel had been destroyed and he needed to create a new one to reach it.

The Raven lit a cigar and took a slow, deep drag, allowing his lungs to fill with the sweet smoke. Damned if he wouldn't have preferred to walk into that house, shoot everyone, and then steal the Stone of Destiny. But his new plan required that Graeme stay alive, at least for a little while longer. The Raven planned to leave tonight without the damned Loch Ness Treasure. Niall was close, and Graeme would see to it that The Raven got the final stone, and then the Kingmaker would be complete.

Finally the boy slid out the back door and ran down the dirt path toward The Raven.

"Did you get it?" he asked.

The boy nodded. He glanced behind him at the house, guilt painfully etched in his young features. He'd learn soon enough that you had to betray everyone in order to get what you wanted out of life. Either that, or wait for them to betray you. It wasn't a difficult choice once you learned that lesson.

The Raven pulled the counterfeit stone out of his bag. His carefully orchestrated theft from Westminster had been a thing of legends, printed all over the newspapers, a crime that had completely confounded the police. Sadly it had all been for naught.

"Here," The Raven said. "Put this one back in its place, and your brother will never know the difference."

The boy looked unsure as he held firmly to the actual Stone of Destiny.

"That belongs in England with Her Majesty. It is a royal artifact, and she would very much like to see its return," The Raven said, choosing his words carefully. For whatever foolish reason, this boy felt a strong attraction to the English aristocracy. "You know your brother is planning to keep that, and it was never meant to belong to anyone, but rather to be protected by the government."

"Go to the devil," Dougal snapped. "I'm not a fool. I know that Graeme would have done right by the queen." He took the counterfeit and braced it under his arm.

The Raven smiled at him. "You've done the right thing."

"You gave me no choice," Dougal said, then turned and walked toward the cottage.

Now his plan was in motion. Eager to convince him of his veracity, Niall had described the other stone's location in precise detail. The Raven needed only to wait until Niall was out of the cave so that he could rearrange the dynamite, setting a trap for the bastard. It seemed a fitting ending. A small explosion would kill Niall, but leave the treasure unharmed and waiting for Graeme. Such a pity

The Raven wouldn't be there himself to witness Niall's ending, but he had plans back in London he needed to attend to. Besides, digging around in the dirt wasn't really a suitable activity for the future king of England.

Graeme would follow him back to London. After all, The Raven now possessed the authentic Stone of Destiny. The only reason that The Raven wasn't killing Dougal right now was that he needed the brat to tell Graeme what he'd done. Once Dougal was no longer under The Raven's influence, the boy would no doubt begin to feel guilty. In no time at all, he'd be running off to big brother to confess.

Chapter Twenty

❦━━━━❧

Graeme moved quietly toward the cave. He knew Vanessa would be unhappy that he'd left without her, but he couldn't trust the stability of the caves with Niall's incessant use of dynamite. He would deal with her anger later. He had a task to accomplish, and he needed to do so without worrying about her safety.

Graeme had her notes in his pocket, crude drawings from the farmer who had originally found the bone that interested her. Her previous fiancé had swindled the notes from the poor man, then proceeded to ridicule his finding in every scientific journal he could. Vanessa had stolen the notes and had intended to discredit her fiancé. Once this business with the Kingmaker was resolved, Graeme fully intended to assist her in doing so. It would give him such pleasure to bring down the man who had hurt her.

Graeme hadn't thought anything of the notes until he'd had that foolish dream. This quest could be utterly futile, but what if that treasure truly was resting in a pile of bones?

• • •

Vanessa muttered to herself as she climbed the slope of the hillside, trying to keep a safe distance from her husband. It was so like him to sneak off and leave her sleeping in bed. But she was not such a heavy sleeper that she did not notice him rustling through her belongings. She hadn't heard him sneak into her room, but she'd heard him take something from her dressing table.

After he'd left the room, she'd waited a few moments, then lit the lantern and realized that he'd taken her notes. She'd seen him out the window leaving the house. She would not be a perfect little wife who stayed behind to embroider or mend her husband's pants. If he was out in those caves, she would be too.

Daylight was fast approaching, which she greatly appreciated as she traversed the damp grass that led down to the caverns. What precisely did he intend to do with her notes? Or more to the point, what plans did he have for the notes that she'd stolen from Jeremy? Did he intend to find the bones for himself? Curiosity beat a wild path inside her, fueling her questions.

She walked softly as she entered the caves, knowing that the sound would echo and alert Graeme to her presence sooner than she'd like. He would notice her eventually. He had highly attuned senses and generally could tell when he was being followed. But she wanted him to get enough of a head start that she might be able to determine what he was after.

She continued to follow him. He moved into the open cavern that had tunnels leading off of it, much like a wagon wheel. He stood still.

If Graeme turned back and looked behind him, he'd see her. So Vanessa hid against the cavern wall, the cold of the stone pressing through the warmth of her cloak and dress. She waited for Graeme to move farther into the cavern.

He held his lantern up, stepped into a tunnel, and disappeared into the darkness. Vanessa started to count; she'd follow on ten.

Before she could reach seven, an explosion shook the cave. Small rocks fell all around her. Luckily none of them hit her directly. Still her heart leapt into her throat.

Graeme.

Fear plastered her to the wall, and she froze. For two long breaths, she was unable to move. Then she ran, arms over her head to protect herself from the falling rocks.

"Graeme!" she yelled.

She ran down into the tunnel he'd selected. She hit something hard and warm and found herself braced against her husband's body. She exhaled loudly, then swore. "You scared me," she said.

"Vanessa! Damnation, woman, must you always follow me?" He held up a hand. "Don't bother answering that."

"Must you always try and sneak off without me?" she asked.

"Twisting the subject around does not get you out of this," he said drolly.

"Where was the explosion?" she asked, changing the subject altogether.

"Over that way. Precisely where I was headed," he said.

"With my notes," she said.

He grinned. "You caught me."

"You weren't very quiet," she said. "What are you doing with them?"

"My dream." He shook his head. "'Tis foolish, I realize,

but I dreamt of that illustration, the treasure lying upon those bones. I thought to find it today."

So he hadn't dreamt of her at all. Her abdomen tightened. "Well, let us go and see," she said. She started off in that direction, but Graeme grabbed her elbow and stilled her. "What?" she asked.

"You are a stubborn woman, do you know that?" But he didn't wait for her to answer. Instead he lowered his mouth and kissed her firmly. "I know I won't be able to convince you to return to the house for your safety, so at least allow me to go in front. And Duchess, be mindful of your step."

She nodded. "I may have been referred to as stubborn a time or two in my life. But I do not believe I am alone in that quality, husband."

He chuckled, looping his fingers through hers and pulling her along. They walked in silence for several moments, their footsteps and their breathing the only sound. Their lanterns lit the way through the narrow cavern tunnel. Then the area opened up, and they could see where the explosion had occurred. Over to the right was a crumbled wall, and fallen stones were piled nearly floor to ceiling. Dust still hung heavy in the air.

Graeme stepped over to the area. He placed his hand on his waistband where Vanessa knew he secured his pistol. "Niall, are you in there?"

"Graeme?" Niall's voice filtered through the crumbled stone. "Is that you?"

"Yes. We're going to get you out." Graeme immediately went about moving stones out of the way. But even as he cleared, Vanessa could see more stones behind.

"No, you can't," Niall said, his tone strained, his breath labored. "It's too late. I'm injured, and I'm bleeding."

"Keep talking," Graeme argued. "I'm going to get you out of there."

"Listen to me, Graeme. I'm a dead man."

But Graeme merely shook his head and continued to move stones, one at a time. But no matter how many he moved, he made no progress. It was as if there was a never-ending wall of stones in that pile. He'd remove one and three more would fall into its place. The small opening on the left was shrinking.

"Graeme." Vanessa put her hand on her husband's arm. "Listen to him. He's hurt. You can hear it in his voice."

"He's got my family," Niall said, his voice cracking with desperation. "Penny and Jonathan."

"Who has them?" Graeme asked, but before he could allow Niall to answer, Graeme knew. "The Raven. That's why you've been working with him." He cursed.

"Yes. I didn't want to, God knows I didn't. But I had no other choice. I tried to find them. For two weeks, I did nothing but search, but I never even found a clue that would indicate where he would have taken them." Niall paused for a moment before continuing. "I refuse to believe they're already dead."

"You could have come to Solomon's. To me. I would have helped you," Graeme said.

"I wanted to. Believe me I did. But he threatened me. Said he'd kill them if I went to anyone to ask for help. It was then that I came here to find the bloody treasure." Niall laughed then, though there was no humor to be found in his tone, only irony and sadness.

"I found it. Here, this morning. I'd set the dynamite up last night to blow through a different wall, and that bastard must have followed me and switched things around. I set off his trap, and now I can't get out. Ironically enough, the explosion opened up the correct area, and there it was. Lying amidst a pile—"

"Of bones," Graeme filled in.

"Yes," Niall said. "How did you know?"

"Doesn't matter, Niall. We'll get you out of there," Graeme said again. "How badly are you hurt?"

"I'm bleeding. A stone fell and hit me on the head," Niall said. "Hurts like a son of a bitch. Several more fell on my leg. I'm trapped on the ground. I think it's broken."

"Graeme," Vanessa said softly. "Look." She pointed down at their feet. They were now standing in a quarter-inch of water. "The loch is coming in," she said softly. "We've got to get out of here before the entire cavern is flooded."

Graeme watched for a moment as the water continued to pour in, first to the toe of his boot, then washing over it to lap at the hem of his pants. Vanessa was right. They were running out of time. He released a long string of curses.

"You have to find them, Graeme," Niall said. "Promise me you'll find my Penny and my son," Niall said, his tone full of anguish.

Graeme stared at his own wife, knowing he probably would have done all the things Niall had done to protect her.

Tears silently slid down Vanessa's cheeks, and she swallowed hard.

"I promise," Graeme said.

"Don't let that bastard kill them," Niall said.

"I won't." But Graeme knew The Raven, and it was likely Penny and the boy were already dead, had been for weeks. Unless The Raven had planned to use them for further leverage—then there might still be time.

"Graeme." Vanessa placed her hand on his arm, tugging on his coat sleeve. Her eyes were wide with fear. The water now came to her mid-calf, and she had to hold on to the wall to steady herself from the burgeoning current.

He nodded. "Niall," he said, but couldn't bring himself to say anything else.

"I know. You need to get out of here. You can't save my family if you wait in here with me. Here," he said as he reached his hand through the small opening. "I can't give you all of the treasure, but this, this is the stone he's after. Use it to get my family back."

Graeme reached for the stone Niall offered, and a large uncut emerald fell into his hand.

"Oh my," Vanessa said.

"I'll save them," Graeme said.

The water tugged at them. The frigid liquid lapped at Graeme's thigh, so he knew Vanessa was now submerged up to her waist. He'd carry her out of here if he had to.

"Now get out of here!" Niall yelled. "Tell them I love them, tell them I tried."

Three hours later, they were on a train headed back to London. Vanessa sat in their private sleeping car and watched Graeme prowl the small space like some great beast caged against his will. Guilt ate at him like a festering sore. She could see the anguish settle in his eyes, the firm set of his jaw.

"You did all you could," she said, knowing fully that her words would make no difference. He would not feel right about leaving Niall there to die until he was able to save his family. She sent a silent prayer that Penny and

Jonathan were still alive and that The Raven had not harmed them.

"I did nothing," he said softly.

Vanessa stood and went to him, stilled him in mid-stride. She put one hand on his cheek to force him to look at her. "There was nothing to be done."

He closed his eyes and leaned into her touch. "I should have known, known that Niall would never willingly work with The Raven."

Graeme met her gaze. The pain in his green eyes tugged at her heart, and she realized with utter clarity that she was hurting with him, not simply feeling sadness at the terrible situation, but empathizing with her husband. More than anything, she wanted to erase that look from his face, to remove the pain that hung heavy in his heart.

She pulled his face down to hers and kissed him fiercely. Gone were her fears about whether or not their lovemaking would alter who she was, or make her forget the woman she wanted to be. In their place was a deep-seated and simple need to comfort her husband. Touch him and make him forget, if only for a moment, that they'd been unable to save Niall's life.

He took what she gave and demanded more. He pulled her tight to him, kissed her breathless. His fingers made quick work of the buttons on the back of her dress, which soon fell from her body in a pool at her feet. She stepped out of it, then pulled her shift over her head until she stood before him in nothing but her stockings and shoes.

"God, you're beautiful," he said. He tore at his own clothes, removing them quickly.

She rid herself of the stockings and shoes, and together

they lay on the sleeping cot. It was much smaller than a bed, but he'd taken her on a desk, so this would suffice.

"Be on top," he said.

She wasn't certain what to do, but in this moment, she would deny him nothing. So she brought one leg across and straddled him. He stopped her before she lowered herself on top of him. Pulled her down and kissed her again, a long, deep kiss that spoke of things Vanessa had never dared dream of. Tears pricked at the corners of her eyes, so she kept them closed to keep the tears from falling.

His hand found her; a finger teased her opening. She was already slick with desire for him. Merely the thought of him touching her had lust coursing through her limbs. Now the touch itself was pure pleasure. One finger slipped inside of her while another found her hidden nub.

She bucked against him, wanting him to remove his hand so she could slide onto him. But she was spiraling now, the climax hitting hard and fast.

"Now, Vanessa," he said. He guided her hips, and she lowered herself onto him. He filled her, so full in this position, as if for the first time she could take in all of him.

His eyes latched on to hers. She moved, tentatively at first, but then she found her rhythm. Over and over again she rocked onto him, keeping her balance by pressing her hands onto his firm chest.

His hand found her again, slid over her sex as she rode him. He was so deep, so full, and with her commanding the pace, she knew when to increase her speed and intensify the force. Deeper and harder she rode him until the world fractured. She shook with her release, but never stopped moving.

And then his hit. He grabbed onto her hips, rocking her

as a guttural groan escaped from his throat. All the while, he never looked away from her, never closed his eyes.

"Vanessa," he whispered.

The intimacy was so great in that moment that she had to look away for fear he would see into her very soul.

Chapter Twenty-one

The sound of the train chugging along the tracks provided a rhythmic backdrop. They lay quietly in their sleeper car, Vanessa snug against Graeme's side, his hand tracing lazily over her naked back. She felt good pressed against him, not only in a lustful way, but somehow she fit precisely in that spot next to him, as if it had been carved specifically for her.

She fascinated him, his wife. She was smart, as smart as any man he'd ever known, and her wit was sharp and clever. He'd never known her to be overly temperamental. Most of the women he'd known were prone to fits of emotion, whether of enthusiasm or sadness; most women lived life by their heart. But not Vanessa, at least not outwardly.

Her sister had betrayed her, yet he'd never seen her shed a single tear over the fact, nor had she ever spoken an ill word about the woman.

"Vanessa," he said softly in case she slept. But he was curious.

"Mmm-hmmm," she murmured.

"Tell me about Jeremy. What happened?" he asked.

She tilted her head and looked up at him, but made no move to leave her spot. "I told you everything. We were engaged, and two days before our wedding, I found him with my younger sister. That's pretty much the entire story."

"You must be angry," he said.

"Of course." She splayed her hand on his chest, her palm flattening against his skin. "Initially I was, but that seems so long ago now, and I can see that Jeremy and I would not have made a good match."

He thought to ask how she thought of their match, but it mattered not. They were husband and wife, end of discussion. There would be no going back. No running away. Not for either of them. "But what of your sister? Are you not furious with her betrayal?"

"I won't lie and say it did not hurt me. But she cannot help who she is any more than I can help who I am," Vanessa said plainly, as if that bit of rubbish explained everything, excused all behavior.

"She betrayed you," Graeme repeated.

"Yes, she did. And it was selfish and cruel. But my family hasn't ever known precisely what to do with me. I've never fit in with any of them. My father, who was also a scientist, thought me a fool and told me so regularly. He didn't see a place for women in the field. He thought us weak-minded and silly. He thought I was naïve to believe I could follow in his path.

"My mother, bless her soul," she continued, "tried her best to turn me into the perfect daughter. She managed just fine with her other two girls, but with me, nothing worked. I couldn't hold my tongue in social settings. I wasn't interested in learning to dance or how to plan a dinner party or run a household. I wanted to read, or go outside and explore."

"Seems to me your father would have appreciated your nature, been able to relate better to it than to that of a girl who preferred frilly dresses and balls," Graeme said.

"I thought that too for a long while, and tried my damnedest to make him see it, but my efforts were in vain," she said with a sad little laugh. She absently toyed with the hair on his chest.

Graeme knew all too well what it was like to try to have a relationship with a father who hadn't given a damn. His own father had been cruel—not so much physically abusive, but he'd given Graeme tongue-lashings more times than Graeme could count.

"In any case, my mother eventually gave up and left me to my own devices. When I started corresponding with Jeremy through a scientific journal, I had no romantic notions about him. As I saw it, he was merely another scientist, and we shared similar views on many subjects. At least initially. After a month of letters between us, he came to London for a symposium. We met for tea and our professional camaraderie continued."

Graeme ran his fingers through her soft hair.

"One day we happened on the discussion of romantic love and realized rather quickly that we both shared the same view of the emotion. One thing led to another, and before I knew it, we'd arranged an engagement, both believing we'd have the perfect union, one built on professional respect. We'd never be bothered or distracted by the frivolous emotions that seemed to consume so many around us."

It was a logical, though naïve, conclusion, but he would

not tell her that. While he wasn't certain that romantic love was a lasting emotion, he knew it existed and had seen two of his friends fall into it. He also knew that, however foolishly, his mother had truly loved his father at one time.

Vanessa chuckled, though the sound was completely void of mirth. "Who could blame the fellow when he met Violet? My sisters are both so beautiful. Victoria is already married with two children, so that left me and Violet. She's barely nineteen, though, and while she's already been a huge success with the men in London, she hadn't garnered any proposals. We all knew it was only a matter of time. She's truly lovely."

"You're lovely," he said.

This time she did laugh, an honest, humor-filled giggle.

He placed one finger beneath her chin and tilted her face to look at him. "I'm serious. You're beautiful. The most beautiful woman I've ever seen."

She opened her mouth to argue, but closed it and smiled. "Thank you."

"Are you sorry?" he asked.

"About what?"

"Not marrying Jeremy?"

"Heavens no. You are much preferable." She gave him a devious grin. "As distracting as I find the lovemaking, I suspect I would never have experienced it in the same way with him." Then she frowned. "No, I'm certain about that. Jeremy was . . ." She tilted her head, searching for the right description, "pale."

Graeme laughed, a hearty, belly-filled laugh. "You are most entertaining, Duchess."

"Well, I'm glad you think so." But he could tell she'd left something unsaid. He wondered if it was that she'd never before belonged anywhere. Well, she belonged now, right here next to him. And in caves when she followed him against his instructions.

He swallowed hard as the realization slammed into him. Damnation if he hadn't fallen for his own wife.

Vanessa wondered if she'd said too much. Perhaps Graeme thought her a fool, too. He hadn't said anything in a long while. Instead they'd lain there in silence, his hand still drawing lazy circles on her back.

It had felt good to say all of that aloud, to express the pain that she'd harbored for so long. She no longer cared if she hadn't impressed her father; he'd been dead for nearly five years. Or perhaps the longing still remained, but she knew how futile it was, considering he was gone. Futile for other reasons, too, she acknowledged, but that little girl in her still popped up every now and again. "Look what I did, Papa!" But she managed to keep those thoughts squelched.

To force her mind in other directions, she pulled herself tighter into Graeme's side. "Tell me about your family," she said, "about growing up in both England and Scotland. That had to have been amazing."

He paused for so long before answering that she feared he might have fallen asleep. "Amazing is not how I would describe it," he said, his tone edged with anger. Again he was silent for a moment before he continued. "I lived exclusively in Scotland with my mother until I was nearly thirteen."

"And then you moved to London? Why?" she asked.

"My father moved me there. I suppose he finally recognized that I was his heir, and that no amount of time would change that. So he forced me to live in London with him so that I could learn the ways of a gentleman and 'lose that awful stench of peat' that clung to me, as he put it."

"But your mother and Dougal chose to stay behind?" she asked.

"Dougal had not been born yet. I suppose that was when he was conceived, when my father traveled up to retrieve me." His laugh was so cold that it spread a chill over her arms. "I don't know why I never noticed that before."

"But you came here to visit?" she asked.

"Yes, he would allow me to return for a couple of months during the summer."

Vanessa leaned upon an elbow to face him. "You don't sound very fond of your father."

"My father was a son of a bitch who never cared for anyone in his life but himself." His jaw clenched, but he said nothing else.

"But your mother loved him, so he couldn't have been all bad," she argued.

"My mother was young when they met, foolish. She saw the error of her ways soon enough. Divorce, though, was out of the question, so she fled to Scotland and remained there away from her husband."

Vanessa frowned. She'd had an extensive conversation with Moira the day she gave her the wedding ring. "That's not the way she tells the story."

"What are you talking about?"

"Your mother told me all about their courtship and their tumultuous relationship thereafter. She has many regrets, but one thing she does not regret is loving your father," Vanessa said.

"Then she is still a fool," Graeme said softly.

"Perhaps you simply misunderstood their relationship," Vanessa offered.

"What are you trying to tell me, Vanessa?"

"Simply that your father never deserted your mother. He wanted her to live with him in England. But she refused. Said she got embarrassed at a silly party and packed you up and left for Scotland. He came up here to get both of you back, but she refused, felt she didn't fit in his world. She wanted to reconcile, wanted to return to England, but never felt she could.

"Then when he came to get you, it was too late. She never got the chance to apologize in person, but she did send him a letter before he died."

"That doesn't explain why he was a bastard to me," Graeme said.

"No, it doesn't. But being hurt can make you do terrible things." Didn't all of this prove precisely how damaging love could be? She wanted to be certain she protected herself from such hurt. "Right now we have a lovely marriage, full of passion and adventure. But were we to add emotion to the mix, everything might fall apart."

Abruptly Graeme stood from the bed. "I need some air." He pulled on the clothes that he had earlier discarded on the floor. "Get some sleep, Vanessa. We still have a few hours left of the trip."

None of what she'd told him changed anything. His father had still been a bastard. But why had his mother never said anything to him? He made his way to the dining car and found an empty table. He ordered brandy, then looked out the window. Darkness was thick, and he saw nothing but the occasional outline of a tree as the train moved south.

The server brought him a decanter of brandy and a glass, and Graeme had poured and downed one before the man could even depart the train car. He was pouring his second when something, or rather someone, caught his attention. Three tables ahead sat someone with very familiar hair. He grabbed his glass and made his way up to the table.

"Dougal, what the devil are you doing here?" he demanded.

"I made a mistake, Graeme." The boy looked out the window, his young features lined with anguish.

Graeme sat opposite him. He didn't ask questions. He just sat and waited. He poured a measure of the liquor into Dougal's glass.

The boy readily accepted the drink and took a hearty gulp, so much so that it made his eyes water. "I've been an utter fool. Just like you said. Trusted the wrong damn people." He took another sip, then leveled his gaze on his brother. "I'm sorry for what I did to Vanessa." He dropped his head onto his hand, his fingers forking through his shaggy mane. "I don't even know how to explain it," Dougal said, his voice heavy with anguish. "The Raven confused me, threatened my family. But when I think about how I could have killed Vanessa, it makes me sick."

Graeme nodded. This was the apology he'd been waiting for. Not so much for himself, but for his brother to finally realize what he'd done, what he *could* have done. Pride swelled in Graeme knowing that his brother was man enough to admit he'd made a mistake.

"You were right about The Raven. He's evil, a terrible man." He shook his head. "But you don't know the worst of it. He's been blackmailing me, threatening to tell you everything. He said you'd have me executed for trying to hurt Vanessa. He said something terrible will happen to Mother." His eyes widened. "I didn't know what to do."

"The Raven is a powerful man, and he's quite skilled at manipulating people. It doesn't surprise me that he'd try to go after someone in my family," Graeme said. "He went after Niall too. He's a dangerous man, and once he's focused on you, it's hard to break free of him."

"I cannot believe Niall is dead," Dougal said.

"How do you know that?" Graeme asked.

"I was there. I saw everything. How you tried to save him, and I heard how The Raven has taken Niall's family." He pounded his fist on the table. "I can't believe what a fool I was."

"It was a difficult lesson to learn," Graeme said.

"Graeme, can I ask you a question?"

Graeme inclined his head.

"Why have you never allowed me to attend school in England? The way you were educated?" Dougal asked.

"It wasn't my choice. I tried to convince Mother that it was a good idea. In case something happened to me, you'd be prepared to take the title. But she wouldn't agree. She didn't want you to have anything to do with England," Graeme said.

"So you would have sent me?" Dougal asked.

Graeme nodded. "I had a spot secured in your name." Graeme frowned. "Is that why you're here now, on the train? You want to go to school?"

"No, I want to help. Come to London and help you and Vanessa catch The Raven and rescue Niall's family." He pounded his fist on the table again. "Anything. I've destroyed so much."

"First of all, you were a complete arse. I'll give you

that. But you haven't destroyed anything. We'll catch him, and we'll save Niall's family," Graeme said.

"But you don't know the worst of it, Graeme," Dougal said.

"What?"

"I gave him the Stone of Destiny."

Chapter Twenty-two

Early the following morning, Graeme paced the length of the meeting room at Solomon's. Only Jenkins and Fielding were currently there. "I promised Niall I would save them," Graeme said. They'd called a special meeting upon Graeme and Fielding's return from Scotland. At the moment, Vanessa and Dougal were tucked safely away at his townhome.

Jenkins nodded gravely. "His family and their safety is a priority. He was one of us."

"Let me go," Fielding said, coming to his feet. "I know The Raven better than anyone here. I can find his hiding place. I'll find them and bring them out safely." He met Graeme's eyes, and his glance spoke of friendship and trust. "You helped me once. Let me help you this time."

Graeme nodded. "Thank you. Now I can go and find the other stones to the Kingmaker."

"Don't forget that he cannot put the Kingmaker together without that third stone. If you don't find him first, he'll be in touch with you," Fielding said.

"Of that you can be certain," Jenkins said.

"Manipulative bastard," Graeme said, then paused and glanced at Fielding.

He held up his hand. "Relation or not, you speak the truth about that man. There is no love lost between us."

There was a moment of silence before Jenkins spoke up. "Niall was a good man—and I wish he had come to us with this matter so that we could have assisted him. I am to blame, too," Jenkins said. "Instead of sending you to spy after him," he said to Graeme, "I should have called him here and inquired about his well-being." He placed a wrinkled hand on Fielding's shoulder. "Go and find his family. The club will see that they are protected and cared for from now on."

With that, Fielding slipped out of the room.

"I'll send messages to Nick and Max, and I have no doubt that they will rush to your assistance," Jenkins said.

"Have them meet me outside of The Raven's estate in thirty minutes," Graeme said. He turned to go, then paused. "Don't blame yourself about Niall. I expected the worst; I doubted him as well." Graeme shook his head. "I could have forced him to tell me, but I didn't. But we will not fail him now."

Vanessa had waited long enough. It was time to face her family, although she really had only come here, to her family's London townhome, to dig through her father's books. If she managed to do so without alerting her family to her presence, all the better.

More than likely she would have to summon Jeremy to locate the information she needed. In his telegram, it had certainly sounded as if he'd found something useful. Was it so wrong to hope that he'd conveniently left it waiting for her in her father's study?

Her mother was alert and roaming the house, instructing the servants, sounding very much as if they were preparing for a party. *Splendid.*

Vanessa rounded the last corner that led to her father's study and found no one else about. Quickly, she slipped through the open door and silently closed it behind her. She started with the books he kept behind his desk in the special case, as this was where she'd instructed Violet to look. If Jeremy had, in fact, found something useful, then chances were it was here.

"Vanessa? Darling, is that you?" her mother said from behind her.

Vanessa whirled around to face the older woman, who stood with her hand clasping the soft yellow material of her bodice.

"Hello, Mama," Vanessa said.

Her mother's eyes rounded, her eyebrows lifting slightly. "That is all you can say to me?" She stepped forward. "Do you know how I have worried for you?"

"I am sorry about leaving the way I did. But I left behind a note, and I believe you received another one while I was gone," Vanessa said. She made no move to walk to her mother, although the urge to fall into her arms weighed heavily.

Her mother straightened. "The one announcing your marriage." She nodded, her features pensive. "To a duke, nonetheless. Well done, my dear." But Vanessa found nothing in her mother's tone that even hinted at pride. Evidently, though Vanessa had, in fact, married quite well, even that was not good enough for the woman.

"Mother, I really do not have time to discuss this right

now." She motioned behind her. "I'm looking for something in Father's books. It's quite important."

"Yes, it is always important," her mother said and turned to leave. Something in her tone gave Vanessa pause. It was not annoyance or impatience, but rather sadness.

Vanessa exhaled slowly. "Wait, Mama."

"If you think I can help you with your little quest, then I'm sorry to disappoint you. But then, I never did know what to do with you." She gave Vanessa a weak smile.

"I beg your pardon?" Vanessa asked. "I'm not certain what you mean."

"You've always been so much your father's child," her mother rolled her eyes heavenward, "even though that stubborn fool never realized it."

Vanessa balked, unable to believe her mother's harsh words. The woman had never even looked askew at Vanessa's father, let alone spoke of him in such a manner. Out of nowhere, a giggle formed, and Vanessa clapped her hand over her mouth.

"Yes, I know, I never said anything of the sort while he was alive, but he was a mean man." She held up her hand in protest. "Of course that's not the similarity the two of you shared. He wasn't always mean; he'd once been charming and handsome and so smart." She pressed her hand to her chest. "Lord, that man could talk of such things I'd never even heard of."

"But you never knew what to do with *me*?" Vanessa repeated.

"I simply didn't know how to relate to you. It was easy with the other girls—buy them a ribbon or a new dress and they were happy. But you"—she shook her head with a smile—"you didn't have a need for any of that nonsense.

You wanted books and tools, and it infuriated your father and confounded me. Then after he was gone, I didn't know how to reach you. I had nothing to offer you. I couldn't teach you anything, and you," her words faltered, and her eyes filled with tears, "you didn't appear to need me."

Years of misunderstanding melted, and Vanessa quickly closed the distance between them. She embraced her mother, and the older woman's arms wound tightly around her. They didn't have to see eye-to-eye on everything to have a relationship. The realization that her mother did actually love her nearly overwhelmed Vanessa.

It was in that embrace that Jeremy and Violet discovered them.

"Vanessa?" Violet said.

Vanessa had thought about this encounter several times over the last few weeks, and every time, she had expected to feel the same way she had when she'd found them in their heated embrace. She'd expected to feel the stab of betrayal and the wash of humiliation. She'd thought her stomach would stir with nausea and that words would fail her. She'd expected to want to run out of the room, but never once did she imagine she'd be in this moment and feel nothing. No anger, no hurt, no betrayal. Vanessa released her mother and turned to face her sister.

"Are you home for good?" Violet asked.

"I don't live here anymore," Vanessa said.

"No, of course not," Violet said. She smiled brightly. "I meant London."

"My husband has many duties here, so I suppose we will reside here most of the time," Vanessa said. *Her husband*. The words had rolled off her tongue so effortlessly, as if he'd always been a part of her life.

"Hello, Vanessa," Jeremy said. He stood next to Violet,

looking very much the same as he had the first time Vanessa had met him. His pale blond hair was tousled in soft curls, making him look more like a romantic poet than a scientist, and his brown eyes were unwavering as they met her face. He swallowed hard and nodded politely.

He was nervous, Vanessa realized, worried about whether or not she would create a ruckus. But facing him now, she felt no pang of jealousy toward her sister. Jeremy was a fine man, but he paled in comparison to Graeme.

"I believe you have something to tell me," Vanessa said to him.

His face blanched, and he stammered several incomprehensible syllables.

"About my father's book, the letter I sent," Vanessa clarified. Although it was somewhat gratifying to see him stumble over an explanation of his indiscretion, she did not have time to enjoy it. "I am in a bit of a hurry."

"Yes, yes, of course," he said, coming forward.

"Vanessa, you and your husband must agree to come to dinner. I would love to meet the man who captured your heart," her mother said.

Vanessa smiled and nodded, but found no words. *Captured her heart?* The thought didn't seem so ludicrous to her as she'd once imagined. One more squeeze of her hand, and then her mother left the room.

"The images you drew in your letter looked so familiar, I knew I'd seen them somewhere," Violet said. "And I shared them with Jeremy and we started looking through Father's books."

"The code is really quite brilliant," Jeremy said. He looked up with a wide grin, and it struck Vanessa that she'd never seen him smile with such ease. In the past it had always been tight slips of a smile, seemingly forced into place to appear polite. "I'm assuming you brought the remainder of it with you?"

"We've been most eager to unravel the mystery," Violet said.

They were an unlikely pair—her rambunctious sister and the buttoned-up American—yet together they were different. Gone was the attention-loving Violet whose behavior bordered on inappropriate, and in her place was a lovely woman whose eyes lit with intelligence and curiosity. And Jeremy seemed far more friendly, less reserved.

"I did bring the entire inscription," Vanessa said. She opened the book to the page in question and revealed the code. Here in her father's study, the hand-drawn symbols looked more than familiar. Now she knew why she'd felt that way the first time she'd seen the decoder.

Violet looked at Jeremy and asked, "Is the book still in the parlor?"

"Indeed it is. I'll fetch it at once." With that, Jeremy dashed out of the room, leaving the two sisters alone.

A moment of awkward silence passed before Violet stepped forward. "Vanessa, I am sorry for what I did," she said.

"And you should be," Vanessa said, then paused. "But it is hard for me to be angry, because if you had not betrayed me in such a manner, I would not have left. And then I wouldn't have met—" Her mind stumbled over how to describe Graeme. The possible labels tripped through her mind. *Graeme. My husband. My own love.*

"Your duke," Violet supplied.

"Yes," Vanessa hastily agreed. That was the simplest description. Yet it was the least revealing.

Violet took another step forward, her hand outstretched as if reaching for Vanessa. "And do you love him?" she asked, sounding slightly breathless. "Do you love him as I love Jeremy?"

The question was fueled by more than mere curiosity. Violet's gaze was lit with regret, but with hope as well. She wanted reassurances, and Vanessa was surprised to find herself willing to give them. Not simply for Violet's sake, but because she had only just realized it herself, and she wanted to admit it, to say it aloud.

"I do love him," she said simply. Then she swallowed back the emotion threatening to choke her. Before she could say anything else, Jeremy hurried back into the room, carrying a large book.

"It's Father's Bible," she said, more to herself than anyone else in the room.

"Exactly," Jeremy said as he placed the large leather-bound volume on the desk.

Jeremy opened the book, and there on the front page, surrounding the title, were small hand-drawn illustrations.

"I loved this book as a girl and always wanted to look at the pictures, but Father rarely allowed me the chance," Violet said.

"I did a bit of research, and it would seem there are less than a hundred of these copies made," Jeremy said. "It would appear to be quite the treasure."

"We deduced that this was a code," Violet said. "If we figure out the corresponding page, then the picture will give us the word on that page."

"But we don't know where to start," Jeremy said.

Vanessa never looked up at them; she kept her gaze on the illustrated Bible. "Kings," she said. "First and Second Kings." She flipped the pages until she found what she sought. "So if we start here," she said, then glanced back at *The Magi's Book of Wisdom*, "using this symbol"—she pointed to the illustration at the top of the page, then found its match shadowed behind one word—"we get the word 'beware.'"

She continued in such a fashion, moving from one book to the other and flipping pages within her father's Bible until she had an entire message scrawled upon a piece of parchment.

Beware any who possess the stones of the Kingmaker, for only the most worthy may hold such a treasure.

The damned code wouldn't have mattered to Graeme's original quest to find the Stone of Destiny, but it could certainly matter now. He was trying to retrieve all the stones in an effort to protect the crown from The Raven.

Vanessa's entire body went alert and rigid with fear. "Oh no, Graeme."

The Raven stood at his study window watching the boy approach. What a fool to follow him here all the way from Scotland. What did he think to accomplish? He could easily send the guards after the boy or even release his hounds. The Raven laughed at his own jest. In the end, he made no move to do anything. This would no doubt be entertaining, whatever the boy's purpose.

"Quite a long journey for a boy your age," The Raven said as Dougal entered his study.

"I am old enough to travel on my own," Dougal bit out. Then he took a deep breath, and his features softened. "I came to help you."

"Help me?" The Raven asked, amused. He relaxed into the large thronelike chair behind his massive mahogany desk and smiled at the boy. "What would give you the impression that I require assistance from anyone, let alone you?" Perhaps the boy could be of use, but it seemed unlikely that he'd come all this way simply for that. He wanted something.

He motioned for Dougal to sit in one of the chairs opposite him. The boy's eyes wandered over his surroundings, and The Raven allowed him to do so. Allowed him to see what kinds of riches could be his if he made the right choices in life. The boy's eyes lit on the heavily jeweled crown that sat on the shelf to the left of his desk.

"Ah yes, you have exquisite taste. That I found in Egypt. It is rumored to have belonged to Cleopatra herself," The Raven said. He clasped his hands together on his desk. "But you did not come here to see my antiquities collection. I believe you were going to tell me how helpful you could be."

Dougal sat straighter on the edge of the leather chair. "I can tell you that my brother has returned to London," he said. "He's already looking for you."

"Something I already knew. I expected him to follow me. Wanted him to," The Raven said. "That had been part of my plan from the beginning." Of course, that wasn't precisely true. He'd been alive long enough to know that plans had to be fluid or else you risked getting caught or losing sight of your goal.

"And he is with his club right now discussing you," Dougal said. "They will, no doubt, come for you."

"Ah yes, Solomon's. Typical. They can't ever do anything on their own. I do wonder if Fielding is there." The Raven felt the contempt rising inside him. He couldn't afford to think about that. He had a master plan in the works. He shook his head. His dealings with Fielding were water under the proverbial bridge. Or rather water beneath the Tower of London, where they'd had their last confrontation. "I'm still missing the point of how it is you're supposed to assist me."

"I can help you get the third stone," Dougal said.

The Raven paused, not wanting to reveal too much. He leaned forward, bracing his elbows on his desk. "He has it? The Loch Ness Treasure? You're certain?"

Dougal nodded. "Niall found it."

"And Niall?" he asked, keeping his tone neutral. "What of him?"

"My cousin is dead," Dougal said, never blinking an eye. "Died in an unfortunate explosion set by his own hand."

Perhaps the boy was telling the truth and was here to assist him. Still he doubted that. Perhaps instead the boy was simply a better liar than he'd first given him credit for. "Pity," The Raven said.

"I wouldn't be so foolish." Dougal crossed his arms over his chest.

And he'd been doing so well. A pity, the boy could have been a true ally. "Never underestimate your own stupidity, boy." The Raven came to his feet, stepped around the desk, then leaned casually against it. "Or mine."

"What is that supposed to mean?" Dougal asked. His arms unfolded, fists clenched at his sides.

"It means I know why you're here. Why you're truly here." He patted Dougal on the shoulder. "I will give you credit for trying to convince me. You definitely have some skills in that area, but your emotions give you away."

"I don't know what you're talking about," Dougal said with feigned ignorance.

"Yes, of course you do. Stand up." He slammed his hand down hard onto Dougal's shoulder. The boy winced, but came to his feet nonetheless. "And I know you're not alone. Shall we go and find your counterpart?" The Raven asked.

Dougal shook his head. "I don't know what you're talking about. I came here alone."

That could have been the truth. "Perhaps, but you didn't arrive alone. Follow me." And in case the boy had thoughts about disagreeing, The Raven withdrew a pistol from the hidden compartment on the bookshelf. "Come along."

Vanessa crept in quietly after Dougal, sneaking in the front door and closing it soundlessly behind her. She waited two heartbeats before moving forward. So far no one had come running, so perhaps she had gone undetected. Dougal hadn't appeared to notice.

She knew the boy had come to help find Niall's family. She'd overheard him speaking with Graeme outside their sleeping car on the train. It had been clear that Dougal was racked with guilt and desperately trying to find a way to make amends. His sincerity had touched her. When she'd arrived back at Graeme's townhome to find her husband gone and her young brother-in-law sneaking out, she had decided to follow him. She simply couldn't allow him to walk into the dragon's lair unaccompanied.

Surely Niall's wife and son were here, hidden somewhere in a locked chamber. A dungeon, perhaps. This house certainly looked as if it boasted a dungeon.

She moved through the hall and up the stairs to her right. She'd check every room on every floor if she had to. She passed by one room as a maid solemnly made the bed, flipping the linens into the air and back onto the mattress. Vanessa spied a feather duster and quickly grabbed it, then sneaked back out of the room. Perhaps if she were caught, they would believe her if she said she was a new maid only just hired and hadn't yet received her livery.

She checked three more rooms in this wing, all empty bedrooms. The other wing was darker, and, if it was possible, colder. She moved in that direction and cautiously opened the first door. This was clearly The Raven's personal chamber, so she slipped inside and closed the door behind her.

The room was ornately decorated, with heavy carved furniture and red velvet and brocade fabrics dripping off every surface. It was easy to see that The Raven enjoyed his wealth. Not surprising, considering what she'd been told of his character. To her, the room seemed oppressive rather than opulent.

Perhaps there was a hidden chamber within this room where she would find Niall's family.

"Penny," she called, trying to speak in no more than a whisper. No one responded. She tried again. Again nothing.

And then Vanessa eyed the dressing closet. When she was a girl, her father had used his own to hide things from the family. Her mother hadn't wanted him to bring his "filthy tools" in the house, so he'd kept them in compartments in the dressing closet, along with some treasures he'd found. Vanessa remembered going in there and sitting amongst his coats and rifling through his mud-caked tools. Perhaps The Raven had similar compartments.

She stepped into the dressing closet. Covering the four walls were a variety of garments: great coats, jackets, shirts, trousers, all sorts of gentlemanly clothes. She swept one side away to reveal the wall behind. She tapped, listening for a hollow sound, but there was nothing. She tried with the next, sweeping the trousers to the left to reveal the wall. She tapped, then paused, then tapped again. It was hollow. Barely detectable, but hollow nonetheless.

Vanessa looked around for some sort of lever that would open the hidden panel, but found nothing that appeared suspicious. She pounded on the wall in frustration and something clicked, then the panel slid aside. However, instead of an entrance to another room, as she'd expected, a small compartment was revealed. Inside she found a simple wooden box.

She reached in and pulled it out, then slowly, cautiously, she opened it. Inside sat two sizable stones, one blue, and the red one that she and Graeme had discovered in MacBeth's crown. A ruby and a sapphire, each the size of her fist, and very similar to the emerald they'd retrieved from Niall. The Raven now had three of the four stones required for the Kingmaker.

"I thought we already tried to kill you," a male voice said from behind her.

"You did try to kill me," Vanessa said as calmly as she could manage. She turned to face The Raven and Dougal. The former held a pistol. "But you missed," she said sweetly.

"That's what happens when you send a boy to do a man's work. I won't make that mistake again," The Raven said.

She was pinned in the dressing closet, and The Raven stood in the doorway, blocking her exit. "So you intend to kill us, then?" Vanessa asked. Her only strategy would be to stall him until Graeme might come and rescue them, because she knew he'd come to confront The Raven eventually. She was certainly not used to being the damsel in distress, but when one managed to get oneself in such a situation, it helped to have a large and strong husband.

"Of course," The Raven said.

"You know that if you harm one hair on either of our heads, Graeme will never give you the treasure you seek. The Kingmaker will never be completed," Vanessa challenged.

The Raven eyed her carefully. If she wasn't mistaken, she thought she might have seen appreciation cross his expression.

"If all you seek are the necessary stones for the Kingmaker, keep us safe, and you can barter our lives for the missing stone," Vanessa continued.

The Raven laughed, a chilling chortle that almost made Vanessa shiver. "You are a clever one, I'll give you that. I fully intend to kill both of you, but as it so happens, I'm late for a rather important engagement. So we must be leaving."

He nodded to her hands, where she still gripped the box with the jewels. "Thank you for retrieving my stones for me. We'll need those where we're going. Carry them gently." He met her gaze, and the complete absence of kindness caused her to shiver. "Drop or damage them, and I'll kill the boy. Understand?"

Graeme would never forgive her if she allowed anything to happen to his brother. She nodded. Briefly she met Dougal's gaze and offered him a smile.

"Now move." The Raven pointed the gun at her and jerked it forward.

She followed his instructions and stepped out of the closet with the box. Together, she and Dougal walked down to the front door. Before she stepped outside, though, she pretended to stumble. She didn't want to appear to have damaged the stones, but she needed a brief reprieve.

"Clumsy fool," The Raven muttered. "Best be careful or the boy dies. Don't test me on this. If I'm not mistaken, you've seen where my talents lie. Fitch and Sam put up excellent fights, but in the end, they were no match for me. Do you honestly think a puny female like you would even have a chance?"

While bending over, Vanessa removed the fossil from her bag and strategically placed it where Graeme would not miss it. If he came here to find The Raven, he'd know the man had her. Hopefully it would be enough to save her and Dougal from whatever horrible death awaited them.

"Hurry," The Raven barked. "I don't have much time."

"Why the rush? Where are we going?" Vanessa asked as she climbed into the waiting carriage.

"Westminster," The Raven said.

"Whatever for?" Vanessa asked.

"There is a funeral today. A highly ranked military leader," The Raven said. He kept the pistol aimed at both of them.

Vanessa wondered momentarily if she and Dougal together could overtake the man. He wasn't extraordinarily large, although she could certainly tell he was athletic. But then she remembered what he'd said about Mr. Fitch. Mr. Fitch had been a very large and strong man, yet he'd been taken down by The Raven's deadly skills. And hadn't Graeme warned her of him?

"And you wish to pay your respects?" Dougal asked, finally speaking up. His brow furrowed in his confusion.

"High-ranking military officer," Vanessa repeated, then she brought her gaze up to The Raven's. "Her Majesty will be in attendance," she said.

"Fancy that," The Raven said.

"You intend to kill the queen?" Dougal asked.

"If I must." Then The Raven smiled. "And I truly must."

Chapter Twenty-three

———※※◦※※———

Vanessa stepped down from the carriage, The Raven's pistol pressed firmly into her back. Dougal already stood on the street. They were a block away from Big Ben.

"Are we to walk all the way to Westminster from here?" she asked. "Why not take the carriage directly there?"

"You see, if you would have killed her when you had the chance, she wouldn't be here now to annoy me," The Raven said to Dougal. "Walk straight to that alleyway." He motioned to their left.

Dougal followed the man's instructions.

Vanessa scanned the street for anyone who might be of assistance, but found no one within earshot. There were a handful of people down the street, but they were too far away. With The Raven's gun firmly lodged between her shoulder blades, she followed Dougal down the alley.

They were heading away from the Thames, but walking alongside Big Ben. Perhaps The Raven expected the funeral to be so heavily populated that he wanted to sneak them in a back door. They kept moving until suddenly The Raven stopped.

"This is it," he said. There was, in fact, a door directly to their left, but instead of opening it, The Raven nudged one of the large stones that made up the street. "Dougal, get down here and move this," he demanded. He eyed both ends of the alley, then stood with his great coat open to block any view of Dougal's activity.

The boy had gotten to his knees and dug his fingers beneath the edge of the stone. It shifted slightly.

"You're going to need to use more force than that," The Raven said. "Prove yourself useful, boy. A strapping young lad like you should be able to do something useful. God knows your cunning intellect isn't going to win you any accolades."

Dougal eyed The Raven, and for a moment Vanessa expected the boy would charge, but he evidently thought better of it. It was a smart choice, Vanessa knew. The Raven might have no qualms about shooting them both here on the street.

With renewed effort, Dougal lifted the stone. Below was an opening that went deep beneath the street. Vanessa could make out the faint outline of stairs.

"Down," The Raven said.

She took a deep breath and did as he instructed. Dougal followed directly behind her. Her initial instinct was to run, run anywhere, to try and get away from him. But she knew that she couldn't leave Dougal to fend for himself. The Raven would kill him, and then Graeme would never forgive her. In addition, she had no idea where she was, and running aimlessly in the dark would not save anyone. She needed to be smart, bide her time, and select the precise moment to escape.

At first, Vanessa expected the tunnel to be part of an abandoned or unfinished section of the underground railway. But she saw no tracks. Once The Raven descended the stairs, he pulled the stone above them back into place, shrouding them in darkness. A match was struck, the flame flickering to life, and The Raven lit a candle.

He retrieved two lanterns from behind the stairs and lit those as well, handing one to each of them. Now, with light, Vanessa could see this was nothing like the underground, where the tunnels were nicely sculpted. This area was crude, carved out probably hundreds of years ago.

Cold and damp, the tunnel immediately reminded her of the caves where she and Graeme had spent so much time in Loch Ness. She hoped that she hadn't seen him for the last time. The thought of never again seeing her husband, never feeling his lips brush hers or his hand stroke her hair, nearly stole her breath. It was as if someone had reached in and squeezed her heart. No, she steeled herself against such thoughts. She would get out of this alive, and she'd save Dougal while she was at it.

She knew in that moment she'd trade everything to be back in Graeme's arms. Yes, she enjoyed her research, but if given the choice, she'd choose him. Because damn it all if she hadn't fallen in love with her husband. Tears pricked her eyes as the realization flooded her. She had to escape because she had to tell him.

"This leads to Westminster?" she asked. When The Raven didn't answer, she went on. "And this is how you got in and stole the counterfeit Stone of Destiny."

"Precisely. You are a clever girl, aren't you?" he said drolly.

Water from the rains yesterday must have leaked below and created a tiny stream flowing inside the tunnel. Her slippers were soaked before they'd walked through the second carved archway.

The three of them walked in silence for several moments, turning twice. Vanessa tried to memorize the route, but the tunnel had several turn-offs, and she wasn't certain whether she'd be able to remember the proper directions. She doubted if she and Dougal could escape, run back the way they'd come, and get to the street before The Raven could reach them. They'd have to disable him in some capacity.

As they walked, Vanessa searched for some sort of weapon—a large rock to hit him on the head or a sharp stick to jab him with. Anything that could be of use. Only rats and the small trail of water occupied the space with them. The foul smell of human waste assaulted her senses, and she winced. The sooner they were out of this damned tunnel, the better. Once they were in Westminster, they could escape or signal for help.

Finally they came to another staircase, and again The Raven sent Dougal first. "Shift that statue of the angel, and it will open the secret chamber," The Raven said. "Make any foolish moves and I'll kill her. I suspect you're like your brother and share his ridiculous propensity for rescuing hapless females, which means you won't raise a hand against me as long as she's here. But in case that isn't enough motivation, remember that if you try any foolish heroics, not only will you and the girl die, but when I find your brother, I'll kill him too."

Dougal nodded, then did as instructed. Once he'd shoved the stone out of the way, he climbed up the staircase and disappeared above them.

Vanessa followed Dougal up, and The Raven followed close behind. Once they were all in the small chamber, he shifted the statue back into place.

"We're in Westminster," Vanessa said, looking up. She knew the stonework of the abbey, having been here on many occasions, although she'd never seen this particular room. It looked to be a room where the choir might gather.

He led them through several other rooms until at last they stopped in one. He closed the door behind them. Vanessa watched The Raven move and stand near a door on the opposite wall. He leaned close to listen.

"Her Majesty will be right on the other side of this door," he said, "once the service concludes. Set the jewels over there." He motioned to a table.

Vanessa did as instructed and placed the gems down next to the Stone of Destiny. Dougal huddled close behind Vanessa, right on her heels like a beaten puppy seeking comfort. He looked dazed, his gaze unfocused. His hands had started to tremble. He had never seemed more like a child. Clearly he was very afraid, and if he didn't get his fear under control, it just might get them both killed.

Vanessa turned to him and grasped both of his hands in her own, giving him something solid to focus on. "Dougal, it'll be all right. I promise."

Finally his gaze met hers for an instant before darting to The Raven, who'd extracted a fiendish-looking knife and was scraping the pad of his thumb against it as if testing the blade.

Dougal shook his head. "No. It won't be fine. He's going to murder the queen, and I've helped him do it. I've helped kill the queen. And I shot you. I can't believe I shot you."

"Nonsense, you have not helped kill the queen," she said sternly, keeping her eyes on Dougal, willing her strength to him. "You are just a boy. You are not responsible for any of this. Besides, he is merely one man and not all powerful. He cannot possibly know where the queen is at any given moment. He may know that she's in Westminster Abbey today for the funeral. He may hope that her guards lead her in this direction. But he has no way of knowing where she is. She's just as likely to be on the other side of the building smelling roses in the garden. And as for me, I'm healthier than ever, and I know you didn't mean it."

Finally, Dougal nodded his understanding. But hers was a brief victory. She'd been so focused on calming down Dougal, she'd forgotten that The Raven could hear every word she said.

Nearly forgotten, that is, until he threw back his head and laughed. Vanessa glared at him, her anger overcoming her fear momentarily.

The Raven's chest shook with his mirth until slowly his laughter died down. "Oh, what kind of foolish amateur do you take me for?" He paced toward her, stopping mere feet away. "Do you really think I would go to all this trouble without first doing my research? Do you really think I would plot and connive for months, that I would kidnap an innocent family, that I would steal from a fellow adventurer, that I would bother to manipulate this mindless dolt"—he gestured toward Dougal—"that I would murder, and then I would waste all of my efforts on an attempt to assassinate the queen if I wasn't absolutely positive I was going to succeed?"

His eyes were lit with a fanatical gleam, his mouth foaming with spittle as he spoke. In that instant, she knew the truth. He was mad, and he would do anything in his power to carry out his plan.

Still Vanessa shook her head. "No. You can't possibly know wh—"

"Of course I can," he interrupted her. "Everyone has his price. Dougal here could be had for a few pandering compliments and a sympathetic ear. Niall could be had for the infinitesimal hope that his family might one day be safely returned." The Raven swung toward the door and gestured broadly. "And one of Her Majesty's most loyal guards had a price as well."

He shrugged as if beset by modesty. "Of course it took time to find the right guard to blackmail. Many train trips back and forth between London and Scotland so I could keep an eye on Niall, visit with young Dougal, and ferret out the information I needed. But in the end, I discovered that one Samuel Bennet has a very embarrassing predilection."

Again The Raven laughed. "Imagine. Being willing to betray the queen merely because you're too embarrassed to admit you're overly fond of young boys. Of course, Dougal, you were willing to betray your queen and your family out of sheer spite. I suppose that is worse."

Dougal lunged at him, indignation radiating from his straining muscles. If she hadn't already held his hands, she never would have stopped him.

"Dougal, no. He'll kill you."

"Of course I'll kill him." The Raven closed the distance between them and ran the flat side of the knife down her cheek to press it against her jaw. "Don't sound so desperate. I already have one undeserving and interfering woman to deal with before I deal with you. And I hear Her Majesty does not like to be kept waiting." He flicked the blade against the skin of her neck casually so that it barely scraped her, but burned fiercely.

"But you know, Vanessa, I just might let you live. How exactly do you imagine Graeme will feel about you once he realizes you allowed me to kill both the queen and his brother? Duty-bound, honorable Graeme married forever to a woman he can't stand. I like the idea of that. That's assuming, of course, that I let you both live. He's coming here, you know, your husband. I sent him a note. Exchanging you for that stone."

In that instant, she'd never hated anyone more. She, who'd always thought of herself as logical and reasonable. As a woman of intellect, she hated this man so fiercely that she wanted to kill him herself. In that moment she even believed that her hatred might allow her to overcome his superior strength.

Vanessa lunged at The Raven, but Dougal must have read the intention in her gaze, and he was ready. Dougal jumped in front of her, pushing her aside so that she fell to the ground as he stumbled into The Raven. The knife grazed Dougal's arm.

The Raven slammed the butt of his pistol down on Dougal's head so hard that the boy slumped to the ground. Blood oozed from the wound, dripping down his temple and onto his cheek.

"Sorry, Vanessa," Dougal gasped, his voice weak. "I couldn't let you get yourself killed. Graeme would never have forgiven me."

She dropped to his side as his eyes rolled back, and her fingers went to his throat, seeking his pulse. It was there—weak, but there. He was still alive. For now.

The Raven bent in front of her, holding the knife. She closed her eyes, waiting for him to slice her the way he'd done to Fitch, but instead she heard the fabric from her skirt tear. He cut two large swaths, then stood to face her. He tucked the knife into his belt.

"You are a pain in my arse," he said. With that he

grabbed her by the hair and looped one of the strips of fabric around her head and tied it at her mouth, preventing her from speaking. "Had I not been so pressed for time, I would have tied you up at my house." The other strip he used to bind her wrists. "Now you can shut your mouth and leave me to do my work," The Raven said.

The music on the other side of the door had had stopped, indicating the end of the processional and the conclusion of the funeral. Men's voices came from the other chamber, more than likely those of the queen's guards as they ushered her into the room. Vanessa knew the protocol of such funerals, as they were often detailed in *The Times*. They would keep the queen there until the remainder of the audience left. She would meet with the family of the deceased and then be taken back to Buckingham Palace. It was during this interim that The Raven planned to make his move. Right now there were too many guards on alert, but once the visitors left, things would quiet down.

Vanessa wanted nothing more than to shout a warning to Her Majesty, but the gag around her mouth prevented her. She tried to scream past the fabric in her mouth, but it came out as an anguished moan. This was enough to garner a glare from The Raven.

"Do not make me regret keeping you alive this long."

His threat was enough to stifle further attempts. Even breathing was challenging, and saliva was beginning to pool in her mouth, making it difficult to swallow.

There had to be a way out of all of this. While The Raven focused upon the door, Vanessa took advantage of his inattention. She stuck her hands into her bag and searched around, but felt nothing useful until her fingers brushed leather at the very bottom. Her tools. She'd never removed them from her bag when they'd gone to the abbey in the hills. Perfect. Quickly she untied the roll and gently felt around for something that could be used as a weapon. They had to get out of here. The queen's guards would protect her, but Vanessa and Dougal were on their own.

She came upon the cleaning pick, a small object with a long, sharp tip. She pulled it out. She tucked it into the folds of her skirt and contemplated her next move. Dougal was still unconscious, but would hopefully awaken soon. She couldn't see him very clearly in the dim room, but it looked like the bleeding might have stopped. Although she hated to leave him in the hands of The Raven, she might not have another choice. And if it meant that she could go and find help, she would do it.

Her hands might be bound, but her feet were still free. She made her way over to where The Raven pressed his ear against the door and jumped onto his back while wrapping her bound hands over his neck. She pulled, stretching the fabric at her wrists against his throat and trying to wrap her legs around his waist to pull him away from the door.

"Stupid bitch," he spat. He bucked, but she held tight, the fabric pulling at his throat. He reached up and untied her hands, releasing the pressure that she'd applied. Now he was able to easily swing her off his back. He tossed her against a concrete tomb, and suddenly he was at her side. He wrapped his hands around her throat.

Vanessa fought for air. Her lungs tightened and burned, and she tried in vain to kick at him.

Dougal stirred but had not come to his feet.

She scratched at The Raven's face, her sharp fingernails leaving thin lines of blood in their wake. She reached into the folds of her bodice and grabbed for her tiny weapon. Without another thought, she plunged it into The Raven's neck. Blood shot out around the wound, and he staggered away from her. She gasped for breath and moved toward Dougal.

"Dougal," she said. "We've got to go. Get up."

He roused immediately.

The Raven held his hand to the neck wound to stanch the bleeding, all the while glaring at them. "This isn't over," he snarled.

But Vanessa and Dougal ran from the chamber.

The Raven didn't have time to waste with those two idiots. He reached up and pulled the offensive thing out of his neck. He might continue to bleed for a while, but he knew he was in no mortal danger. Although the injury hurt like a son of a bitch, he felt as clear and sharp as ever. His lucidness meant it was unlikely that Vanessa had hit a major artery, but warm blood oozed down his neck, across his clavicle, and down his sternum.

Little bitch.

But he had more important women to deal with. He could see Queen Victoria through a crack in the door. Dressed in mourning black with a small plumed hat, she was older now, her skin wrinkled with age. But he had no qualms about killing a defenseless elderly woman; she was the queen.

Without further ado, he kicked open the door. Her Majesty was within reach, so he immediately grabbed her and pulled her close to him. His own blood dripped onto her flesh. Perhaps it would soon mingle with her own. He held his knife up to Victoria's neck. The pistol he held out in front to ward off the guards.

"Don't come closer or I *will* kill her," he warned.

The three guards eyed one another, then looked back at him as if waiting for someone to give them guidance. Fools.

"Listen to him," the queen said sternly. Her eyes darted to the side to glance at him. "Why don't you tell us what you want?" She lowered her voice as she spoke to The Raven.

"What I want." he chuckled. "Where do I even begin? I want the throne. Let's leave it at that for simplicity's sake."

The guards collectively grumbled and moved a few steps toward him.

"I said stay back!" The Raven yelled. He knew what would happen if he did kill her now. They'd open fire on him and riddle his body with bullet holes. No, he had one more step to complete, and then he needed to get her out of here. Away with him until he could put the Kingmaker together. Then he would watch her die a slow death.

"Now. One at a time, I want you to turn and leave the room." When they made no move to leave, he ran the blade across the queen's delicate skin, slicing her. Blood trickled down her throat.

"Do as he commands," she said. Her voice betrayed no fear. She spoke with ultimate authority, and part of The Raven respected her for that. 'Twas a pity she'd have to die.

The guards did as he said, turning and evacuating the room, one at a time. Until finally he was left alone with the monarch.

"I've waited for this moment for so long," The Raven said.

Chapter Twenty-four

❧~~❧

The guards scrambled, still trying to decide what to do next when Graeme and the others arrived. Graeme did not bother to explain anything and instead simply ran past them into the room where he knew The Raven held the queen. The bastard had a bloody blade against the queen's neck, and a thin cut slashed down from her ear to her neck. Blood trickled from the wound.

Graeme saw no fear in Her Majesty's eyes. This was not the first threat that she'd endured. But her pulse beat rapidly beneath her pale skin.

"Let her go. You know you can't get out of here alive if you harm her," Graeme said.

"The hell I can't. When I leave this building, she will no longer be the ruler. I will. You know what I want," The Raven said. "Give me the last stone and I'll let her go."

"That's not a bargain I can make, and you know that," Graeme said.

The men of Solomon's stood behind him. Graeme could feel their presence and knew they would not only protect him, but protect his wife and brother as well. Currently Max was searching Westminster to find them.

Graeme knew Vanessa had been with The Raven; he'd found her fossil at The Raven's house. Now he desperately wanted to know that she was safe and unharmed, but he dared not ask. He couldn't afford to show any weakness with The Raven when the queen's life was in jeopardy.

"I see you brought your own army," The Raven spat. "Where is Fielding, I wonder?"

"He's recently returned from rescuing Niall's family from your nasty little hiding place, in the same spot where you'd held Esme at one point. Clearly your creativity is waning," Graeme said.

The Raven smiled, a deadly, chilling grin. "If anyone could have found them, he could. If Niall would have only asked, sought Solomon's help, it would have saved him so much woe." He clucked his tongue. "But Niall was too independent, too proud to ask for help. Pity."

Graeme felt the emerald weighing heavy in his pocket. He could so easily toss it to the man and move the queen to safety. That was what truly mattered. But what would happen when The Raven put the Kingmaker together?

"Let her go," Graeme said. "You can negotiate with me. And only me."

The Raven shook his head. "No. Look." He motioned with his head to his right. "It's all there. All the pieces necessary, but the one you hold. Give it to me."

"You lugged all that down here with you?" Graeme asked. The individual gems were not heavy. No bigger than small apples, they could easily fit in a man's jacket. But the Stone of Destiny would have been demanding to carry down here with two hostages.

"You underestimate me. Suffice it to say I'm always

prepared. I brought it here last night. The rest is courtesy of your wife. Now enough!" The Raven said. He tilted the blade until the tip pricked the queen's skin. "I will kill her. Give me the stone. I know you have it."

"What could possibly happen?" Victoria spoke up.

"Dreadful things," Jenkins said from behind Graeme. "We are unsure of the power of the Kingmaker."

"I'm not," Her Majesty said. "This man does not possess the requisite virtues of a monarch. I believe the stones are even representative of those very characteristics." She met Graeme's gaze. "Courage, wisdom, and authority. Give him the emerald."

Graeme eyed her for a moment, wanting her to further explain. She nodded encouragingly.

"Only if he lets you go first," Graeme said.

"I give you the queen, and you give me the stone," The Raven said.

"Agreed." Graeme withdrew the stone and showed it to The Raven. "Release her and I'll toss this to you."

The Raven paused, but only for a moment. He dropped the blade from the queen's neck and shoved her forward. Graeme tossed the stone, and The Raven caught it with one hand. He wasted no time in grabbing the Stone of Destiny. He cradled the sandstone block as he dropped the emerald into place. He glanced around waiting for something, anything to happen.

"Get her out of here," Graeme said as he moved the queen behind him. Once she was safely under her guards' protection, the men of Solomon's stood in a line, all leveling guns at The Raven. "It's over this time," Graeme told him.

Then the ground shook. The Kingmaker burned bright red as if The Raven had held it over hot coals, and he yelled in response but did not drop the block of stone. The shaking increased, and Graeme grabbed onto the wall to steady himself. There was a great noise that sounded as if it emitted directly from the center of the Stone of Destiny, and then in a blast, the Kingmaker shattered into countless pieces, and The Raven fell to the ground.

"He's dead," Nick Callum said, kneeling by the body. Other members of Solomon's gathered around him.

"The Kingmaker is only for those who are worthy to hold the throne," Victoria said, stepping forward. "I knew his plan would not work. Admittedly I suspected he would have to be shot, but this," she eyed the body at her feet, "worked as well." Then she turned to face Graeme and the rest of the men of Solomon's. "I believe I once again owe you a great deal of gratitude."

Graeme pushed Nick forward. "You have Nick here to thank." Then Graeme turned to leave the room. He still had yet to see his wife, to hold her and know she was safe. "Has anyone found my family?" he asked.

"They're over here," Max called. His voice came from outside the chamber, across the sanctuary.

Graeme looked to find his wife and brother sitting with Max. Both had blood on them, and Dougal still looked fearful, his smile a little brittle.

"Graeme." Vanessa stood and ran to him.

When she reached him, he wrapped his arms around her and squeezed. Then he held her out in front of him to look for signs of injury. Bruises were beginning to form at her throat. So The Raven had tried to kill her. The thought soured his stomach. "I thought I'd lost you," he said. He ran his hand down her cheek.

"I left you a clue so you'd know where I was," she said, her smile shaky.

He pulled the fossil out of his pocket. "It was a perfect clue." He held it out to her.

"No, you keep it." She shook her head. "I don't need it anymore," she said.

"But it's the beginning of your collection," he argued. "How can you be a paleontologist without fossils?"

"It's our collection. I suspect this was only one adventure, and we'll go on many more together," she said. She smiled and it nearly brought him to his knees. "Besides, I don't need any of that. I thought I belonged only in the science community, but I know the truth now. I belong with you. Wherever you are, I belong at your side."

He ran his fingers gently across the bruises forming at her neck. "I don't know what I would have done if I'd lost you."

"But you didn't. I'm here, and I'm not going anywhere," she said.

"I love you, Vanessa," he said.

She smiled. "Aye, I know," she said, mimicking his brogue. "And I love you, too."

He kissed her soundly, his woman, his wife.

Her warm palm pressed to his chest. "Graeme? What about Niall's family? Did you find them? Are they safe?"

"Yes," he said with a nod. "Fielding was able to locate Penny and Jonathan earlier today. They're home resting now."

"Thank goodness," she said. "And I deciphered the code from *The Magi's Book of Wisdom*."

He wrapped his arm around her waist and pulled her snugly to him. "Did you?"

"Though I don't suppose any of it matters now. It was merely a warning against those who might seek the Kingmaker. Evidently it only works if you're worthy."

"And destroys you if you aren't," he said. "The Raven is dead." She nodded and snuggled closer to him.

"I think perhaps its time I met your family, considering you've met all of mine. I believe I have some choice words to share with a few of them," he said.

"You'll meet them in due time. Besides, I've already seen them today. Right now, I just need you to love me," she said.

"Always, Duchess, always."

Don't miss the first book in the
Legend Hunters series!

Fielding Grey is a treasure seeker
with a taste for danger...

Esme Worthington has favored
dusty tomes over society balls...

*Please turn this page
for an excerpt from*

Seduce Me

Available now.

Chapter Four

Fielding had followed the sound of voices all the way to the innermost part of the ruins. The Raven's men had a woman with them, and she was quite the talker. He'd managed to find a ledge where he'd situated himself to see how many he was up against. Peering over, he wished they had a bit more lighting below.

"I will give you no such thing," a woman's voice said.

Where was the woman? He spied Waters standing in the middle of the room, and Thatcher looked to be walking directly toward Fielding. He crouched farther down to make certain he wasn't seen, then peered back over the edge. There, chained to the wall, was the woman, wearing nothing but a flimsy nightrail. Since when were The Raven's men in the habit of abducting women? Evidently his uncle wanted this artifact badly.

Well, this certainly complicated matters. It would have been nice had Jensen and his Solomon's friends warned Fielding about the possibility of having to rescue a woman in addition to the box.

Of course he had no obligation to save her. She hadn't been part of his original agreement.

"Where is it?" Thatcher asked, his voice coming from between tightly clenched teeth.

"I don't know what you're referring to."

"The key to open this bloody thing." He held up the box in question.

"Let me see the box closely; it might jar my memory," the woman said.

"I know you have it. The Raven said the Worthington woman had the key. That's you, ain't it?"

There was a long pause before she answered, as if she'd been considering a lie. "Yes, that's me, but I don't have any keys with me. If you take me back to London, though, I'll be happy to retrieve all the keys I own for you to dig through."

Worthington. That was the name of the scholar on Mr. Nichols's list. Fielding again peered over the ledge. He'd imagined an old matronly figure with grayed hair and a shapeless body, her nose firmly implanted in a book. Not the slip of a woman below him. Even in the dim light, he could see her tantalizing breasts under the nightgown.

Fielding wondered if the men of Solomon's knew about this supposed key. And if they did, why hadn't they warned him? There'd been nothing about a key in the notes they'd given him either. Bastards probably didn't share all their information with the hired help.

"Get your filthy hands off me, you beast," she said.

Thatcher was indeed putting his hands on her, searching her for some sort of key, from the looks of it. Although why he thought the woman could hide anything beneath her almost transparent nightgown, Fielding didn't know. He rolled his eyes. He'd never liked Thatcher, always felt the man took pride in being as vile and contemptuous as possible.

"What do we have here?" Thatcher asked. "That's an unusual pendant." He pulled his hand back, yanking the necklace free, and stepped away from the woman.

"That is nothing," she protested. "A frivolous gift from my father is all. It's not even real gold; I believe it's made of painted steel. It will probably rust in another month or so."

All Fielding could see was a slight glimmer against the lantern light. A bit of jewelry perhaps. So she *had* been hiding something.

"We'll see about that. Waters, get over here. And hold that light still."

"You have no idea what sort of trouble you could be in for," the woman warned. "That box is quite likely very dangerous. And I'd wager that your employer is paying you to retrieve it, not open it."

She was a smart one, Fielding would give her that. However, her common sense was sorely lacking. It was she who didn't realize the danger she was in.

While he'd never known Waters to harm a woman, Thatcher was the kind of man who took what he wanted regardless of what the implications might be.

"Look there," Waters said. "See that notch? It looks just like her trinket."

"Go ahead," she said loudly. "Open the box. All that lies within the walls of that box are evils. Death, destruction, pestilence. The plagues of Egypt. The ruination of humankind. Go ahead," she said again. "Unleash terrors upon yourself, it matters not to me. But I cannot watch."

She sounded remarkably like Mr. Nichols. Fielding shook his head. He'd never understand adults who believed in such fairy tales.

"Perhaps she's right," Waters warned, his voice wavering with nerves. "The Raven did ask us to get the box, steal her key, and bring them back to him."

"You wouldn't want to disobey your employer's instructions," she said.

"We won't know if her key is the correct one," Thatcher ground out, "unless we try it."

"But she has all those books in her library. All of them were about this box. She knows something," Waters said.

"That's right," she agreed. "My library is extensive." The last word came out in a yawn. "I might be a woman, but I know of what I speak."

"Your incessant chatter is grating on my nerves." Thatcher hitched up his pistol and hit the woman hard on the head. "I said shut up!"

Fielding gritted his teeth as if he had been the one struck. The woman's head dropped and her body went slack, dangling from the manacles that affixed her to the wall.

Thatcher dropped the necklace into his pocket and walked away from the woman. "We'll wait in here for first light, then we'll take her to The Raven and he can decide what to do with her. Waters, build a fire over there."

From his perch, Fielding watched the two men build a makeshift camp, complete with a fire and ratty blankets to lie upon. Once the woman came to, her arms would ache fiercely from being shackled in that position, but the knot on her head would no doubt hurt worse. She was so small, her body frail and limp. He forced his eyes back toward the men. Fielding kept his post for another hour, waiting for the duo to settle in for the night.

Thatcher was unable to leave the box alone, though. He went back and forth, picking it up to further examine it, then setting it back down and trying to fall asleep. Once more he picked up the box and held it close to his face. He nudged Waters with his foot.

"Waters," he whispered.

The other man sat bold upright. "What?"

"Listen. Do you hear that? Do you hear the voices?"

"Only your voice," he said groggily.

"Here, listen." Thatcher held the box out to the other man, who, in turn, took it and held it up to his ear.

A moment later Waters threw the box away from him as he sat up abruptly. Thatcher caught the box before it fell to the ground.

"You heard it, didn't you?" Thatcher said.

"Bloody 'ell," Waters said. "I heard my name."

Thatcher dug into his pocket and pulled out the woman's necklace. The pendant caught the fire's glow and cast flecks of light around them.

"What are you doing?" Waters asked.

"Opening it."

Thatcher pressed the metal pendant against the box, and a latch audibly released. Even from a distance, Fielding could hear it. He shook his head, certain he must have been mistaken. His own mind must be playing tricks on him from lying still so long.

In one swift movement Thatcher popped open the lid. Both men sat for a moment looking around them, presumably waiting for the terrors to be unleashed upon them, but nothing happened.

Fielding rolled his eyes. Damned superstitions.

"There's nothing in here," Thatcher said.

"Let me see," Waters said. "What's that on the bottom?"

Thatcher dug his hand in, perhaps searching for hidden compartments, then pulled his hand back. "Nothing."

"What's that on your wrist?" Waters asked.

Thatcher held his arm up to the firelight, and a thin band of gold shimmered against his dirty flesh.

"A treasure," Waters said. "Give me the box." He too put his hand in the box and pulled back with a band of gold on his wrist as well.

They eyed their matching bands for several moments. Thatcher laughed. "Why, that's a pretty find. But we'd better take them off. Don't want to damage them before we can get the box back to The Raven." Then Thatcher tried to remove his bracelet. "It won't come off," he growled.

Waters attempted to remove his own, and his bracelet would not budge either.

"What do we do?" Waters asked, his voice rising a notch.

"We'll get them off tomorrow," Thatcher said. "The Raven will help."

"We can't tell The Raven. He'll kill us for trying to steal from him."

"I can make him understand," Thatcher assured him. "Now go back to sleep."

Fools.

The Raven would never understand. And he didn't deal lightly with those who betrayed him.

Fielding wouldn't have to wait much longer. He needed them to doze off for only a little while before they'd be too bleary-headed to fight him. He checked his waistband for the pistol and found it snugly in place. Ten minutes later Thatcher's loud snores echoed through the dungeon.

Fielding waited a little longer before he crept down from his ledge and into their makeshift camp. Snagging Thatcher's bag with the box hidden inside proved easy enough, as was snuffing out their lanterns, leaving only the remnants of their fire as light. But as Fielding turned to go, he saw her.

Her frail body hung limply from the manacles, and her brown hair was matted with dirt and a small patch of blood. Her nightdress was covered in Thatcher's muddy handprints.

Blast it all.

There was no way Fielding could leave her here. He glanced over his shoulder. The two men were still sleeping, so he slowly moved to stand in front of the woman. He tightened the cinch on the bag to ensure it was secure over this shoulder before placing one hand firmly against her mouth. Her eyes flew open, but his hand muffled the sound she made.

He shook his head. "Be quiet," he whispered. "I'm not going to hurt you. I'm going to get you out of here. Nod if you understand."

Her wide eyes rounded, but she nodded nonetheless.

"If I move my hand away from your mouth, do you promise not to scream?"

She nodded fervently.

He waited a few heartbeats, then he slowly took his hand away.

"Please hurry," she urged.

Reaching up, he worked on the right brace, nudging the pin out of its confines. The rusted metal scraped and groaned as it moved, but it eventually gave way and he was able to remove her hand. Being hung from the wall as long as she'd been, her movements would be unsteady and sluggish. He couldn't afford to be slowed by her. As she lowered her arm, she winced, confirming his suspicions.

The men stirred. Fielding and the woman froze, waiting to see if either man awoke, but the snoring continued.

He moved to remove the other pin, but unlike its counterpart, this one would not budge.

"He had trouble with that one," she whispered.

Fielding nodded and continued trying to work the pin out, but it remained lodged firmly in place. If he'd had a sword he could have snapped the chain in half, but seeing as he wasn't in the habit of carrying swords around with him, that wasn't an option. There was something he could do, although it would most certainly wake Waters and Thatcher. He didn't even know this woman, and already she was more trouble that he'd wager she was worth.

But damn it all, he couldn't leave her.

With brusque motions, he began to run his hands along the skin of her arms, massaging the tender flesh there.

She gasped. "What are you doing?" she asked in a whispered hiss.

"Kneading your muscles."

"Well, I insist you stop at once. It's most improper! Furthermore, I can do it myself once you release me."

"Once I release you," he explained with forced patience, "we are going to have to move quickly. A cramped muscle could mean the difference between life and death." He paused to meet her gaze. "Understand?"

Her eyes were wide in the darkness, her breath coming in nervous pants, but she nodded.

He returned to the task at hand, working on her arms first and then turning his attention to her legs, which were longer than he expected for a woman of her diminutive height, and surprisingly sturdy. Supporting her feet, he bent first one knee and then the other, massaging the muscles of her calves and thighs as he did so. Her sinewy flesh convulsed beneath his touch.

He worked quickly, since there was no time to waste.

But even so, he couldn't help noticing her generous curves and the enticing flesh beneath his hands. His body leaped in response, though he tried to stifle his reaction. Much more of this, and she wouldn't be the only one moving slowly.

"I believe, sir, that my muscles are quite relaxed now." Her tone was both husky and tense, whether from the situation or his ministrations, he couldn't tell.

Fielding reached into his boot and withdrew a dagger. He handed it to the woman. "If they come after you, do not hesitate to use this, do you understand?"

She looked down at the knife in her free hand and nodded, but he was uncertain as to whether or not she could actually follow through with such a task. There was no room for error at the moment, else he and the woman would both find themselves prisoners of The Raven.

"Do not bother slashing at their arms. Go straight for their bellies, where you'll do the most damage," he instructed.

She shuddered but nodded.

He stepped away from her and aimed his pistol at the top of the chain.

"Are you mad?" she hissed.

He ignored her and took the shot. It did the trick and the chain broke free, but the ricochet rang throughout the room and Thatcher was on his feet in a matter of seconds. Fielding had already grabbed the girl, though, and they were making their way up the stairs.

"Where do you think you're going, Grey?" Thatcher snarled. The man searched for his gun, but Fielding had already removed it. Just as he'd also disabled their carriage outside and sent their horses running.

"Thatcher, it's not your style to abduct unsuspecting

women." He slid another bullet into his pistol and leveled it at the men.

Thatcher took a step toward them but stumbled in the darkness. "Grey, you and I both know you're no different than us, despite that title of yours."

Waters felt around the camp, crawling on his knees, searching under their bedding, no doubt also looking for a weapon.

"Ah," Fielding said, "but there is no difference. I have the box and the girl."

Thatcher snarled. "Give us the box." He took another step forward. "We'll split our share of the money with you."

"Don't make another move, or I will shoot you," Fielding said as they backed their way up the stairs. "We'll be leaving now." And with that, they turned and ran.

Fielding dragged the woman behind him, knowing that her slippered feet were taking a beating against the cracked stone, but that wasn't his concern. Carrying her would only slow them down, and he could already hear the men scrambling after them.

He and the woman reached the outside, and the chilled night air slapped at them. With one arm, he jumped onto his horse, then pulled the woman up in front of him. Facing him, actually, which proved a bit awkward, but there was no time to rectify it. He kicked his horse into action, and they rode off just as Thatcher and Waters appeared outside the ruins.

"Thank you for rescuing me," she said breathlessly.

It was hard not to look at her face when she spoke to him, as she was sitting directly in front of him. And the moon hanging above illuminated her perfectly. She was close enough for him to see the freckles that splattered across her nose, and her large, thickly lashed, river-green eyes. Her hair smelled of lilac, despite the mud covering her.

He merely nodded and returned his attention to the landscape before them.

"Won't they come after us?" she asked.

"Probably." Her legs brushed against his, and he looked down—milky white thighs straddled his own. He couldn't help remembering how those thighs had felt beneath his hands. Firm yet pliant. His senses stirred as his body once again responded to hers. Damn it all.

He could only imagine her indignation if she happened to notice his growing erection. He'd heard more than enough of her prattling earlier to know she was a well-bred lady. A prim one at that, despite the fact that her body was obviously made for sin.

They couldn't very well ride back to London this way. It was more than twelve hours away, and if she noticed his reaction, chatterer that she was, she'd no doubt preach to him the whole way about sins of the flesh or some such nonsense. The ride would be interminable even if his body didn't have a mind of its own.

They needed to either take the train or find a coach. He eyed her mud-splattered nightgown. Clearly they couldn't take the train and avoid being seen, even with a private car. He didn't even know who this woman was. The last thing he needed was some angry papa coming after him demanding Fielding marry the girl. That left finding a carriage. He'd seen a sign for a carriage house on his way to the ruins.

As he turned his horse down the appropriate road, he detected the sound of pounding hooves behind them.

He did his best to isolate the noise, to be certain of what he heard. Definitely horses coming their way.

"Hold on tight," he told the woman.

"Why?"

"Because we're being followed."

THE DISH

Where authors give you the inside scoop!

♥ ♥ ♥ ♥ ♥ ♥ ♥ ♥ ♥ ♥ ♥ ♥ ♥ ♥ ♥

From the desk of Hope Ramsay

Dear Reader,

Picture, if you will, a little girl in a polka-dot bathing suit, standing on a rough board jutting out over the waters of the Edisto River in South Carolina. She's about six years old, and standing below her in the chest-high, tea-colored water is a tall man with a deep, deep southern drawl—the kind that comes right up out of the ground.

"Jump, little gal," the man says. "I'll catch you."

The little girl was me. And the man was my Uncle Ernest. And that memory is one of those touchstone moments that I go back to again and again. My uncle wanted me to face my fear of jumping into the water, but he was there, big hands outstretched, steady, sturdy, and sober as a judge. He was the model of a man I could trust.

I screwed up my courage and took that leap of faith. I jumped. He caught me. He taught me to love jumping into the river and swimming in those dark, mysterious waters, overhung with Spanish moss and sometimes visited by snakes and gators!

I loved Uncle Ernest. He was my favorite uncle. He's

been gone for quite a while now, but I think of him often, and he lives on in my heart.

There is even a little bit of him in Clay Rhodes, the hero of my debut novel, WELCOME TO LAST CHANCE. Jane, the heroine of the story, has to learn that Clay is the type of guy she can always trust. A guy she can take a leap of faith with. A guy who will always be there to catch her, even when she has to face her biggest fears.

And isn't love all about taking a leap of faith?

I had such fun writing WELCOME TO LAST CHANCE, because it afforded me the opportunity to go back in time and remember what it was like spending my summers in a little town in South Carolina with folks who were like Uncle Ernest—people who made up a village where a child could grow up safe and sound and learn what makes a life meaningful.

I hope you enjoy meeting the characters in Last Chance, South Carolina, as much as I enjoyed writing them.

Y'all take care now,

Hope Ramsay

www.hoperamsay.com

♥ ♥ ♥ ♥ ♥ ♥ ♥ ♥ ♥ ♥ ♥ ♥ ♥ ♥

From the desk of Cynthia Eden

Dear Reader,

Have you ever wondered how far you would go to protect someone you loved? What would you do if the person you loved was in danger?

Love can make people do wild, desperate things…and love can certainly push people to cross the thin line between good and evil.

When I wrote DEADLY LIES, I created characters who would be forced to blur the lines between good and evil. Desperate times can call for desperate measures.

The heroine of this book is a familiar face if you've read the other DEADLY books. Samantha "Sam" Kennedy was first introduced in DEADLY FEAR. Sam lived through hell, and she's now fighting to put her life back on track. She knows what evil looks like, and she knows that evil can hide behind the most innocent of faces. So when Sam is assigned to work on a serial kidnapping case, she understands that she has to be on her guard at all times.

But when the kidnapper hits too close to home and her lover's stepbrother is abducted, the rules of the game change. Soon Sam fully understands just how "desperate" the victims are feeling, and she vows to do anything in her power to help Max Ridgeway find his brother.

Anything. Yes, desperation can even push an FBI agent to the edge of the law. Lucky for Sam, she'll have backup ready to help her out—all of the other SSD agents are back to help track the kidnappers, and they won't stop until the case is closed.

I've had such a wonderful time revisiting my SSD agents in this book. And I hope you enjoying catching up with the characters too!

If you'd like to learn more about my books, please visit my website at www.cynthiaeden.com.

Happy reading!

Cynthia Eden

♥ ♥ ♥ ♥ ♥ ♥ ♥ ♥ ♥ ♥ ♥ ♥ ♥ ♥ ♥

From the desk of Robyn DeHart

Dear Reader,

There have always been certain things that fascinate me—the heinous crimes of Jack the Ripper; why cats get up, turn around, then settle back into the exact position they were just in; people who can eat only *one* Oreo cookie; and the ancient legend of the Loch Ness monster. Recorded sightings of the creature date all the way back to the seventh century, and not all of these sightings have been water-based—there are those who claim to have seen the monster walking on land.

Regardless of what you believe, it's interesting to think that there just might be some prehistoric animal hiding in a loch in the Highlands. It was this interest that compelled me to write TREASURE ME.

Another interesting tidbit about this book is that it was actually the first romance novel I ever wrote. Okay, that's not entirely true, but the concept of a couple who fall in love near Loch Ness, centered around adventure and action and danger, well, that was all in that first book—even the characters' names stayed the same. But I didn't keep anything else. When it came to the third book in my Legend Hunters trilogy, I took my basic concept and started from scratch.

If you've read SEDUCE ME and DESIRE ME (the first two books in the series), then you might remember meeting Graeme, the big, brooding Scotsman who looks and sounds remarkably like Gerard Butler. Graeme has been after the authentic Stone of Destiny for years, because he believes the one sitting in Westminster is a counterfeit. He's gone back to his family's home in the Highlands to do some research, and meets with trouble in the form of a delectable, self-proclaimed paleontologist named Vanessa. She's just run away from her own wedding and is determined to make a name for herself as a legitimate scientist.

Add in a marriage of convenience, a deadly nemesis,

and some buried treasure and you've got yourself a rollicking adventure full of intrigue and seduction that will leave you as breathless as the characters.

Dare to love a Legend Hunter . . .

Visit my website, www.RobynDeHart.com, for contests, excerpts, and more.

Enjoy!

Robyn DeHart

♥ ♥ ♥ ♥ ♥ ♥ ♥ ♥ ♥ ♥ ♥ ♥ ♥ ♥

From the desk of Kira Morgan

Dear Reader,

It's easy to write about a match made in heaven. Cinderella meets Prince Charming, they fall in love at first sight, and they live happily ever after.

But for my latest book, SEDUCED BY DESTINY, I wanted to take on the challenge of star-crossed lovers, characters like Romeo and Juliet—a man and a woman cursed by fate and thrown together by chance, who have to overcome their tragic history to find true love.

In SEDUCED BY DESTINY, set in the time of Mary Queen of Scots, Josselin Ancrum and Andrew Armstrong each have a dark secret in their past and deadly peril looming in their future. They have little in common. They should avoid each other like the plague.

She's Scots. He's English.

She likes to stir up trouble. He likes to fly under the radar.

She's a tavern wench who loves to play with swords. He's an expert swordsman who'd rather play golf.

Her mother was killed in battle.

His father was the one who killed her.

Talk about Fortune's foe . . .

All this would be fine if only they hadn't started falling in love. If they hadn't felt that initial spark of attraction . . . if they hadn't begun to enjoy one another's company . . . if they hadn't succumbed to that first kiss . . . their story might be a simple tale of revenge.

But Drew and Jossy, unaware of the fateful ties between them, are drawn to one another like iron to a magnet. And by the time they discover they've fallen in love with their mortal enemy, it's too late. Their hearts are already tangled in a hopeless knot.

This is where it gets even more interesting.

To make matters worse, outside forces are working to drive them apart. What began as a personal mission of vengeance now involves their friends, their families, and ultimately their queens. Suspected of treason, hunted by spies, they become targets for royal assassins.

The uneasy truce between Queen Elizabeth and Queen Mary is mirrored in the fragile relationship between Drew and Jossy. The lovers are swept into a raging battle bigger than the both of them—a battle that shakes the foundation of their union and threatens their very lives.

Only the strength of their fateful bond and the power of their love can save them now.

Of course, unlike Romeo and Juliet, Drew and Jossy will triumph. Nobody wants to read a historical romance with an unhappy ending! But just how they manage to overcome all odds, when their stars are crossed and the cards are stacked against them, is the stuff of nail-biting high adventure and a story that I hope will keep you up all night.

To read an excerpt from SEDUCED BY DESTINY, peruse my research photos, and enter my monthly sweepstakes, visit my website at www.glynnis.net/kiramorgan. If you'd like to read my daily posts and interact with other fans, become my friend at www.facebook.com/KiraMorganAuthor or follow me at www.twitter.com/kira_morgan.

Happy adventures!

Kira Morgan

Find out more about Forever Romance!

Visit us at
www.hachettebookgroup.com/publishing_forever.aspx

Find us on Facebook
http://www.facebook.com/ForeverRomance

Follow us on Twitter
http://twitter.com/ForeverRomance

NEW AND UPCOMING TITLES

Each month we feature our new titles
and reader favorites.

CONTESTS AND GIVEAWAYS

We give away galleys, autographed copies,
and all kinds of exclusive items.

AUTHOR INFO

You'll find bios, articles, and links to personal websites
for all your favorite authors—and so much more.

GET SOCIAL

Connect with your favorite authors, editors, and
other Forever fans, and share what's important to you.

THE BUZZ

Sign up for our monthly romance newsletter,
and be the first to read all about it.